LINCOLN McKEEVER

Lincoln McKeever

by

ELEAZAR LIPSKY

Appleton-Century-Crofts, Inc.

New York

To
Jacob and Augusta Kohn

Acknowledgments

I am indebted for information and advice in various ways to Carlos Escuaderos, Maurice Firth, Gerold Frank, Leonard Dal Negro, Mrs. Alice H. Rossin and Dr. Sol Weintraub, all of New York City; Miss Mary Rose Allen of Salt Lake City; the Hon. Lowell C. Green, Clerk of the Supreme Court, Santa Fe; Herbert K. Greer, Esq., of Socorro, New Mexico, and Alexandria, Virginia; Mrs. Dorothy Hughes of Los Angeles; Morris Kight of the New Mexico Art League and Prof. T. M. Pearce of the University of New Mexico, both of Albuquerque. Various other persons connected with government agencies and public bodies have been uniformly kind and helpful in indicating sources of information.

Chapter I

It was a drowsy hot day in spring toward the end of the century. In Washington the government pursued its business with languor and the bureaucracy was at peace. At the Capitol, the corridors were quiet except for a few tourists drifting through, perspiring, chatting, accepting the impressive statements of the guides, aging war veterans, as to the cost of the treasures adorning the structure. Under the great dome, a family from Iowa was testing the acoustics. The fact that a whisper at one place could be heard across the rotunda seemed to point somehow to the nation's fundamental greatness.

At that time the Supreme Court sat in the old Senate chamber. Several scores of lawyers were assembled in the lounge, chatting and bantering in low tones. They wore cutaways, low-cut black vests and dark striped trousers. With their pleated shirts, Gladstone collars and large bow ties, they were in the proper regalia of the profession before the high court. An attendant announced that the court was about to sit. They trooped in with brief cases and found seats in low benches of severe design. A group from New Mexico, awkward in formal dress, found seats and gazed about with fierce legal belligerence. One of them, Florence Hogarth, a clear-faced woman, glanced at a notation and leaned forward.

"Mike," she whispered to her senior.

A massive red-faced man with a bald head turned. "Yes, Floss?"

"Will you *please* remember that California citation, the Rodriguez case?" she said urgently. "I still say that's in point."

The man, Mike Taft, glanced at her humorously. "Now, Floss, I don't want that case," he drawled, "but if it'll make you happy, I'll try to weave it in. Meantime, just sit back and get the feel of things. We don't argue till tomorrow."

She smiled and put aside her notes and gazed about with frank curiosity. The long bench with its nine seats, upholstered in black leather, dominated the chamber. A row of Doric columns supported a marble elevation. In the center stood an arch hung with formal black drapes.

1

A placid clerk entered through the arch and inspected the bench with an expert eye. He examined and replaced a quill pen with a critical air. A schoolgirl looked in with a merry face only to open startled eyes and withdraw with a giggle. Florence absorbed the details with the thought that the impressive decorum could never be forgotten. Her attention was drawn by a cough to a pale twelve-year-old boy at her side.

The boy's serious eyes darted about with delight. "Oh, Dad!" he breathed. "This is wonderful!"

A lawyer in a rumpled cutaway at his side murmured indulgently, "Indeed it is, Jeff." His leathery face, touched with a sad humor, seemed familiar to her. He looked about forty. There was a clear resemblance between father and son. The same broad strong features were in both, but the boy's mouth had the sensitivity of earliest adolescence. He whispered eagerly and pointed to a printed calendar. "What's that case after yours, Dad—Carlos de Niza and all that stuff?"

Florence cocked an ear. *De Niza v. Alamo Land Development Company, Inc.* Now why, she wondered, was this of interest to the youngster?

"Just another case, Jeff, the Land Grant Case," the lawyer whispered. "Now stop asking questions."

"Oh, all right!" The boy subsided and then bobbed up again. "Dad?"

"Yes?"

"Will you argue first?"

"Yes, I told you so!"

"You know—" the boy broke off and coughed. His father looked at him anxiously.

"What's wrong, Jeff?"

The boy shook his head. "Nothing—just a tickle."

"Do you want to leave?"

"No—I'm all right."

"I wish you'd change your mind," the lawyer urged.

"I don't want to miss the opening," the boy said doggedly.

"Well—" The lawyer scratched his chin dubiously, then caught the woman's glance. He smiled uncertainly and returned to a printed brief.

Florence closed her notes and sat back. Perhaps her senior, Mike Taft, was right about the California case, she conceded reluctantly, perhaps it was best omitted. In the meantime, there was no reason for her heart to be beating with excitement. The dim light filtering through stained glass was beautiful, the decorum was satisfying.

The clerk tapped the gavel and announced that the Supreme Court of the United States was in session.

The murmur died. Eight justices in robes entered with slow leisure and quietly stood at their places. One chair decorated with brass studs remained empty. At a nod from the Chief Justice the bench sat.

The countrified lawyer glanced at a heavy gold watch. The court had come to order precisely on the hour. It was a courtesy to the many lawyers assembled from all parts of the country, and for some reason, this simple fact moved him. His eyes began to water and he wiped away the moisture with a thick rough finger. His expression was strained.

The voice of the clerk rang out as he called the first case on the calendar. "Samuel Stern versus Georgia."

The lawyer arose and went forward to meet his opponent. Florence was suddenly aware of the man's clumsy girth. He lumbered up, grasping his papers in a large speckled hand. He placed them on the lectern. When his adversary was seated he bowed to the Court.

The Chief Justice, Amos Tucker, made a notation and nodded gravely. "We are honored to have you with us again, Mr. McKeever." He spoke with a strong New England accent.

Florence felt an immediate stir of interest. The whisper of the lawyer's name spread through the chamber, and even the judges looked up with anticipation. Of course, she thought, this was Lincoln McKeever! The leathery face had been familiar, but now somehow —unexpected! He looked more like a weary farmer than the foremost trial lawyer of the day.

The justice in the junior chair, a tiny man with pointed nose, Simon Tolliver of Illinois, whispered to his neighbor.

If McKeever was aware of all this, he gave no sign. He stood at the lectern, hands thrust in hip pockets, waiting for the attention of the Court with a pleasant air of outward assurance—an assurance he did not feel. He had in fact a sense of dread that his words might not come in the form needed, and the aching pulse in his temples distracted him. But none of this had to do with his sleepless night, nor even with the difficulties of the appeal. No, it had to do with his son seated in the rear.

He fingered his printed brief, for at least that part was all right. Whether the oral argument went well or ill, the bench would retire with the printed argument in its best possible form. Nothing more could have been said, nothing better written, the authorities had been impeccably marshaled by his assistants in New York. But even this thought was no comfort. Like the facts of record, the cases were against him. He wondered that he had agreed to argue this hopeless appeal, especially with this other great fear upon him. He glanced at the array of lackluster faces. The argument would depend wholly on striking the first right note of emotion.

The Chief Justice closed his eyes and seemed to doze. He said, "You may proceed, sir."

The lawyer replied in a friendly way, "I am waiting for the Court's attention."

Simon Tolliver looked up with a disagreeable expression, shrugged and settled back with his toes reaching for a footstool. McKeever drew a shuddering breath and began, and in the accustomed swing of argumentation felt enheartened.

He came to a simple point. A state prosecutor and a howling mob had created an inflammatory atmosphere which had denied the defendant—a mill bookkeeper charged with the murder of his mistress —a fair and constitutional trial. The proof lay in the record. When the verdict was rendered, the defendant had remained cowering in jail while the mob had surrounded the courthouse.

"May the Court please," he drawled, "I had some surprises during the past weeks in the exchange of briefs with my learned colleague. Until today I thought there was a Constitution of the United States which the Federal courts are supposed to maintain against unlawful invasion, even by the various states of this Union. But our friends seem to feel that although the Constitution is a splendid document, it's up to each man, even when on trial for his life, to look out for himself, and they would have the Federal courts even in such case remain neutral between citizen and state. Well"—he rumpled his hair with a deploring grin—"that's like the mountaineer who came home one day to find his wife wrestling in the kitchen with a ferocious black bear attracted by the smell of her delicious cooking. He studied the situation and decided to take a neutral position between woman and bear . . ."

He finished the anecdote in a broad twang, easily and pleasantly, grasping his lapels and peering at the bench with shrewd eyes. Another lawyer would have been struck by the wrath of the bench, but he was a privileged wit, and under his light touch a wintry smile rippled across the bench. He hunched forward and went into the facts with earnest concern.

His clumsiness vanished in the charm of his expression. His physical warmth was infectious. He spoke with simple common sense with a chuckle at the state's folly and indignation at its wickedness, and his baritone rose like a trumpet to a pitch of urgency. A rebellious

4

cowlick thrust forward as he swept the courtroom in a blaze of indignation.

Tolliver broke in. "Sir!"

McKeever looked up. "Your Honor?"

"As I see it, trial counsel agreed that the defendant for his own safety ought to remain in the security of the prison—so that all this was done with consent." The little justice flipped through the record. "I call your attention to folio 1,060."

McKeever retorted, "The reason is indicated. Trial counsel was persuaded that the mob might storm the courtroom. This is exactly the point I am making."

"As I recall, sir"—Tolliver sucked his pen meditatively—"the state court decided that none of this had any effect upon the trial of the issues."

"A trial where a man's life was at stake!" McKeever interrupted.

"I'm quite aware of that!" the justice said acidly. "But where do you question the sufficiency of the appellate review below, sir?"

McKeever answered with a note of anger. "We wish to correct the error which the state courts refuse to admit. We are here to save a man's life."

Tolliver favored him with a tolerant smile. "So far as I can see, both trial and appeal below were regular. On what ground can we intervene? We have ruled on this point many times, as you must be aware"—his ironical glance was obvious—"for I see you attempt to distinguish our earlier decisions in your brief on pages 25 to 30." He sat back with a pleased air.

McKeever's face darkened. "The question is one of substance," he said strongly. "The record may be good in form, but the state courts are taking the man's life without due process!"

"Under our system of jurisprudence, what can we do?" Tolliver asked gently. "We do not know it as a court!"

There was a silent moment.

McKeever extended his arm toward the bench. He was astonished that his hand was trembling with anger. "This Court can change the rule! It has done so in matters of less importance! It can do so now!"

"Oh, sir, you ask too much!" Tolliver said with regret. He sat back and lost contact with the footstool. McKeever drew a deep breath. The death of the man in the Georgia prison could be seen in the array of unconvinced faces. The dim light filtering through the windows, the ornate carvings, the portraits, the green-shaded lamps—all gave him a thick sense of the history of this room. "I do not agree," he began, and at that moment a racking cough in the rear split the silence.

5

Uh! Uh! Uh!

McKeever went white. It was a sound he did not want to hear and he tried to continue. "As I said—" He broke off with an expression of pain, unable to proceed, as the coughing went on, but he did not turn his face to see.

The Chief Justice opened his eyes and said quietly, "Mr. Tate." The clerk rose. "Yes, Your Honor."

"See if that boy would like this glass of water." Tucker handed down a glass which the clerk took to the rear. As all eyes turned the boy went into a paroxysm of coughing. Florence received the glass and passed it over.

"Here, son," she whispered. "Take a sip."

The boy pressed a handkerchief to his mouth. "No," he managed, "I'll be all right."

"Take it," she said firmly and the coughing broke out again. The boy arose scarlet with embarrassment and walked out. At the lectern, McKeever turned with a look of pain. Florence caught his glance, arose, and followed the boy out.

The court was silent. McKeever kept his eyes on the printed record before him, thick in its gray covers and smelling faintly of glue. He dared not look up, and then the Chief Justice said:

"Please continue the argument, sir."

McKeever raised a face of distress, but it was no use. He had come to the end. "I have concluded, Your Honors. I urge that judgment of death be vacated and that this case be remanded to the state court that justice may be done in accordance with law." He hesitated, then resumed his seat and his opponent, a lanky man with sandy hair, advanced to the lectern.

In the nightmare which followed, McKeever's thoughts were elsewhere. He made no rebuttal. When finally the court arose, he went quickly to the corridor. A crowd at the water fountain alcove attracted his attention and he pushed through. The boy was seated on a marble bench, pale and sweating, with his head thrown back. His forehead was being daubed by the young woman lawyer, there was a strong smell of cologne. McKeever knelt.

"Hello, Dad," Jeff said guiltily. "I'm sorry!"

Florence looked up cheerily. "Oh, Mr. McKeever! I wouldn't worry too much. This boy looks right as rain."

"How is he?" McKeever asked anxiously.

"He's just having a little fun," she drawled. "All that attention in there, oh my!" She smiled sunnily for the boy's benefit and McKeever got an impression of a handsome positive face, slightly freckled, with perceptive steady green eyes. Her head was small and graceful with a crown of russet braids coiled neatly on a slender neck. He said, "Here, let me see!" He took the handkerchief and exclaimed at the pin-point fleck of red spray. "Oh dear!" he said with dismay.

The boy averted his eyes guiltily. "I couldn't help it, Dad," he muttered. "It just happened!"

"No one's blaming you!" McKeever folded the handkerchief in paper and gave a fresh linen to his son.

"I spoiled it! Now you're going to blame me!" Tears trickled down the boy's cheeks.

McKeever put his arm around his son's shoulders. "It was all right," he said with distress. "Really all right, Jeff! I wanted you in court."

"No you didn't!" the boy wept.

A motherly woman in the crowd clucked and offered advice and then McKeever said worriedly, "You've got to get back to the hotel, Jeff. The trouble is, I've got to stick around—"

"I'll get back myself," Jeff said. His eyes squeezed water as he suppressed his coughing. They discussed the matter until Florence broke in. "Suppose I take him back to the hotel," she volunteered. "Where are you staying?"

McKeever looked at her dubiously. "We're at the Willard, but we can't impose, Miss—?"

"Florence Hogarth!" She introduced herself with a smile and gave him a strong hand. "I wouldn't mind one bit!"

"Are you sure?"

She thrust a hatpin through a trim straw hat with a firm air of authority. "It's only the friendly thing, Mr. McKeever," she said easily. "Back home you wouldn't ask twice. If you've got some business keeping you here, I'm more than glad to help out. I'm at the Willard too. It's no trouble at all."

"Well—" McKeever rubbed his face uncertainly. This young woman was good-looking, richly dressed, and her manner was direct. She met his glance quizzically. "I'm a lawyer," she remarked. "You can trust me!"

"It's not that," he said uncomfortably. At this point, a dignified elderly Negro in livery came to say that the Chief Justice was ready to see him in chambers. He turned to his son. "Do you mind, Jeff?"

The boy glanced at the smiling young woman and shook his head. "You stay here, Dad. I'll see you later."

McKeever smiled and gave in. "Well, since you're a member of the bar, Miss Hogarth, I yield. Let me put you in a cab."

"So stipulated," she said humorously. "Jeff, let's go!" She took the

7

boy's hand and they left the building. They found a cab waiting in the hot sun. Jeff sank back weakly while his father paid the fare and turned to Florence. "I'd like to thank you," he said worriedly. "May I see you later?"

"I wish you would," she smiled. "My whole crowd's at the Willard and I know they'd like to meet you too. We've heard about you even in New Mexico, you know."

"I'd be pleased," he agreed.

The boy's mouth quivered. "I couldn't help it!" he muttered.

McKeever turned to him. "Never mind that now, Jeff!" he said sharply. "You get off your feet and into bed. I'll ask for a report when I get back. Now mind!" He waved them off and watched the carriage disappear through the shaded streets. His son's pale sweating face was in contrast to the sunny open vigor of the woman lawyer. Damn! he thought. Why had he ever given in to the boy? He stared at a pigeon hotfooting on the pavement, then disconsolately returned.

The building was emptying in the recess. At the head of the stairs, knots of lawyers were chatting and discussing the proceedings. A sallow man smoking a cigar detached himself from a group and came over. "Sir, may I say that your argument was splendid? It had the authentic note!" He spoke with a marked Spanish accent. "I shall not forget your remarks!"

McKeever halted. "Why, thank you, sir. You're most kind!"

"I am called Dominguez!" The man fumbled in a thick wallet and handed over a card. "José Dominguez! I imagine you don't remember me."

The ornate script proclaimed that José Dominguez, Counselor and Attorney-at-Law, maintained offices in the Valdez Building, Cuatro Rios, Territory of New Mexico. McKeever turned over the pasteboard. He said quizzically, "I'm sorry—?"

"Sir, about six years ago, when you gave that lecture in Harvard—I listened!" The lawyer laughed heartily with self-appreciation and slapped his thigh. "I listened!"

"Harvard?" McKeever wondered.

"I'm an alumnus. Class of '59. I may not look it, but I am." The dark ugly grin displayed a row of gleaming white teeth with infectious humor. McKeever smiled and snapped his fingers.

"Of course!" he recalled. "You were in the third row on the aisle seat. You were taking notes and later you invited me to New Mexico to lecture in some town or other—"

"Cuatro Rios!" the other supplied.

8

"Exactly!" They shook hands and chatted and McKeever asked, "Well, sir, what brings you here?"

The New Mexican lawyer lost his delighted expression. "Our celebrated Land Grant Case, I'm afraid. We'll be reached for argument tomorrow. Are you familiar with the matter?"

"I'm afraid not, except for what I've read."

Dominguez sighed. "It's been dragging for years. Ah well! If you'll be here tomorrow, I would appreciate your reaction. The matter is most important back home. May I invite you to attend?"

"I'm afraid I've got to get back to New York," McKeever murmured.

"Perhaps it's as well," the other said deprecatingly. "The fact is that I'm nervous as a cat. We daren't lose this appeal. I don't know how you manage to be so eloquent, sir, but it seems to come easy to you!"

"Does it seem easy?" McKeever smiled faintly. "Well, if you'll excuse me!" With an abstracted nod, he went into the cool building. He retrieved his papers, and set off for chambers, sunk in thoughts of his son.

McKeever found the Chief Justice of the United States in shirt sleeves in his study, a room lined with calfbound legal tomes. Early Supreme Court reports were hidden behind glass, and McKeever surmised that these were volumes originally owned by John Jay and Oliver Ellsworth and John Marshall and Roger Taney and the rest who followed the author of the Dred Scott decision with all the mischief it had brought in its wake. Amos Tucker stood behind a teakwood desk littered with memoranda and opinions in progress, a tall stooped man with a thatch of white hair and a neat vandyke. He was holding a magnifying glass.

"Well, Link," he said genially, "would a julep strike you right?"

"A julep would be fine," McKeever admitted wearily, and they shook hands. "I haven't tasted the real thing since last time."

"The secret is the mint," Tucker said precisely. "Let it soak, that's the trick. Julian!" He rang a bronze bell which brought the dignified Negro, who took the order and left.

"Now, let's see." Tucker gazed up sharply. "Suppose you sit there where I can see you. My eyes are getting damn blurry these days. Can't see without glasses."

McKeever sat with his back to the bookcases which rose the height of the ceiling. He had a special feeling here for the continuity of things. He said aloud:

"Why not wear your glasses then, sir?"

9

"Hate the things," Tucker said shortly. "The world looks better through a haze, at that." His eyes were weirdly Cyclopean behind the magnifying glass. He put it aside and swiveled about.

"Off your feed today, Link?" he asked abruptly.

"Oh, I touched the main points."

"H'm!" Tucker gave the despondent lawyer a curious look of affection mixed with disapproval, but he had no intention of discussing that point till after refreshments. He smoothed his vandyke. "Sorry about the boy," he said sympathetically. "Isn't he a little young to bring to court? Or was this some sort of puberty rite?"

"He'll be all right," McKeever said shortly. "He's resting at the hotel. I didn't want him to come, but it seems as though I can't manage him these days. I couldn't keep him away. He was bound to hear me argue an appeal in the Supreme Court and I had to give in."

"Ah!"

Tucker closed his eyes and for a moment he seemed asleep, then as suddenly they opened. "Saw that Hogarth girl follow him out. Damn good-looking woman—and they tell me, a good lawyer."

"I didn't suppose you'd not notice," McKeever drawled.

Tucker chuckled. "No, Link, my salad days are past and done. I knew her father, Dan Hogarth. You know, *the* Hogarth. Fought with him at Shiloh during the War. Hell of a soldier."

"Oh yes, the Land Grant Cases." McKeever nodded intelligently and took a cigar from a carved box. He mentioned his encounter with the New Mexican lawyer, Dominguez. "That matter's been up and down the Ninth Circuit for twenty years. Why not put the poor devils out of their misery?"

Tucker grimaced, "They're crazy down there, Link. Bitter-enders. Never settle a case. I'm going to propose a new rule of court. We shoot the next set of fools who bring those issues here."

"Hogarth, eh?" McKeever struck a match and brought the cigar to life. "Seems to me he got burned a bit in Wall Street last year. Got in with a fast mining crowd, and they caught him in copper, I believe. Young Guggenheim had a finger in that pie."

"Let's not worry about Dan Hogarth." Tucker sat back and let the clouds of blue smoke drift lazily out the window. McKeever waited patiently for the old man to get to the point.

"Damn it, Link," Tucker growled, "the work here is getting out of hand. We keep getting the wildest kind of appeals, things we ought never to get. We're swamped. Would you believe it—" He broke off as Julian entered and served juleps in frosted glasses of Venetian design. "This job was once supposed to be a sinecure. When

10

John Jay was appointed, they thought they were putting him on the shelf. He had nothing to do. They just met and adjourned. Went on that way for years till he got out and went to England as ambassador just to keep busy. Marshall had ten cases the first year he was appointed. Ever hear of that?"

"Of course." McKeever sipped the iced drink, the sprig of mint was pungent at his nostrils. "But Marshall sat here for thirty-four years. He made it quite a thing."

"So he did."

McKeever could understand the justice's thoughts. These chambers were a second home in which he had lived for thirty years. Portraits of a score of secretaries were on the wall, Yale men mostly, many now jurists themselves. A bronze bust of the old man stared across the room at a dark portrait in oils. He was evidently getting ready for posterity. McKeever nodded at the painting. "That's well done, sir."

Tucker tapped his cigar with a grunt. "They say it looks like me. Can't tell myself. Some fool woman got me to sit for it. Don't know a thing about painting, but she was a good-looker and I didn't mind one bit. Finally wanted to marry me till I told her, no, thanks—one wife was enough for one lifetime!" He raised the frosted glass and squinted. "Pure bourbon never hurt an old man, Link. That was the one thing Abel Greene taught me when I came to this town. I'm just beginning to understand how true that is."

"Greene wasn't much of a judge," McKeever remarked acidly.

"Don't be heartless, Link, it's not your style," Tucker smiled. "When it came to cards and liquor, he was a good man to have on my left. What if he was a little mad about states' rights?"

Julian entered quietly and brought fresh juleps. McKeever gazed out at the tree-shaded streets surrounding the lawn. Washington was shabby and provincial, he thought, but one could live well here.

Now why the oblique reference to Abel Greene? He thought he understood. There was a story that when Justice Greene, a prideful man and one of Lincoln's appointees, had taken to dozing at the bench, his fellows had deputized Tucker to urge retirement, a nasty job but necessary. Tucker had been persuasive and at a farewell banquet, Greene had blubbered and wept like a child. He had retired to pasture in Baltimore where, perversely, he had lived on in bitterness, unreconciled to fate, writing fiery articles on the decline of the judiciary until his death from overeating at eighty-nine.

"Link." Tucker put aside his cigar and sat back with hands folded across his paunch, and suddenly he seemed frail. A button of his shirt had come open and McKeever could see the white curls of hair beneath and this, more than anything, struck him as evidence of age—he could not have said why—and he felt a pang. This was a process of nature but it was related suddenly to a feeling of his own these days and his anquish was encompassed in what he saw.

Tucker said quietly, "I finally had breakfast with the President last Saturday."

McKeever sat perfectly still. This was of course the point, and so many things were surging within him. He saw how fine Tucker's eyes were, gentle and intelligent and touched with pain under the white shaggy brows. But what were they telling him? He drew a breath.

"Yes?"

"I told him there would be an empty bench in this Court after all." Tucker sighed despondently. "He didn't act surprised at all. Seems that damn clique in the Senate was pushing him to talk to *me!* I've never seen the politicians more bold. They were trying to force the issue, putting out rumors, especially that fellow from Ohio, and no one ever told me. I thought it was our secret. You were the only other one I told, Link, and I don't suppose you spilled the beans. How do these things get around?"

"I'm sorry to hear this," McKeever murmured.

Tucker shook his head. "Don't be. It had to come, but I did feel I had a few more decisions to write." He studied the cigar meditatively. "Takes a long time to make a good judge, Link. I'm not sure one lifetime is enough. Never an end to learning. It's a damn silly thing. You think there's never going to be an end, and then there you are! No, I've got to resign."

McKeever said nothing.

"But it doesn't matter, not since Dolly died. It's a pretty empty life without your wife. We were married fifty-one years." Tucker turned. "You ought to know, Link."

"Yes, I know," the lawyer said somberly.

The old man closed his eyes and his head drooped. They sat in silence. A black bird with crimson shoulders whistled at the window sill and the sound brought him back and he said abruptly:

"When I got this appointment, Link, I thought it was the most important thing in the world, at least to me. I knew it was coming. I was supposed to replace old Judge Allen. He was from Vermont, and up there they like to live forever. It was touch and go and I thought it would never happen. And then—" Tucker arose stiffly and placed his hand on the mantelpiece of Carrara marble with eyes sunk in the past—"then there was news that the old boy had pneumonia. I had my heart set on this job. That night I dreamt that I was attending his funeral. I was in the graveyard throwing clods in his face. Never forgot that dream." He lit a paper spill at the grate and with a thoughtful air rekindled his cigar. "When you look inside yourself, Link, you can shudder. There's a bit of the murderer in all of us, don't you think?"

"Perhaps," McKeever murmured.

Tucker waved the spill and it fluttered out. "Link," he said directly, "is it terribly important to you to fill my place?"

McKeever rubbed his face.

"That's a hard question, sir, the way you put it." He felt a curious turn within him. He was not sure which way this talk was going, but he seemed to be standing suddenly outside himself, gazing at his own image on the bench in robes of office, his head cocked to the argument, and he could not tell at that moment what he felt. "I wish you could stay forever, you know that. No one can fill your place."

"Nonsense!" Tucker slumped into a red brocade chair, and folded his hands over his small paunch. "I'll say this much, Link, your name came up before I got there. The President knew all about it." He smoked meditatively. "Good set of fellows, this Bench, except that varmint Tolliver. Not too bad a life. Don't blame anyone for wanting it."

"The Supreme Court—" McKeever murmured. Through the window, a maple began to sway violently as a breeze kicked up, and then Tucker extended a frail hand and came to the point.

"There's no chance for you, Link," he said quietly. "The President has his own ideas. I'm sorry but there it is."

It came as a shock. "No chance?" McKeever said stupidly. "Are you sure?"

"He was pretty definite."

"But I thought—?" McKeever paused aghast. "But I had it from Tom Fletcher. Otherwise I wouldn't—"

Tucker smiled grimly. "You'll never learn, Link, not to take a politician's word. I don't think there was ever a chance. Are you disappointed?"

"I don't know." McKeever rumpled his hair. "I'm bewildered. Fletcher told me you could swing it. Didn't you urge it?"

"I promised to take it up, Link, and I did," Tucker said sharply, "but the President has his own ideas, and I must say I agree with him. He has no reason to appoint you to this bench."

"Is that what you told him? That you agreed?"

"I gave him an honest opinion."

McKeever could not grasp this. "No chance!" he said with wonder.

"This was never a position you could get, Link, don't you understand?"

The lawyer thought this over. "You didn't say that three months ago!" he said with some resentment. "I wouldn't have gone out on this limb without your promise. I never asked for anything in my life!"

"I didn't understand that," the judge said with regret. "I'm sorry."

"Sorry!" McKeever turned away with a breathless feeling. "I wouldn't mind if only those others weren't such—" He paused. "Who's getting the appointment?"

The old judge hesitated. "I can't tell you, Link."

"It's not Waring, I hope."

"No—not him."

"It doesn't matter," McKeever muttered. "I know the whole pack of them. They're not lawyers. They're just working for the railroads! I thought I could do something useful here. I thought I could bring something to this court." He paused as it struck him that this sounded hollow. "It doesn't matter what I thought. I just hoped for more than that from you, Judge. This way, well, I guess it is a disappointment." He stared out at the red sunset beyond the Potomac with the thought that there would be rain. The truth was that he felt slightly sick with hurt vanity.

Tucker raised a finger.

"Now let me tell you," he said firmly, "you're a fine fellow, Link, but that's got nothing to do with it. The woods are full of fine fellows. What the President wants is a judge, not a maverick lawyer. No one knows where you'll stand on anything, and there are a lot of new problems coming along you're not qualified to consider. The frontier's gone. The country is changing. We see it all the time. You're an old-style court man, and these new things are complicated. It's the office lawyer we need now. You've spent a lifetime chasing rainbows, bucking the courts, that sort of thing. It's made you popular in some circles, but that's no qualification here. You should have been a preacher, not a lawyer. Take this appeal today! What did you expect to accomplish?"

"I thought—" McKeever muttered.

Tucker made a strong gesture. "I know what you thought! That poor devil's wife or mother or aged father got you to take this appeal. You know there's nothing in the record to hang your hat on. Those state judges are getting devilish cunning these days when they want to hang a man. But why didn't you turn the case down? No—let me tell you. They worked on you and your heart turned to water. You couldn't refuse. You took the appeal with the prayer that you might

14

get us to change the rule just by force of your personality. Perfect nonsense—even for you!" The judge puffed strongly on his cigar. "How do you think we feel when you throw your bleeding heart in our faces? We know that Georgia situation was an outrage—but what can we do? If we were to listen to fellows like you, the whole system would collapse." He paused. "I don't know why you've got me excited. It's all too elementary."

McKeever was silent.

"The fact is—" The judge puffed at his cigar, and went on in a lower voice. "You've got a warm and compassionate heart, Link, that's why the country loves you, but don't mistake its function. The heart isn't the mind. That's the difference between a trial lawyer and one of us. You come pleading for a man's life. That's easy, that's the hero's role. We've got to make the decision. No glory in that and a lot of heartache. This kind of work isn't really your field. Now isn't that a fair statement?" He raised his hand for a crusher. "And it's not as though you had any real political support. I don't care what Tom Fletcher told you, your position is weak. Two New York Senators don't go far these days. If you'd ever done anything for the party, the President might have gone along. He loves a low-down reason when he makes an appointment. Like all of us, he's only ashamed of his better instincts. But you've never once taken time out to mend your fences. Now tell me, did you get so much as a decent fee in this case?"

McKeever shrugged.

"I thought so," Tucker nodded. "Let me tell you about that defendant. What's his name—Branch? Stern? He may be just a book-keeper but his uncle owns that mill. You could have named your own price. How can the President put a softie like you on this bench? You're just not fit!" He paused. "You're not convinced?"

"You don't mean that," McKeever said resentfully.

"Perhaps not—but that's the rough idea."

The lawyer kept staring toward the sunset. The sky was still crimson and the first lights in distant windows were appearing. He was trying to sort out his thoughts. The first tide of shock had receded, leaving him drained of feeling except for this other matter of Jeff which never left him. He felt—what was it? He gave the old man a curious glance.

"Is that how I strike you, Judge? A damn fool rushing around?" Tucker smiled.

"Of course not," he said soberly. "We're talking about different things. You're an emotional man, that's all. It's not to your discredit." He put out a hand and McKeever could see the delicate red tracery in his eyes. "This isn't your place," he said softly, "at least not yet. You're a trial lawyer and you belong out front—buzzing away, stinging where it does the most good. Up here you'd get restless. You're too young to get on the shelf." He snorted. "Now why must every lawyer want to be a judge? Perfect nonsense!"

"You don't understand me at all," McKeever said in a low voice.

"What is it, Link?" Tucker asked gently. "You've had other disappointments. What else does a lawyer get out of life?"

McKeever's eye picked out details of the room, the red blotter, the heaped letters with British postmarks, the portrait of the Lord Chief Justice of England, the green-mantled desk lamp, the bird life whistling on the lawn. The odds and ends of Tucker's long and rich and honored life pointed to what had slipped through his hands. Perhaps if he had made a more strenuous effort? No—nothing could have helped! He saw that now. He raised his eyes.

"I've been giving you a hard time, Judge, and do you know," he said gloomily, "I feel relieved."

"Eh?"

"The fact is I've decided to retire."

"Retire?" Tucker exclaimed. "Are you serious?"

McKeever nodded.

"I must say!" Tucker arose and walked about the room, disturbed. "I don't understand you at all, Link, I vow I don't! You're young enough to be my grandson, yet one disappointment and you're talking like a child. Really!"

"It's not just this business today," McKeever said, "it's a lot of things." He picked up his cutaway and felt the damp shoulder pads with the feeling that the humidity was more than he could bear. "I made up my mind three weeks ago. I'm through with the profession. In a way I was afraid to get this appointment."

Tucker studied the downcast face and his anger receded. "Is it the boy?" he asked gruffly.

"That's part of it," the lawyer said in a low voice.

"I thought that was just a coughing spell. Something going down the wrong way."

"No, it's his lungs." McKeever raised a white face. "The left is clear, they say, but there's a bad patch in the right. It's been getting worse for months, and I never knew." He added savagely, "I was too busy with my work!"

"I didn't realize, Link. That's hard to take, I know." Tucker fumbled at his desk. "Are you sure of all this?"

"We've had the best," McKeever said despondently. "Reuben Loewy came in from Denver for this case. You ought to remember the family. His father ran a dry goods store in Salem." He sighed heavily. "It's just taken the starch out of me."

"What are you going to do?"

McKeever shrugged. "Loewy wants us out in Denver. There's some talk of a hospital out there, or a sanitorium they're going to build. Meanwhile—he says there's a good chance, but I don't know. It's a nightmare. I was hoping against hope, then the answer came through this week."

"Are you going out there with the boy?"

McKeever nodded. "He won't travel without me."

"Does he know how sick he is?"

"I don't know. I suppose he does. He's become so difficult, it must be on his mind. He's a boy with black moods these days. He must get that from me." McKeever's smile was a fixed grimace. "Oh, Lord! I had to let him attend this argument today. He just put his heart into coming."

"I wondered at that."

"It might have been his last chance," the lawyer said simply. "I couldn't refuse."

They faced each other, each with his own thoughts.

"But you'll be back?" Tucker suggested.

McKeever shook his head heavily. "No—I'll find something else to do. I don't want the law game any more."

"Was it this disappointment today?"

"Not entirely, no." McKeever sighed. "I've simply had no taste for the practice since Liz died."

"Ah!" Tucker was silent a moment. "Is that what was troubling your argument—Liz? I felt something wrong."

McKeever shrugged. "I have such a sense of mortality these days. Time is just rushing past. When I went back to Boston for the funeral, I went to my old chambers with Uncle Rufe. Hadn't been there in eighteen years, not since I was a clerk. The shingle was still flapping in the square, there were the same cobblestones, and the brewery smell. Well, the street was the same, but different. One of the old clerks—you remember Ellery Prentiss—came running to greet me and I almost broke down. Oh, Lord!" He shuddered and stared out the window. "This feeling of time!"

There was a silence.

"You're not much past forty, Link," the judge observed gently. He lit a match and held it aloft with an inquiring glance. "You're not expected to mourn forever, you know." McKeever followed his gaze to a portrait of his wife, a woman with large features and a

17

humorous twinkle in her eyes. It struck him that the old couple looked remarkably alike.

"It's not only that!" He turned fiercely. "Why should the boy be so sick? What purpose does it serve? You give your life to others, you sacrifice your wife, your son, everything—and then this happens! I thought this appointment might change my feelings, but it would have made no difference. The boy's got to live!" His eyes glowered with dismay and wrath. "It's not fair!"

Tucker waited. "You'll change your mind," he murmured. "You're too young to pull out."

"No!" McKeever said stubbornly. "I've never given the boy anything, and now I'm going to make it up to him. This was my last case. I've always been chasing after one damn case after another. When I started clerking in Boston, I expected to inherit a quiet practice—you know, estates, real property, that sort of thing. I used to eat lunches at home with Liz. Sundays we went fishing. We were having a happy time of it. Then I got into a case with a moral issue, and I never drew an easy breath again. Never had a minute for Liz, or Jeff either, after he was born—"

Tucker glanced up. "Your ice is melting," he suggested.

McKeever's somber thoughts were in the past. "Lord, that first case was almost twenty years ago," he murmured. "It was a little farming town in Cape Anne. A poor ignorant Irish lad was charged with rape. He wasn't much older than the girl, but her father worked up a lot of feeling among the Yankees. That wasn't hard then. The Irish were coming in droves after the famine. Got the boy off though. It took an appeal but I did it." He sighed heavily. "D'ye know, I've forgotten the boy's name? Patrick something."

"Not Patrick—John," Tucker suggested. "John Mahon."

McKeever showed surprise. "How can you remember?"

The judge smiled. "Old Bassett, J., used to talk about that trial. He never forgave that blistering summation you made. He always felt Mahon was guilty."

"Bassett was a hangman," McKeever said bitterly. "He never knew what a fair trial was. A regular Jeffries. It seems to me I've been fighting Bassett ever since. I never did get back to that quiet practice. When Liz died after all those wasted years, we were strangers. She never forgave me, you know. As for Jeff—!" He stared into his glass. The refreshing smell of mint had gone.

"You're too young to crawl into a shell," Tucker said with curious affection. "'The war horse smells the smoke of battle from afar,'" he quoted gently, "'and paws the ground and cries, Ha! ha!' You'll come running when you hear the trumpets."

18

"I don't think so," McKeever said stiffly.

Tucker brushed his beard as a thought struck him. "Then let me ask a fair question. How could you have filled this post away in Denver?"

"I don't know." McKeever rubbed his neck. "I suppose the main thing was to get the offer," he admitted ruefully. "I guess I'd have appealed to you to hold your resignation until Jeff got well. But at least"—he raised his head defiantly—"at least I'd have had the choice."

Tucker shook his head in despair. "Oh Link, Link!" he exclaimed. "You're a child!"

McKeever had in mind a vision of the night Liz had died, and this was something he could share with no one. They talked briefly of other things, but it was only a pretense, their thoughts were elsewhere. The judge was not happy with the President's notions and he wished to suggest his own successor. McKeever pointed out that the law schools might well provide a candidate—Harvard, for example. This book by the junior Holmes on the Common Law, it showed a poet's eye in the field of scholarship, almost mystical in its insights, especially in the chapter on primitive notions of criminal liability. Quite good and original, he thought.

Tucker cocked his head sadly. " 'The lunatic, the lover, and the poet,' " he quoted, " 'of imagination all compact'! I like my law solid, Link. Ah, well, I'll think about it. Holmes!"

McKeever glanced at his watch and exclaimed at the time. At the door, Tucker took his hand. "This may be the last time," he said softly. "I'll say good-by."

McKeever said reassuringly, "Now, sir, Kent wrote his *Commentaries* after he retired. It was a long time writing."

The judge smiled feebly. "Kent was sixty, Link, not eighty-seven. It makes a difference. I wouldn't want to start a long book." His handshake was light and feeble. "My best to the boy."

McKeever left and took a four-wheeler to the hotel. The hot sun made his head ache. The forlorn old judge was in his mind, mixed with images of his own early days when he had come down from Boston with Liz to start the practice in New York, the modest house on the square, the night they pulled Jeff through an attack of diphtheria, the other many nights—

He paid the driver off, and entered the old Willard Hotel and went up to his son.

Jeff was eating raspberry ices with Florence in the suite. The sound of his laughter came through the slatted door as his father entered to find him seated on the sofa covered with a light blanket. The boy saw his father's face and his gaiety died.

"It didn't go, Dad, did it?" he asked.

McKeever hung up his hat. "No, it didn't," he said briefly. This was not to be discussed, his manner said, and the boy subsided soberly. He asked, "How do you feel, Jeff?"

"All right, I guess," the boy said slowly.

Florence arose and patted her hair. She saw something between them as she began to pull on white gloves. "He's been fine," she said agreeably. "The only thing, Mr. McKeever, he's too worried about the fate of the vanishing buffalo. He can't understand why we're not doing much more to solve that problem." She smiled and the boy blushed furiously.

"Oh?" McKeever gave him a dry humorous look. "Jeff worries about more than the buffalo. Wait till he gets on the fur-bearing seals of the Pribilof Islands. Do you realize how fast that species is vanishing?"

She laughed. "No, I didn't."

"Something's got to be done!" Jeff said hotly. "It's like the passenger pigeons. Just ten years ago, there were still millions of 'em. Now what's happened? There's not one. You see—"

"Now, now." With a fond look, McKeever turned. "Would you care to stay for tea, Miss Hogarth?"

"No, I think I'd better get along!" With a good-natured smile, she excused herself. He showed her to the elevator, where she said soberly, "He's a fine boy, Mr. McKeever. You know, it wasn't all just talk about the buffalo. It was mostly about you."

"Good Lord!"

"There's a lot of hero worship," she smiled. "He seems to know every case you ever tried. He had your argument today at his finger tips. He was quite fascinating."

"Oh, Jeff's bright enough," McKeever agreed. She lingered a moment, clear-faced and handsome, and he was aware of a fresh scent. He had no idea of women's clothes, but her light tailored suit seemed expensive and sophisticated. Her interest in him—or was it only the usual curiosity?—was obvious. "Too bright, I'm afraid," he added.

She saw the cloud on his face. "Tell me, is there anything seriously wrong with the boy?" she asked.

"No, not a bit!" He must not neglect his manners, he thought. Something was called for—flowers perhaps. But Liz was no longer there to deal with this, he realized with a pang—he would have to call the florist himself. He caught himself staring and said, "I'm very grateful, please be sure."

"Not at all. Would you like me to look in again?"

He shook his head. "We're leaving in the morning, but if you're ever in New York, let me know. My offices are on Pine Street."

The elevator door opened.

"Perhaps." She smiled. "Well—good-by." She gave him her hand and stepped into the elevator. McKeever lit a cigar. He returned to Jeff and a vehement discussion of the dangers threatening the giant redwoods of California.

In the morning, they took the train for Denver. Some weeks later, his office in New York telegraphed that the Supreme Court had unanimously and without opinion affirmed the judgment of death of the court below.

Chapter II

A year after McKeever had settled in Denver, a man named Tom Canty got off the Pullman at Cuatro Rios, a small lazy town several hundred miles south in New Mexico Territory. The ancient city had an historical importance, but it had not yet felt the full effect of the railroads pushing in from the East and North. It slept as it had for four hundred years since the first conquistador had passed in search of the seven cities of gold located in the indefinite regions beyond.

Each spring for a million years, the river which meandered past had been fed by the melting snows of the surrounding ranges. At this point, it ran broad and shallow, boulder-strewn and dirty with silt, marked by willows and cottonwoods along its banks. But in the mountains, it began as a gushing spring, it rushed through stands of evergreen trees, it watered grassy meadows and mountain brakes. The Indians still drew water for irrigation in their ancient primitive style. Along its lower reaches, it dwindled and sank into the Gulf of Mexico, warm and turgid and exhausted.

Cuatro Rios got its name from four streamlets which converged at a point called Puente de las Estrellas—the Bridge of Stars. In the remote past, Fray Augustin, a Jesuit, had established a mission among the Pueblos who then occupied the area. The Indians then raised corn, fished a bit, hunted in the surrounding ranges and pursued a peaceful life. When the *encomienda* system with its enslavement of the natives was introduced, a bloody revolt was staged and suppressed, and the land returned to peace. Here Don Francisco de Niza, a nobleman of Spain who had lost his arm in battle, had established his house, secure in the belief that title to the lands of the four rivers—by grant of the Crown of Spain—lay vested in him and his heirs in fee simple forever. But the charred hearthstones of the great white *casa*, still visible at the river's bend, marked a later day when war bugles had sung in the plaza and a new flag had mounted to the blue sky.

Cuatro Rios had changed little since the land had passed to the

United States. Steep grades caused the railroads to skirt the Valley, but a spur had been put through the Cluny Junction and a train ran thrice weekly to pick up ores, cattle, timber and passengers—in that order of importance. The line connected with the Santa Fe system and thus south and north to El Paso and to Denver, but it was not ordinarily a traveled route. On this day, the activity was unusual for the time of year and a large influx of passengers was attracting attention.

"Cuatro Rios! Cuatro Rios!" the conductor bawled as the train squeaked to a halt. "All out."

Canty swung off before the train had stopped completely. Buckboards and traps were clustered at the depot in unusual numbers. He sauntered to a carriage whose driver was in earnest conversation with a hulking man of unusual height. He threw his carpetbag into the carriage and the driver, old Pedro, twisted around with a reproachful air. "Señor, where do you go?" he asked.

Canty got in and settled back. "Let's see, what's the best hotel?"

"The Conquistador."

"That's what I want then."

"They are full up."

"Take me anyhow," Canty said stolidly. "I'll talk to 'em personally."

The tall man who had been leaning with folded arms against a post stirred. "Better listen, mister," he drawled. "Pedro's right. You can't get a room now."

"Maybe," Canty smiled, "but I figure they'll listen to reason."

"I'm telling you!" the tall man said sharply.

Old Pedro broke in. "It's all right, *jefe!*" he said hastily. "I will take this man and make my dollar. Why not?"

"Now that's better," Canty said pleasantly. He sat smiling at the sun-drenched scene, a group of Indians in tribal costume, the garish brick structures, the old adobe buildings, the carriages, the sidings piled with lumber, the smell of hot dust, the sharp outline of remote mountains—

The tall man, Sheriff Max Kyle, gave him a sharp look of suspicion, then shrugged and returned to his study of the scores of passengers who were claiming baggage, laughing, joking with old friends. His stetson dipped low on his nose, his eyes were in shadow, and a sharp long chin projected like a challenge. He said sourly, "It's all right with me."

"*Hai!*" Pedro cried, and the mare ambled into action. The passenger, he decided, was a drummer perhaps, a portly man with a short nose and fattish flat eyes. A high forehead and gray temples gave a distinguished appearance, but his mouth was lipless and his gaze

23

was disconcerting. He seemed pleased like a man looking at his own property—which was odd, Pedro considered, since he was a stranger. "*Hai!*" he cried. They left New Town and crossed the bridge and came finally to the large rambling hotel on a hill. "Here we are," he announced and caught a silver dollar. "*Gracias!*" he grinned.

Canty leaped down on light feet. He strode to the desk and in a loud voice demanded a room.

The clerk shook his head with regret. "I'm sorry, mister, but I need a reservation. We're full up."

Canty wiped the sweatband of a straw hat with a critical air. "I'm an important mining man," he announced pleasantly. "I guess you can do better'n that."

The clerk made an entry in the guest book. "I've got six important mining men ahead of you. I'm just that sorry."

Canty made no move to go. "I just come five hundred miles," he said. The clerk looked up with annoyance. "Now what good does that do when I've got all these reservations?" he asked impatiently.

Canty smiled. "I can't help it about other folks. I want a room. I didn't get any sleep on the Pullman. Train does that to me. It's the pitching and bucking."

"You could try some private family."

"You might as well give me what I'm asking," Canty said pleasantly. "I never change my mind. I ain't going to leave and you ain't putting me out, young feller."

They stood at an impasse. The stout smiling man seemed immovable and the clerk was young. He hesitated and called for the manager:

"Mr. Collier!"

An older man with a peeled red face came out of the office. "Yes, Buddy?" he asked with a harassed air. The clerk explained briefly and he turned to the importunate visitor. "Lands! Don't you know the situation?" he exclaimed. "These rooms were taken last year, mister!"

"Is that a fact?" Canty seemed unimpressed. "That don't help me!"

"I don't see what I can do," the manager said resentfully, plucking his lip. "These are Dan Hogarth's guests—come for the birthday fiesta at the Ranch. We're too busy to argue. Now if you were on the list—"

"Well, I'm not on the list," Canty said stolidly.

The upshot was a compromise. With some head-scratching, the manager recalled a room in an old wing near the servants' quarters. It was not elegant but it had a bed.

"I'll take it!" Canty said with disgust.

"This way," said the porter, hefting the luggage, and left at a trot for a white clapboard outbuilding behind the kitchens.

"Well, it ain't much!" Canty remarked sourly when the door was swung open. The small hot room smelled of plaster, but it had an iron bedstead and a massive walnut dresser. There was no closet. The window was cracked. Across the patio were the kitchens where the help were at work and where frightful squawking could be heard.

He raised the blind and looked out. An old man was chasing a frantic rooster with the aid of ragged children, dogs, and a screaming woman. The kitchen help were calling encouragement in Spanish. "*Olé! Olé!*" called a fat greasy man in a white hat beating on a kettle. The panting woman caught the bird by its legs and threw it on the chopping block and the old man swung an expert ax. There was a gasp of silence and the rooster was hurled headless to the dust. It scrambled up, its legs working like pistons, racing madly, butting into adobe walls, its neck spurting bright gouts of blood.

Canty blinked and licked his lips. "*Oye, linda!*" he called.

The woman stared at him. A loose blouse showed naked shoulders and the outlines of heavy interesting breasts. There was excitement in her dark features. "*Sí?*" she responded, panting. She wiped a smear of blood from her bare calves. "What's on your mind?"

He winked. "I could eat that chicken!" he said cheerily.

She burst into laughter. "Suppose you order it for supper."

"And you too—I could eat you!"

The woman looked about at the grinning help. A fat woman shelling peas called out in Spanish and there was hooting laughter. She flirted a skirt provocatively. "I'm a special order, but for you I put on shoes. No extra charge!"

The chef appeared at the kitchen door and began to swear. "*Borrachos!* What the hell out here?"

"*Sí, patrón!*" The old man deftly caught the kicking rooster and began to pluck its feathers with haste. "*Sí, sí!*" The woman swaggered into the kitchen and Canty pulled down the blind and turned to the porter. "Who was that?" he asked.

"Juana, señor. A whore. You want her tonight?"

"I got other things on my mind." Canty tossed over a silver dollar. "Just remember, *niño*, I'm an important mining man. Treat me right and you get one a day."

"*Gracias, gracias!*" The porter caught the coin, grinned, bit it, and ducked out.

Canty closed the door and threw himself on the bed and stared at a train of ants on the ceiling, unmindful of the heat.

Hours later, when the room was dark, he arose suddenly and

opened his carpetbag. Two store suits came out; these he brushed and hung on nails. Underwear went into the dresser with shirts, a celluloid collar and woolen socks. He spread a Spanish newspaper, *La Luz,* on the bed, studied its columns, and placed it under the straw mattress. He counted a dozen shotgun shells, weighed the metal pieces, replaced them in a sack. A massive beetle, attracted by the lamplight, flew in and crawled on the dresser. Thoughtfully, he mashed the thing with his thumb and his eyes flickered as the carapace cracked. With a last satisfied look he went out to dinner as the first stars were in the sky.

The Conquistador was a comfortable old hotel with wide porches on which invalids and honeymooners rocked and gossiped in twangy Kansas voices about home and politics. Its four main wings enclosed a lovely garden through which a clear rill of water ran. Not only visitors but local residents patronized the cuisine, which was inexpensive and abundant and ideal for large families. With all these and the fiesta guests, the dining room was filled, but Canty managed to get a table from which he could watch the scene.

He looked about intently. Numerous brass lamps hanging from oaken beams cast a warm light. The guests were family men—prosperous ranchers, cattlemen and farmers, some mine owners, all dining with wives and children. There was a mood of joking humor among tables, he observed, and then the waitress placed a menu before him. He looked up and an amused grin broke. He said:

"The chicken girl, no?"

"The very one," she winked. "Juana Malina."

"I see you're wearing shoes."

"Why not? It's a rule of the house."

She gave him a bold stare until with a grunt he returned to the printed menu.

"Now"—he plucked a thin lip—"I'll have the pepper pot, broiled trout, steak with fried eggs, mushroom sauce, any kind of potatoes, canned peaches and coffee."

She noted the order, went to the kitchen, and returned with the hot soup. He was staring intently. As she put down the plate, he asked, "Could I make a mistake?"

"How do you mean?"

He nodded toward the rear. "Who do I think that is?"

"What kind of question is that?" She followed his gaze to a table at the hearth where piñon logs were blazing against the chill. A well-groomed elderly couple were joking with a roly-poly fat man with a good-humored face. Canty nodded. "Who are they?"

"Them?" Juana asked with surprise.

The old man placed his fork down and laughed till the tears came, a hearty booming sound, and all eyes turned, smiling. His ruddy complexion and large stern face were distinctive. "Oh, Lordy, Lon, not in mixed company!" He wiped his eyes, scarlet with amusement.

"That's Judge Hanna," Juana said. "Why?"

"I'm thinking that's old *General* Hanna, that's why," Canty remarked in a low voice. "That's who I think that is!"

The waitress was struck by an oddness of his glance. Douglas Hanna was a notable. As Chief Justice of the Territorial Supreme Court, he sat with his associates in Santa Fe, but like each of them, he presided over the District Court of his own judicial district. As the county seat, Cuatro Rios saw him regularly on court days, when he conducted the proceedings with an air of icy precision. The fat little man was Lon Wilby, publisher of the *Herald*. Juana said with asperity, "I don't get what you're driving at, Mr. Canty."

"Let's say I'm a stranger." He attacked the food, feeding himself faster than he could swallow, and the grease collected on his chin. He paused only once.

"We'll see," he said cryptically.

"See what?"

He blinked. "We'll look into a lot of things."

He did not explain and she served the next course and retired to the kitchen. Sadie Chavez, a waitress, remarked, "That one's got a touch of *indio*, I can tell."

Juana squinted. "Who hasn't, these days?" And indeed, something in Canty's bluff face had a Mongoloid cast. "He's kind of unpleasant the way he eats," she said cheerfully. "But then I like a man to be disgusting up to a point."

Sadie jingled a pocketful of small silver. "You aim to make him?"

"No, why? I'm kept busy. Besides"—Juana caught his signal—"I got a feeling something else is on his mind."

"Such as what?"

Juana said stolidly, "Such as minding his own business."

"He's a ten cent tip," Sadie remarked.

"Fifteen cents," Juana replied and went off. She brought dessert and coffee. Canty stirred his cup and looked up as she was about to leave. "Juana?" She grinned. "Yeah?"

"Don't run off like that," he said slowly. "How do you think I feel?"

She was about to reply with a joke, then her grin vanished. She asked cautiously, "What's your question?"

He blinked. "Would you be free one of these nights?"

"Which night?"

27

"I'm not sure, but pretty soon."

She poked a pencil behind her ear. "Mister, I'm working down at Tía María's, if we mean the same thing. I'm there any time."

"Are you regular?"

"I just help out."

"Tía María's," he nodded. "I'll find you there."

She went back to her station, balancing a tray, and unaccountably, she shuddered. "*Va!*" she exclaimed. "That man gives me the creeps!" She found that Sadie Chavez and Francisco, the chef, had gotten up a little pool on the question of Canty's tip. As it turned out, Angelo, who had guessed that Canty would leave fifty cents, won the pool. It struck them as a prodigal and pointless tip, but then, perhaps he had reached for the first coin in his pocket in his haste to follow the old general out. Juana thought of this later when she saw Canty intently watching the old couple stroll hand in hand in the garden. But there was a rush of business at Tía María's and she put the matter from her mind.

The hotel continued to fill with guests assembled for Dan Hogarth's fiesta. They came from as far as San Francisco and St. Louis and even New York, making railroad connections through the Santa Fe system. Local visitors came from all parts of the Territory, using their own mounts or fancy carriages or the old Barston and Oakes Stage which still ran down the Valley, carrying passengers, freight and mails to Cuatro Rios.

For several days, Canty lounged about in a purposeful manner. He seemed bound to attract attention as he sauntered through the town, drinking sweet Spanish beer in the saloons, asking pointless questions, winking and nodding with an air of gaiety. At night he appeared promptly for dinner at the same table. He gorged on meat dishes, greased his face, and kept his own counsel. Not for some days was there to arise reason for Juana to recall the strange intensity of his face on that occasion in the garden.

On the night of the fiesta, the stars were brilliant and the full Mexican moon turned the landscape into magic. At the bend of the river, music and laughter came from the great stone building of the Hogarth Ranch.

In the shadow of an oak tree overlooking the main building, Canty stood concealed, peering at the entrance. He stood knee-deep in rich grasses behind a hedge of honeysuckle, a sweet smell of shrubbery in his nostrils. A double row of giant cottonwoods twisted high into the night. Strings of chinese lanterns were hung across the formal gardens.

28

The Hogarth Ranch proper was spread over eight thousand acres of rich alluvial soil, but this was only one part of its hundreds of thousands of acres stretching along the river. It was here given to apple and peach orchards and blooded stock feeding in the millet planted by Hogarth for experimental purposes.

A night bird whistled liquidly. The silhouette of a night rider passed between the building and the watching man.

Canty slid the bolt of his rifle back. His face twitched, and he shrank back into the deeper darkness of the hedge.

The door opened, and a small group came out. Canty reached into a boot leg and took out a field glass. It had a low magnification, but he could make out the faces of the old judge, Douglas Hanna, and his wife, Virginia, as their lips moved. They were smiling and bowing as they shook hands with a stocky older man. A younger woman, wearing a black velvet gown with bare shoulders, joined them.

Canty nodded. This must be Dan Hogarth, he decided, and from the way the young woman slipped her arm in his, she could be his daughter, the one they called Florence.

Hogarth raised his hand and presently from the stables an old Spanish servant drove a buggy. The couple in cheerful good humor got in and were driven off at a trot behind a pretty Morgan mare. The clopping disappeared in the direction of Cuatro Rios, ten miles away.

"*Bueno!*" Canty muttered and withdrew into darkness. The night rider, or perhaps it was another, passed slowly behind him, the hooves of a stallion padding in the mulch of decaying oak leaves.

When there was quiet, he ran at a crouch along a dry irrigation ditch, knee-deep in drifting leaves. At the river, he ducked under a fence and got caught on a barb. He tore away impatiently, and scrambled down in a slither of soil. A tuft of wool remained behind.

He approached a gray cob tethered in the shadows at the river's edge. At his smell, it reared and rolled its eyes.

"Easy, boy, easy!" he murmured.

With quick skill he untethered the animal and mounted. He walked a stretch and then roweled into a frenzied gallop along the river path. He passed occasional sleeping adobe *casas,* then came to a halt at a stone bridge. He patted the cob, looked about, decided he had time to spare.

"First a smoke," he muttered, "then we see."

The bridge was a simple type of a design which went back through Spain to ancient Rome. A series of arches, built of granite brought on muleback from the mountains, bore its weight. The span was narrow and not more than one carriage could pass at a time—and this, he decided, was proof that things were going his way.

Scrambling down, he cut two thick withes of willow and peeled the bark with strong shredding motions. He climbed back and went directly to the granite coigns at the far end.

"*Ya, ya!*"

He muttered with satisfaction as he found the two holes gouged by him earlier that night in the cement between granite blocks on each side. With a strong thrust, he jammed a withe into each hole and flexed them strongly. The withes held.

The hup-pup of a trotter caused him to freeze, then the sound faded off and the sound of crickets filled the night. He snapped his fingers, he had lost the train of thought. Ah, yes. The saddlebags. He took out a horseshoe and wedged the steel tip between two blocks and levered it back with a stout pole. There were crumbs of cement to be scraped, and then the block gaped open under his powerful heave. He repeated the operation on the opposite side. His breath was whistling in his nostrils.

He slipped two heavy shotguns in the gaps, facing each other, elevated to have their fire meet at a point in the center of the bridge. His armpits felt wet in the cold breeze, but he finished quickly with no mind for this, nor for the trembling in his legs. A hank of twine went around the withes, formed a loop, and returned without snag or hitch to the triggers.

And then he waited.

The night was luminous at the river's edge, the Milky Way glowed in the limpid air. The mountains were dark silhouettes in the distance. A purling sound arose from below. Beyond the bridge the road, shaded by willows, made a turn toward the Hogarth Ranch. And along that road he heard a clear old woman's voice singing:

> "*There is a lady sweet and kind*
> *Was never face so pleased my mind;*
> *I did but see her passing by,*
> *And yet I love her till I die.*"

He began to shake violently.

He had nothing in his mind. There was only the road dappled with moonlight and the thud-thud of a trotting mare coming to the point of rendezvous.

The carriage approached. In the darkness the mare snorted softly and entered the bridge. The sound of her hooves changed as they struck the wooden planks. The firefly glow of a cigar came nearer.

He could see them resting, affectionately entwined, the old man and his wife, and then his buttocks knotted in a muscle spasm as the shotguns roared.

"*Dios!*" the stableboy screamed. "*Dios! Dios!*"

Canty stepped forth and stood stiff-legged in the moonlight. The mare reared and whinnied and backed as the stableboy sawed at her mouth, screaming his terror into the night as he saw the rifle.

"*Por favor,* señor, please!" he begged.

Canty peered into the carriage with a thoughtful look. The old man's face was torn away but he was alive and moaning. "Oh, God, oh, God, oh, God—"

His wife was groping for a handkerchief, dazed by the pain. "I can't see!" she whimpered. "What is it, Tomás?"

"Oh, God, oh, God—"

The woman spread out her hands. "Don't hurt my husband," she begged. Shot had raked her cheek and breast and a spattering of blood was oozing through her bodice. "Tomás! What has happened?" she cried.

"Oh, señora!" the stableboy gasped. "He has a gun, this man!"

Canty raised his rifle and counted. "*Uno!*"

The stableboy stared with amazement into the black muzzle. "He is standing there!" he screamed.

"*Dos!*"

"He is pointing the gun!"

"*Tres!*" Canty fired and with a low grunt the stableboy sat back, open-mouthed, and died.

"Not my husband," the woman cried. "Let my husband live—"

With a look of thoughtful concern, Canty fired again. The bullet struck the old man's neck, the blood spurted, and again death came at the river's crossing.

He raised the rifle a third time and hesitated. The old woman was groping about, blinded—and this made a difference. After a moment, he turned and untethered the cob and galloped back to town. Without rousing the hostler, he returned the cob to its stall in the livery stable.

Soon after, he knocked at a wooden frame house in Old Town. He was ushered to the parlor where he asked for Juana Malina. She came down in a wrapper, yawning and rubbing her eyes. She paused.

"Oh, it's you! What's on your mind?" she grumbled. "Sort of late, ain't it?" He stood with a hand on the piano, gay and smiling, in exuberant high spirits. "It's never too late!" he said and threw back his neck. "There's ten dollars in it, *chica!*" he grinned.

31

Her eyes turned up. "I don't know," she said dubiously. "I just had a full meal! I feel pretty stuffed!"

He laughed and threw aside his hat. "I don't mind one little bit! Just so's you put your heart into your work!" He took her arm and led her up the stairs.

An hour later, he entered the hotel, strolled past the sleeping clerk, and went to his room where, with a slack mouth, he fell into a sound sleep.

Tía María lay asleep in a heavy cotton nightgown, dreaming of love, a fat motherly woman with a mustache, when she seemed to hear a mewing cry through the warm gelatinous haze. The sound crept into her dream, turned it to a thing of pain in which her lover, a shrimp fisherman she had known as a girl in Tampico, became a cat snarling in her face. She awoke with a start.

The sound came to her again, and again, and she looked out into the street. Across the way, the Cantina Imperial was closed. Nothing was in sight but a buggy and a pretty mare in the moonlight waiting patiently between the saloon and her bagnio.

"Funny!" she thought.

The town was silent, it was hours yet to the dawn over Gidding's Pass in the distant hills. What was up? She knew the mare and the elegant trim buggy. It had no business on this side of the tracks, she thought, and then she saw that something was wrong.

"*Madre mía!*" she cried.

She threw back the covers and went out into the ill-smelling hall. "Katie! Louise! Carmen! Josie!" She banged on the cubicle doors and roused her girls to the cry for help. They sleepily followed her into the street where they clustered about the buggy, hitching wrappers about their bodies.

The old woman was standing with groping hands. "Something is wrong," she whimpered. "I can't make my husband talk. Somebody please help me."

"Señora, what happened?" Tía María cried.

"Oh?" Mrs. Hanna turned to the sound. "Who is that?"

"I am called Tía María."

"I don't know you, do I?"

"No, senora, you do not."

"I can't see," the old woman said querulously. "Why isn't there a doctor?"

"*Válgame!*" cried Tía María.

The women clucked at the bloodied flesh with horror and sympathy and they crossed themselves. Stabbings and shootings were commonplace enough, but the circumstances were strange. "What do we do?" They stood about uncertainly in the waning moonlight, a bunch of untidy sodden drabs, until one, a bony red-haired woman, thought of the fire alarm, a large iron ring hung in the plaza. "Wait here!" she cried. She ran to the plaza, seized the clapper and with powerful blows set a brazen clamor in the night.

The alarm bell woke the Valley. In small adobe *casas* and in outlying farms, men and women came stumbling to their doorways to stare into the night, with only the clucking of chickens and perhaps the snufflings of a pig to reassure them against the evil riding the winds.

At the Hogarth Ranch, Florence flung back the covers of her bed and threw up the casement window. The fiesta had quieted and the house was dark. About her, windows were opening. The alarm had aroused her house guests, some of whom, the Dabneys up from El Paso, were still hilarious. To her right, she heard the squeak of pulley wheels.

"Is that you, Pa?" she called softly.

"Yes, Floss!" Dan Hogarth answered. He bore his great head to one side, as though he were passing under a low arch, as he peered into the night. She asked:

"What do you suppose it is?"

"Couldn't be a fire," he said in his deep voice. "If it were, we'd see the flames from here. Remember that time Walker's house was burned?"

Her mind went back to her childhood. The Walker place at haying time had gone up like tinder, and the entire valley had bathed in the light of flaming haycocks. But now there was nothing out there, only stars and a black sky.

"Shouldn't we send help?" she wondered.

"No, I wouldn't think so," Hogarth mused. "It's coming from Old Town. Can't be much." His tone was odd and she asked, "Do you have any idea what it might be?"

"This is news, whatever it is."

"Is it, Pa?" she said skeptically. Her father usually had a clear idea of things, even before they happened. The Dabneys called from below, they were answered, windows closed, she returned to bed. The fiesta would resume tomorrow, she thought wearily; this year it was more tedious than ever. She made a mental note to go over the soprano's program—and it occurred to her that the Walker burning had been an arson job. The iron clamor went on and she could not sleep.

33

Max Kyle turned in his bed and groaned.

"Oh, God damn!"

He sat up, scratching and yawning, swallowing the bad taste on his tongue. If a bunch of drunken cow hands were taking apart the town, he thought, that was hardly worth his while. If it was a fire, that was for the volunteers, not for the sheriff.

His wife continued to snore gently. He smiled at her dark face pouting in the moonlight. Nothing could awaken her, he thought with affection. However else he had lost out in all these years in the Territory, this was the thing he had—Consuelo, a girl from a good family, the one he had taken to marry that year he had killed the Williamsons. He grimaced at the sour recollection.

That year!

It was the watershed of his life. Before that, he had been a boy hulking down from Kentucky, looking to find his way in the Territory—a discharged veteran of the armies of the South, hungry like a million others, his lust for glory unslaked by the last desultory fighting in the Kansas hills.

He reached for his shoes.

He was living too much, he realized, in the past. In his mind there lingered the day of the Williamsons. He had known then he could not miss. The hour came when they stood in surprise before him— two men taken at dawn on the porch of their mother's house in the bottomlands, rocking on bare feet, spinning and collapsing. Then out of the drifting mists, the big dogs came howling at his throat.

He had killed the dogs and gone home. The Williamsons were a dirty litter, feared and detested in the Valley, and their death had brought applause and fellowship and the governor's reward in Santa Fe. He had won his re-election, and he had married Consuelo.

Consuelo, a dark girl, married in the church of her fathers.

He sighed and reached for his shirt. It had not worked out. The whispers had started and everything had gone downhill. How could things have gotten so twisted? The rat-faced Williamsons had been transformed by the ballad scribblers into gallant smiling outlaws, friend of the poor, all that swill. He scowled at the thought of his own poor role, a coward who had killed from a hayrick ambush. Was that how the future would remember Max Kyle? And why a hayrick? Where had that come from? Ma Williamson never let so much as a privy stand in the approaches to the house. He finished dressing and wondered what had happened to the image of his youth.

There was a tap at the window. A voice whispered, "Sheriff!"

He raised the sash. "Bob?"

A thin young man looked up. "You coming, Mr. Kyle?"

"Right along," he whispered, and behind him Consuelo struggled to her elbow. *"Quien es, Max?"* She flattened the sound of his name to the Spanish "X." It was a sign between them of her love.

"Just Bob Ames," he said softly and she drowsily fell back to sleep. He left through the kitchen door, and set off with his gangling young deputy, Bob Ames, toward the commotion. He could see many figures hastening to the plaza.

"Oh Jesus Almighty!" he exclaimed.

Sam Goldman, Ike's boy from the dry goods store, was holding a kerosene lamp aloft, his mouth agape. Faces were turned toward the woman in the buggy. Tía María held up her arms in entreaty. "Please, señora, come down!" she begged.

"No, no!" Mrs. Hanna held her hands to her face, moaning with pain. Her hair was smeared with blood. "Oh what happened?" she cried. "I can't see! I can't see anything!"

Kyle approached the buggy. "Mrs. Hanna."

"Who's that?" she asked.

He said gently, "This is Max Kyle, Ma'am."

"Oh?" she gasped with pain. "How is my husband, Sheriff?" she asked faintly. He mounted and the buggy swayed under his weight. He examined the staring body briefly. "I'm sorry about this, Mrs. Hanna," he said with regret. "I wish I could say something good."

"Then he's dead?" she whispered, incredulous.

"I'm afraid so."

"Oh my God," she said in a small voice. "Oh dear God!" Her hands fluttered with the shock of finality. Dried blood encrusted her eyes. In a childish voice, she said, "And Tomás?"

"He's dead, too."

"Oh dear! His poor family!" Her face quivered as she turned toward the body. She whispered, "Douglas—"

Kyle glanced at the crowd. These were railroad hands, bindle stiffs, a wrong bunch. The snarl-up was beginning. They were pressing in, open-mouthed, waiting to hear, eyes dark and sullen. He put his mouth close to the woman's ear. "I hate to ask this, Mrs. Hanna, but can you answer a few questions?"

"Not now," she moaned. "It hurts—"

He grimaced and persisted, she gave her few facts in a weak voice. She knew little. "It was so dark at the bridge—" she whimpered.

"What lingo did he use?" he asked urgently.

"I don't know!"

"Try!"

"He just counted!" She twisted her hands. "That's all!"

Kyle paused. "Was it by one, two, three?"

35

"No," she said doubtfully.

"Was it by *uno, dos, tres?*"

"Yes! Only let me go!"

"Then he spoke Mex!" the sheriff exclaimed.

"Yes, yes!"

The crowd muttered restively. A lanky man in a bathrobe said angrily, "Sheriff, you let up on that woman! Can't you see she's hurt! She needs attention!"

"He talked Mex!" Kyle muttered to himself. "Well, that's something." He sighed and looked up. "Maybe you're right, Fred," he admitted, and turned. "Bob, suppose you take Mrs. Hanna to the hotel. I'll send a man for Doc Kimball."

The woman groped about and found her husband's hand; the first rigidity could be felt. "Oh darling! Why, why?" she whimpered. "What was it about?"

"*Qué lástima!*" wept Tía María and her girls joined in. "*Ay de mí!*" they blubbered. Bob Ames took the fainting woman in his arms, the crowd parted as he carried her off like a child. His long strides took him through the light of a street lamp and he disappeared.

Kyle turned now with a scowl. "Tía!"

"*Sí?*" she responded.

"Get those whores back to the crib! Keep 'em there! I want to talk to each one!"

"Whores?" she cried resentfully. "My girls?"

He seized her arm. "Don't waste my time, Tía," he said with soft menace. "I give you a lot of rope, but don't take advantage!"

She was about to retort, then the words died at something she saw in his wicked small eyes. "Come on, girls!" she exclaimed haughtily. They returned to the house, where they stood bridling and exclaiming at the misfortunes in life even to the best.

More deputies arrived, first Tom Simpson, a grizzled old range rider, then a fat no-account cousin of Consuelo Kyle's named Sotero Gomez y Gomez, then others. More lamps were brought from the cantina, the body was examined with shrewd surmise. Finally Simpson raised a hand. "The sheriff wants to say a few words."

Kyle stroked his killer mustache with a sense of pleasure. It had been a long time, he thought, but now it had come. The circle of faces were waiting, expectant.

"Who did it, Sheriff?" a drunken voice called. "Let's git the mother-raping son of a bitch!"

Kyle tilted back his stetson. "Let's not rush it, Davy," he said easily. "There's a lot of work ahead. I'm going to need a dozen possemen, maybe more. I want volunteers."

36

A bushy-haired man in overalls flicked a finger. "Count on me, Sheriff," he drawled and a score of hands went up. "You, you, and you!" Kyle made a selection and swore them in. "I want no fooling around," he said grimly. "Public business comes first. If I say do a thing, no stopping off for private business! Now we'll take a view of the bridge. Gomez y Gomez stays here with the buggy. We'll need trackers. Steve Tender, suppose you hit it for the Agency. Tell Colonel Strong I want Willie Bear and Manuel. I'll pay a dollar a day."

Steve Tender nodded. "Right." As he rode off, a light carriage drove up and Lon Wilby jumped down. The plump newspaperman elbowed through the crowd and stared at the twisted bodies. He swore softly. "The old general was the salt! Kyle"—he looked up with tears trembling in his eyes—"I saw the old man off to the fiesta just this morning! Now this!"

"It's a shame," the sheriff agreed stolidly.

Wilby went on, incredulous. "We had a nice dinner just a few days ago. We were sitting there at the hotel. I just can't believe it!" He looked up with a sharp glance. He was a clever journalist with abilities suited for a larger field, but he loved the Territory he had made his own. He wrote extensively in the national magazines, his salty editorials were widely quoted. His sharp-nosed, bland, good-natured face was known everywhere. He said, "Does Dan Hogarth know?"

"Not yet," Kyle said.

"What are you waiting for? They were brothers-in-law, for God's sake!"

"I'll get to it," the sheriff said sourly.

"Better not fumble this one!" Wilby cocked his head. "You got any ideas I can print?"

"Not just yet."

Wilby pointed a fat little finger. "Sheriff, I'm the AP man here and I want this story. I've got a clear wire to Washington, and they tell me the President's got a statement in the morning. I can get you into the official story."

"I don't know," Kyle said doubtfully.

"I'll quote your very words. Won't change a one."

"All right," the sheriff decided. "You can say I know the killer comes from the Mex elements. I'll turn him up in no time."

"Mex elements?" Wilby exclaimed. "Sheriff, you know what that can do to this mob? You're sure?"

"Just quote me right!" Kyle said savagely.

The same drunken voice called, "What Mex would that be, Sheriff?" Kyle turned to a knot of toughs behind him. "Why, Davy, I wouldn't be surprised," he drawled. "The peaceful Mex has got nothing to worry about in my county. We're after the guilty party—which one I ain't saying. We'll wait till Mrs. Hanna can tell us."

Wilby turned and strode off.

The crowd broke into knots, discussing the matter in low tones. Bob Ames returned driving a buggy with an angry hatchet-faced man, Dr. Ulysses Kimball. While the young deputy hitched up the doctor's mare, the doctor as county coroner went directly to his task, shaking with wrath. He gave the bodies a quick look and wiped his fingers. "Well, Kyle, soon as it's light I'll start the post mortem, then I'd like you to draw me a jury. I could hold the inquest now."

"What do you mean?"

"This was an ambush." The doctor gave his reasons emphatically. "Shotguns, then a rifle! The man was waiting there! The first didn't work, and he finished the job. You can see where the bullet entered."

As the word spread, an angry mutter went up.

"Come here, Doc," Kyle said. They stood aside and he asked in a low undertone, "How's the old lady, Mrs. Hanna?"

The doctor stared grimly. "It's just lucky she'll live. I found shot in her scalp, and some raked her eyes. If her head hadn't been turned, she would have died."

Kyle touched his mustache. "Is she blind?"

"I don't know yet—but there's damage there."

"Can we talk to her? Can she tell us anything?"

"Not now. I put her under sedation."

"It's a damn shame!" Kyle muttered savagely. "Why, I remember when she came to the Territory back in 'sixty-eight. She used to run those country dances when she was a girl. She was real pretty." He sighed heavily and glanced around. "Does anybody else know about her eyes?"

"Of course not," the doctor said stiffly. "I know something too."

"Well—" Kyle spat thoughtfully between his boots. "Let's keep this to ourselves. Maybe she'll be able to pick out the man later. We'll see what develops." He turned. "Bob, get back to Mrs. Hanna and stick with her. I don't want a soul talking to her till I say the word. I'm going out to view the scene."

The young deputy gulped with disappointment. "Can't I come with you?"

"Not this time, Bob," Kyle said softly. "It's important enough. You stay with the old lady."

The doctor broke in. "I'll need a lot of ice."

"Why ice?"

Kimball continued to wipe his fingers on a handkerchief. "I expect

38

they'll want a big military funeral in Santa Fe," he said gloomily. "I'd like the undertaker to get him there in good shape. The other body won't matter, I don't suppose."

"All right," Kyle agreed. "That's got nothing to do with me. It'll be up to Mrs. Hanna to say." With this and other arrangements made, they left. Tom Simpson drove the sheriff's buggy easily and at dawn they reached the bridge at Vale's Crossing.

Kyle's attention was drawn to a heap of horse dung beside the bridge. He squatted and sniffed and poked about with a twig. The graining was yellow and crumbling.

"That's a livery animal," he decided. "We'll look into that later. I'll want every stable checked."

A deputy named Art Train made notes with a stubby pencil while the site was examined. They found the massive shotguns clamped in the granite blocks. The killer's skill was evident.

Kyle drew a deep breath at the ugly sight. In the gray quiet, only the faint croaking of frogs could be heard. The muzzles of the guns were elevated to a high trajectory. He touched the metal and sniffed the muzzles gingerly. "These things were fixed to tear off the old man's head!" he swore. He was angered by the thought, for he had known and liked the slain man, but nevertheless he felt a surge of well-being. "Now this is a case!" he muttered with relish.

Simpson leaned forward and exclaimed, "Sheriff!" He pointed to an elaborate floral design on the stock of each gun which enclosed the letter N. The weapons were a matched pair. "That's something we ought to be able to trace, Sheriff!" the deputy said. "These ain't the kind of guns to forget."

The letter N!

Kyle nodded. "Tom, it's your job. I don't want anybody stampeded, but that could take us to the killer. Find out on the quiet who brought the guns into these parts. It might be the killer himself, then again it might not."

The guns were elaborately designed, the workmanship looked Mexican. "Now why," Simpson wondered, "would the killer leave these behind to be picked up?" He scratched a bristly jaw and yawned. "Got any ideas, Sheriff?"

Kyle stared at the distant hills. "I've got ideas, Tom," he said grimly. "I just don't want them blabbed around."

Additional details turned up, including two shells of a Henry rifle. The trap was carefully dismounted, samples of blood and soil were put into paper bags, the layout was studied with care, careful notes were made by Art Train. Then Steve Tender arrived at a gallop with his Apache trackers, Manuel, an old Army scout, and Charlie Bear, a phlegmatic middle-aged man.

Before they left the bridge, the pounding of a large horse was heard and at the bend came a roan stallion. Florence Hogarth slid off and looked around. Her lips had been bitten through and a trickle of blood was on her white blouse. Her hair was flying.

"Max, is it true?" she demanded hoarsely.

Kyle nodded soberly. "Sorry, Floss, I would've liked to tell you myself, but I just had too much to do!"

She gazed at the tranquil scene with wonder.

"I just can't believe it!" she burst out. "Who would want to kill Uncle Douglas—or hurt Aunt Ginnie? Who?"

He told her what he knew. She stood beating a switch against her suede split skirt with a look of nausea. She stared unbelieving. "I put them in the carriage myself, just last night," she muttered. "They were so happy, laughing. Next month was their anniversary!" She paused, irresolute, and rubbed her eyes. "Oh dear, we've got those house guests, and I ought to look after Aunt Ginnie—" she trailed off. "Where is she?"

He told her and patted her shoulder. "Now why not let Tom Simpson here take you to town?" he said gently. "Your aunt needs you and you'll feel better. I'd go back with you, only I've got this job of work."

"That's all right." She looked up, dazed. "Somebody's got to tell Pa. It's a terrible thing. I don't know how he'll take it."

"I'll do it myself," he promised. He watched her as she rode off in a daze with his deputy. Her hair fluttered in a gust and she passed out of sight. He turned and gave orders. Some were to follow the trackers. Others were to scatter for information. "Remember," he growled, "the average Mex won't give you the right time. I don't want any excuses on that account. I just want information, I don't care how. What strange Mex were sniffing around these parts?"

It had been a long time, he thought grimly, almost too long, but this was the day for which he had been made. He left a man on post and drove off for a talk with Dan Hogarth before taking the moves already shaping in his mind.

They buried him on a peaceful knoll overlooking the valley, in the private cemetery of the Hogarths. All around was the sweep of endless vistas while a hot sun stood in a blue sky. They were assembled from all parts of the Territory, the family, the dignitaries, the military in heavy blue uniforms, sabered, brass buttons gleaming, bearded men with hard faces.

40

Hogarth stared at the coffin under the flag. His mouth worked convulsively. "They killed the best man who ever lived," he said in a rich full voice. "He was a good judge, a good soldier, and a good friend to every man in the Territory. He was one of the first to come to these parts. He wrote a lot of history in his time and now they killed him. This isn't the time and it isn't the place to say more. I can only say for the family that we won't forget this. Virginia"—he looked at the frail woman in black weeds leaning on his daughter's arm—"you have the love of everyone here."

The minister stepped forward, the coffin was lowered into the trench. The intonation began.

> *"As for man, his days are as grass,*
> *As the flower of the field, so he flourisheth.*
> *For the wind passeth over it, and it is gone;*
> *And the place thereof shall know it no more. . . ."*

It was the loveliest of days, and for this Florence was grateful, for otherwise, she felt, her heart would burst with grief. This was her mother's sister whose eyes were swathed in bandaging, from whose lips moaning sounds were slipping. Florence glanced at her with anxiety. Her aunt's weight was heavy on her arm. She had come against doctor's orders and she stood shivering with pain.

"Floss," she whispered. "I may faint."

"No, Auntie!" Florence said firmly. "You'll be all right." She looked at her father across the trench of black moist soil. His yellow eyes were flecked with red and they stared at a point in space.

> *"The Lord giveth, the Lord taketh away,*
> *Blessed be the Name of the Lord—"*

The earth trickled on the box with a hissing sound. The widow sank to her knees. She cast a sprig of lilacs and remained blindly there while others did the same. At a sharp order, the bugler lifted his high note. The blue-clad guard fired three volleys into the sky.

The flag was folded smartly, hand over hand, into a small triangle. The guard saluted and withdrew with precision. The ceremony was over.

Chapter III

There was a sound of coughing on the sun porch. McKeever put aside his copy of the Denver *Post*. Jeff should be asleep, he thought uneasily, he did not like this. But the paroxysm he feared did not come. Instead there was a liquid sneeze, and he sank back with relief. This was merely a cold, something to be watched, nothing more.

He considered the view of the city. Denver was an overgrown mining town, a center for speculation and smelting, its houses were substantial and the streets shaded by trees. Life here had been pleasant and slothful. On the hill opposite, he could see the gingerbread castle of a lively young widow named Sophie Muller.

He smiled with a wry picture in his mind. He had met Sophie soon after his arrival in Denver at a talk given to the Delphian League. After the lecture she had found him at the punch bowl, the center of an admiring circle, and somehow she got possession of him. She was a fluffy thing, a bit of a chatterbox, but she had a ringing laugh, adoring eyes, and a soft feminine hand on his wrist.

As he thought back, he realized that he had not been quite fair, but there had been the bleak need for a woman's solace, and he had reached out for her. The winter with its heavy snows had passed, and then, only two weeks earlier, he had come to the unhappy realization that there was no hope or profit in the affair, no matter how sweet she was, not until the time would arrive for something to thaw within him.

That time had not yet come.

He had made his decision that afternoon after a brisk canter through the trails of the city's outskirts. They had returned exhausted to her house and she had called for tea. As she poured, gossiping busily, he had gazed somberly at her thick corn-silk hair. It had done no good to warm himself in the gaiety of her spirits, he reflected, for the despondency of an unslaked thirst was still on him. He took her hand.

"Sophie—"

"Link, darling?" she murmured expectantly. She opened brilliant violet eyes with a fond smile. "Gosh!" she exclaimed. "I'm all black and blue! That's the last time you'll get me to go riding, let me tell you!" She saw the unhappy look in his eyes and put aside the cup. "What's wrong?" she asked with sudden concern.

It had not been easy. The delicious smell of her hair made it hard to tell her that he would not return the day following, nor the next, nor at any time. The affair of six months was over. She was dismayed. "Is it me, Link?" she asked anxiously. "Is it something I've done?"

"No," he said softly, "it's just—" He had had no words. How could he explain about Liz? She was a dear thing, he murmured, but the icy pall hung over him still. She wept a bit and blew her nose and forgave him. The portrait of Ezra Muller, an iron-faced man of sixty, stared grimly and disapprovingly.

"Poor Ezra!" she sighed. "He always said to remarry a good lawyer. All that bank stock, all that voting control! Oh my, it'll probably slip through my hands. You're sure you wouldn't marry me?"

He patted her cheek. "No, dear," he smiled tenderly, "not even to own a bank." He held her close. Her body was warm, the sun was pouring into the bright living room, yet he felt nothing—nothing at all.

The roaring hearth in the library brought back his thoughts. It was a dark paneled room, pleasant but chilly at times, and a blaze was welcome. His eye went to Prescott's *Conquest of Mexico*, the Encyclopedia Britannica, the great eighth edition, the *Harvard Law Review*, more of the same—and all unread for a year. He had drifted lazily, reading innumerable novels, gardening a bit, corresponding with Amos Tucker, letting the tranquil beauty of Colorado seep into his soul while Jeff took his sunshine and crawled slowly, oh, so slowly, back to health.

Jeff!

There was another sneeze on the porch and he turned. The boy's mind was expanding and he was reading omniverously. He had discovered the library. A frankly illustrated edition of de Maupassant had called for much talk about the mysteries of womanhood. With his son reaching an ineffable romantic stage, McKeever found himself surprisingly shy and reticent, but he had tackled his duties manfully, and, he hoped, with some success.

He yawned and returned to the newspaper dispatch from Cuatro Rios. The embittered local correspondent, Lon Wilby, wrote with a strong personal touch. There was color and vivid interest in his description of the growing violence. The town was milling with stock-

43

men and miners in an ugly mood. Armed men were patrolling the streets, but there was doubt that their numbers were sufficient.

McKeever put aside his cigar. He read quickly and absorbed the facts, but more important were the underlying implications. He was not pleased at the plea of the authorities for law and order; it came too hard upon their baleful promise to find the killer in the Spanish population.

The slain man, it appeared, had served the Territory a long time. He had first come as a full colonel of cavalry during the Mexican War. In the Civil War, he had served with distinction at Shiloh with Grant. On his return to the Territory, he had studied law and soon acted as special prosecutor of federal land frauds during the 70's and 80's. He had put down cattle thieves with a heavy hand. He was involved in the intrigues of the Territory, financial and political, and through the influence of his brother-in-law, Dan Hogarth, he had been appointed to his last judicial post, where he had written the decision in the most noted of the Land Grant Cases.

This last decision had had the effect of destroying titles of the old Spanish families to millions of acres of land. Resentment had flared, violent threats had been made. Certain implacable elements, Wilby wrote, had refused to accept the decision as valid even though confirmed on appeal by the Supreme Court in Washington. The authorities were claiming that these elements were behind the assassination.

McKeever turned to a paragraph from Santa Fe. The Spanish population had called upon the governor to ask for Federal troops from Fort Nolan, one hundred miles south of Cuatro Rios. The governor, Lloyd Sullivan, a recent Presidential appointment, had taken the matter under advisement and the committee had returned to their homes dissatisfied.

On the obituary page, a portrait of Douglas Hanna stared out like a Roman senator, his high brow and silvery hair lending an air of glacial distinction. It was the face of a martinet. An old instinct stirred and McKeever felt his hackles of dislike rise. No doubt, he thought wryly, if the judge were alive, the feeling would be mutual.

The Land Grant Cases!

McKeever closed his eyes. He recalled clearly that appeal in Washington a year earlier—the western lawyers with their bow ties and fierce expressions, the Spanish lawyer he had met. What the devil was his name—Dominguez?

He threw aside the paper and fitfully returned to a worn copy of *Anna Karenina.* It was a work Jeff too was reading with a heart

44

wrung by poor Anna's fate. He found it hard to concentrate. After a time, his eyes blurred and the book slipped from his hands.

"There will be killings," Don José said simply. "They are coming from all parts of the Territory."

Emory Martin gave him a troubled look.

"I know all that," he agreed, "and I'm not happy, Joe, but there's nothing I can do."

"You are the district attorney," Don José pointed out. "You could call the grand jury."

Martin stood at the window. He was a lanky young man with a stubborn face. In the plaza below, groups of men were talking in low tones. They were in store clothes for the most part, but some wore chapparals white with dust. A Civil War veteran in threadbare blue was haranguing a crowd of grinning men. A shingle at the Valdez Building caught his eye—a white board with gothic lettering.

JOSÉ DOMINGUEZ
Attorney-at-Law

He had seen that shingle since he was a boy. In those days the Spanish lawyer had seemed to him the embodiment of jurisprudence. And now, with a drawn oily face, the older man was looking for something he could not deliver. He turned.

"What would I ask the grand jury to do?"

Don José wiped his eyelids before replying. "If this sheriff has proof that our people are responsible, let him present it. If not, he should be exposed. These statements of his are reckless in the extreme. The Anglos are inflamed. There have been incidents already. If they continue, I cannot answer for our people. They will not submit, Emory! I assure you that there are limits."

"Incidents?" Martin frowned. "I wouldn't exaggerate, Joe. That just makes it worse. A window breaking, a burning hayrick, two kids in a fist fight? I wouldn't call that anything!"

Dominguez did not smile. "These things will get worse. There will be killings, and then reprisals!"

Martin grunted. "They'll submit," he observed. "Always have around these parts. Might be different elsewhere, but this is Hogarth County, Joe, you know that. Besides, I don't know what the sheriff's got. He might be on the right track. Can you guarantee every one of the Spanish?"

Don José dropped his eyes.

"I have no idea who killed the general," he said evenly.

Martin took a turn around the office. It was barely furnished with an oak desk and a swivel chair, a Kansas law school certificate, a bookcase with the Territorial laws and reports, spittoons, a feed-and-grain calendar and a portrait of the Territorial Supreme Court autographed by the justices. A large signature sprawled, "With Affection —Douglas Hanna, Ch. J." He studied the picture, then turned a grim face.

"If you do get an idea, would you let me have it first, Joe? You pick up a lot of information."

Don José took his high-crowned hat.

"Perhaps," he said unsmiling. "If the killer is a Spanish man, which I refuse to accept, I will without doubt be called upon to represent him. I will consider the position at that time. But one thing—" He pointed a light cane.

"Yes?"

"Tell Dan Hogarth to be extremely careful. I can understand why you avoid the grand jury. They are Hogarth men, just as the sheriff is his man, just as you are his man. I say this with regret, Emory, because I have affection for you, and not alone for your father's sake. I am sorry you are part of all this." He paused. "But I see you will do nothing."

Martin showed him to the door.

"I don't control the sheriff," he said helplessly. "They're just out searching. I've got nothing legal yet."

"You could inquire why none of the guests at the fiesta have been questioned," the lawyer said pointedly.

"Kyle claims that they're accounted for."

"Ah!" Don José gave the troubled young man an ironical glance. "Accounted for by Hogarth?"

Martin lit a cigarette and considered this.

"Let me give you a piece of advice, Joe," he said thoughtfully. "Hogarth's been pretty peaceful for some time, but I wouldn't tangle with him. It's not only the killing, it's what happened to Mrs. Hanna. Now that's just an idea."

Don José lifted his cane, and in the harsh light his pallid face had an oily sheen. He said grimly:

"I would not predict where this will end. Go with God, Emory."

He left the young district attorney alone, swearing softly. There was a subdued hubbub in the corridor and a raucous drunken voice below the window.

"Damn!" Martin said helplessly. He slumped wearily into his swivel chair and stared at the crowd in the plaza.

46

The influx of guests had raised too many trails to follow with ease. Nor were the events on the night of the fiesta clear. Only one person's suspicions turned at first to Tom Canty.

Juana Malina brought her views to Tía María in the kitchen where coffee was being served. "What do I do?" she asked in a troubled voice. "I hate to take this up with the sheriff." She hitched her wrapper about her thighs and began on her nails.

Tía María ran a quiet and orderly place. The old days were passing and with a strict sheriff it was necessary to watch her step. She gave Juana a sharp glance. "Aside from that night, what makes you suspicious of this man?"

Juana continued to buff her nails. "It's the way he sticks to his room. He claims he's a mining man, yet he don't look like any mining man I ever saw. Then there's that way he kept looking at the old judge that day. Now should I tell Kyle what I think?"

Tía María was playing solitaire. She slapped a card down. "Let him find out for himself! You'd just put yourself in the middle. Besides, I don't forget what he called my girls that night!" she said viciously.

But this was not her reason. The town was filling with rough characters attracted from the four corners of the Territory and she needed every girl to handle the landslide business. Time enough to help the law.

"I wouldn't get involved, Juanita. A thing like this could lose you your good name," she said wisely. "That's the one important thing, your good name! Without that, what has a girl got? With it, there's no telling what could happen!"

"That's very true," Juana agreed soberly.

A customer called and she left to take the trick. Her mind was abstracted, but she put in an honest hour of work, and there were no complaints.

Canty remained in his room staring at the ceiling. At intervals the maid came banging at the door only to be told off. He was resting, he shouted, and he wanted to be alone. He ate nothing and for water he drank from the pitcher which otherwise stood unused in its basin. The window faced west and toward sunset his room heated up, but he seemed not to mind as he lay on the bed, sweating slightly, stinking his flannel underwear as he watched the bluebottles on the windowpanes. A smile was on his lips; his eyes were impassive. Occasionally he made a buzzing sound in imitation, than sank back into his thoughts. He lay spread-eagled, gripping the rods at the head-stead, moving only to mash a bluebottle when, attracted by the smell, it crawled across his face.

The second day, Juana Malina peered through the cheesecloth curtains at the window. She had come to verify the account of the maid about the slops in the chamber pot. But although their eyes met, he gave her no sign of recognition and she dropped back out of view.

In the evening, Canty arose and got dressed in his cheap black store suit. He soaped himself with the last water in the pitcher; he lacked enough to rinse, and he wiped the lather on his shirt. He stared in the fly-specked mirror. He was unkempt, but he used neither comb nor brush which lay on the walnut dresser. He unhooked the latch and strode out. To the disgust of the kitchen women, he urinated at the tamarisk in the courtyard. This was not unusual—the stench at the bole told its story—but the unclean act was forbidden. It surely was not seemly for guests of the management.

"*Va!*" Sadie Chavez exclaimed. "That pig!"

Juana gave a hard laugh. "I am not surprised."

"Why not?"

"He has not moved from his bed for days! Phew! Who could wait!" She clutched her nostrils and grimaced.

"Still," said Sadie Chavez thoughtfully, "he is a good-looking man."

"I know what I know!" Juana said wisely, but she did not enlarge on this.

Canty went on to the dining room where he took a seat and waited. The room was empty except for the bus boy, Angelo, who was placing silverwear for the breakfast service next morning. Although the dinner hour was over, he was able to order a plate of ham and eggs and fried potatoes which he ate hungrily to the last morsel.

"Say, that's a big business!" Angelo remarked. "Some doings!"

Canty looked up. He had been in bed for two days with a cold, he explained. "What business?" he asked with an agreeable smile. When Angelo with some enthusiasm went into the murder, he sucked his teeth with distress. "That sounds awful!" he exclaimed. "That nice old man?"

Angelo nodded vigorously. "They're checking on all strangers. I would stay at the hotel till they call, if I were you."

"You might be right." Canty shook his head. "The old general? Jesus! Now who would want to do a thing like that?" His eyes were attracted to a napkin ring, lacquered, painted in a tourist-Indian design. He slipped it on his thumb and suddenly walked out, jiggling the trinket.

Angelo spat carefully between two fingers.

48

The sun was going down in a crimson sky. Canty strode down the gravel path. He passed the church, now deserted except for old Father Hilario standing helpless at the entrance.

Large numbers of armed men were out, military uniforms could be seen, there was activity at the saloons. The sound of hammer against anvil beat a cadence at the blacksmith's. None of which Canty seemed to notice; indeed he was almost ridden down by a troop of cavalry as he crossed the courthouse park.

Here was a drowsy twilit loveliness. Lofty cottonwoods rustled their leaves, willows more than eightscore years old trailed the ground. A fountain played before a statue of the Virgin, the overflow running like a brook through a garden planted to flowers. Facing the courthouse were dry goods stores, the most notable of which was surmounted by a wooden six-pointed Shield of David, a landmark of hospitality to peddlers, tourists and traveling salesmen throughout the Southwest, possibly the only port of call for barreled salt herring south of Denver. Its owner, Ike Goldman, was seated on a rocker and as Canty trudged across the park, he breathed with distress as unheeding boots trampled a bed of anemones. Ike was a snub-nosed man with wispy hair and honest tender eyes. He loved the flower beds and at that moment he conceived a dislike for the destroyer of the beautiful things.

Canty found the lockup closed. The ugly brick structure had been a center of activity during the day, now it was dark. He considered a moment and turned the corner and paused at the sheriff's quarters.

Max Kyle heard the knocking from the dining room where Consuelo was serving pork and beans. "*Quien es?*" she called. There was no answer. Kyle went to the door, holding a plate of food in hand. "What do you want—?" he began with a scowl, and then he saw the scar cutting the right cheek.

"Yeah?" he grunted.

Canty smiled. "At the hotel I heard you're questioning strangers," he said with his candid air. "I understand you might want to see me. My name's Canty."

Kyle wiped his mouth. "I might."

"Well, I'm here."

"All right, let's get to the office." The sheriff motioned him in and said, "Sit there." Canty obeyed while Kyle thumbed through a worn book of wanted men circulated by the Texas authorities. He paused at "Q."

"Where'd you get that scar?" he demanded.

Canty touched the whitish line which ran down his cheek. "An

49

arrow," he said slowly. "I was prospecting. This Apache buck ambushed me. I got him though. Back in 'seventy-four."

"Take his scalp?"

There was a pause.

"No, why should I?"

"You were a bounty hunter, weren't you?"

Canty shook his head slowly.

"Not me."

"Ever answer to Quantico?"

The fixed smile became one of pity.

"Quantico? No!"

"Joe Quantico—Joaquin?"

"My name is Canty."

"So your name is Canty," Kyle said heavily.

"That's right."

Kyle tossed the book into the roll top. "All right—Canty! Now, how do you figure to help?" He tilted the lamp and in the yellow light, the man's tongue slithered out and returned, dry and gray.

"About this killing," Canty began carefully. "It was an awful thing. I came to see if I'm under suspicion."

There was a pause.

"Go ahead," Kyle said.

"Well, I had nothing to do with it."

"Who says you did?"

"Oh—" Canty looked off vaguely through the window, and this was all the reply he made, although the question was put in several ways. He seemed not to hear until finally he leaned forward earnestly.

"I'm a stranger in town, Sheriff. I would figure this way. Now who has been around? There was all these guests at the fiesta. They knew the old general for sure. Then at this time a lot of men come drifting through. Who? I'm one of them. I'm a mining man. I might want to look over some locations. If I was just to head out you might wonder. So I came in."

The sheriff nodded thoughtfully as though all this had meaning —as indeed he was beginning to feel it might. He continued to pull at his pipe, tamping the glowing tobacco with a horny thumb. He opened a locked closet and some legal forms tumbled from a shelf. These he kicked impatiently as he turned back holding two objects.

"Know what these are?"

Canty nodded. "Shotguns."

"All right." The sheriff sat and beat one of the weapons in his palm like a wand. "I'll tell you these guns were used to kill the old judge. How did they get here to Cuatro? I'd like you to tell me."

Canty scratched his head, puzzled. "I don't know."

"I'll tell you they were brought by burro. Whose burro?"

"I don't know."

"I'll tell you it was Trister's burro."

Canty looked up. "*Sam* Trister?"

"The very one!"

"Trister?" Canty sat blinking, a beading of sweat showed at his temples. "You think this man Trister killed the judge, Sheriff?" he asked with wonder.

The sheriff continued to beat his palm with the gun muzzle, slow, menacing. "Trister's an old man! Somebody gave him these guns to carry into Cuatro! Now he's skipped!" There was a sound of snoring from the lockup. He said suddenly, "What did you want with Trister?"

"*Sam* Trister?"

"You were heard asking for him down in Old Town. I don't mind telling I was getting around to you. What's the answer?"

"Well!" Canty scratched his head. "I just needed a guide. I understand he's an old-timer. They tell me he's in with the Apaches, and I don't want trouble where I'm going. Feller down at this cantina recommended him. A regular desert rat, so I heard. That's right," he nodded intelligently, "*Sam* Trister."

"That's the whole story?"

"That's right!"

Canty wiped his eyelids and waited, his smile fixed, facing the menacing stare. Kyle returned the guns to the closet and knocked the ashes from his pipe.

"Guess that's all," he said. "You don't mind if I make a search? I guess I ought to cover that part, if you're leaving town."

Canty shook his head. "Sam *Trister!*" he murmured, as though to fix the name in mind. "Beats me!"

With a quick motion for so large a man, Kyle arose and took his black felt hat from the hook. "We'll take the buggy." He paused only to give his wife a kiss, and left with Canty—holding the man's arm in a strong grip as they drove off to the hotel.

While Kyle methodically searched the room, Canty leaned against the door without change of expression. He seemed disinterested as the peace officer went through the bureau, the closet, and all hiding places. He had no explanation for the Henry rifle, nor for the box of shells matching those taken at the bridge. The livery stable receipt was a surprise.

"I swear!" he said earnestly. "There's some big mistake! Those things wasn't here when I left just two hours ago! You've got my word on that, Sheriff! Would I be fool enough to come to you if I had this stuff here?"

Kyle studied him wickedly. "I don't know, Canty!" he said softly. "I'm going into all this later." He turned back the lumpy mattress. "Meanwhile—what's this?"

"Just a newspaper," Canty protested.

"Do you read Mex?"

"Why sure!"

The Spanish newspaper was dated months before the murder at Vale's Crossing. *La Luz*, a four-page flimsy published in Ciudad Jardín, carried banner headlines and a savage caricature of the slain man, Douglas Hanna. At the masthead, besides an emblem of the *quetzal*, the bird sacred to the Aztecs, appeared a name in bold type:

CARLOS DE NIZA: *Editor and Publisher*

Kyle felt a sense of exultation surge within him. Sure—the letter N on the shotguns! The crest of the House of De Niza! This was the thing! He read the text avidly. "*Ojo por ojo! Diente por diente!*" Eye for eye and tooth for tooth! The editorial outburst of rage attacked the original decision of Douglas Hanna in the Land Grant Case, and called with unbridled violence for the extermination of its author.

Don Carlos de Niza!

Kyle felt his hands trembling as he gazed around the sleazy bedroom. "Turn out your pockets!" he said savagely. Canty complied, and from his coat tumbled a silver ring with the *quetzal* emblem. It looked like Mexican work. Kyle hefted the object. "All right, Canty," he said in a low voice. "This is between you and me. What's Carlos got to do with this?"

Canty said stupidly, "I don't know any Carlos, Sheriff."

"I'll ask you again in a nice way," Kyle repeated.

Canty protested, "What Carlos?"

Kyle waited a moment, half smiling, half scowling. He turned, and then wheeled and smashed Canty's face with a gun butt. The man fell prone. Kyle kicked him until a rib cracked and then, panting, dragged his prisoner back to the lockup.

A face at the window retreated.

Toward midnight, Juana Malina slipped away. In the darkness she ran through the streets to a house near the courthouse plaza, and with a quick look around, she knocked on the door. A light showed and the door opened.

"*Señor Abogado!* It's me! Juana!" she whispered urgently. "About the murder! The Anglos have a man!"

A stocky man looked at her. With a quick head motion he opened the door wider and she entered to tell the lawyer, Don José Dominguez, of the happening at the Hotel Conquistador.

Chapter IV

McKeever brought his cigar to life with small puffs and stretched his feet to the hearth. "I haven't taken a case for a year," he said uneasily. "Have you tried anyone else?"

"There is no one else," Dominguez said simply. His eyes were shining in the flames, moist with anxiety. "I respect your reasons, sir, but I'm at my wits' end. I need trial counsel. Why else would I come to Denver?"

"I'm sorry." McKeever rumpled his hair with a sigh. The brandy was wearing off. This would be his fourth or sixth since dinner. He had lost count. Damn! Why had he let this fellow into his house? He should have known better. His eye fell on the telegram on his desk lying on the litter of unanswered correspondence. "I regret you've made this trip for nothing," he murmured, "but I don't want to take on a major trial. Besides, this is just a routine case."

"No, sir, you're mistaken," Dominguez said nervously. "If that were the situation, I wouldn't be here." With a touch of resentment, he added, "I don't like to be put in a beggar's position. Of course, this can't add to your reputation. I didn't think of that, I'm just a simple country lawyer."

"Oh, come now!" McKeever protested with annoyance.

"That's what it amounts to!"

"I wish—" He stirred uncomfortably. He was seated in a deep chair, feet extended, arms dangling, luxuriating in the warmth at his slippers. The sarcastic humility put him at a disadvantage, and it was unfair. He loved to mingle with the bar, to feel himself within the fraternity of practitioners. He had no sense of his eminence. This sarcastic humility was not warranted. Oh Lord! He would have to see this through, he thought wearily. He scratched his cowlick. "Well, go ahead, sir, I'll try not to interrupt."

"Yes, of course." Dominguez fell into a brown study, rubbing his fingers, while McKeever smoked his patient cigar. "I'll be quite frank, sir," he muttered. "I can't offer your usual fee. I've got to appeal to your sense of justice."

McKeever grunted and gave him a long stare. "I'm not a public servant," he said drily. "Why does everybody think I don't care for money? I'm as interested in a fat fee as the next man."

"But I thought—"

"You're mistaken, sir, much mistaken!" McKeever said firmly. "I look to my reward in this world, not the next." He returned to his cigar, sucking thoughtfully. "Do you represent a committee of some sort?"

Dominguez paused. "Not yet," he said warily.

"But you may?"

"Perhaps."

"Well!" McKeever shifted. "Suppose you go ahead. Let's call this a friendly talk." He held up his goblet, only too conscious of the other's worried face. He roused himself. "I doubt if we'll get to the problem of fees. I sometimes wish," he murmured wistfully, "that people would remember that I'm primarily a civil trial lawyer. A few criminal successes and that's all one gets."

Dominguez loosened his string tie nervously, fumbled, let the ends drop. "Where to begin? There is so much—!" He plunged ahead, index finger quivering, eyes moist, evidently in distress. The situation at Cuatro Rios had deteriorated rapidly. Word was out that the lid was off. Livestock had been stampeded, a woman raped, a building burned, with the death of an infant, there had been knifings. The most peaceful men were sleeping on their guns.

McKeever moved restlessly. "You say a child was burned?" he asked, incredulous.

Dominguez halted. "I knew that child, sir. Four years old. The son of a peaceful small *ranchero*, a client of mine. I don't say the Anglos meant murder, but they meant arson."

"Was an arrest made?"

"There wasn't even an inquiry!" Dominguez said bitterly. The devil was loose in the land, he added with a look of hate, and someone would have to put him in the box. He did not enlarge and McKeever broke in. "This background is interesting, but what's the bearing? All this is political."

"Exactly!" the New Mexican said darkly. "If this were a robbery or a cow theft or any of those things, I wouldn't be taking your time. On that level I can handle the Anglo." He paused under McKeever's keen glance. "The Territory's full of old hates and grudges. You don't know where they begin or end. A lot of blood's been spilled over the years, and now there's this last struggle for the land. If they convict this man Canty"—his hesitation was subtle—"we'll face the 'seventies and 'eighties over again."

55

"I see." McKeever settled lower, staring at the flames. In the recesses of his mind, a thin violin note of warning sounded. He saw a house blazing, a child screaming.

"Has this prisoner Canty retained you yet?" he asked.

"No."

"Then aren't you premature?"

"Not quite." Dominguez made a helpless gesture. "You see, his mother was Spanish, and he's one of us, even though he uses an Anglo name. You must picture the Territory. We are still two people, sir!" He raised two fingers. "Two tongues, two faiths, two ways of life, one strong, the other weak—and only one land. One day it will change, but that time is not yet. In these circumstances, the weak help each other or they perish. There's a certain feeling. In trouble, they stand together."

"Even the criminals?"

"Criminals? That depends on your view. In any case, compared with the Anglos, they are few." The smile was ugly. "These people don't feel that Anglo law is their law. When one is in trouble, the rest make a defense, put up cash, hire a lawyer—and I'm usually elected!"

"And you respond?"

"Yes."

"And if you don't?"

"I've described a strong feeling. Even the criminal element expect help. If it isn't coming, they can get pretty vindictive." Dominguez blinked. "I know it sounds peculiar, but the Anglos feel the same where we predominate."

"I don't quite understand," said McKeever doubtfully.

The New Mexican lawyer grimaced with distaste. "Our local Anglos are mostly from Texas. A dangerous lot. They've brought all their contempt for Mexicans and they confuse us with that element —which is ridiculous." With faint arrogance he added, "We are not Mexicans. We are Spanish."

McKeever poured a brandy, sipped, let the liquor suffuse his palate, felt his head spinning. "I appreciate these feelings," he said drily, "but I don't see that they're my concern. Canty seems guilty enough. What's your special point? Why me?"

The Spanish lawyer said unhappily, "It's important that he be told that he'll have the best possible defense."

"Why so?"

Dominguez hesitated. "If he feels revengeful, it won't stop with him. The Anglos could use him against the rest of us. They'll raise a lot of feeling. Wipe us out. Take the land. He's a dangerous man."

56

"Oh, come now! That sounds far-fetched!"

Dominguez gave a harsh laugh. He had been standing at the fireplace, earnest, gesticulating. Now he flopped down in the leather chair opposite. He pointed a quivering finger.

"You don't know Hogarth County. How long ago was it the frontier? The Anglos came in from all their wars—wars against us, against the Indians, against each other. Death and killing are nothing. I don't say we won't fight back, but we're disorganized and they hold the power." He looked up. "This murder can put us back forty years!" he cried passionately. "Who else can I come to but Lincoln McKeever?"

There was a pause.

"Well!" McKeever thrust hands in pocket. "That kind of talk can't get a lawyer sore." He smiled humorously. "But as I told you, my son's health comes first. I wouldn't dare move him without the doctor's consent. That couldn't be for a few weeks more."

Dominguez seized the opening eagerly. "Then why not bring him too? The climate is as good as Denver. You'll find the same facilities. We've become a health center, you know. Every bit as good as Colorado," he added with local pride.

McKeever raised his hand. "No!"

Dominguez drummed his fingers, then burst out, "Mr. McKeever, I won't ask you to take on the whole trial. Just make an appearance. Show up for the preliminaries, the arraignment. They'd pay attention to you, and that's all I'll ask."

"Sorry!" McKeever arose with an air of finality. "You've got my answer."

"I can't believe this," the Spanish lawyer cried with wonder. "If you had a legal reason, yes! But how can you refuse?"

McKeever opened the door.

"I'm sorry!" he said with regret, but then as the pallid lawyer stood in stunned disbelief, he felt resolution oozing out of his palms. Damn this! It was a mistake to talk, or explain, or argue! With a wretched feeling that he was the weakest man in the world, he said angrily:

"I don't think you're interested in Canty, sir! You're afraid the man will turn state's evidence—name accomplices or principals, isn't that it?"

Dominguez wiped his eyes. "I'm only asking you to listen!"

"Then what's this about? You've been chasing your devil around the stump all night." McKeever closed the door, irresolute, then turned back to the room, considering the matter. "Well, I'll do this much. In the morning, I'll ask our doctor whether my son can make

57

the trip. But I won't commit myself." He grasped his lapels and turned. "Dominguez!"

"Yes?"

"Just what do you want?"

The Spanish lawyer drew himself up with dignity. "Simple justice," he said. "Is that too much to ask?" They faced each other, and then he went to his portfolio and drew out a sheet of notes. "Let me show you some more facts. This is the background—"

"Well—" McKeever gave in grudgingly. He listened with an attentive ear, striding the length of the library, grasping his galluses, his cowlick thoughtful. He arranged the facts swiftly in his powerful orderly mind. "Just exactly who is Carlos de Niza?" he asked at last.

"Don Carlos?" Dominguez's face softened. "He is a pure flame among us!" he said fervently. "He's the best man I know. His family was in the Territory three hundred years ago." He nodded at the gold-stamped row of books. "You'll find the name of De Niza in Prescott. Let me show you something." He unrolled a large canvas map. With interest McKeever studied the lithograph issued by the General Land Office in Washington. Large sections, colored and marked, were a striking feature. Mora Grant. Sandoval Grant. Baca Location. Beaubien and Miranda Grant. De Niza Grant. A dozen more. He murmured:

"Where's Cuatro Rios?"

"There." Dominguez indicated a point touching the vast section marked De Niza Grant. "Good Lord," McKeever breathed. "That's larger than Rhode Island! Did one family hold all that?"

"Yes, they did." Dominguez rolled up the map. "Until the Supreme Court spoke at Washington. *De Niza v. Alamo Land Development Co.* An action in ejectment to recover possession of more than a million acres in the drainage of the Rio Amarillo."

"H'm. Now who is the Alamo Company? That sounds Texan."

"The majority of shares are held by Dan Hogarth. A minority interest is owned by his daughter. She inherited the shares on her mother's death eight years ago. They are Texans indeed, the Hogarths."

"Florence Hogarth?" McKeever paused and thought back. "Is she a lawyer?"

"You know her? Oh, of course," the New Mexican nodded. "That time in Washington."

"Yes, I remember her quite well." McKeever slowly poured a brandy. The picture of that day was still much in his mind. He tossed off the drink and turned. "Does this man, Carlos de Niza, have a connection with Canty?"

58

Dominguez hesitated. "Not recently, I'm sure."

"But he formerly did?"

"Yes."

"How long ago, then?"

"More than twenty years ago, Don Carlos formed a little land league to protect these titles, not only the De Niza Grant, but scores of others. Our best families were involved. There were a lot of killings. Not only sheep and cattle either. At that time, Canty was hired."

McKeever looked up.

"Hired by Carlos de Niza?" he asked slowly.

"Exactly." Dominguez licked dry lips. "But Canty didn't last."

"What were his duties?"

"He was a guard."

"Do you mean gunman?"

There was a pause.

"Yes," Dominguez admitted.

McKeever strode the length of the library. "Is there anything else you want to say?"

"I omitted a point!" The Spanish lawyer smote his forehead. "In my distress, of course!" He glanced at his notes. "The distinctive feature of the shotguns—the rosette designs enclosing the letter N."

"What does that mean?"

There was a breath of hesitation. "An unfortunate construction could be placed on the fact."

McKeever paused in his lumbering walk. "Are those guns the property of Carlos de Niza?" he asked quietly.

"I'm afraid so." Dominguez nodded, his eyes shining suddenly with fear. "I recognized the description myself at once. But how Canty got his hands on them, I do not know."

A log crashed in the hearth, then another.

"But that doesn't sound like much—a pair of shotguns," McKeever said slowly. "It's not decisive at all."

"In a high wind," the other raised a quivering finger, "a spark can start a prairie fire. They'll find or invent other things, you can be sure."

McKeever grunted.

"Where was De Niza at the time of the murder?"

"In Mexico City."

"Can that be proved?"

"Beyond question! He was testifying before a commission on a matter of Church lands. The Mexican government dislike him, but they accept his testimony. He's an authority on the subject."

"Where is he now?"

59

"Still in Old Mexico. He's been living near Ciudad Jardin for the past three years. That's some distance south of El Paso."

"Then why are you so concerned at this time?" McKeever asked curiously. "If all this is true, he's safe from extradition."

"Theoretically."

"Well then?"

"You don't know Hogarth!" Dominguez said grimly. "He hates Carlos de Niza in the worst way. Canty's a miserable dog. I've got no idea why he committed the crime, or what he had in mind, but while he's in Hogarth's hands, we're all in danger!"

"Well!" McKeever continued to pace the library, worrying, slouching its length. Dominguez had touched only the surface, he surmised, but this did not disturb him. It was the silences, the things unsaid, which he heard with an inner ear. At a sound, he looked up with sudden surprise. Hot tears were brimming in the Spanish lawyer's eyes. He stood at the fire clutching his throat, grotesque, weeping.

"I regret," Dominguez choked convulsively. "You have no conception!" He averted his face. "I can't seem to make you understand! Unless something is done, this can mean hundreds of dead. And it won't be fair, because we've tried to live with them, we really have! I've done my best to head this off, but I'm only one man."

"Oh Lord!" said McKeever with dismay. "Dominguez, please!"

The Swiss clock chimed nine.

There was a tap on the door and a short old woman looked in. Her broad flat face was kindly but utterly humorless. Her hair was iron-gray. She said, "Jeff would like you to kiss him good night."

McKeever said stiffly, "In a minute, Mrs. Blanchard." The door closed and he resumed his walk. He was entitled to his peace, he thought resentfully. He had put more into twenty years of law practice than most men put into three lifetimes, years of agony, for the law did not come easy, not to him, not in these life and death struggles, not in the glare of publicity with tension at fever heat. One man against the power of the state! He knew what that could mean! Still—a restless anger was stirring. He paused.

"You say a child was actually burned?"

"I saw it with my eyes!"

"Can't understand how things like that can happen," McKeever murmured. He resented the dark moist desperate eyes fixed on him. He wanted none of this. He sought nothing but the slow passage of the days, the work in the garden, fishing, the hours with Jeff, the sense at last that time was standing still.

"Dominguez," he said uncertainly.

"Yes?"

The portrait of his dead wife was on the wall. Liz with her cheery tart common sense, a long-faced, gray-eyed leggy girl from Bangor with braids and a poke bonnet, amused at his abstract remote mind, proud of his brilliance, vexed at his self-doubts, in despair at the queer compulsions in him. She would have hated this.

"I don't know," he muttered. "I just don't."

He paused at a circular ebony mirror. There was fat in his jowls, a sprinkle of salt at the temples, a nose like an amiable plough horse, a strong pugnacious mouth, shrewd serious eyes with a friendly sad twinkle—by gosh, not a bad face at all, come to think, a good strong courtroom face! And what had he done with it? He gazed with dissatisfaction at the litter of papers on his desk. What was this life in Denver? An aimless routine, a brainless affair with a younger woman? No, he thought, and then, perhaps because it was the brandy, perhaps because some voice was talking through him, the words came hoarsely of themselves.

"Do you absolutely need me, Dominguez? Are you sure?"

"If they must have Don Carlos, let's give them a fight!" the Spanish lawyer said fiercely. "I swear to you he is an innocent man!"

McKeever sighed.

There would be Jeff and the talk with Dr. Loewy in the morning and a final farewell to poor Sophie, and so many things. He stretched his great frame and wriggled the stiffness from his finger tips.

"Well, suppose you give me the rest of the facts," he said gloomily. "I haven't said yes, and I won't take the case until I'm satisfied, but I'll listen." He pointed a finger. "And don't think I'm the kind who can be talked into things," he added crossly, "because I'm not!"

"Oh sir!"

With a look of joy, Dominguez began to spread his notes on the desk.

Hours later, McKeever paused at Jeff's door. There was a sound of light regular breathing. The room faced south and during the day it would be drenched with sunlight. Now the windows were black. They looked to the lofty mountains of Colorado, capped with snow, beautiful with their mantle of evergreens, which for a year had been doing their healing work. In the dimness, a spiky head of hair was on the pillow and there was the outline of a thin body. The walls were decorated with Harvard pennants and trophies. A baseball mitt rested on the cover, a book was on the table.

"Jeff?" he asked in the lightest whisper.

The boy turned. "Dad?"

61

McKeever sat and took the boy's hand. It was warm but normal and dry. "Weren't you asleep?"

"No."

"How are you feeling?" he asked. "All right?"

"Yes, Dad," the boy mumbled. "What happened? Are you leaving me?"

McKeever touched the thin cheeks. They were wet with tears. At fourteen, this boy was himself at the same age, he thought. There was the same despondency, the moodiness, the strange strong feelings.

"Of course not, Jeff," he said firmly. "I told you I wouldn't. Don't you know that?"

The boy raised himself on an elbow. "That lawyer wants you to take that case in New Mexico. I heard him telling you. Don't you want to go?"

"Not without you. I won't go unless you can come with me. That's what I told him. He's catching the midnight train back. Now in the morning, we'll ask Dr. Loewy."

"Oh!"

McKeever could hear the anxious sigh of relief. "I was worried," the boy admitted and his voice was strange. "I was afraid."

"What's wrong, Jeff?" his father pleaded.

"I don't know," the boy said with despair. "I'm sick of being sick. I want to get better. I want my mother." He wept silently in the darkness.

"Jeff!" There were times, his father realized with a helpless sense, when he forgot that he had a child on his hands and that all this was part of the disease. "We won't go except together," he repeated. "Now that's a promise."

The boy wiped his eyes. "Do you think I can travel?" he asked hopefully.

"There's a good chance," his father said. "Why not? You've been coming along fine."

"Gosh!" The boy sat up eagerly. "I'd just love to go! I've been reading so much about it! Why, it's a wonderful case!"

"Well, we'll see." McKeever smiled and patted the boy's hand and talked softly and after a time he returned to his own room and went to bed. He lay still until the sheets had taken the warmth of his body. The amused sardonic eyes of Amos Tucker were on him.

Lincoln McKeever—Collector of Lost Causes!

All the same, as he drifted toward sleep, he was rather pleased with himself for the first time in a year.

Chapter V

I f a stranger were set down in Ciudad Jardin, he would have been able in a moment to lay hand on shoulder of Don Carlos de Niza. Any child could give directions. Even without aid, he was not to be mistaken.

"Don Carlos de Niza?" The name would be drawn out sibilantly, with respect and fondness. "*Ah sí!* He is taking *cafecito!* I can show you! You are friend, maybeso?"

If ever a man dressed to match his role in life, that man was Don Carlos. He wore an outmoded courtly garb—tight high-waisted *pantalones* gathered by a sash, a short velvet jacket, silk shirt with lace cuffs. A flourishing cape and a low sinister dark-brimmed hat completed the ensemble—without mistake, the costume of a political conspirator. Beneath a flowing cravat lay a gold crucifix, for he was a fierce churchman in a land lapsing into secularism. He was also a royalist in the republic, a mystic among materialists, a poet among philistines, and many other things.

He was not always to be found at the cafés. There were times when he disappeared into the north in altogether different dress— riding a strong white mule, sombrero nodding, serape drawn, guitar in hand, singing in a beautiful tenor the nasal melodies inherited from Old Spain. His gaunt frame was to be seen silhouetted against the sky in obscure villages throughout the lost territories across the border. He traveled in a world of lunar fantasy—great canyons cut through deserts, lava beds of the badlands, the malpais, drifting gypsum sands without life, vastness, solitude, elevation, little rain. Here men lived by the river ways, the Hondo, the Pecos, the Canadian, the Rio Grande—some flowing richly, others dwindling to nothing in the summer. Here were people whose tongue was Spanish, whose Faith was true. He passed by a charm among the Apache, the Navajo, the Zuñi, as he had done even in the time of Vittorio and of that mountebank Geronimo.

Don Carlos de Niza!

The church bells would ring, the children come running, a house swept and cleaned, a room set apart. A fine meal would be prepared, for he was a noted trencherman, a lover of spiced foods and red wines. He would eat alone, while the village gathered to marvel at his fine manners. He ate with hearty appetite, joking drily, inquiring of each child and its growth. "Learning!" he would counsel. "That is the future—the education of our children!" The gnomic wisdom would be murmured with respect by all. With the ache of travel sloughed off, he would change to elegant garb and call his followers in meeting, perhaps in some humble dirt-floor church. His orations were magnificent. One might accept or reject his vision, but still it was valid within its boundaries. He was a legitimist in all things—politics, philosophy, religion, art and business. All rights, he held, derived from the past through clear succession or not at all. Especially were rights and title to land within this order. He could make proof with irresistible logic, drawing on a copious knowledge of canon and civil law and international practice, that the vast realms about them still of right belonged to the Crown of Spain based on the Papal decree which had granted the Western Hemisphere to Spain and Portugal. The intrusion of the Anglos into this logical scheme, so clear and orderly and manifestly right, was a thing to be fought on all levels—in the realm of ideas, in the courts of law, on the field of battle.

Whether his listeners grasped even the rudiments was doubtful, but they sat entranced at the magnificent tapestry of boisterous humor and brilliant irony, of savage invective and fearless appeals— all with the promise of a day when their humiliations would be ended, the Anglo powers destroyed, their ancient lands restored, when each man would sit under his own fig tree with the woman of his heart. As he warmed to his theme, sweat poured from him, he shook with paroxysms as he hammered at the concrete foe, the one who held the strands of power, the despoiler of the land—Dan Hogarth. For they knew the man, they had felt his cruel hand, they had been impoverished by his courts and his hirelings.

Hogarth! Hogarth! Hogarth!

He returned to the name like an incantation. It was a strong counterpoint to a main theme of hate. The people nodded. The quarrels of the giants were beyond them, but the seizure of lands, the corruption of courts, the exactions of tax collectors, these indeed were things to make the heart burn.

Tales of horrors made them shudder. Women exclaimed with terror. Broad scatalogical jokings brought their laughter. He held them in his palm, playing like a master on their simple emotions. It was worthy, he was aware, of a bigger stage, but this was of no moment.

The idea was the thing. When the vision took possession, he would stand aside in his own mind to let the fury boil, surprised and delighted at what came gushing of itself. It was not vanity but the gratification of an artist who feels the beating of eagle's wings about his head in the moment of creation. The effect could almost cause him to forget the main purpose, the collection of funds for the *Partido* of which he was founder and *presidente*. Almost, that is, but not quite. Out would come the coppers and the meeting would end with pleasant exhaustion, a midnight repast, and a discussion of violent plans for the unspecified future.

The other purpose of his journeys was not to be discussed except in whispers. In the far hills were bands of self-styled revolutionists and border ruffians, the scourge of two governments. There were obscure canyons where they might be met—places where spring waters seeped, where primroses were waist-high, where antelope could be taken. Other men were not safe, not against these bandits, nor against the occasional Apache, but Don Carlos rode unmolested, and conversations took place. No one ever knew what might be said. Records were not kept and nothing seemed to result—nothing except impossible demands for money. Neither oratory nor vaulting ideals could move the scoundrels. It was cash or nothing. It was maddening, but the brave days were past and in the end Don Carlos would return to the cafés of Ciudad Jardin or Mexico City with empty hands.

Don Carlos de Niza?

One need only follow his ears to the sound of disputation. In the cool of evening the gatherings in the cafés with his followers were his meat and drink. They were aging men, opinionated, fanciful and devoted, veterans all; none were young. Pamphleteers, gossips, busybodies—they burned with wrongs too many to count. He loved the endless talk. He could sit for hours, *cafecito* after *cafecito,* smoking countless *habanos* sent by admirers from Cuba, plunged in the heat of debate.

He was unmistakable. His eyes flashed, his beard and whiskers bristled, his voice roared with abuse of followers and enemies alike while with his left hand he scribbled his polemics. His correspondence with Spain and Hispanic America was voluminous. In his grand scheme, the prime goal was the recapture of the territories plundered from Mexico by the shameful betrayal at Guadalupe-Hidalgo. Thereafter would follow the union of Hispanic America under leadership of Spain and a destiny of glory forever.

It could not be said that these were practical politics, but then, Don Carlos was a despiser of practical man.

65

"*Oigan!*" he would remark, forefinger up, whiskers bristling. "They say this is a dream, the practical ones, but who knows the power of a dream? The true Spaniard will not lift one eyelid to gain an advantage in commerce, but he will go to his death for an idea. A dream is a torch in the night. The moths, the birds in flight, however many, the torch draws with irresistible power. We are few, we are poor, we are divided, we are in the night, but if we raise our torch, it will be seen, and they will come, the millions of the Spanish blood and true faith—they will surely come!" His eyes would gleam with a fixed purpose, the banter would abate, the talk falter. "One Idea, one People, one Faith!" he would mutter with fanatical zeal. "The Land cannot contain two!"

The Republic despaired of him. These blistering polemics, expressed in his paper, *La Luz*, were insulting to a friendly government. They were libelous to important citizens of a powerful neighbor. It was embarrassing to diplomacy. The government could only deny sympathy for the raving pro-Church, pro-Royalist clique in Ciudad Jardin.

To no avail.

The hostility of the *politicos* was heady wine to Don Carlos of the cafés, for he was a born actor. He savored his own ferocity. He wore his cape with a swagger, conscious of the admiring glances of the ladies, young and old, for truth to tell, he still had the key to many boudoirs. The embers were burning low these days, but many a sigh still heaved for him. There was something in the fierce eyes, the rich voice, the bristling whiskers, the violent humor which neither they nor he could resist. "*Dios!* What a devil I am!" he would mutter, trimming his beard at the mirror. "Carlos, Carlos!" his followers would grin—for in these matters they were with him to a man.

Between love and politics, he was a trial to Doña María de Niza. He was never home. Day would pass into night at the shabby hacienda while dinner would grow cold. Gossip of his affairs left her heart aching, yet she understood the swagger which drove him to those conquests. It was in a way expected of him. No—what hurt was something else. It was that no woman could be mistress of his heart. First came the Idea. The fixed purpose of his life. The one goal. The redemption of the despoiled lands of the North.

That—and the hate for Dan Hogarth!

On a certain day, Doña María left the hacienda with her Yaqui servant girl and drove to market. Women of richer means went north to El Paso for fancy goods, canned fruits and better cuts of meat, but her purse was limited. The market consisted of small sheds in which vegetables, fruits, dried meats, household goods and tourist items lay exposed to dust and flies and the hot sun—an institution inherited remotely from the Moorish *suq*.

As she was selecting green chiles, she heard a man behind her ask where to find her husband. She turned and observed an Anglo, a red-necked toothless man whose suit bulged under his shoulder. The question had been put to a market woman who ran her fingers through a tub of horse beans and squinted. "Don Carlos?" she asked fondly, then gave crackling directions. The Anglo nodded, lit a cigarette, and walked off. Doña María returned to select *cordero* for a dish of roast lamb, and put the episode from mind.

The following day at the hacienda, one at a time, troubled and agitated, the leaders of the *Partido* gathered, summoned at the urgent request of Don José Dominguez. The old building was shabby but gracious, the remains of a prosperous estate. There was a small orchard, a garden with numerous benches, and many rooms. It was well suited to Doña María who never knew what guests would stay the night.

They talked endlessly through a hot afternoon, broke off toward sunset for a hasty supper, then resumed in the living room. Doña María sat in the dining room sewing. The door was open and she listened with heavy heart. How many years, she thought, had she not heard this talk, not lived with this hate of the Anglos? The tumult of excited voices rose and Don Carlos broke in.

"I will not bargain at the counter of redemption!" he shouted in his throaty roar. "What is it Don José tells us? That this Canty was once in our employ? That he is expected to name us as his paymasters in murder? He can prove nothing! Don José trembles at shadows, ancient things, dead and forgotten! Pah! Anything ever done to the Anglos was in fair retaliation—as the record will prove. Our conscience is clear. I am ashamed only when I think of indignities and crimes still not revenged. The defiling of women, the murder of old men—who brought such things if not the Anglo? It is perfect nonsense to accept the defensive. The pest take the Anglo with his law and his courts!" He paused for breath. "War is war!"

A deep voice broke in. "This is all very well, *Presidente*, but what is the motion?" The question was put by Prof. Juan Negra, a teacher of languages, a pedantic fellow.

Don Carlos hesitated. "I will state the issue," he said, mopping his forehead. "Don José asks that we form a committee of notables to defend this Canty. He moves that we find the money, engage lawyers, and take the lead to obtain his acquittal of this expected charge of murder."

"Permit me," Negra smiled painfully. "Is it proposed that we appear as a party? If so, I am against the resolution. We cannot afford to be tarred with this brush."

A hand shot up. *"Presidente!"*

"I recognize Don José," Don Carlos said.

The lawyer arose wearily. He stood for a moment with closed eyes. His greenish pallor seemed to deepen. "We are already tarred, Professor Negra," he said finally. "The situation is bad, and it will get worse. The Anglos have created a dangerous mood, and we are already convicted by public opinion of this crime. Only the acquittal of Canty in open court, or"—he hesitated subtly—"a prudent and careful defense can disassociate us from the crime."

Negra said, "You have not answered my question."

"Ah!" The lawyer rubbed his eyes. "My resolution asks that we appear as a group of notables, not as a party."

"I recognize Don Adolfo of District Seven," Don Carlos said.

A narrow-chested man with inky hair and beady eyes, Don Adolfo Toza, a dealer in hides from Mesilla, arose and stated in a cutting voice, "We still do not know, Don José, if your McKeever will accept a retainer."

"I am not discouraged," Dominguez said wearily. "His letter is kind, but he is still undecided. It all has to do with his son. He writes—" He fumbled and brought out a letter.

Denver, Colorado

My dear Dominguez:

After thinking the matter over, I am afraid I cannot leave Denver yet. My son is doing well but there are more tests before his doctor will make a final decision.

Aside from this, I am still not persuaded about Canty. I do not completely accept the newspaper accounts, but the known facts point to a cold-blooded assassination. The wider issues which we discussed apparently have not yet arisen.

I have meanwhile written to my friend, Jos. Choate, in New York, on your behalf. He is the kindest of men, and a far better trial lawyer than I can hope to be. Perhaps he will take another view of the matters. Why not try him?

Jeff sends his regards.

Faithfully yours,
Lincoln McKeever

P.S. Is your De Niza the same who contributed an article last June to the *Edinburgh Review?*

"The *Edinburgh Review?*" Don Carlos fluffed his beard. "H'm!"

68

"I do not see how that letter helps," Don Adolfo said. "It is a refusal to act."

Dominguez shook his head. "I believe the door is open. The letter invites further correspondence. I feel that he may yet be persuaded."

Don Adolfo sat with an unconvinced look on his face. "I wish, Don José, that you had not acted without our consent. We are either an Inner Committee, or we are not. We cannot permit our affairs to be managed loosely."

"*Presidente!*" said a hoarse voice.

Don Carlos nodded to a clumsily dressed bore, a landowner from Bernalillo whose refusal—or inability—to sell his lands to the Santa Fe Railway gave him a claim to prestige. "I recognize Don Stefano."

Don Stefano Anza recalled his many sacrifices to the Cause at length before he came to the point. "I agree that we need a lawyer if only to ensure that we are not betrayed by some treacherous Anglo appointed by the court. That's common sense! However"—his wattles shook—"how much will it cost?"

Don Carlos interrupted.

"I should like to ask Don José why we are obliged to grovel before this Lincoln McKeever?"

Don José arose to reply.

"*Presidente*, it is not a matter of any lawyer!" His shoulders sloped with fatigue, but he faced his friend with a temper of his own. "This trial will test whether we can live in honor in the lands of our fathers, or whether they drive us out. A lawyer of stature must be secured. I have tried others and they have refused. The entire western bar is in fear of Hogarth!" He paused. "I do not understand, Don Carlos, how you can cavil. Of course I may not grasp these things. I am merely a lawyer. Perhaps the experience of a lifetime has befuddled me."

"Spare us these sarcasms," Don Carlos said angrily. "This McKeever is an Anglo—he is not to be trusted!"

"He is not an Anglo like other Anglos," Don José retorted.

There was a thoughtful silence.

Doña María caught the sound of a child's whimper. She put her sewing aside and went into her son's room, a boy of fourteen, to stroke his head. The Chihuahua nights were cool, she closed the shutters.

"Mama?" the boy muttered.

"*Duerme!*" she whispered. "Sh!" She covered him and returned to the dining room, where she continued to sew with short quick strokes. The same slogans, she thought with a heavy heart, the worn-out ideas, the historic resolutions, the flaming platforms, the call to arms, the threats, the promise of terror—and now this! Her once delicate hands, now brown and ropy, were a blur before her eyes.

"Let us vote," Don Adolfo demanded.

"We are missing the point," Don Carlos stated. "We should take advantage of the situation to advance our interests. As you know, I have taken the liberty from time to time to talk with certain armed men in the hills. Most of these talks have been fruitless, and for this reason, I have never reported to this committee. Their ideas run solely to rapine and robbery—they are simple criminals. But others—" He broke off impatiently. "I beg of you, Don Adolfo, do not interrupt. It is highly offensive!"

Don Adolfo said nastily, "*Presidente*, we go by rules of procedure. You are out of order."

"Then I am out of order!" Don Carlos roared. "I have finally found men who will strike a bargain. At the cost of preparing a stupid legal defense, five hundred to a thousand men would be willing to raid the border. With stealth, they could reach Cuatro Rios, free this prisoner and turn him loose. It has been done before. I move that I be authorized to take such action. This substitute motion will negate Don José's resolution which calls for a purely legal defense. It calls for the force of arms—the only thing the Anglo understands!"

"And if we fail?" Don Adolfo asked coldly.

Don Carlos drew a breath. "We shall still have struck a blow, and that will be something, let me tell you. Is there a second to the motion?"

There was a moment of silence, then hubbub. Don Stefano got the floor.

"*Loco!*" he shouted excitedly. "This is insane! Excuse me for saying this, Don Carlos, but you are living in the past. How can a military incident help our cause? What chances are left that the European Powers will intervene? France? Germany? Spain? Once, yes! What Maximilian did was proof. But those days are over. I believe in our program as much as any man, but I am living quietly with my family in Bernalillo, and we are doing nicely. Let me tell you something. Not all the Anglos are against us. There are good fellows among them if only you grasp their peculiar mentality." His wattles were purple with the exertion of thought. "I advise you to drop this nonsense. Let us stick to the spiritual aspects of our program! If your motion is carried, I shall resign. Besides, I believe the *Partido* owes me some money I shall try to collect."

Don Adolfo hunched his narrow shoulders. "Of all the ridiculous things I have ever heard, Don Stefano," he said brutally, "it is the thought that you can get your money back from the *Partido*."

All laughed except Don Stefano.

70

Don Carlos broke through with staring eyes. "Is there a second to my motion?" His voice took on a tremor. Some eyes were dropped, but no hand went up. "I see!" His face darkened. "Señores, I must regard this as a matter of confidence."

"*Presidente!*" Prof. Negra protested. "Please do not!"

Don Carlos stood at the little table on which a silver mallet rested. His back was arched, his great magnetic eyes went slowly from face to face. He had a curious odd smile as though he saw them for the first time. He felt a sudden desolation as though his life were suddenly without purpose or design. The years had gone, the golden years, the years the locusts had eaten. Was this the work of his hands? Were these his comrades—a handful of ordinary stupid men scratching their noses? Had he given his heart to be eaten by pigs? He nodded slowly. The day of Carlos de Niza had passed. He saw that clearly. It was the day of Stefano Anza.

"Carlos—" said a low voice.

Doña María was at the doorway with a tray of wine and fruit in her hands. Her mournful eyes were on him. She stood with her head bowed, wearing her shabby black dress with grace. She understood the desolation within him, he thought wretchedly, although later she would not say a word. He tapped the gavel and addressed the meeting in a shaking voice.

"There being no second, my substitute motion fails. We will now vote on the motion made by Don José. Do not let me influence you, señores. We will be guided by the majority. However feeble we become"—his irony was heavy—"let us preserve the last remaining virtue of unity. Don Stefano?"

The landowner cleared his throat. "I am for Don José's resolution," he said defiantly.

"Don Ishmael Carmel?"

The red-haired rotund delegate from Sonora peered up nervously. "For the resolution," he said finally.

In the end, the vote was unanimous.

Don Carlos turned to the secretary, trembling. "Please note that I am against the resolution. Also, record my resignation as *presidente*."

In the guilty silence, Prof. Negra stretched out a hand.

"Carlos!" he pleaded.

"Yes, Professor Schoolmaster?"

"You are our leader. You have our love. Why must you resign? Can you not accept our judgment?"

"In this matter? No!" Don Carlos raised his gaunt head. "I am ashamed for my blood." His voice shook. "We should be wolves, but we are sheep. They spit upon us, they kill us, they traduce our honor, they violate our women, they pollute our sanctuaries and we—we talk of courts and lawyers and crafty devices. Our sons will forget our ways. We will sink into the dust of history. We will die tamely at the hands of hangmen and judges. I have called for a last attack on the enemy while yet some strength remains in our arms. I have had your answer."

They sat meditating, ashamed of themselves, until Dominguez arose. "I may assume, *Presidente,* that I have power to act in this matter?"

Don Carlos threw down the silver mallet violently. "I am not *presidente!*"

Dominguez stared resentfully.

"No one will accept your resignation. Please remember, dear Carlos, that Hogarth has the initiative. There is work to be done. I need funds and authority for many things. The land is in flames while you sulk. I must try McKeever again."

"Then go to the Anglo!" Don Carlos said fiercely. "I wish you well!"

Dominguez shook his head. He picked up his coat and walking stick, gazed at the silent circle, then turned. "Carlos, my dear friend, a final word. Under no circumstances are you to cross the border! Now I must go back tonight."

"Sheep!" Don Carlos spat. "I am to be a leader of ewes and lambs?" With a washing motion of his hands, he strode out to the garden.

Doña María entered the room. Her face was impassive as she set the tray on the sideboard. "Señores, I think you will like this wine." In the foreboding silence, she poured a glass of muscatel and then looked up. "Don José," she said hoarsely, "I beg you not to let the case go beyond this man Canty."

"I will try," he said soberly.

She stared. "Go with God, Don José."

Dominguez left. And then, since these matters have no end, the others adjourned to the garden where the argument lasted till dawn and continued thereafter for many days.

"Carlos!" she whispered.

He looked over in the dimness. On the wall a small candle flickered and he could seek out the dusky lines of her face. "My dear," he said in his troubled voice.

"Please sleep," she said in her low voice, and there was a trace of the huskiness he had loved since she was a girl.

"No," he sighed. "These thoughts are bursting! They prevent!"

"It is three weeks now you are like this," she pleaded. "What can I do for you?"

72

"There is nothing!" He flung a gaunt withered arm aside. "I should kill that man. It troubles me that I cannot! Hogarth! Hogarth!" he said savagely. "I have lived with him all my life! What if I should die before him, who will spit on his grave?"

"Oh, Carlos!" she begged.

They remained quiet while the warmth of her body was with him and the dimness of the room was a mantle over them and some time passed. Somewhere beyond the netting a mosquito was whining.

"María," he said suddenly. "Listen!"

She sat up on an elbow and her hair fell like a sweet-smelling cloud at her breast.

"The dog barks," she said with wonder. "Nothing more."

He touched her wrist.

"There was a horse," he whispered. "I felt the step."

"I heard nothing."

"A big horse," he muttered. "I have a feeling!"

"Carlos—"

He swung out of bed and with haste pulled on trousers and shirt and shoes.

"What is it, Carlos?" she pleaded.

"Listen!"

An insane barking stopped as suddenly as it had begun. He reached out and her shallow breast met his hand. He drew her close with a strong grip on her arm and she winced.

"*Querida*," he said in a low voice, "take the children quietly and make your way through the trellis. When you come to the ditch, lie there till the sounds pass. If I do not come for you, write to Don José. There will be money."

"No!" she cried. "I will stay!"

"And Miguelito?" he said impatiently. "And Juanito?"

"I will not go!" she said stubbornly.

He seized her wrist and dragged her, half-resisting, to the children's room. The sound of clinking steel outside somewhere in the fields had awakened Miguelito, the older boy. He struggled up in bed.

"Papa!" he whimpered.

He drew them together. "*Oigan!*" he said sternly. "You will go through the small door in the cellar I have shown you. Wait for nothing until you come to the ditch. If I do not come, you will know what to do when you are men. Guard your mother." He kissed them fiercely. "Now go with God!"

"Is it *they*, Papa?" the boy asked.

73

"Yes!" he said grimly, his face to the window. "It is *they.*"

A hoarse voice in the cornfield said something in a low obscene tone and there was a chuckle.

Don Carlos led the boys and their mother through the kitchen where a door led to the cellar, into which they disappeared. He paused and from its shelf among a heap of chile peppers and dried corn and utensils, he drew a rifle and a box of shells. He retreated to the living room and opened the shutters which gave him a view of the stables. The moon was high shedding a brilliant white light on the scene.

One might read fine print, he thought, and cursed his luck. Not thirty yards away was the stable with his fine-blooded mare and her companion mule. Why had he not permitted guards to be posted?

In the distance were the lights of the town. A wailing hoot of the railroad came drifting over the horizon.

He felt no fear, nothing more than the exultation of the moment, and regret for his wife and the two boys. He felt his pulse to count the time. The slow strong beat pleased him. He would count to three hundred, he told himself, then he would, God willing, make his move. The mare would be fleet and she needed no saddle, nothing more than the sound of his voice. He thought of this and muttered a Pater Noster.

"—ninety-one, ninety-two—"

This hacienda had been a good temporary refuge, he thought, a poor but gracious place set in the hills. Quail could be taken, and occasionally venison, and the garden and the arbor were fruitful. There was schooling for the boys—

A shrill neigh burst from the stable, and the sound of hooves beating the stall, then the bray of the mule.

He stood erect and fired once toward the stables, and the flash and deep roar of his heavy rifle burst out.

"*Señores Ladrones!*" he shouted. "Thieves in the Night! Depart! I am armed! I will shoot to kill!"

There was a silence.

"*Ladrones!* I have friends!" he shouted. "They will come to the sound of shooting."

A voice called out.

"Don Carlos?"

It was a Mexican voice and he answered.

"*Quien es?*"

"*Soy*—Manuel Esposito."

"I will hold fire," he said, and out of the clump of willows a man reluctantly advanced. He wore the dusty uniform of the *Rurales.*

74

His elderly features in the moonlight seemed to ripple with unhappiness.

"*Buenas noches,* Don Carlos," he said formally.

Don Carlos laughed grimly. "Indeed, Manuel! What is it?"

The officer showed that his hands were empty. "Please understand," he said miserably, "I am under orders. My captain gave me instructions to come with these men."

Don Carlos waited.

"I have a paper to read," the officer said. "May I come in?"

"No, you may not," Don Carlos said decisively. "What is the paper?"

The officer coughed apologetically. "It is a warrant for your arrest."

"Ah—and on what charge?"

"Murder!" the officer said deprecatingly. "It relates to the murder they are talking about in the United States. The one among the Americans at Cuatro Rios."

"What is this nonsense? This is Mexico!"

"It is a warrant of extradition!"

Don Carlos was incredulous. "And you, a Mexican officer, arrest me?"

"No, Don Carlos, these are American peace officers. I don't understand this procedure, but my captain tells me it is regular. He does not like it either, but there were orders from Mexico City, and I think someone big is throwing the weight around with the government down here. This paper commands your arrest, and you are to be turned over. They say that this man Canty has made a full statement, and that you are named by him. That is how it is."

Don Carlos waited in silence.

"Are you finished?" he asked icily.

"Yes, you must come with me."

"And these men?"

"They are assisting me. It is all proper."

"And then?"

"We will appear for a hearing at the district court on Monday. In the meantime, you will stay with me at the barracks at Nuevo León."

"And if I refuse?"

The officer shrugged. "I will never arrest Don Carlos de Niza, you may be sure of that. I told my captain so when he gave me this assignment. But I cannot answer for the Americans. Please do not be rash. They are heavily armed."

Don Carlos was silent for several minutes.

"I would never live to see the district court," he said slowly. "It is a trick."

"I am sure they want you alive."

Don Carlos said violently, "Tell them to go to the devil!"

"Don Carlos!"

"I shall give you the count of ten. One! Two!—"

The officer said, "Here is the warrant." He dropped a piece of paper at the portal and retreated hastily to the willow clump. At the count of Ten, Don Carlos fired in his direction. He aimed high and his hand was trembling but it made no difference. His purpose was to draw fire. Three flashes from the arbor! One from the clump of willows ahead! Two to the left! Nothing, he thought with relief, had come from the ditch, and then from that direction came three or four sharp cracks of a small-bore weapon. His heart sank at the thought of his wife and children.

"Thieves—depart!" he called fiercely.

A bullet crashed into a precious jar of majolica ware behind him. He returned the fire and cursed his shaking hand. In the silence the crickets were shrill.

"All right, Carlos," a deep voice called in English, "let's use some common sense about this thing. This *Rural* claims you're afraid to surrender to us. Now you ought to know better. I've got an order to take you home."

"Who is that?" Carlos called.

A tall figure came out of the willow clump. Evidently this was their point of command.

"This is Sheriff Max Kyle of Hogarth County, Carlos. You remember me. I'm here to take you back to Cuatro Rios, and that's all I want. Now you know you can trust me!"

Don Carlos laughed mockingly.

"As you were trusted at the Cañon de los Angeles by Don Porfirio Gallegos? Shall I throw out my rifle as he did?"

"Jesus Almighty," Kyle replied after a moment, "don't you ever get a thing right? That was a plain mistake about Gallegos. Anyways, that was twenty years ago!" He paused and added with exasperation, "Maybe this might convince you—the reward specifies we bring you back alive!"

"That is more convincing," Don Carlos agreed with irony.

"I've got nothing personal against you, Carlos," Kyle called. "I just don't want trouble. Now this whole thing is legal. Under this warrant of extradition, I can assist in this arrest. What do you say?"

Don Carlos remained silent. Kyle continued to lament that he was not trusted and then stepped cautiously into the moonlight. Don Carlos raised the rifle and got him into the sights. It was almost as good as sunlight, he told himself, and then the image began to blur and slip out of focus. He could have wept with rage—and then he fired.

"Damn you, Carlos," Kyle shouted. "You're just making this trouble!"

A voice from the arbor called hoarsely, "The hell with this old bastard, Sheriff, let's rush him!"

Another voice growled, "Let's fire the place!"

Don Carlos fired at each voice and then a fusillade broke out. A bee came whining out of the darkness and smashed his palm and he grunted with the shock. He looked down.

"*Ay, Madre!*"

In the moonlight, all blood is black, he thought, as the liquid bubbled and came dripping down his sleeve. He was in a state of wonder at this mutilation when he heard a whisper behind him.

"Papa!" Miguelito cried hoarsely.

He turned with dismay. The older boy had returned and was crouched on the floor, and at the door was the younger, clasped to his wife's breast. She looked at her ankle—it was bandaged—and there was fear in her eyes.

"Carlos, they shoot at everything," she whispered starkly.

"Lie down," he cried.

There was a lull broken only by the whimpering of Juanito. This was not for María, he thought with despair, she was too gentle, too filled with fears for the children. He stared at the flattened field in which each stalk of wild grass was distinct. He could imagine the rustle of field mice. Somewhere a night bird whistled liquidly. Kyle called across the clearing in his complaining voice:

"We're just wasting time with this foolery, and I'm not going to stand it. Carlos—come out or we'll fire the house!"

Don Carlos wrung his wounded hand.

"*Bueno!*" he spat. "You show your hand, Anglo! You would not dare!"

To this there was no answer. The pain surged and he feared that he would faint. He heard a rough voice growl—and how distinctly the sound carried in the night!—"Let's take the son of a bitch up on that, Sheriff!" There was more of this, and then in Spanish the *Rural* called:

"Don Carlos, they will start with the stables—the mare!"

In the dark a torch went swaying toward the stables. Don Carlos fired again and again and again and his only reply now was a throaty chuckle.

"Anglo!" he called hoarsely. "If you have come to kill, then kill! But not the animals, not the children!"

77

There was a shrill whinny of terror.

Kyle called, "You're just being stubborn. You're wanted for trial, Carlos, you know that. I promise no shooting. Now you got my word on that. After this, I can't be responsible."

Don Carlos slumped down weakly. His breath was coming in gasps. He looked about the pleasant room and at Doña María and at the children of his old age. The hand was useless. He cursed himself weakly. He had known this would happen! Why had he not taken to the hills when the warnings had come from across the border?

"Have you decided your mind, *querido*?" María asked gently.

He stared at her in the darkness.

"I cannot say the words," he whispered hoarsely. "*Madre de Dios!* They will not come!"

She drew herself along the floor, painfully, and kissed him, then dragged herself to the window. "Señores, it will be all right," she called. "You may enter my husband's house."

There was a silence.

"Come on out, Carlos!" Kyle said. "We won't come in."

He stepped finally out of the shadows, his back arched; there was blood on his beard and the men came advancing. He stood there quietly. He thought:

"*Dios!* How beautiful is the night!"

The surrender was a formal matter. He listened with bitter comprehension as the warrant of arrest was read in detail. In his mind was the thought that money and lawyers could drag out the proceedings for many months. "*Bueno!*" he said decisively. "Take me now before the district court."

Kyle snapped on the manacles.

"Let's not worry about details," he drawled with good humor. "You'll get exactly what's coming, Carlos. No more, no less."

Don Carlos looked at his sons and at his wife. Then they carted him off in the shallow wagon smelling of hay and dung. He turned for a last look at his home and he muttered:

"*Mientras en casa estoy, rey soy!*"

A tousled thin deputy scratched a match and yawned in the quick blue spurt. "What's that, Carlos?" he asked in a friendly tone.

Don Carlos stared at the young man.

"It is a saying," he replied bitterly. "It means that a man's home is his castle."

An older deputy chuckled. "They're full of sayings, these Mexos. You just can't stop 'em. Now we got that saying too."

They drove on to the siding where a locomotive was making steam, sending up hoots of coarse black smoke.

Don Carlos drew back. "This is going north," he said suspiciously. "I demand to be taken to the district court."

"They're closed for the week end," Kyle said stonily. "Let's not waste time."

He objected violently. "No!" Two deputies seized him and dragged him into the coach in a furious struggle in which his bandage slipped and he began again to bleed.

"Now, you going to behave?" Kyle demanded, panting.

Don Carlos spat at his face. The sheriff slowly wiped his cheek and a broad genial grin spread. "All right," he said, and with a gentle touch he patted the prisoner's knee. "If it gives you satisfaction, why, I don't mind one bit. We all got a long ride. I'd advise you to try to get some sleep."

He pulled a cord and the train started. The last thing to be seen was the dejected *Rural* standing alone at the deserted siding.

For a day and a night, Don Carlos ate not at all. When they crossed the border, he answered a call of nature. For the rest he sat erect and proud, dry with hate, wearing his irons like honorable things.

And in Denver a receiving telegraph key began to chatter.

Chapter VI

Denver.
 Not less than a flying carpet, a whaling vessel, Bucephalus, a river boat, the submarine *Nautilus*, a prairie schooner, a windjammer in the China trade, the railroad was a thing of enchantment to Jeff.

Midnight.

A yellow glow in the ticket office. Gleaming track stretching into illimitable distance. Crickets strident. The desolate dampness and a man high-stepping the ties swinging a red-green-yellow lamp. Two men in work clothes laughing quietly about the things which railroad men know among themselves.

The lonely stars setting the course.

The chill.

The gang of laborers squatting mournfully, sombreros down on patient faces, serapes wrapped against the cold, bare feet, an occasional huaracho, laborers off to work the sugar beet fields beyond the Divide. The priest among them. A straggle of section hands setting a handcar and the pump-pump-pump into the swallowing darkness.

The alley clear and the vast smoker blowing fog. Hoof-hoof-hoof-sssh! Sssh!

Doctor Loewy shaking hands. Beard and shoulders of an Assyrian bull. Warm meaty hand on forehead. Teeth through red lips like gleaming white scimitars. *Look after this boy, George!*

Yes, suh! Sure *will!*

The white clean warm smell of starch and wool and smoke and a strange pillow in the darkness. Then sleep.

And suddenly the light.

Past meadows of columbines, around the peaks, blue towering ranges in the distance, then smelter stacks, and lead and copper and the wait at Pueblo. Fields of haying grass. La *Hoon*ta. The Harvey House. The waitress with dresden china-blue smiling eyes.

Bo-ard! Bo-ard! Bo-ard!

Trinidad.

Drill, you tarriers, drill! Squint-eyes, rags, steel bars, hold the rail, the blinding sun, the Liner thundering by, curious eyes as the windows pass. Drill!

Raton Pass and then New Mexico.

The friendly world of travelers. Mining men. Railroad men. Cattle men. Tall rangy men with fixed eyes and slow way of talking. Family men with stringy fussy wives and gummy children. An Agency couple hating the heathen Indian tribal ways. A missionary. A Carlisle College Comanche with a bitter mouth. Government men. A knot of unpleasant men, silent, alone, with guns.

Everywhere the name of Dan Hogarth.

McKeever never slept on Pullmans and during the run down from Denver, the smothering sense of curtains and walls kept him tossing. He filled the upper berth exactly, feet flat against cold iron, head painfully against headplate, ventilator whistling—he hated the whole business. At about three he got up in a cold sweat but in the lower berth of the compartment, Jeff was sleeping with a gentle snore, his head dim against the pillow.

He looked at his son a long moment. He was still bewildered at himself. What was he doing on this train? What compulsion brought him at the last moment? His only reward was Jeff's high glee at the trip. He smiled and withdrew. He lay rocking with the train, turned fitfully, snapped on the light, opened his brief case. His notes were sparse, but enough for the moment.

LAND GRANT CASE: Actn in Ejectmnt. In Dist Ct, 6th Jud Dist/ New Mex. To recover poss. of De Niza Grant in Counties Mingo, Galway and Hogarth. Pltffs: Carlos & Maria de N.; Deft: Alamo Land Co. (Dan. & Flo. Hogarth)

Yes, those were the parties. He stirred slightly at the recollection of Florence Hogarth. He had assumed in Washington that her interest in the appeal was a lawyer's. Now, he saw, her stake in the outcome was greater then he had supposed. Well, the situation was interesting.

De Nizas claim through grant of Governor of New Mex. and King of Spain 1818 to cover earlier revoked grants of 1688 & 1743. Conditions re estab. of settlers not filled. Not confirmed by King. Not enforced under Mex. laws after Republic est.

There it was, he thought cynically. Idealism and politics rooted

81

in property rights now under cloud since the revolt. Who would not be a royalist?

> Hogarths claim title through later Flores Grant 1843 by Gov. Armijo. 2,000,000 acres on Rio Amarillo. They further claim adverse possession from 1866. Proof: pasturing cattle, horses, hogs and haying plus testimony one Morgan and Holahan.

He raised his brows thoughtfully. If the Hogarths had kept De Niza so long out of actual possession, how had the latter managed his finances? These cases were desperately expensive.

He skimmed an intricate summary in which verbal testimony was hotly in dispute.

> Held: Error to allow in evidence talk with Holahan. See, Recopilacion de las Indias, La w29, Liber 8, Title 13–16th Century Code (Pope v. Simons, 2 Cal. 319) All sales real property must be made before Escribano (Notary) etc. Fuero Juzgo (6th Cen. Visigothic Code) requires writing except in case of executed contract and livery of seizin. But cf. Schmidt's Civil Law of Spain and Mex. (Publ. New Orleans, 1851)

And so forth. He came to a more solid point.

> Held: Claims must be filed to be known to Land Office.

And finally.

> Held: *Statute Limitations*. Comp. Laws, New Mex. Sec. 1881 Uninterrupted occupancy of land for 10 years by person with no title (if done adverse to true owner extinguishes title of true owner and vests title absolutely in occupier. (See, Lord Coke, 1 Inst. 153: "A disseisin is when one enters intending to usurp possession and to oust another of his freehold; and therefore *querendum est a judice quo animo hoc fecerit*, why he entered and intruded.") So inquiry is reduced to fact of entering, and intent to usurp possession.

A cunning statute of limitation! McKeever thought. Short enough for smooth talk to lull a claimant into a false sense of security. The years would swiftly pass. The rules were strict. The courts would turn deaf ears to the victim's outcry. Now who, he wondered, controlled what legislature?

> Jdgment for Hogarths per Hanna, Ch. J. Appeal to U S Sup Ct. dismissed. While motion to reargue pending, Hanna murd!—????

He read the last line again. Unless De Niza was totally mad, the murder of the judge could not have been more inopportune.

On the other hand, he thought ironically, to slay the judge was a way to end litigation. Who would not sympathize? There was that California lawyer Healy who had attempted to shoot Justice Wiggins in the Ninth Circuit. Drastic, yes, but effective. Brother Healy had had the unavowed sympathy of the entire suffering American bar.

Well, all this background study felt familiar. He smiled faintly and snapped out the light. The ventilator was whistling as he drifted to sleep. He awoke with the tap on the door.

"Last call for breakfast."

"The country's sure changing."

"I remember when there was just a handful of shakedown houses, adobe, knotty frame, that kind of thing. Now they've got these brick buildings."

"I remember White Oaks. Man, was it tough! Men came from all over the world. There was even one feller in from South Africa. Now that's where there's mining! They've got these natives lined up. All you got to do is set in the shade with an eye out. Pack of Dutch farmers around with these fat tow-hair girls for fun."

"Do they talk English in Africa?"

"Better'n you. Take that Babcock who's been buying all these herds, he's from there. Jo'burgh, they call it."

"Thought he was English."

"Nope—just talks that peculiar way."

"All this talk about remittance men, hell! They tell me they're buying up every spread along the Pecos. They're just a pack of bankers, getting so they've got all the range in sight. Even Guthrie's selling out."

"Well, the real money's in England. These boys hereabouts might just as well get it. Better than letting it get down to South America."

"It's not that, it's the principle. A lot of white men went through a lot to get this land away from the dons. Those old dons just had to pack up and git. Can't blame 'em for a lot of feeling, come to think."

"Oh, I don't blame 'em, only there comes a time. When you take a court trimming, they ought to let it lay. I just can't see this ambush."

"Guess that's so. Still, I was talking to a lawyer up in the old Indian Territory. He claims this judge handed Carlos out a raw deal. Said it was just foolery not to admit his family's been sitting there for three hundred years, then along comes Hogarth and boots him off. I can see it Carlos's way too."

"You really think Carlos is behind Canty?"

"Don't you?"

"I say it don't make any difference. He's just messing with old Dan Hogarth and that's foolish. When you touch a buzz saw, you can't look surprised when you got no hand left."

"Say, that's a good one."

"I got it from an Indian medicine man."

"A buzz saw!"

"What I say is, a judge is a judge. He don't ask what the case is. He takes what comes along. Now supposing two men get to quarrel and jaw and there's a lot of fighting around, and they take off to law it out. Maybe it's nothing. Maybe it's something. What's the judge got to do? He can't duck out. Can't satisfy both. He just sets on it and when the burr works high he lets out a yowl and by guess and by God out comes some decision or other. You mean to say after that this judge's just fair game?"

"Why not? I've run into judges I could just as soon drown. You take this son of a bitch Parker. Now I wouldn't want this to get further, but when I was dodging around in the Chickasaw Nation I would've been a dead duck except a smart lawyer named Norman Provett alibied me out."

"You got away from Parker—say!"

"It was just old Norman Provett done it. But I spent a year on bread and water. That jug was tough. Twenty of those boys got strung up while I was waiting trial. They went with a smile though."

"How do they do it—a smile? I've wondered about that!"

"Sometimes a deputy will slip you a pill. You get enough of that in your crop and you don't know a thing."

"Is that how it's done?"

"You think anyone likes his neck stretched?"

"It's crossed my mind. I mean, how would I feel comes the day? Though generally I don't worry. I don't work where you can't square the beef. Now before Parker came wasn't nothing you couldn't fix. Things sure is changing."

"Sure is! They tell me they've even got Pinkertons down in Cuatro on this case."

"Hell, no, just Charley Longo and some boys from Dallas."

"Charley worked down in Texas for the Association, I seem to remember."

"Yeah, he's writing a book about it. How it breaks his heart to betray the poor cow thieves after he's worked among them."

"Well, I don't care for cow thieves. How can a poor old range cow defend itself? It's plain cowardly. You give me a bank or a post office any time."

"Cowardly? Say, that's good! But I don't look at it that way. Take

84

a plain cow. It ain't so different from an ordinary deer or antelope. Just because it's got itself branded a little don't make it property to my way. Cowardly?"

"That's good too."

"Oh, well, I was born original. If I could write, they tell me, I could make a writer, I've got that kind of a mind. Now there's quite a market for good writing. I know the West just as good as Texas Sam, for example, and he's making a fortune peddling these stories."

"*Texas* Sam? I knew him when he was calling himself Sam Slobodkowitz or something. Just a plain immigrant. They's a pack of 'em working themselves up from Galveston. Started selling gew-gaws all down the river bottoms, now they got all these stores. But I give 'em credit. Still, they tell me even Geronimo's getting set for this story peddling up at the new Fair."

"They's a pack of writers down in Cuatro. This feller on the train McIver was telling me yesterday the Hearst papers got a man from Frisco coming in especial. No, they'll never get the Fair set. Been talking too much too long. Besides why would they pay good money to see that flea-bitten blanket Indian? Can't sell me Geronimo!"

"They tell me you dasn't lay an Apache woman without feeling around for the knife first. They got a funny sense of humor when they get high."

"Do they cut before or after?"

"Why?"

"It sure would make a difference to me."

"More of a difference to her!"

"You've got a point. Well, this McIver's got a slant. I was listening how he was telling his kid they waste too much time fussing around. Said they ought to revive the Star Chamber in this country, whatever that is. Why accuse a man of a crime maybe he can prove he didn't commit? The better way, he was saying, is just accuse him of being Carlos de Niza—and how does he plead to *that*, guilty or not guilty?"

"Sounds like a peculiar sense of humor."

"This kid of his was laughing like there was some point or other, the which I didn't get. Still, it makes sense. Why not get it over? That's what all these prosecuting cliques are after. They make up their so-called minds there's a man they're out to get. Like Eli Swade in the old Panhandle days. I know for a fact he was on the scout in Missouri at the time this stage was robbed, but they was sick and tired of Eli, so they dug up some half-wit witness and that was it."

"You've got to admire the way they got Carlos. His mistake was squatting below the border. I read some of this stuff he was writing about Dan Hogarth. It was kind of amusing, except he should've drifted off into them hills. But no! He's the kind that's got to have the last word and that strikes me stupid."

"This Santa Fe paper don't think much of Carlos. They can't see those old dons are just naturally sore."

"I wouldn't care if he'd shot Dan Hogarth, but not the old judge."

"My only guess is, it was a demonstration of some kind. The Mex has got a funny mind, in my experience. I'd just as soon kill the best like I would a dog. I don't see the difference."

"That's what this fellow McIver was saying back there. Why don't they hang the Mex half of this Tom Canty and keep the other half for a witness against Carlos? Claims that's what he would do was he Kyle—only he was fooling with the idea. Can't make him out. He's got a way of telling these stories, I got to admit they're agreeable, but he sounds like a confidence man. Now what would he be after in Cuatro?"

"McIver? Looks like a drug store keeper to me. Say, where you staying? They're putting me up in this hotel."

"Well, us special deputies are supposed to get room and board with private families. I'd just like to bed down in some farmhouse with two girls the right age. I figure this job could be some fun in it beside bonus money."

"Ain't two girls hard to manage at one time? I'm asking because I got that offer once in a house in Matamores."

"I'll tell you this. It's tricky but it can be done."

"You sure?"

"I learned it the hard way."

"I want to think that one over."

"This whole idea of a badge feels funny."

"Most of the boys don't mind. They need men, and why not? In my case, I aim to get on the credit side comes sentence time. Fact is, this marshal in Sweetwater recommended me for this job. Says a good word from Kyle could help with the judge, and I'm not so young. Still—riding herd on a pack of Mex! Things are getting tough!"

"Tough is the word."

"Now where's that gun? I had it here— Say, ain't that Cuatro Rios?"

The blaze of noon.

The hoo-hooing at Gidding's Pass drifted over the Valley as the train labored around the shoulder of the mountain.

The sun-drenched platform was covered with a thin coat of yellow dust. Silent men in jeans and rough work clothes were standing about carrying guns. Harvey girls were smoothing their aprons, women with serious eyes, working women. Leaning against the posts were newsmen and a man with a wooden box camera. One of the kitchen help, a swarthy man, was hefting a cleaver.

The stationmaster glanced at his timepiece. "They promised to make it on time," he worried. "I hate to keep this liner waiting."

The distant train slackened speed and descended through the great stands of fir and spruce into the grasslands of the Valley. It rolled through the poor outskirts, adobe houses, tin sheds like chicken runs, children tumbling in the dust, sleepy burrows, wash hanging on fences, neglect and poverty and then the center of town. A jerk and a sigh and the diamond stacker clanked to a halt gushing smoke.

"Cuatro Rios!" the conductor bawled. "Cuatro!"

Two heavy-set blue-jawed men carrying sheepskin coats crept down wearily from the coach and went directly to the toothless man with the badge. There was a low-voiced conversation.

"Sheriff?" the taller man asked. "We come down from La Junta."

The deputy sheriff, Tom Simpson, removed his corncob. "You Cody?"

"I'm Joe Hurley. This is Cody."

Simpson made a note. The two men stood yawning and scratching before they got into the sheriff's buggy and drove off. The stationmaster turned to the conductor.

"Now who were those birds?" he grunted.

"Special deputies," the conductor said laconically. "This Irish valentine came with 'em. See it gets to Max Kyle." By which he meant the green traingram received at La Junta from the peace officer who had paid their fares. He puffed his cheeks. "Lands, we've hauled in twenty-five of these deputies I know about. Now I'm overdue, Bill. Don't hold me up."

At the Pullman, the porter leaped down, grinning at a quip, and placed his footstool at the step. "Yes, *sir!*"

McKeever stepped down into the sun.

He stood with the breeze ruffling his hair. This was a scene he had lived through before. Among the faces, a lantern-jawed man with splintered teeth snarled. A knot of toughs had hoisted hostile signs and a tattered effigy with a plug hat hung on a makeshift gallows. He stared at the grotesque caricature of himself and chuckled.

Jeff called down, "What is it, Dad?"

The lawyer stretched his galluses and looked about with an amused fearless glance. "Guess they think I'm Daniel Webster, Jeff," he drawled in an ironic affected nasal twang. He turned back and raised his arms. "Come on, down you go!" The boy crept down weakly and stood beside him, squinting in the glare. Mrs. Blanchard followed. "Lands!" she exclaimed at the sight of guns. For an uncertain moment they stood under the gaze of strangers.

McKeever turned to the stationmaster. "I was expecting to be met by a committee," he said. "Do you know Mr. Dominguez?"

"Oh, I know Dominguez all right," the stationmaster said curtly. "The question is whether he'll show. There's quite a mood here."

"What's wrong, Dad?" Jeff asked anxiously.

"It's nothing," his father said reassuringly. "Nothing at all."

"Oh Link!" a high-pitched voice called. "Link McKeever!"

"John Bellew!" McKeever exclaimed with pleasure. A tall smiling man, a New York journalist, pushed through the crowd, leading a cameraman. John Macy Bellew was one of *McClure's* brilliant staff of contributors. His mouth had a soft girlish pout, his cheeks were rosy, bangs covered his forehead, but there was clear purpose in his manner. He was smoking a meerschaum. "Welcome to Cuatro Rios!" he exclaimed and stood back beaming to savor the return of the prodigal. "Back to the hustings, Link?"

"So it seems," McKeever admitted and they shook hands.

"The press has missed you." Bellew smiled. "I never put stock in that retirement *canard.*"

"Put out by my competition, I guess," McKeever smiled. "Trial men are a jealous lot."

Other journalists, knowledgeable traveled men, came clustering and were introduced—Glen Wyatt of the Dallas *Star*, Henrique Clementis of the *Picayune*, Ida Montgomery, a rising muckraker, a Hearst man, and others whose names eluded him; only the local press was absent. McKeever greeted them pleasantly and introduced his party. He was both genial and elusive, but he knew nothing of the facts, he protested. He had no opinions. He would make his first statement in court. "Now where's my baggage?" he wondered with an anxious eye to Jeff. Someone took the baggage checks from him, and he drew Bellew aside. "How long have you been here?" he asked.

"About four days." Bellew smiled, recalling their last *cause célèbre* together in Pennsylvania. He was the product of a sheltered life, who had found the study of Metropolitan crime and political corruption a delectable field. "You'll like this town, Link, it's the legendary West. It's marvelous, absolutely the real thing!"

McKeever looked about at the ominous circle of onlookers. He murmured, "Is this turnout for my sole benefit?"

Bellew's face clouded. "Not entirely," he said briefly. "Your committee will be along. They'll explain."

"What's wrong?"

"Well, Link, this time you picked quite a situation, I'm afraid." Bellew pressed his nostrils like an anxious spinster, and this seemed to underscore his next remark. "Virginia Hanna took a bad turn yesterday."

"Mrs. Hanna?" McKeever was startled. "What does that mean? I thought she was recovering."

"Oh, no, it's not that. It's just—" Bellew shook his head grimly. "You'll see in a minute. The local press is pretty bitter." He indicated the conductor and stationmaster in earnest conversation. "They're holding the train for her now. They're taking her on to New Orleans."

The crowd muttered and stirred.

A voice called McKeever's name in a heavy accent. With a familiar flash of gleaming teeth, Dominguez came through, leading a small committee of dignified rigid sallow men. He was panting slightly and evidently nervous, for his clasp was convulsive. "Thank God you got here!" he said hoarsely. McKeever murmured deprecatingly and he went on, "Well, I'm delighted! I hope you had a good trip. Ah Jeff! And Mrs. Blanchard! You look well, all of you." He turned. "May I present my friends? Don Adolfo Toza, from Mesilla. Dr. Leon Sandoval, an outstanding dentist, as I promised. Don Stefano Anza, a leader from Bernalillo. Señor Pete Morales has come from Santa Fe in your honor. Señor Casimiro Morales, editor of *La Vox del Pueblo*." And so on. "Gentlemen," McKeever murmured. They shook hands Spanish style, once up, once down, men soberly dressed in store clothes, hair oiled, shoes gleaming, their uneasy white faces impassive. They bore themselves well, the red-necked crowd might have had no existence. "Señor," they murmured, "be welcome among us."

Photographers with wooden box cameras came swooping and McKeever posed with the committee, scratching his hair, genial and humorous. He was nevertheless disquieted. His committee were few, dismayingly few. Nor did they seem like men of large affairs, not the sort he would need for the struggle ahead. It was a weak start, he thought, as he bantered with the newspapermen.

A freckled boy perched in the window above them called down. "Mr. Torrence!" The stationmaster looked up. "Yes, Buddy?" With a squint the boy pointed. "Here they come."

"All right now!" The stationmaster pulled up his gartered shirt sleeves. "Let's make some room, folks. I can't keep this train all day."

"Here she comes, Link," said Bellew.

McKeever followed his glance. The street which ran from the

station was lined with arcades of stores selling harnesses, general merchandise, and the like. In the distance a surrey came into sight led by a man in a white shirt. Inside, across the seat, a stretcher had been laid. A wagon piled with bales of wool paused to give the right of way.

Jeff exclaimed eagerly, "Dad, there's Miss Hogarth!"

The frail figure in the stretcher moaned.

Florence patted her aunt's wrist. "We're almost there, Aunt Ginnie," she said in a low voice. She sat wan and exhausted from a vigil which had lasted now beyond endurance. Her forehead was wet and cold in the light breeze. She did not trust herself to speak.

When they reached the platform, willing hands went to work and the stretcher was handed down. A stocky sharp-faced man with a medical air of authority, Dr. Kimball, bent over the figure. "Virginia, this is me," he said softly. "I'll be going all the way, so there's nothing to worry about. You'll be fine, just fine."

The platform was quiet.

McKeever managed to glimpse a head swathed in heavy bandages. A single white curl peeped out at the neck. The blue veins of a wasted old hand plucking weakly at the blanket were clear in the sun.

"Why don't you tell the truth?" the old woman moaned. "I'm going to lose my eyes, I know I will!"

"No, you're not!" Florence said strongly. Her face, ravaged with grief, was unseeing and stony. "You're not to think that at all! This man in New Orleans is the very best, Auntie!"

"Come with me," the old woman begged.

"I'll come down in a few days," her niece promised. "You'll be all right, I know you will."

"Well, it doesn't matter." The hands fell helplessly. "I don't care what happens. Oh why didn't I die too?" she moaned.

The conductor snapped his watch. "I'm afraid we've got to start, Doctor—"

"Well, here we go!" The doctor squeezed his patient's limp hand. "This old girl is a wonderful patient!" he said firmly. "Floss, I want you to get some rest now. There's nothing more to do."

With the porter's help, the stretcher was lifted into the Pullman and out of sight. A sigh went through the onlookers. The doctor and a uniformed nurse mounted the step and the conductor wagged his hand.

"Bo-oard! Board!"

The pistons picked up thrust, the great driving wheels turned, the semaphore winked green, the train pulled slowly down the yard.

Out of the crowd a blue-eyed man wearing a bandanna stepped forth.

"Miss Hogarth," he said respectfully.

Florence turned. "Yes, Jim?"

"Everybody says her eyes are going to come out. Is there any truth to that?"

She put a hand to her throat. "There's a chance, Jim," she said huskily. "This surgeon in New Orleans might help her. He just might. We won't know for a little."

The distant train whistle howled its low note and the plume of smoke disappeared. Florence remained motionless, and then she saw the McKeevers.

She hesitated.

They were standing in the sun only a few yards away. She could almost touch them, but the distance seemed insuperable. The structure of the boy's face was heavier, she saw. His brows were thicker, his nose had become prominent, a faint down masked his sensitive lip. Under a pallor, he had the promise of his father's attractive animality. She saw all this, quite detached. They faced each other and there was nothing to say. Then after a hesitant moment, she inclined her head graciously and the boy smiled.

"Hello, Jeff," she said soberly. "You're looking well." His eyes lit with pleasure and he took her hand awkwardly. "Mr. McKeever," she said formally. "I'm glad to see you again."

It was a strange moment, McKeever felt, and not the most comfortable. This was merely good manners on her part, he felt, nothing more. They shook hands. She nodded to his committee, who bowed stiffly in return. But she remained aloof, tugging at her black gloves, eyes pinched and remote. Her kindness was directed pointedly at Jeff and away from himself.

"I'm sorry to learn this distressing news," he said. "It must be difficult for you."

"Yes, quite difficult," she said frozenly. Her mouth twitched. "Perhaps I'll see you again, Jeff," she said huskily. "But I'm afraid you must excuse me now." She got into the surrey. The man in the white shirt took the reins and they drove off.

"Well!" said Bellew softly.

"Dad, I'm really tired," Jeff begged.

"And now," Dominguez nervously rubbed his hands, "I have a carriage waiting. We will drive home. We have arranged lunch and I know Jeff will want to rest. Dr. Sandoval will see to the baggage." They drove out of the silent plaza and only then did the crowd begin to disperse. McKeever barely saw the city. He had an impression of gracious adobe structures and ancient cottonwoods, and it seemed to him that a bridge was crossed. The mood of violence at the station was disquieting.

"That's pretty!" Jeff breathed with tired delight when they drew up before the rambling old house which Dominguez had rented for them. A clump of poplars arose, dark and swaying against a blue sky. The clear air was like wine. Mrs. Blanchard gazed through square-cut spectacles. "Now *that's* worth while!" she decided.

They found it spacious and charming. The adobe walls were several feet thick. They would be cool in summer, warm in winter. The owners had left a good library and excellent paintings. Heavy colonial Spanish pieces of furniture in this setting seemed only too appropriate.

The boy was entranced with his bedroom. Navajo rugs made the room bright. His bed was a huge fourposter with an inviting feather mattress and quilts of down. A fuzzy puppy came scrambling from a basket as he opened the door.

"A gift!" Dominguez smiled. "Your papa wrote that you loved animals."

"I certainly do!" Jeff held the puppy to his cheek and thanked the Spanish lawyer with his eyes. The room was stocked with Indian artifacts and books. "And now," said Mrs. Blanchard with her air of decision. "I want this young man in bed at *once!*"

Jeff crawled weakly under the quilts. Through the window the horizon was the widest he had ever seen. It was one of those rare days when in one distant corner of the sky purple thunderheads were piling. In their inky depths lightning was flashing and across the vast spaces came the faint rumblings of thunder. The rest of the sky was clear in the hot sun.

He ate a light lunch, petted the puppy, and fell asleep.

When Florence reached the ranch, she went to the sickroom where she had kept her long vigil. She stood a moment with her aunt's effects, things to gather and perhaps to send on to New Orleans, slippers, a piece of tatting, a book, a photograph with a loving inscription. She found a white hairpin on the dresser and it seemed pitiful beyond words. She stood in thought. Her father, she sensed, was prowling below in his great library, rummaging through his collection of maps, smoking his endless cigarillos, his great eyes questing voraciously through old texts. He was waiting for her, but at the moment she did not want to see him. She did not want to see anyone. She returned to her own room where she sat quietly at the window until it was dark.

The living room seemed dim and empty, but after a moment,

McKeever made out Dominguez standing at the window. The Spanish lawyer looked up with a ghastly smile and pointed. "The Fortress of San Felipe," he said simply. "They are holding him there."

McKeever looked out at sun and space and a vast blue sky. Thunderclouds were still towering in the distance beyond a pile of masonry from which a plume of smoke was rising. San Felipe was an old fortress built after the ominous futile Pueblo Revolt in Santa Fe two hundred and fifty years earlier. Now it was an historical site and a tourist lure.

"Good Lord!" McKeever was reminded of the antiquity of the Spanish settlements in these lands, far older than Jamestown. He asked, "Why is he held there?"

"Why?" Dominguez laughed harshly. "They can hold him incommunicado there. Just as they held Canty." He stood breathing heavily with a vengeful look on his face. "The miserable sons of bitches! What in God's name are they doing to him?"

"Incommunicado?" McKeever exclaimed.

The other gave him an ironic glance. "Exactly!"

"Have you tried to see him?"

"I've been there every day for a week. Three days ago I drove through a dust storm. They kept me cooling my heels."

"That sounds incredible!"

Dominguez pursed his protuding lips. "Mr. McKeever, I warned you. This is Hogarth County. You've got some unpleasant surprises coming."

In the distance, a carriage came out and turned down the river road toward a darker green in the distance. This, Dominguez indicated, was the great Hogarth Ranch. The road was the same one taken by Douglas Hanna the night of his murder. McKeever studied the unfamiliar terrain and looked up with a thoughtful face. "Dominguez, what's the situation?"

"Bad enough," the Spanish lawyer said somberly. "When they broke Canty, all his old connections with us began to come out. Our own people are divided. Some would like to throw Carlos to the wolves. The younger element are talking war. There's a lot more in this than just a trial." He paused. "We'll need armed guards!"

McKeever laughed. "I must say that sounds extremely refreshing. There's nothing like a hint of violence to spice things up. In a way, it's a form of flattery. Shows respect for the legal profession."

The Spanish lawyer was not amused. "I could tell you stories, Mr. McKeever, but I see you wouldn't believe me."

"I'll believe!" McKeever smiled faintly. "Now the first order of business is dinner. Then we'll see if I still know how to frame a petition for a writ of habeas corpus. Is that satisfactory?"

"Better make sure of the form! Dan Hogarth's daughter is a stickler for the technicalities."

McKeever raised his brows inquiringly. "His daughter?"

"She's the judge's law secretary," Dominguez explained. "God knows what she's been feeding him in chambers. The Hogarths!" he said savagely. "They're everywhere!"

McKeever paused.

"I don't understand this," he said slowly. "I was surprised in Washington to find a woman lawyer, but I didn't think much of it. Can't say I approve or disapprove. Why would she want to practice law?"

Dominguez shrugged. "She'll be a rich woman some day. She took this job when her uncle was still judge with that in mind. It's a sure thing she's not interested in the practice itself. She's a good lawyer," he added grudgingly. "You'll see."

"Can she actually influence the Court?" McKeever wondered.

"Oh, I don't think so, but there's a bad atmosphere in chambers. Judge Millikan won't do anything illegal, but he won't help. He's just naturally a hard man to please."

The door opened. Mrs. Blanchard announced that their newly hired cook, Rosaria Duran, a vast cheerful woman of ample bosom, had dinner ready. "Something called *arroz con pollo*," she said with humorless disapproval. "And other things I'm *not* too sure of!"

"Let's explore!" McKeever looked up with interest. "I may not know painting or music, but cooking is an art I understand." He felt famished and went in rubbing his hands. But even the hot new spices could not keep his racing mind from the tasks ahead.

After dinner, fortified and rested, he worked late into the night. He moved through the maze with a sure touch, for although the terminology was strange, he rested on the fundamentals of law familiar everywhere. Many eastern forms, he discovered, were in good local usage. The New Mexican lawyer was competent and sensible, and by dawn the papers were completed.

They paused to yawn wearily.

"If that doesn't do it," Dominguez pronounced with satisfaction, "nothing will."

McKeever smiled faintly. "We'll see," he said cautiously. "Now let's get some rest." He had been completely absorbed in the satisfying work, and it was not until he was undressed and in bed that a stirring in the next room brought him up short. He realized that he had not said good night to Jeff.

He waited for quiet but he could not sleep. He put on a robe and sat on the terrace and watched the stars fade. A light was flickering in the Fortress of San Felipe.

94

Chapter VII

The District Court of the Sixth Judicial District of the Territory of New Mexico, County of Hogarth, sat in a two-story wooden frame structure, white with fresh paint, utterly without style. On the first floor were offices for the county officers, the clerk, sheriff, treasurer and district attorney, the usual courthouse ring who managed local politics. Courtroom and chambers were on the second floor. A corral provided facilities in the rear. Outdoor privies for both sexes were decently spaced apart. It stood adjacent to the county lockup, a modern red-brick structure as plain and ugly as ingenuity could devise.

A stroll around the square would find the Palace Bar, patronized in ordinary times by a mixed crowd, now only by Anglos. Ike Travis's Gunsmith Store. Buffalo Hall, a combined saloon and licensed gambling house, above which the Knights of Labor had headquarters. A boarded-up home of a small contractor. Old Gallegos Building where the Police Department was housed. An empty lot owned by the Methodist Church. The Valdez Building where Dominguez had offices. Ike Goldman's dry goods store and that of his rival, Herman Sinzheimer. Adobe fences and an alley leading to a dry arroyo.

All these enclosed the lovely gardens of the plaza in which nodded ancient willows.

Promptly at nine, McKeever and Dominguez drove up in a buggy, brief case in hand. In some mysterious way, the word had gone around and a group of newspapermen and citizens were clustered at the steps. Smiling and friendly, McKeever brushed aside questions and entered the old building. At once, at the familiar smell of dusty corners and mice, he felt oddly excited.

On the second floor, they peered into the empty courtroom. The bench was so long that while the judge sat near the witness stand, the other end was out of his direct sight. Not long ago, Dominguez remarked, a main witness, a drinking man, had been discovered curled up under the bench, asleep. The floors were wood, well worn and oiled. A rickety railing divided the court from spectators. At the moment, a gaunt elderly bailiff was setting a privileged row of rickety kitchen-like chairs inside the rail. There were stoves for heat in winter and naked bulbs for light.

"It's not much, is it?" Dominguez murmured deprecatingly.

McKeever smiled grimly. " 'Not so deep as a well, nor so wide as a church door, but 'twill serve,' " he quoted. The truth was that his heart was beating strongly at the sight. The bailiff met his glance stolidly and went on with his work. He looked like a thousand others in courts all over the country—reserved men with their own estimate of the worth of a lawyer's efforts. To McKeever's mind, the approval of one good bailiff was worth more than the acclaim of multitudes. "Well, let's get on," he murmured.

In the rear they knocked on the door marked "Chambers." A woman's voice called:

"Come in."

They entered and Florence arose to greet them. Her cheeks were pale but she seemed refreshed by sleep. A neat shirtwaist with starched cuffs and a spruce lace jabot relieved the severity of a black suit. Her manner was cool enough as they shook hands. She said, "I imagine you're here to see the judge?"

McKeever nodded. "We're applying for a writ."

There was an awkward pause.

It was strange to deal with a woman, but not disagreeable, except that her manner held a hostile challenge. McKeever rubbed his chin ruefully. There was no hint of the warmth of their prior meeting in Washington. Ah well! It was natural enough. The photograph of her uncle on the desk, enclosed in a massy silver frame, told its story.

"I'll show you in," she said formally. "This way."

The sunny inner room was large and sparsely furnished with an oak desk and black leather furniture. A man of middle years arose to greet them. "Come in, gentlemen!" he said in a commanding voice. His piercing blue eyes stood in contrast to a full brown vandyke beard and mustache and luxuriant hair. This was Associate Justice John J. Millikan. He put aside a cigar to shake hands. "You can be seated," he indicated.

"Thank you."

The judge sat with a grunt and favored them with a stare. "Is this another application, Dominguez?"

The lawyer folded his arms. "Afraid so, Judge."

"Let's see the papers." Millikan put out his hand. "No, don't go, Miss Hogarth. Now, I suppose, McKeever," he said heavily, "you're accustomed to a lot of polite talk before business. Well, you won't find it here. We're pretty plain about this thing. I don't mind saying the Court has strong feelings in this case." His lurking smile was without humor. "Hope this set of papers is better than the last, Dominguez. Wouldn't look good for counsel if it weren't."

"My last set was good enough," the lawyer answered evenly.

"Was it?" With an air of irascibility, the judge put on his glasses and ran down the averments of the petition, then flipped back to the writ itself. The language peremptorily commanded the sheriff to produce the body of Carlos de Niza before the court with a statement as to time and cause of the imprisonment. To take effect, the writ required only the judge's signature, which by law he was compelled to affix.

Florence sat at the window with a remote look.

"Seems all right," the judge said finally. He handed over the papers and sat back smoking. "Miss Hogarth, would you mind?"

"Of course." She studied the petition swiftly, her eyes grasping the significance, paragraph by paragraph. She looked up to raise a technical objection. "I don't see how the writ can apply to the governor. If he wants to withhold his records, that's his prerogative. The form is too broad."

McKeever answered, "I've made it broad, Your Honor, because the situation calls for it. The governor is equally responsible for issuing the request for extradition."

"Furthermore," Florence added coldly with a touch of color in her pale cheeks, "portions of the petition are insulting to the Court itself. It ought to be stricken." She returned the papers.

"I'm only called to sign the writ," the judge said drily. "I've decided to disregard the innuendoes. I'll bear them in mind at the right time."

All this, challenge and response, had gone swiftly. McKeever hesitated. This was no time for argument, nor did he care too much which way it went. He glanced at the angry woman and placed his palms on the conference table with a firm gesture.

"Your Honor, I'm afraid I must insist on your signature now. Or you can refuse. I'd just as soon take appropriate action at once."

The judge flushed.

"The Court has no intention of not signing," he said harshly. "You'll get strict justice from me, sir, nothing less. I don't care who or what you think you are. But when you go to trial, McKeever, don't forget that the murdered man was a judge of this very court!" The lurking hard smile touched his mouth. "I'll be interested in your argument. When will it suit you?"

McKeever arose. "Forthwith!"

"Nine o'clock Monday morning." The judge scrawled his name and handed over the paper. He sat back and patted his finger tips, smiling, a neat stern man whom no feelings could touch. "Miss Hogarth, kindly show the gentlemen out."

McKeever took the paper and bowed ironically. "Your Honor!"

Florence showed them to her outer office and he followed, writ in hand. He was blessed—or cursed—with a strong sense of history. He looked at the formula fully aware that great wars had hammered out the force of its words. It was a simple piece of paper, this writ of habeas corpus, but much more. It went back to the mists of antiquity beyond Magna Carta into Roman Law. He liked to think of himself as a man of hard-headed stubborn Scot ancestry, but his soul was a deep romantic chasm in which, as always, a chill of deep feeling shivered at the power placed in his hands by law.

He looked about the sunny office. It was a room where a woman's touch was evident. A vase of rosebuds stood on the desk. A misty water color of Montmartre hung on the wall. A delightful elusive scent was in the air.

Florence turned at the door. "Mr. McKeever."

He looked up from his abstraction. "Yes, Miss Hogarth," he said stiffly, not too well pleased with her reserved hostility. He felt vaguely dissatisfied. He was a man of strong intuitions—they served him well, more so than the pure powers of reason, a function vastly overrated, in his legal opinion—and something, he felt, was wrong. The lurking smile of the judge was still disturbing. Yet he eased off slightly. This grave young woman, handsome and clear-featured, appealed to him. She was less the lawyer, less the efficient bustling doer of things, he thought, than she imagined. He added courteously, "Is there something?"

She hesitated. "I'm sorry I was obstructive in there."

"Not at all," McKeever smiled. "You were right—my application was too broad. Never mind, I got more from the judge than I expected."

"Oh?" She did not respond to his humor. "I'm afraid I'm not being too nice about things. I haven't really welcomed you, have I?" She looked up seriously, the shock of tragedy still lurking. "I just hope you didn't mind me too much, yesterday at the station."

He smiled faintly. "I think I understand." He felt easier at the touch of intimacy. "This whole business must be painful."

She sighed.

"Well, it was good to see you again, Mr. McKeever." She gave him a cold hand in farewell. "I know I oughtn't to take this personally. A man is entitled to his defense"—she returned his smile sadly—"but it's hard not to resent things. We were a close family."

98

His large hand enclosed hers warmly. "Well, of course," he said sympathetically.

Dominguez coughed with annoyance.

She tossed her head and looked up. "And Jeff? I was glad to see him looking so well. I didn't realize his condition in Washington. I'd like to invite him—I mean both of you, of course—to the Ranch. It's worth seeing, you know, quite a show. But—" Her hand went to a broach on her crisp shirtwaist, a beaten silver pin of Navajo design. "I'm afraid it would be, well, kind of difficult."

"Perhaps you can visit us," McKeever said smiling. "It would put Jeff in seventh heaven. He's talked about nothing else since we left Denver. He'd love to see you."

"Really?" she said with wonder.

"Jeff's a McKeever," he said humorously. "We drink little and we smoke little, but that doesn't exhaust the possibilities."

She laughed.

McKeever hesitated. "He's a lonesome boy, I'm afraid. He needs friends and I'm not always enough, though I let him cling to me more than I should. Can't help it, I suppose." He waited awkwardly. "Please drop in. He's got a theory about the chinook salmon he's dying to explain."

"He's a sweet boy," she agreed, half laughing, and then her face clouded. "I'd like to come, but I'm afraid not for a time. I've got to leave for New Orleans tomorrow. My Aunt Ginnie." She paused with feeling and her eyes began to fill. McKeever saw this and said, "Good-by, Miss Hogarth."

"Give Jeff my love." Her voice was husky as she closed the door and turned to the next caller waiting. In the corridor, the lawyers exchanged glances.

"Well?" said McKeever.

"I've got nothing to say," Dominguez muttered stiffly. "She's not our friend. We've got our writ. Let's serve it."

"Why do you suppose the judge was smiling?" McKeever mused uneasily.

The building was deserted as they clattered down the stairs. A body had been found with a knife through the heart in the privy vault of the boarded house next to the Old Gallegos Building. Wood chips, sawdust and barnyard filth had been piled in to conceal the crime. The officials were taking the corpse to the stables for identification and autopsy, and about them was a circle of Anglos. They had been amused enough at the news until it appeared that the man was not Spanish, as at first supposed, but a ranch hand named Joey McMullen.

99

All this information was excitedly brought to them at the corral by one of Dominguez's clients, an elderly shabby stonecutter. "Are you sure the dead man is Anglo?" the Spanish lawyer demanded.

"There is no doubt!" the stonecutter grinned. Across the plaza, there were cries of rage, and he spat with satisfaction. "An Anglo with yellow hair like wheat! A young one!"

"*Ay, ay!*" Dominguez muttered somberly. "It begins, it begins again!"

He cracked the whip viciously and they drove off. At the Fortress of San Felipe, the small gate opened. A scowling guard stepped out, gun in hand, to receive the order of the court.

On the return day of the writ, the courthouse square was filled with men in a mood of violence, but the situation was in hand. The militia had mounted gatling guns behind sandbag emplacements. General Turner Prescott, a square-cut regular, resplendent in blue, patrolled the grounds on a handsome chestnut, his springfield athwart the pommel. A flag was rippling in a gentle breeze.

Loose talk about a jail delivery was at a minimum, due in part to Max Kyle's cautionary efforts. The hulking sheriff issued a warning to known troublemakers. "This is one man," he said dangerously, "who's going to get what's coming in open court! Anyone don't understand that is going to deal with me personally. These newspapermen are going to get a good impression about the way we run things down here."

Luther Guthrie, a lantern-jawed man, the eldest of four brothers, all ranchers and active in the local "White Masks," a hooded secret fraternity, passed the word along. These were Dan Hogarth's wishes, he understood, and he was satisfied. The Territory had a sound judge, a special prosecutor, a local jury in prospect, and a strong case. Moreover, the gatlings had a steadying effect.

"Just so they don't change the venue, Sheriff," Guthrie stated. "We all go along with that." His brothers nodded agreement.

Kyle said somberly, "This trial stays right here in Cuatro. Even Lon Wilby sees it that way for once." He was referring, as they knew, to an editorial in the *Herald* against a change of venue on the ground that its advertisers, the local merchants, were entitled to the windfall business. Further, a match between the eastern trial master and the special prosecutor, Mike Taft, would be a sporting event of importance.

Guthrie explained this to the waiting newspapermen. The Territory took its court battles seriously. The western bar was filled with cantankerous men, vain and opinionated characters. The trial men had their followers and admirers, *aficionados* conversant with the finer points of style and technique. The local taste ran to roaring and stamping and soaring eloquence, and in this school Mike Taft was outstanding. He was a strong courtroom man and a shrewd tactician who had learned the tricks of the arena in the early frontier days. How the eastern style would match this was an open question.

"I'll take ten dollars on McKeever," said John Bellew, eyes twinkling. A gnarled old rancher spat liquidly at his boots. "Don't be too cocky, mister," he drawled. "Your man's going to learn a few tricks in there, no matter what! Taft's fast as a wildcat and twice as mean! He's Hogarth's own boy!"

Bellew laughed. "Oh yes, I know that. I wouldn't come this far for nothing." His effeminate face was rosy with pleasure as he smoothed his bangs. "Now let's put up our money."

The court was packed and stifling as McKeever arose for the opening skirmish. The hot sun was pouring through the windows. Every seat was taken by visiting notables, not only the jury box, but the well of the court itself, and he stood in a tangle of sprawling feet. As he gazed about in the sudden quiet, his temples were throbbing with excitement, as though the fallow season had lasted too long, but this, he knew, would quickly pass. Unsmiling, he affixed his spectacles and with a studious air bowed to the bench.

"The petitioner is ready," he said quietly.

Millikan made a notation in his minute book, looked up, and slipped back the sleeves of his robe. His florid handsome face, framed between two brass lamps, was baleful. He turned to the bailiff.

"Bring in the prisoner."

The door in the rear opened and the prisoner was brought in from the corridor. McKeever turned for his first view of his client.

Carlos de Niza was superb, he thought, a tall gaunt giant with eyes burning in pools of umber. He stood erect, bristles uplifted, holding his manacles close to his breast. His linen was spotless. Except for the deep lines of a graven sneer, he seemed indifferent to the hostile sea of faces. With an air of leisure, he strode down the aisle.

Dominguez arose to open the gate in the railing and saw the streak of white in the black beard. "Oh my friend!" he exclaimed.

Don Carlos paused with a sad smile. "Ah, dear José," he said with weary humor, "I did not take your advice. I should have taken to the hills while there was time. I apologize for my folly."

The lawyer swallowed convulsively. "Never mind that now, Carlos, I wish you to meet Mr. McKeever."

This exchange had been in Spanish in low voices. The prisoner

measured the eastern lawyer. In the large horselike features he saw
strength and honesty and a quiet anger to match his own. He murmured, "This is your Anglo lawyer, José?"

"Yes, Carlos."

"This was against my wishes," Don Carlos said somberly. "Well,
let's get on with the farce." Like an old hand, he took his seat at
the defense table and placed his manacles before him. "Ah, the
Anglos! The Anglos!" he muttered heavily, then turned ironically.
"Since we are in this together, Mr. McKeever, I will hear you out. I
am interested in what you may have to say." He threw back his
head and stared at the lazy bluebottles looping about at the hot ceiling.

Millikan leaned forward. "Mr. Kyle, you will remove the irons."

"Yes, Judge!" The sheriff complied grudgingly. Three deputies
squeezed into seats directly behind the prisoner, who sat rubbing his
wrists. McKeever objected strongly and the deputies were ordered
to sit further back to permit counsel and client to confer. This done,
he arose and grasped his lapels in a familiar pugnacious pose.

"Ready for argument!"

Emory Martin arose smoothing his light panama with a nervous
hand. His stubborn honest blue eyes were troubled. "May it please
the Court, Mr. Taft will argue for the Territory. We understand that
some question may be raised—" he turned inquiringly—"raised con-
cerning the governor's prerogatives."

"That may become necessary," McKeever conceded stolidly.

"In that case—" Martin hesitated and sat. A chuckle arose from
the fierce older man at his side. The special prosecutor, Mike Taft,
lifted the wrinkled hoods of his eyes like an awakening bird of prey.
His naked skull was remarkable; it seemed divided in two, a sharp
sloping crown ending in a bony shelf. Greasy black locks curled at
his neck, reminding one of a Shakespearean actor. A sharp chin
pressed back a goiterous throaty protrusion, and his mouth was like a
knife. He threw a friendly arm about the district attorney's shoulder.
"Just note I'm here," he boomed at the clerk.

The rear door opened and Florence entered. She glanced at Mc-
Keever, then placed a sheaf of white paper, legal caption in size, on
the bench and whispered to Millikan, who nodded briefly. When
she had taken a seat, he tapped his pencil. "Proceed, sir!"

Now what the devil, McKeever thought, was all this about? Well!
He threw down a typed brief. He was weary but his mind felt clear.
He could see the argument before him, like a chess expert visualizing
the board and all possible combinations. The sense of the unac-
customed was draining away. There was formality, yes, but the self-

conscious formality one finds when people well known to each other assume a hands-off attitude for a special occasion. There was an atmosphere, the excitability of the Spanish, the toughness of the Anglos, an assumed legal courtliness which might not stand the strain of grim necessity. In the mixed bloods, the stoic Indian strain mingled with fierce Spanish emotion gave rise to a complex character.

He read all this at a glance. There were first polite formal flourishes, a few preliminary motions were disposed of, his admission to the court's roster of lawyers was noted, then he began:

"May the Court please, we have before us the writ of habeas corpus on which the petitioner has been produced. Also, a petition to discharge him from the custody of the sheriff on the ground that he was arrested in violation of the Constitution of the United States and of its laws, and of the laws of this Territory. The petition is based on the fact that his original arrest was illegal and void, and that his present detention is contrary to law. To this petition, we have the sheriff's return subscribed by him and served last night. Nothing stated in that return contradicts the petition. With the Court's indulgence, I will not go into the facts of the crime in detail. Those are matters of public knowledge."

Millikan stirred. "Mr. McKeever, the shorter you make this, the better. The Court approaches this argument with irritation amounting to extreme exasperation. The Court would like you to come to the point."

They exchanged stares.

McKeever paused to wipe his hands on his handkerchief. This was more than mere discourtesy. "I may return to the facts," he said with rising anger. He touched briefly on the murder and on the circumstances through which the confession of Tom Canty had been developed. He spoke without notes and with a surprising familiarity with the devious facts.

"Go on, sir, go on!" Millikan interrupted with asperity. "I am aware that the press is here! I tell you to get to the case."

Mike Taft cupped his hand and whispered to the young district attorney, and his chuckle was loud.

"As the Court pleases!" McKeever flushed. "Let me turn to the incredible facts surrounding the arrest in Mexico. The sheriff knows all the ins and outs which govern extradition. No request for extradition can be made by the governor without proof that the wanted man is a fugitive from justice. What proof? The standard is clear and simple enough. One must show that the man was in the jurisdiction *at the time of the crime*. One must then show *that he has fled the jurisdiction to escape arrest*. The rule is elementary. It is not technical but substantial. It is designed to protect the citizen in his most basic rights. Without such a rule, who would be safe in his home? Who could protect himself against malice? Who could be secure among his friends? In this case"—he removed his glasses—"the rules of law have been grossly violated by the sheriff of this county, deliberately and with malice and beyond any shadow of doubt."

He paused for effect.

"How did the sheriff get the governor to issue the warrant of extradition? This Court knows the answer. Weeks ago, he came into this court with certain affidavits and secretly applied for a warrant of arrest. One affidavit he made himself, a formal document, and the other was made by a man named Sotero Gomez y Gomez."

The judge broke in. "I know the affidavits, sir!" he said icily. "I issued the warrant of arrest myself. Go to your next point."

"Indeed!" McKeever glanced at the row of newspapermen. Bellew was tapping his teeth, covertly amused at the open-mouthed interest of the local man, Lon Wilby. The woman muckraker, Ida Montgomery, sketching the scene swiftly, looked up with the barest well-bred flutter of an eyelid. He resumed. "Was the Court aware that Gomez y Gomez is not only in the sheriff's employ, but also is a cousin of the sheriff's wife?"

The judge went scarlet. "This is an impertinence!"

McKeever bowed.

"My impertinence is addressed to the sheriff! I'll revert to this point. Once this sheriff got his warrant, he paused only to confer with a certain gentleman." He paused an ineffable moment. "A gentleman well known in this county. So well known that the county bears his name. That same day the sheriff took a train to Santa Fe and hastened to the governor's mansion. Now I don't know what message he carried. I wasn't there. But effect follows cause. The Law's delay? There was none! Someone with a long arm reached out to Washington and then to Mexico City. Perhaps the facilities of certain mining interests were employed. Within two weeks, Carlos de Niza saw his home surrounded by armed men. They came after midnight. Shots were fired. He was threatened with burning. His wife was almost killed. His children were put in terror. He was wounded. You can still see the shattered hand he will never again use."

In the silence, Don Carlos stared at the twisted flesh before him. His expression was judicious, a critic of rhetoric.

Millikan said, "Was there not a mandate of the Mexican authorities to make the arrest?"

"So they say," McKeever retorted indifferently. He resumed his spectacles, picked up a note, threw it down. "All these acts took place in the petitioner's home—a place where he had the right to feel safe from any knock on his door. Was this violence necessary? I don't know. Again I was not there. But having done all this, the arresting officers had a clear duty. They were required to take their prisoner to the Mexican court. He was entitled to have the documents translated and explained, to make a defense, to obtain bail. But the sheriff forgot this detail!"

McKeever raised his pitch.

"Forgot? Nonsense! He had a strong reason to avoid the Mexican courts. In defiance of Mexican law, and of the laws of this country, the prisoner was hustled across the border by special train. Who paid for the train? Was it the treasurer of this county? Or was it the same private gentleman who is not in this court?"

Florence Hogarth looked up, white-faced, at this clear reference to her father, and her mouth tightened.

Millikan sank back. "You're here to make proof, sir," he said grimly. "I shall hold you to account for loose unproved insinuations at a later time."

McKeever tossed his head. "Well, I won't press the point. Everybody knows who paid the railroad. If necessary, their books will be brought here. In any event, none of these factors are denied." He sat back against the table with folded arms. "Let's come to the affidavit made by the sheriff's cousin, Mr. Gomez y Gomez." He held up the copy with disdain. "The sheriff's cousin claims that he saw Carlos de Niza at Polk's Spring in this county with a man named Sam Trister *at the time of the crime.* Now will counsel concede," he turned slightly, "that without this sworn statement the warrant of extradition would not have issued?"

Mike Taft took his hands from a formidable paunch and raised the hoods of his eyes. He boomed:

"Brother McKeever's late with his smart legal stuff and he knows it. Why don't he get to the real issue?"

"Late?" McKeever watched the scribbling pens race at the press table. "Your Honor knows the point. I offer proof that Carlos de Niza was in Mexico City at the time of the crime, twelve hundred miles away." He turned and received from Dominguez a thick sheaf of papers, sealed, stamped, ribboned. "Exemplified copies of proceedings of the government commission before which he was testifying, before, during and after the murder! Proof that the affidavit made by the sheriff's cousin is wilful perjury. That the warrant of extradition was gotten by fraud! That the arrest was false! That the petitioner is entitled to be remanded to Mexico to test the legality of his arrest in the courts of that country."

105

The judge drummed the bench, loud in the silence. "I examined the affidavits myself, sir, before I issued the warrant," he said curtly. "Are you charging the Court with connivance?"

"I refuse to be embarrassed," the lawyer retorted. "I said nothing to reflect on the Court. I charge this fraud to the sheriff's account."

"And the governor?"

"Ah, the governor! He was careless. He should have made inquiries. He must know who pulls the strings in Hogarth County, and why—why was no hearing ordered? There are people in Santa Fe who could have set him right. He let himself be used and abused. So did Washington. So did Mexico City. That's why they kept Carlos de Niza from the courts of Mexico—to prevent exposure of the fraud!" McKeever was beginning to sweat heavily.

The judge sank back ominously, "Don't raise your voice, sir, not to me, and don't wag your finger. Have you further proof?"

"I ask that Gomez y Gomez be produced!" McKeever turned to Taft and repeated the demand twice. The special prosecutor pulled in his paunch complacently, and said, "He ain't in court."

"Where is he?"

"I can't say."

"Can't or won't?"

"Have it either way you want! When we need him, if we ever do, he'll come in!"

McKeever turned. "Unless Gomez y Gomez is produced, Your Honor, I submit that deliberate fraud must be assumed on the part of the peace officers who made this arrest. Who paid for this perjury? Who procured it?"

"I will assume nothing," the judge said. "Are you done?"

McKeever raised a finger sternly. "The fact remains that Carlos de Niza was kidnaped from his home. The arrest was in violation of law, both ours and Mexico's. If the Court wants more proof, I have witnesses from Mexico City to show that these affidavits could not have been made in good faith. I move that Carlos de Niza be discharged from custody or that he be returned to Mexico for a proper hearing. I think, Your Honor"—he removed his glasses and pressed his burning eyes—"I think that these issues transcend the mere charge of murder. They touch the entire fabric of law enforcement in this jurisdiction."

Someone hoarsely cleared his throat. McKeever went on in the same vein, and then finally the judge turned to the prosecution table. "I will hear you now, sir."

Taft arose and strolled forward with a humorous air. "May the Court please, I'm sorry Brother McKeever decided to stop," he drawled. "I thought he was putting on a good show. I could see why he gets those big fees back East. Fact is, I and the rest of us poor country lawyers here were picking up quite a few pointers." He chuckled complacently and faced the prisoner, who had assumed an air of boredom. "Carlos here must be awful guilty to put out that kind of money. Trouble is, Brother McKeever's too late with that crooked alibi somebody put into his mind."

He waited for amusement to die, wiping his protruding eyes. "The plain issue here is murder. It don't matter if Carlos was here personally at the time, or if he sent in the killer from outside. The fact is, Carlos de Niza"—he stabbed an accusing finger and his voice rose like a scream—"Carlos de Niza paid Sam Trister to carry the guns here to Cuatro to deliver to Canty, and he paid Tom Canty to take those guns and kill a former justice of this court. That makes Carlos de Niza as guilty as Cain. That's what the Territory stands ready to prove. All this smart talk can't change the issue." He remained poised, quivering, then subsided.

McKeever broke in strongly.

"No question of guilt can arise until the petitioner is legally before the Court! How does Mr. Taft answer the fact that the petitioner was illegally kept from the Mexican courts?"

Taft gobbled sardonically. "Your Honor, it strikes me that Brother McKeever is still new around here. He's got some funny ideas about the border. I won't go into that now. We got our understanding with the *Rurales,* and they got theirs with us. We did a lot for this man just going to the trouble we did in getting a warrant up. I don't admit a thing, and I'm not going to answer that point." He cleared his throat and affixed a formidable pair of shell-rimmed glasses and took up a paper with the air of a man about to explode a bombshell. "Your Honor, I'd like to submit an amended return executed by Sheriff Kyle this very morning."

The clerk stepped forward, took the legal paper, handed it up to the bench, stepped back with a significant look at McKeever. Taft inspected a copy and passed it over to his opponent, twirling his glasses. He resumed:

"I'd like to forget about the extradition. Fact remains, Carlos is here in Hogarth County. Nobody's talking extradition any more. That's all passed."

"All passed?" McKeever exclaimed. "I don't understand—" But of course he got the point at once. Only too well. The hard smile on the judge's face. Florence's averted eyes. The paper in his hands. The guilty flush of the honest-looking young district attorney, Emory Martin. Taft drawled on:

"It now appears, Your Honor, that the grand jurors voted to indict Carlos de Niza and Sam Trister for murder right here in this court last night. Thereupon, Your Honor issued a bench warrant which was placed in the hands of the sheriff. That same bench warrant for murder was executed this morning at sunup at San Felipe Fortress. I was there when it was done, so there's no question. This arrest is the sticking kind." He hoisted in his paunch. "Carlos ain't here on the arrest made in Mexico. He's here on the fresh arrest made this morning in this county. If he's got any complaints, let him take 'em up in Old Mexico. I understand they got a regular department down there."

The judge set his desk in order. He placed aside the worn Bible from which he drew inspiration at sentence time. Before him, neatly piled, he placed the original indictment handed up by Florence, and above it, the sheriff's amended return reciting that the original arrest had been superseded. He said harshly, "Well, Mr. McKeever?"

The eastern lawyer stepped forward with an angry look. "I'm shocked, Your Honor! I was prepared for hard blows, but not for foul ones! This maneuver is unbelievable! This is the first I hear of this new arrest!"

"Hasn't your client informed you?"

McKeever turned. The prisoner was reclining, chin in palm, finger tapping a sunken cheek, savagely amused. The lawyer said, "No, he has not."

"Do you wish more time?"

McKeever stood foursquare, his great hands opening and closing, a shaggy man of wrath. "Our petition relates to the original wrongful arrest. To let the wrongdoers legitimize their acts by this morning's shabby trick would constitute a travesty on justice. Let me call the sheriff to the stand now! Or the governor! Or Hogarth himself! I will agree to a continuance. Eh? What about it?"

In the breathless silence, the faint ringing of a spittoon in the rear could be heard.

The judge leaned forward. "Sir, the Court has not listened to this harangue with any degree of patience, but rather with some spirit of indignation. The Court however will not take action now, since he is mindful of the grave issues involved." He paused. "You are directed to deal with the fresh arrest made this morning."

McKeever shook his head. "I press my original motion."

The judge stroked his luxuriant vandyke. "Very well, sir, the Court will rule." He took up the brief which Florence had prepared and began in a loud firm voice, conscious of the scrambling furious pencils of the country's press. He summarized the facts concisely, then came to the meat.

"Thus this case does not differ in principle from prior decisions of sister jurisdictions and of the Supreme Court of the United States. The argument amounts to this, that the relator was brought to this jurisdiction unlawfully before he was placed under arrest. If such is the fact, the Court regrets the situation. The remedy however lies elsewhere."

He brushed aside a crawling fly and went on. "In *Starr v. Indiana,* the fugitive, charged with larceny, fled to Chile and thereafter Indiana requested extradition. For some reason, the messenger of Indiana saw fit to abduct the fugitive and to take him at gun point to an American warship lying in the harbor of Santiago. The prisoner was brought to San Diego where he was turned over to the peace officers of Indiana. Ultimately, the Supreme Court ruled that the prisoner was not excused from standing trial."

He turned a page.

"A similar rule was laid down in *Hoskins v. Ohio.* In that case, a mob of armed men crossed from Ohio to Kentucky and there forcibly removed the prisoner from the local jail and delivered him to the authorities in Ohio. There too the prisoner was nevertheless required to stand trial." He went on to discuss a dozen such precedents and brought in an English decision with a flourish. McKeever's professional ear was forced to concede a sound craftsmanship. How much of this was the judge's work? How much Florence's? How much done by the prosecution?

The harsh voice went on. "In this case, the petitioner, Carlos de Niza, is detained on a valid warrant of arrest issued on an indictment for murder. The charge is serious in the extreme. A more atrocious crime cannot be imagined. It is no answer that he was prior to arrest brought into this jurisdiction through guile or trickery. The Court cannot question the steps taken by our sister republic to deliver him to our authorities. Nor can the Court question the good faith of the Executive. There is nothing in the laws of this Territory, nor of the Constitution or laws of the United States which can help the petitioner. The claim of forcible abduction or illegal extradition cannot cloak him with immunity for the crime of which he stands accused. The writ of habeas corpus may not therebefore be used to avoid trial for murder." He continued with the vehement discussion, his voice rose, he cited many authorities until he was ashen and sweating with the effort.

At the conclusion, McKeever arose:

"Your Honor, in the cases cited, the lawless acts were done by private individuals. In this case, as the Court pointed out, the sheriff was the messenger of the Territory. He himself was guilty of fraud in the inception of the process. Can the Court let this happen? Can the Court denude the petitioner of all rights guaranteed under the laws relating to extradition? The right to resist extradition is not technical. It relates to the fundamental right to be free from molestation. Since the petitioner was prevented from raising these issues in the courts of Mexico, he should be granted relief here."

There was a moment of silence while the judge thirstily drank a glass of water. A strong voice rang out.

"Sir Judge!" Don Carlos arose. "May I be heard?"

Millikan eyed him severely. "You'd better keep your mouth shut! You've got a good lawyer. Two of 'em, in fact."

"This is a personal matter!"

"Well, go on," the judge said, putting aside his drink. "Nothing can surprise me this morning."

"*Dios mío,* Carlos!" Dominguez muttered. "Guard your tongue!"

"Nonsense!" The prisoner strode forward, flicking a handkerchief. "I don't agree with Mr. McKeever, although I want to thank him for his efforts. He means well, but he should have known better than to expect a fair decision." He paused a deliberate moment. "It's simply this. I'm perfectly willing to stand trial. I don't care whether you discharge me from custody or not. I don't want an appeal taken. I want no delays. I want to come to grips with this thing. There's no reason to delay my vindication."

"Carlos, Carlos!" Dominguez muttered in a stricken voice. There was shuffling of feet and the petitioner's rich warm voice rang out in perfectly modulated tones.

"Let me add this. I'm something of a newspaperman. I see that the press is here and I'm interested in what they'll tell the world about Cuatro Rios. I'm dealing with Hogarth lackeys from top to bottom. From the governor down, they're no better than a pack of pimps. All this is sheer waste of time." He raised his stiff beard to the highest elevation. "I ask the press to note that the confessed assassin, this Tom Canty, has been omitted from the indictment for murder—the reward, no doubt, for services rendered."

Millikan arose. "Mr. McKeever, the writ is dismissed. The petitioner is continued in custody of the sheriff." He faced the disdainful prisoner. "Carlos de Niza, you will get a fair trial in this court."

"An Anglo court?" Don Carlos said ironically.

The judge tapped the gavel.

"This court stands adjourned."

There was a murmur, and then the crowd slowly dispersed. Old Carlos had guts, it was agreed, and that maybe was a point in his favor.

Chapter VIII

The argument had ended late. McKeever suggested a press luncheon at the Hotel Conquistador. He was aching with exhaustion, drained. Perhaps it was the altitude, perhaps the heat of battle. Yet in the circle of good fellows, in his accustomed role as host, he was at his charming best.

It was a pleasant relaxed interlude. About them arose a hum of conversation and clinking of silverware. The solid cuisine produced oysters, a thick soup, sirloin steak and fried eggs, strong bitter coffee. The writing men brought news of the outside world. Graft trials in San Francisco. A Wall Street breach of promise suit brought by a Brazilian demimondaine. A scandalous railroad reorganization. All the growing pains of the country's swelling dimensions.

McKeever cocked an eyebrow. "Any changes in Washington?"

No, the Supreme Court bench was still intact. No one had resigned. He sighed and over cigars told the old one about the Vermont farmer who had released a chicken thief caught in the night red-handed, a fat pullet in each hand. He was a perfect mimic, he had each character pegged, down to the squawking birds. Perfectly sound decision, he twinkled. In six months time, what would folks say around the cracker barrel? Perkins? Wasn't he mixed up *somehow* in the robbery of a hen roost?

There were chuckles before Bellew started the ball rolling. "Well, Link, you made a strong impression. Did you actually expect to win?"

McKeever studied his cigar ash. "The Law is an old lady. She hobbles along but she does make progress. Yesterday's dissent is tomorrow's law." He looked up blandly. "I'll reserve other comments for the court."

"Will you appeal?"

"If we do, you'll be informed in good time. It certainly won't rest here. The whole thing is too shocking. Why did they include this poor devil, Sam Trister, in the indictment? Where is he? If they had faith in their case, they'd try to get him here as an additional witness.

No, it's pretty clear they don't want the truth. Either that, or he's a myth!"

"Oh, he's no myth!" Lon Wilby spoke up. He had been silent in the midst of gaiety, his plump face troubled, dubious. He produced a clipping from his billfold and passed it over. "I'm running a line cut of this picture tomorrow."

McKeever looked at the photograph with interest. It had been taken at Socorro at a barbecue reunion of old-timers. A rawboned group stared stiffly in assorted styles of store clothes. Max Kyle loomed high, eyes shaded by his stetson, shoulders awkward, discontented. Grinning beside him was a bewhiskered toothless old man, ridiculous in a four-in-hand and black felt hat. "Sam Trister," said Wilby with faint disquiet. The photograph went around. "Now why," asked the *Picayune* man, "would they wish to indict that poor old one, *hein?*"

McKeever tapped his ash into the coffee dregs. "Why indeed?"

Ida Montgomery examined the picture with blurry myopic blue eyes. A woman in the background caught her interest, a wrinkled crone in calico, hobbled and dark-skinned. She asked, "Who's that?"

"Trister's wife," Wilby explained. "Woman named Guadalupe."

"She looks Indian."

"She is! Navajo!" Wilby tucked away the clipping, then asked whether McKeever had seriously intended to call Dan Hogarth. The lawyer smilingly declined the gambit. "It's perfectly clear what's happening here," he said warily. "You've got a man with power who's using the Law to satisfy a grudge. It's no secret and I'll bring it out at the right time. Once that starts, nobody's safe. It's the beginning of no law at all."

"If there's a grudge," Wilby said sharply, "Carlos has kept it alive! He's been offered all sorts of deals. Never would take one!"

"It's got to end somewhere," McKeever said. "All I ask is a chance to talk to the jury."

"Fair enough!" Bellew arose with his look of amusement. "I must say, Link, this is turning out better than I hoped. All this local color! I think sometimes they're just putting it on for our benefit. I never quite believed that men walked around with six-shooters, but they do, they really do! I think it's marvelous."

"Yes, marvelous!" McKeever arose and left Bellew with Dominguez, scribbling notes. He drove off with some relief at finding himself alone at last. He was amused at the public figure he had carefully nurtured—plain simple Link McKeever who wanted nothing but twelve fair men. He had laid it on thick. If he could judge, they had responded along expected lines.

The shadows were lengthening when finally he put up the mare in the stable. As he walked to the rear gate, he heard squeals of delight coming from the garden.

"*Ven acá, Niña!*" a boy's voice cried. "*Ven acá, pobrecita!*"

A younger boy piped, "*Azúcar!*"

The rose vine on the adobe fence was in full bloom and its sweet smell drifted toward him. He heard Jeff respond gaily, "Let her come to me!"

McKeever opened the rear gate. Two olive-skinned boys with black hair and lustrous eyes were romping on the grass with a trembling fawn, so young that its white spots had not faded. Jeff was sitting on the hammock with a wool blanket over his legs, smiling, holding out a lump of sugar. "Here, Niña!" he called. "Here, girl! Gosh, how do you say it in Spanish?"

The older boy smiled, "*Acá! Acá!* You must say it, Jeff!"

Jeff called, grinning, "*Acá.*"

"Hello," McKeever said, and the boy looked up with shining eyes. "Dad, look what they brought me!" he cried. "All the way from Mexico." He held his breath with pleasure as the pretty creature wabbled over and licked the lump of sugar, "Her name's Niña!"

"Don't overdo it," McKeever said, and joined the boy at the hammock. He squatted and smoothed the fawn's moist muzzle. Pablo, the puppy, came frisking and a warm tongue licked his hand. He smiled as the residues of the day's tension eased. "Who are these fellows, Jeff? You'd better introduce them."

"Oh!" Jeff introduced them. Miguel de Niza, fourteen, bowed gravely and put out a slender hand. Juan, eight, chunky and enthusiastic, followed suit. They had their father's hawklike features and his mannered air of remoteness, but their pleasure was evident. Their father had married late, McKeever thought, to have sons so young. He asked:

"Where's your mother?"

"Inside," Miguel said. "She is waiting, sir."

Jeff stroked the fawn. "Can I keep her, Dad?" he pleaded. Pets were still a mad passion. In New York, he had kept dogs, cats, worms, goldfish, white rats, rabbits, snakes, turtles, guinea pigs, white mice, a toad and a bantam cock whose morning screech had brought out the police of New York on the run more than once.

McKeever smiled. "Just take good care of her, Jeff, that's all I want. Maybe we can get her a milch goat."

He left the boys in play and entered the living room. The woman standing at the hearth turned to face him.

"I am María de Niza," she said simply.

113

He liked her at once. Her hand was cold and wet, but her face had a look of strength. Her black dress was threadbare and she wore a single gold ring as ornament. "I am sorry to come like this," she said with a marked accent. "But as I wrote, I must know about my husband. His friends tell me nothing, or they tell me lies."

"I'm glad you came," he said with sympathy. "Would you care for something? Sherry?"

"Please."

As he got the decanter, McKeever reflected that Doña María was unlike the few Spanish women he had met so far. Those of the better families for the most part wore an air of humble resignation. Although Doña María had an air of reserve, she showed a determined dignified carriage. She was his own age, he judged, not much more than forty, a full-fleshed woman with sad level eyes.

He poured the sherry deftly. "Those are fine youngsters," he said warmly. "I want to thank them for the fawn. My son"—he handed her a glass—"my son loves animals. Trouble is, he's inconsolable when they die."

"It was nothing." She sipped slowly and a touch of color returned. She asked urgently, "How is my husband? Have they treated him badly?"

"I don't believe so," he reassured her. "He seemed well enough in court. He was under a strain, but that's to be expected." He explained the legal situation in simple terms, and said, "I didn't get a chance to talk to him, but I'll do that tomorrow."

"I see." She stared at her hands. "I would like to see him."

"I'll make the arrangements," he promised. He waited for something more and finally she looked up. "I am afraid for him!" she cried starkly.

"Why do you say that?"

"He is a stubborn man! He will not help you, sir!"

"Why won't he help his lawyer?"

"Ah, why?" she asked bitterly. "He has his own ideas, my husband! He won't listen to his wife, or his lawyer, or to anyone with sense. He has something inside." She tapped her breast. "The thing inside! That tells him what to do!" The load of misery suddenly overcame her and she wept noisily. "I'm afraid he will do something foolish!" she cried, walking about in agony. She tried a pitiful smile and wiped her eyes. "I am sorry," she apologized. "It is that I have no one to talk to! No one!"

The anguish of the family, McKeever thought, was the lawyer's heaviest burden in these cases. "You have your friends," he said gently.

"Friends?" she laughed harshly. "We have no friends! Would friends let my husband throw away his life for nothing?"

"I don't understand," McKeever frowned. "I was told that your husband is a greatly loved man, the leader of a party, a political organization."

Her mouth was twisted with scorn. "The *Partido!*" she cried. "The Ideal! The Congress! The Platform! I am sick and tired of that nonsense! What has it got us? The children are in rags. We are without a penny. We owe money to everyone—and they talk of things which died forty years ago. How can they be friends? They are tiresome fools, all of them. Who are left? Men who use him. Men who sucked the life from him! And now see what it has brought us!" She walked about the chamber, twisting a handkerchief in agony. "Oh, I'm the stupid one because I can't stand their talk-talk-talk! I'm only a woman! I have none of his education! I never went to the university! My father was a grocer! I was not educated to live in the clouds! Oh, no! I'm good only to keep the house and raise the children and to give him comfort when he turns to me. The *Partido!*" She faced him with an overflowing heart. "They will kill him!" she cried hoarsely. "Señor McKeever, the Anglos will put him to death! I cannot bear the thought!"

McKeever took her shaking hands in his own. "I'm sure it's not that bad," he said reassuringly. "You mustn't talk like this, for your own sake."

She stared and her eyes suffused with misery. "He is an old man!" she said in a low voice. "You must find a way to let him live! Find the way, Señor McKeever!" She covered her face and stood mute. "I am sorry," she said finally. "I am not a help this way."

He smiled faintly. "I think you're behaving very well," he said with warm reassurance. "Now, I'd like to ask a few questions. Are you up to it?"

She nodded. "I will try."

He opened a door. "Please come into the study."

She entered the inner room and sat in a hard-backed colonial Spanish chair sipping sherry while McKeever put the last of the afternoon to use. He explained the situation patiently. He was sure that the prosecution would not pursue their claim that her husband had been in Cuatro Rios at the time of the murder, for on this point the documentary proof from Mexico City was too strong to be shaken. No, the attack would come from another direction.

"We don't know the details," he said grimly, "but we can expect that they'll try to prove a conspiracy to commit murder. This man

Tom Canty will swear that he met your husband before the crime took place to arrange the assassination."

"But if he was in Mexico at the time of the murder?"

He shrugged. "They can reach out no matter where the conspiracy was hatched, so long as the killing took place in this Territory."

"But he was in Mexico City at the time!" she insisted. "That will be proved!"

He smiled wearily. "It makes no difference, but we must know when your husband met this man. Do you know?"

"Of course not!" she cried resentfully. "But *if* they met—!" She paused and bit her lip. He studied her and went on quietly.

"When did your husband leave home?"

She searched her memory. "He did not leave for Mexico City until New Year's Day," she frowned. "It was April when he returned home. I remember I was cutting the children's hair that day. I felt trouble here"—she pointed to her breast—"but that was after the murder was in the newspapers."

"Did he seem surprised at the news?"

"I cannot say. He was with one of his followers, a man named Ishmael Carmel, and they discussed the matter in private. Then my husband wrote an editorial for *La Luz*. You have read it?" she asked bitterly.

He nodded. "I thought it wasn't sensible, but from the legal point of view"—he put aside his glass—"it has no bearing. Except, of course, that it will not help him on cross-examination. Now let me ask: Did they discuss this man Tom Canty?"

"I find these Anglo names hard," she said doubtfully. "It is not a Spanish name, you appreciate. Smith, Brown, Jones. They are so difficult." She almost smiled at her private joke and he thought her fleshy features attractive.

"Did your husband mention Joaquin Quantico?"

A wary look came to her face. "After the arrest, I heard that this was a name used by Canty."

"Did you ever hear talk of Canty before the murder?"

She studied her hands. "I am afraid so," she said reluctantly. "But it could be nothing, I am sure."

He drew his chair close.

"Please trust me, Mrs. De Niza," he said earnestly. "They have this man, Canty, in their hands and he'll testify as a witness for the Territory. He'll say that he was hired to commit this murder by your husband."

She exclaimed, "How can you know?"

"Without Tom Canty, they've got no case," he said grimly. "But the fight will be about the details. What other witnesses were present? Where did they meet? How much was paid? All such things. It's a tedious business, but I can't take anything for granted. When did you first hear of Tom Canty?"

"Let me see." She thought back. "At least a year ago last Easter," she decided. "My husband was on one of his trips into the hills. I think I should tell you that such trips were frequent because he was always meeting with one group of *politicos*, or the other. It was hard to keep track, since they were thick as flies. He would meet them with hopes, but always it would end in nothing. Usually, they would want to use his name for some personal adventure. They were working to be bought off, or to get themselves taken into the Army. Fortunately my husband was not deceived. He is foolish about many things, but he can see into the hearts of men. This comes from his years of raising funds for the Cause. He has a saying. There is no better way to separate the sheep from the goats than to touch the pocketbook. Well, during this absence, a letter came from this Tom Canty."

"Who brought the letter?" the lawyer asked.

"This old man they mention, Trister. He waited a day with his burro, then disappeared."

McKeever drew a deep breath. "A year ago?"

"Fifteen months," she corrected. "My husband was disturbed, I know. He came into the kitchen and asked me excitedly when it had been delivered. I was embarrassed for the servant. She is only a Yacqui girl but I do not like shouting before her. It is against her idea of politeness. It was unusual to see my husband so annoyed." She looked at her hands. "Perhaps I should not tell you these things without his permission," she muttered.

There was a pause.

"What was in the letter?" he asked.

"These were matters my husband would not discuss." She shook her head. "Later there were other letters."

"Where did they come from?"

She searched her memory. "I cannot say. A town in Texas called Anson, I recall. One from Breckenridge. Also from Colorado. I was curious."

"Why so?"

She smiled sadly. "Because my husband was disturbed."

"Did you ever ask him about Canty?"

"Only once."

"What did he say?"

117

She stared at him. "My husband is a man of silence. I have learned not to ask."

"Did you know who Canty was?"

She shook her head. "Not then. Later, I understood that he was used by the *Partido* when the Anglos were driving them from the land. But that was many years ago."

McKeever took a sherry, his third, and walked about. His head was swimming a bit. It had been a long day, he realized suddenly, and he wanted dinner badly. He looked up. "I want to know whether your husband met Canty just before he went to Mexico City?"

"Before New Year's Day?"

"Yes."

She fell into a brown study. "I cannot say," she said in a low voice. "My husband was frequently away from home. There were times when he was alone in the hills for weeks."

"Then your husband could have met this man Canty before he left for Mexico City?"

"It is possible," she admitted.

"Is it probable?"

She drew a deep breath. "I think so."

"Why do you think so?"

She burst out, "My husband would meet anyone who would offer to advance the Cause. Bandits, Indians, thieves—anyone at all! It would be easy to pretend an interest in his affairs, and he would go out of curiosity, or to see which way the wind was blowing. Everyone knows Carlos de Niza."

McKeever stared at her for a dismayed moment.

"Is there anything else I should know?" he demanded.

There was a silence while she tried to control the shaking of her hands. "The rifle and the shotguns they talk of," she finally said hoarsely. "He took them with him before Christmas. When he came back, they were missing. How did the guns come into this thing? I am afraid of what that means."

"Yes, I see!" He paced about, then turned. "That's a thing to clear up. Do you have any idea?"

Her control was beginning to slip again. "I know only that my husband used them to shoot quail in the hills on these trips, but they were missing when he came back from that occasion."

"Is this when you think he met Canty?"

She nodded miserably.

"I swear that my husband is an innocent man," she burst out hoarsely. "I swear it on the soul of my sainted mother. I swear it on

118

the head of my children." She trembled violently, her hands twisted the handkerchief with agony.

He stared with the thought that the strongest line of defense had just washed out. The Mexico City alibi was incomplete.

"Do you know what this means?" he demanded.

She nodded. "I felt I must tell you, for my husband might not. In many ways, he is strange. You will have to find the answer yourself."

"Do you know why Canty wanted to see your husband?"

"No."

"Do you know why he should wish to implicate him in this murder?"

She shook her head mutely. "Only to serve some reason of Hogarth's. I can imagine nothing else."

"Is there any reason other than that?"

"I do not know!" She clutched his arm. "Go to Hogarth, Señor McKeever! I beg of you! Tell him how it is with my children!"

They faced each other a long moment.

"No, Mrs. De Niza," he said finally. "I'm sure your husband would never agree. As far as I'm concerned, he's innocent and we've got to see this through."

Her sons' laughter came from the garden. They paused to listen and then she bowed her head.

"Of course," she muttered, "that is the only way." He let her wipe her eyes before he spoke again. "Do you have a place to stay?"

"*Ah sí!*" She nodded. "I have been invited by Señora Sandoval. She is my good friend."

He hesitated. "I would like you to stay with me," he said suddenly.

"Here?" She was surprised. "I had not thought, señor."

He overruled her objections. It was only common sense. His housekeeper, Mrs. Blanchard, was finding it hard to cope with the household, and help was needed. Later there would be clerical work and other problems of the defense committee. "To tell the truth," he urged persuasively, "I have a selfish reason. I'd like you to stay here with your sons for my boy's sake. I'll be forced to leave him from time to time, and it gets lonely without boys his own age. I'd be most grateful. Listen!" There was a volley of giggling outside.

She stared at his bleak face. "Yes, of course," she said after a moment. "If I can help, I will do what is possible." Her head bowed and she muttered bitterly, "That we should reach this! That my sons should know that men will come one day to put their father to death!" She clasped her hands to her breast. "*Madre de Dios,*" she whispered. "Look after my husband! Guard and protect him against this thing!" She stood swaying with closed eyes.

McKeever patted her hand.

"And now you must stay for dinner! I'll help you with your luggage. After dinner, I've got more questions. How do your boys like roast chicken and apple sauce? Good! Oh Mrs. Blanchard!" he called.

Doña María smiled feebly and went out to give her sons the news.

McKeever met his committee in an evening session.

"We're going to need preparation for this trial, gentlemen. The work we do today will determine the outcome tomorrow. Facts, facts, and more facts! We can't skimp on effort. Now—" He continued to slouch about, talking aloud, throwing his ideas to the sallow unsmiling men. "Now, we'll need records and documents and letters from two thousand miles around. We'll have hundreds of false trails. We'll get rumors and tipsters and crazy men and women, and we can't take a thing for granted. We've got to build a picture of Tom Canty from the moment he was born."

The meeting had taken place in the living room, a large chamber supported by black oak beams. Mrs. Blanchard had gotten up a batch of sweet cookies which his guests munched listlessly. They refused to smile and one, Leon Sandoval, a fat good-natured elderly dentist, raised a finger.

"But I don't understand, Señor McKeever," he said with a foreign lisp. "How can they ever believe a man like that? Canty! He's a murderer! He admits it! I know the Anglos and in my opinion they've got no use for that kind."

McKeever smoked thoughtfully. "I'll agree with that, Dr. Sandoval," he said slowly, "if you take each man, one by one. But when you've got them whipped up into a mob, they'll vote black is white. We can't come to trial with empty hands and expect them to hand us the verdict on a platter. Justice doesn't come that easy."

Dominguez broke in. "I'd like to hear what Pete Morales may think."

A swarthy man with small cunning eyes threw a cigar into the hearth. "How much will this cost?" he asked bluntly.

"It depends." McKeever did some hasty calculations. "I'd want as many good men as I can get. There's a detective agency in Dallas, Art Roberts, who can let me have about thirty men. At eight dollars a day, you can see where that takes us. Then we've got to consider legal fees."

"Of course," they murmured uncomfortably.

He smiled faintly. They were decent fellows, faithful and dour and impassive, willing enough to defray small expenses, but appalled at the costs he had outlined. He said drily, "As to fees, I propose to be moderate, but it's an item we must cover. We'll need to hire more lawyers. So far, we haven't had any luck."

"We are trying," said Dominguez uncomfortably.

Morales started a stogie. "I told you so, Joe. Like everybody, the lawyers are looking out for number one." Unlike the others, he spoke in a broad western style with no trace of Spanish accent.

McKeever drew the discussion back to the costs and showed that two thousand dollars a week for six months would be a moderate estimate. "Well, gentlemen, that's the goal."

The committee unhappily stared into their wine glasses. Fifty thousand dollars!

"It's the man's life!" McKeever reminded them.

"Oh, sure! The man's life!" Morales was the first to rise, grinning sourly. "McKeever, this is a tough one, it sure is. Maybe we can't afford this kind of defense."

McKeever said slowly, "Then perhaps I can't be responsible for its conduct. In a case like this, you've got to understand that we can't pinch pennies."

"Can you use volunteers? That would cut costs."

"It would help."

"Well!" Morales took his stetson and placed it on his sleek dark head with a flourish. "I'm not one of Carlos's crowd, McKeever. In fact I'm opposed to the *quetzals*. I'm just a plain politician. My business is to deliver the vote and to make both sides happy. I aim to get along with everybody. But I'll do what I can. Put me down for a thousand. I'll try to shake a few of the boys in Santa Fe when I get back." He paused quizzically. "You don't need to know where it comes from, I hope?"

"I won't ask questions," McKeever promised.

Morales turned to Dominguez. "I think you got a good lawyer here, Joe. Coming?" They adjourned on a decision to set up a defense committee to carry on the work. Dominguez was elected chairman and McKeever was given power to draw checks for expenses in his discretion.

It was midnight when they left, driving off into the darkness one at a time. McKeever felt excited by the exertions. He had in mind reading in bed, a good book, Zola's latest perhaps. As he closed the outer door, Mrs. Blanchard in a dressing robe hobbled down with a disturbed look.

"What is it?" he asked anxiously.

She hesitated. The dark mustache on her broad lip quivered. "I'm not sure, Mr. McKeever, but I think there's some fever. I thought you ought to know."

He turned stupidly. "Fever?"

"Now, now, it's just a trifle," she reassured him. "I don't think it's much. He's sleeping quietly."

"Oh my God!" Dr. Loewy had warned him back in Denver to expect this, but Jeff had been well for three months. Even the train ride had not set the boy off. He felt sick. "What should we do?"

She made the decision. "We'll let him sleep. At least he's not sweating. In the morning we'll call the doctor."

The house was empty and quiet. There was only the last faint swirling of tobacco smoke. He looked about and after a moment he went up to bed. This was after all something he had learned to live with. That doctor at the station—what was the fellow's name?— had had a competent look about him. That would be the morning's first order of business.

When he opened his eyes, the sun was high.

There was a tap.

"Yes?" he asked irritably.

"You've got a visitor," Mrs. Blanchard called through the door. "Mr. Martin!"

McKeever thought. "Do I know him?"

"The district attorney."

"I'll be there in a minute," he said after a pause. He stood yawning and scratching with a savage feeling that before coffee life was not worth living. He went to the window. The smell of roses was strong. The De Niza boys were on the lawn playing a knife game with Jeff who was counting in Spanish.

"Jeff," he called softly.

The boy turned with a glad smile. "Yes, Dad!"

At the cheery grin and the bright sunlight, the anxiety of the night diminished. McKeever reminded himself that these fevers were still to be expected.

"Did you have breakfast?" he called.

"An hour ago," the boy said, and returned to his game with a look of enjoyment. McKeever shaved and washed and he felt better when he entered the living room. He found Emory Martin with a perplexed look on his stubborn face, tugging at his goatee. They shook hands.

"Well, come in," McKeever said grumpily. "Let's have coffee."

Martin demurred. "I didn't mean to impose—"

"Come in, sir, come in!" McKeever led him to the sunny dining room. He felt in a better purposeful frame of mind. "If I miss anything, Martin, it's my morning *Times*. Unless I get my headlines laid out by a familiar hand, I've got no opinions at all. Feel fuzzy the whole day. Waste of time, come to think. Ever read Thoreau on the pleasures of *not* reading the news? Well, you should. Ah, here we are!" His cook, Rosaria Duran, although aggrieved that he had ruled against the customary breakfast in bed of sweet rolls, the eleven o'clock of *caldo colado*, and the four o'clock of chocolate and sweet cakes, was ready nevertheless to do justice to a man of large girth. With single-minded concentration, he tackled a platter of ham and eggs and black coffee before he patted his lips with satisfaction, ready for business.

"Now, sir, what can I do?" He struck a match and looked up inquiringly. "Is this official or private?"

Martin with an unhappy air removed his rimless spectacles. "I had a talk late last night with Joe Dominguez," he said hesitantly. "He told me I could come to you."

The older lawyer lit his cigar. "What's your trouble, sir?"

"Can we talk as lawyers? I mean, in the confidence of this room?"

McKeever glanced at him keenly. "That depends, Mr. Martin. I've had my confidence abused in the past. I am however"—he sat back and studied the curling smoke—"I am willing to listen."

The young man rubbed his face glumly. "Well, I don't blame you," he muttered. "You're up against a tough outfit. A lot of things are happening I'm not responsible for. They don't seem to know who's supposed to be district attorney around here. I had quite a set-to with the old man."

"Do you mean Dan Hogarth?"

Martin nodded. "It was at a big meeting at the Ranch. Whole Territory was there, from the governor down. I told them that they couldn't extradite Carlos. I said it wouldn't stand up. The old man started to bawl me out till I felt like two cents. Then they told me they were going to get Carlos for trial, one way or the other. I swear," he said with perplexity, "I never figured Millikan to rule the way he did. How could that be the law?"

McKeever almost smiled at the picture of unhappiness. "The judge made the only decision he could," he observed. "It's a good rule to read the cases before you form an opinion."

Martin stared in wonder. "But you made sense in court. I never thought they'd get away with it. That's why I went along as far as I could."

"I didn't say the judge was *right*," McKeever remarked slowly. "We're in an unlucky period now. The forms are still congealed, still rigid. There's work going forward in the law schools that ought to change the climate of opinion, but that takes time. These developments in England, for example, show the way. Trouble is, the crim-

123

inal law is old. It resists change. Too many feelings are involved." The honest blue eyes across the breakfast table blinked unhappily. He smiled suddenly. "Don't let me get started, Martin. I'm naturally talkative and I'll keep you all day. I've got something more urgent this morning."

Martin remained staring in his cup. "I don't want to fight all my friends," he muttered. "I've got to live in this county and I've got good chances to get ahead. I could get to represent a lot of important interests here. Only—" He paused.

"Yes?"

"The old man is off me and Floss is mad as hell. And nobody wants to do the right thing. They just want to get Carlos." He smiled ruefully and drank his cold black coffee. "I guess I'm not much of a prosecutor."

"Floss?" McKeever asked finally. "Who's that?"

"Dan Hogarth's daughter—Florence. Oh I forgot, you wouldn't know, but that's what we call her down here, ever since she was a kid. We were good friends in school."

"Really?" McKeever remarked with some dry amusement at the younger man's self-absorption.

"Oh sure. Some things are changing, but this is a small town. I mean, all the kids who could afford it went to the same one academy, it didn't matter who anyone was. We had a good time here. Hayrides, picnics, all that. We covered all the *bailes* in the county together."

"Spanish and Anglos?"

"Oh sure," Martin said with surprise. "Except some of the *ricos*, the rich Spanish families, they're likely to send the children east to school. St. Louis or Europe. But Floss didn't go off to this school in Switzerland till long after."

"I heard somewhere," McKeever said, buttering a hot biscuit, "that you two were once engaged."

"Engaged?" Martin looked up, startled. "Gosh, no! I just got her to wear my pin when she came up to the senior hop, but that was just being friendly. Since she came back from Europe," he sighed, "she's sure changed. We're still kind of friendly, but she's pretty remote. I guess she's got some idea now what it means to be a Hogarth."

"What does that mean?"

"Well, when it comes to a thing like this case, she's just like the old man. She's so damn sure! And then she's sticking to the law. I know she's smart, but for a girl that rich, why should she want to be a lawyer?"

McKeever's cigar had gone out. He started the stub anew, and gazed up sharply. "Martin, there's something specific you've come to tell me. If you want to discuss matters frankly, I won't take unfair advantage. Does it have to do with Sam Trister?"

The younger man stared. "How did you know?"

"I've got a sensitive nose," said McKeever drily.

After a moment, Martin nodded.

"Sam Trister wouldn't hurt a fly!" he muttered. "Everybody knows that. But Canty claims that Trister was part of the conspiracy. Says he was there when money was paid over. Carried the guns to Cuatro Rios. A lot of things. Now why?"

"Why indeed?"

Martin unhappily rolled a bread crumb into a pellet. "I'm not satisfied they want to bring Trister to trial. Kyle's been delaying the circulars. He told me he notified the Rangers in Texas—but I know he didn't. And then, none of the wanted posters carry his name. The whole thing is fishy. Worst thing is, the word's been passed unofficially to take him dead or alive! Why? It's Carlos we're supposed to want! Sam Trister is no good to us dead!"

"Aren't you answering your own questions?" McKeever asked mildly. "He may be extremely valuable to someone—dead!"

"Yes, I've thought of that."

"Well then?"

Martin came to a decision:

"Dominguez told me you're having trouble rounding up local counsel. Is that right?" he said abruptly. "I mean Anglos, of course."

"Do you think we need one?"

"Oh yes! You're up against a peculiar mentality here!"

"Seems I find a peculiar mentality everywhere. Well, we ought to get some answers to telegrams today."

"I know all those telegrams," Martin said grimly. "We've been keeping close tabs on you since you hit this town. None of those men will go along. Mallon in Las Cruces, Wernick in Santa Fe, Phil Judson—not one."

"What do you suggest?"

Martin tugged at his legal goatee which made him look younger than ever. "I could hitch up."

"You?"

"Why not? I'm an Anglo. I sent the governor my resignation this morning. I just couldn't stomach that lying extradition affidavit they got from Gomez y Gomez. The sheriff's cousin! I told 'em it was perjury when Kyle brought that affidavit in. Fact is," he burst out with stubborn anger, "I don't even believe he's in good faith. He'll eat dirt for Dan Hogarth, or anything to hang this on Carlos!"

125

"Would you say Hogarth planned this personally with the sheriff?"

The younger lawyer said grimly, "He doesn't need to do more than bat an eyelash, and Kyle knows what it means."

They faced each other a moment.

"Where is Sam Trister now?" McKeever asked.

"I don't know. He was hanging around town before the fiesta, and then he disappeared. Kyle can't or won't say where. Trouble is, they know I'm green and I can't control the sheriff. He's seen too many prosecutors come and go to worry about me. But all this is just too raw."

McKeever smoked thoughtfully.

"You might as well hand in your license," he observed. "Few of us can buck the tide you'll face."

"My pa used to say, if you're not here to do the right thing first, don't call yourself a lawyer." Martin smiled faintly. "I'm not trying to prove anything. It's just the way I feel. My pa used to know Carlos, and I can't believe he's guilty. I don't care what kind of a case they make."

"You sound like a foolish young man," McKeever observed, "throwing away a career."

"Somebody's got to do something," Martin said simply.

McKeever rumpled his hair with perplexity.

"Then let me warn you. If this keeps up, you'll always be poor. You'll quarrel with your clients and starve your children, and neglect your wife. You won't find gratitude. You'll die battling for some obscure lost cause, and when they bury you in potter's field, those you helped will be on hand to spit on your premature and unlamented grave." He smiled faintly. "My legal advice is to stick to the fleshpots."

Martin said stubbornly, "I've made up my mind. The question is, whether you want me."

"Well, at least you *sound* like a lawyer," McKeever grumbled. "But I don't like it, Martin! If all you fellows turn noble, what happens to us? Just steals our thunder and lightning! Ah well, if the Court won't object to a switch of allegiance, I won't." He looked at his cigar with distaste. "Confound it! Why can't I stop smoking these things?"

They drove off together. The day was fresh and McKeever felt some relief at the first crack in the walls of hostility surrounding him. Martin's disaffection was bound to help. There were ticklish aspects but nothing a special rule of court could not cure. He enjoyed driving along the dirt roads, the conversation and the soft thud-thud of his mare. They parted at the courthouse. He went on and pulled up before a house with a white shingle on the lawn:

ULYSSES KIMBALL, M.D.

He strode up the path, and after a moment of knocking, the door opened.

"I'm McKeever," he said gravely. "Do you remember me?"

Dr. Kimball stared out ungraciously. "Oh, come in."

The sitting room, with its antimacassars and threadbare furniture and steel engravings, might have been anywhere in the Middle West. There was nothing of local color except that the doctor's license to practice was posted in a Spanish translation. A worn copy of *Gray's Anatomy* was displayed, and there was a medical smell. The doctor sat back behind his desk and listened stolidly to a description of Jeff's condition, and when McKeever had finished, he shook his head.

"I'd rather not go out on that case," he said abruptly.

McKeever was taken aback. "Not go out?"

"That's right."

"Didn't Dr. Loewy write to you from Denver? He told me you had a good record at Johns Hopkins. That's why I felt safe in coming down from Denver!"

"Yes, he wrote."

"I don't understand this," McKeever murmured. He felt the beating of a pulse in his throat. This was a thing he had not counted on. "Reuben Loewy's a personal friend of mine, not just a doctor. He said I could rely on you."

"Loewy said that?"

"He said you were outstanding."

"Well!" Kimball kept drumming his fingers on the desk. "I never refused a sick call in my life, McKeever," he said angrily, "not even in the old days. And I won't tell you how tough they were. What you don't seem to understand is how close we all are here—especially the first of us who came to the Territory."

"I don't see what that's got to do with my son."

"Don't you?" The doctor looked up resentfully. "I just came back this morning from New Orleans," he muttered. "I was with Virginia Hanna all this time. I had to watch her eyes fester, and I was there when they came out. It's a wonder she's alive."

"Oh my dear God!" the lawyer exclaimed. "The poor woman!"

"Exactly! The poor woman!" The doctor glanced impatiently at his watch, then burst out savagely, "Why don't you go back to Denver? You're not wanted down here. I guess you mean well, but you've got a bad case. Defending the man who did all that!"

The lawyer arose, disturbed. This development was something he had feared. The ominous scene at the depot was still fresh in mind. But now, here it was. He placed his hand on the bookcase, felt the dust, rubbed his fingers abstractedly. "Does the town know this news?" he asked.

"Not yet, but they will. Wilby's putting out a special edition right now." The doctor slumped back. "When she was a girl, she was the prettiest thing you ever saw," he said in a low voice of wonder. "A real beauty. I delivered her twice, and the babies died of diphtheria, and I saw her through other things. Never complained. Always a good patient. Yes, I knew her well." He looked up blinking. "Have you got any idea what she's going through? Or how this town will feel? Why don't you just go?"

The lawyer shook his head. "I can't do it."

"I don't see why not. Your boy can keep on this way for months, or it might clear by tomorrow. That fever last night doesn't sound too serious. You say he was playing this morning?"

"That's not it."

The doctor refused to understand. "Then what is it?"

"What?" McKeever looked at his hands in dismay. Nothing ever worked out simply in these matters. "I've taken on this trial," he said. "I can't leave these people in the lurch."

"I don't see why not!"

The lawyer said grimly, "The same reason you can't leave a patient."

"It's not the same thing at all!"

"Isn't it?" McKeever laughed harshly. "It's a marvel to me how deep the medical rut can get! What did they teach you at that St. Louis Medical College?" He stared at the medical diploma framed at eye level. "How to make money? Or how to heal the sick?"

The doctor sat swinging his watch fob, and then from an inner room a woman's voice called him to breakfast. He drummed resentfully, opened a drawer, swept his desk clean of its litter, and gave in. "I suppose you're right," he sighed. "One thing's got nothing to do with the other, I suppose. It's just that this has been upsetting. You never met Mrs. Hanna, otherwise you'd understand."

The lawyer arose. "Well, I am relieved."

Kimball showed him to the door. His wife called again, he responded with annoyance, then turned, unsmiling. "I'll get there about sundown. Don't worry. These fevers come and go. They've got to be expected, but I'm sure your son is all right. I'll send Loewy a report myself."

McKeever turned. "Doctor—"

"Yes?"

"I'm deeply grateful."

Kimball studied his face. "Yes, I suppose you are."

They shook hands and McKeever left. The trial, he realized, as he drove through the lazy shaded streets toward the center of town, would be vastly more complex than he had expected.

Chapter IX

The spring of the desert passed.

In the brief rainfalls, the wild flowers sprang up, turned faces to the soft blue skies, formed endless carpets of white and lavender and orange, went to seed and disappeared. The loveliness of primroses and verbenas and poppies was gone.

The hot winds blew steadily.

Drawing on their reservoirs of water within, the cactus bloomed. Giant saguaro put forth white waxy blossoms. Water seepages nourished clusters of small plants called devil's gardens.

Tall bristling ocotillo dropped crimson fingers to the hot sands.

Pink beaver tails.

Yellow encilias.

Among the patient vegetation crawled animal life. Lizards and the deadly banded coral snake.

The summer passed.

In the mountains came the promise of torrential rains.

The trail climbed slowly into the hills dark with giant fir and larch. McKeever felt the stark beauty of the land move him strangely. The months of riding into the countryside to get the feel of the jurisdiction had strengthened his muscles and he took pleasure in the heat of the animal between his thighs. He turned to look at the now familiar valley.

As far as the eye could see, the great Hogarth Ranch clung to the river and spread out to the surrounding hills. The land was black with grama grass in which blooded stock fed shoulder-deep—Durhams and Polled Angus and such, mild-eyed beasts, a far cry from the Long Horns which had come driving up from Texas only three decades earlier. In the farther distance, Cuatro Rios sat on its four streams like a toy village. The October sky was overcast with a suspicion of rain.

He sighed heavily with the thought of the difficulties he had left in Dominguez's hands. Defense headquarters had become a hive of activity in the months which had passed. The first small committee had been enlarged, funds were being sought, public opinion was being agitated and the turmoil was going along expected lines.

Turmoil it was. The humble followers of Don Carlos began to come soon after the word had spread that he was in the hands of the Anglos, and they seemed to know that McKeever's house was the place of pilgrimage. They came in ones and twos from the remote places. From Sonora and Chihuahua and Texas and Colorado and all the lands where the Spanish tongue was spoken. They squatted against the house in the hot sun, humble copper-skinned men, sombreros tilted against the glare, ragged serapes about their shoulders, ankles naked, mute dark eyes following the advocate as he went about his errands.

"Send them away!" Doña María urged with distaste. "They are nuisances, every one! Look how filthy they are! It is not Christian! They are a dirty bunch to have around the house!"

McKeever surveyed them somberly. Their mute adulation made him uncomfortable. "What do they want of me?" he wondered.

"Who knows? I'm sick of them! In my opinion, they make a bad impression on the Anglos!"

"Perhaps." He was inclined to agree, but in the end their silent patience won out. He set up a field kitchen where the peasant women made the coarse foods to which they were accustomed. Ragged children ran about screaming, while the smell of cooking drifted over the house. The gentry of his committee too were distressed, but since all this was at McKeever's own expense, they could not well protest. Nor could they with grace urge that their poorer compatriots reflected on their own dignity.

The teeming Spanish life had another advantage, McKeever reflected, if only to fill Jeff's footless routine. When he got tired of reading, or of playing with the De Niza boys—and this was often, for under the strain, Miguelito and Juanito were frequently moody and quarrelsome—he would spend hours in the kitchen, plying Rosaria Duran with questions about the strange cookery. "Ay, sí, niño!" she responded with amused hearty laughter. "It is a thing!" She recalled the early days. Before the railroad came through, they had nothing like lemons or oranges or ice or white sugar or sea food. Coffee, chocolate, spices came by wagon from Old Mexico. Whole bloody carcasses of beef and mutton were bought at the butcher's. Jerky was a staple, and for relief there were fresh venison and wild turkey and fish from the mountain streams. For winter, pumpkins, melons, grapes, plums were dried on sticks, all varieties introduced by the early Jesuits. Yes, she recalled those days, and some customs remained. Baking was still done in outdoor adobe ovens, as he could see, and the old iron and copper pots were still best. In the great kettles, the stews bubbled for hours, blending their flavors subtly, for time was the thing! Corn and wheat and chile—the king of vegetables—were still ground on stone *metates*, old-fashioned, perhaps, but the way of *los padres*. And outside—*"Mira, niño!"* Chiles hung in festoons, red and green, not to be touched for fear of blistering the hand. And the spices—*orégano, culantro, chinajá, anís!* He would sniff the warm kitchen smells, munching her brown sugar *pilones*, trying his hand, to her amusement, at the simpler recipes.

From the humblest of them up, everyone was kind, for they understood how it was, but of course the high point for Jeff was Florence's visits. In early August she rode up for the first time, glowing and vigorous, bringing the breath of the wind with her. She brought him gifts from New Orleans and books—an original Audubon overwhelmed him—and over a game of chess resumed the friendship casually where they had left off in Washington. "Now, Jeff, what's this about the chinook salmon?" she teased. "Is it going the way of the buffalo?" He half laughed and gulped with pleasure. "Oh no, it's not that!" He went on earnestly to explain his theory. The chinook salmon had a life cycle which required that the young fish descend the river into the Pacific, follow the Japanese current in a vast circle north to the feeding grounds, then back to the point of origin. But two per cent invariably departed south to be lost forever in the sea —a violation of the basic life instinct of the species. "Now why?" he argued. "If Darwin's right, it shouldn't happen! The wrong instinct ought to kill 'em off! I mean, how does it keep getting transmitted? Can't be environment. Can't be heredity. Then what?"

"I have no idea," Florence responded, slightly amazed. The boy sat forward on the couch, hands clasped between his knees, an almost comical replica of his father. The ruffled cowlick, the absorbed earnest manner, the air of abstraction caused her to smile faintly. The bookcases, she saw, held a mixture of titles from Jules Verne to Thomas Huxley. She murmured, "What's your answer, Jeff?"

"Well—" He scratched his head worriedly, then at her air of amusement broke off with an abashed grin. "Dad says, all I'm proving is that it takes all kinds to make a world—even the fellow we think is a freak."

"That's quite true," she agreed, laughing, and moved a rook to checkmate.

During her first visits, there was a constraint between her and McKeever. She was still harrowed by her aunt's condition, and her visits were a cause of comment at defense headquarters. On his part, he felt clumsy and awkward with her. He was once again completely absorbed in his work, and his mind felt icy and remote. Nevertheless, it was remarked, as the months had passed, that his eyes followed her in the courtroom and on occasions he managed to meet her on his rides into the countryside. At these times—since they could not possibly discuss the trial—he felt a sense of ease, riding with her through the high wooded trails of the surrounding hills. If he kept the talk in the realm of abstract ideas, he was the last to realize the fact.

It was a letter from Sophie Muller which had brought an awakening. It had been brought to the study by Emory Martin late one afternoon in a bundle with hundreds of others from points as remote as Copenhagen. The envelope with its childish scrawl, strongly scented, light blue, with its Denver postmark, lay on the pile. He put down a batch of reports from his Dallas detective agency and rubbed his eyes wearily. He turned over the envelope, hesitated, then with impatience opened the flap. He had almost forgotten who Sophie Muller might be.

She had married again, she wrote, the treasurer of poor Ezra's bank. All things considered, this seemed the sensible thing. The depositors were reassured, the bank examiners had sent congratulations, and only the vice-president, the runner-up, had been disgruntled. The wedding had been splendid, and she was happy. She begged her *dearest* Link to forgive her.

McKeever smiled faintly. He had a dim warm feeling for Sophie—like that for a clean puppy tumbling in a tub—but the news left him feeling odd and lonely. It had been a delicious affair, he recalled. Silky hair and brilliant violet eyes, brainless and empty but a delight to the senses. Good Lord! How long had it been since he had held a woman? Or even thought of it?

He sat there at his desk, surrounded by files and stacks of papers, staring at the letter, and his gaze went toward the ceiling. Jeff's room was there above. It was getting late and Florence soon would be down. He thought of this and an artery in his throat began to beat thickly.

"Is it anything important?" Martin asked.

McKeever brought his gaze into focus. "Eh? Oh no! Just personal." As Martin left for the living room, now converted to a main office, he began to compose a warm letter to Sophie, more tender and emotional than his feelings or even the occasion warranted.

But of course when Florence came down to leave he had nothing to say. He arose awkwardly as she entered the study, her warm green

133

eyes dancing, and as they shook hands he was conscious of her touch. "Good-by, Link," she said, reading his expression, "until next time." "Until next time," he agreed.

She hesitated. "You ought to spend more time with Jeff," she said. "He misses you."

"Yes, of course." The litter of work caught his eye. "Just as soon as I can. I'm just so busy!"

He had let her go without a word more. All that had taken place in early September and now it was late October, he reflected. He clucked and continued on the path until, at a point of moist seepage, he saw the impress of the steel shoe he had been trailing. The extra flange was unmistakably that of Florence's great roan stallion. Was it accident or design which brought him on this path? He could not be sure. He paced on slowly, and then he heard an excited child cry out. He halted at a small adobe house.

"*Mamacita!*" the child cried. "*Un hombre!*"

There was a deal of excited chattering among the family as he dismounted and the *ranchero*, a young broad-shouldered man with a sunburned face, bowed humbly.

"Señor McKeever?" he asked. "*El abogado?*"

McKeever smiled. "I'm the feller," he said good-naturedly. He was used to this. As the summer had passed, he had taken to the countryside on these trips, partly to clear his mind, partly to get the feel of the jurisdiction. He had talked to cattlemen, and farmers, coal miners and woodsmen, railroad workers and all those who could tell him something of the currents of the land. His name had spread throughout the borderland. He was the lawyer who had come to defend Don Carlos de Niza.

"Will you have food with us?" the *ranchero* said humbly.

"Why sure!" McKeever dismounted and entered the poor little hut. Silently he prayed for an absence of frijoles swimming in bacon fat, red and hot with chile peppers. He joined them, grateful that at this altitude the usual swarms of flies were absent. Pottery decorated the walls, and a large adobe oven, fired with hardwood, gave a pleasant heat in the morning chill. The woman made sweetened wheat cakes and smiled while McKeever admired the shrine at which a candle was burning.

"What is the thought in the *campo?*" McKeever asked when finally they were seated about the crude table.

The *ranchero* sucked his teeth with somber foreboding. He was illiterate but intelligent, with a clear grasp of the forces at play. "I feel with the archbishop," he explained earnestly. "Unless there is peace,

134

they will hang him, the Anglos. Without Don Carlos, they know we are in the darkness." He touched a finger to his forehead. "They are too many, too strong, and what are we without a leader? I am an ignorant man but I know they will kill him." His face flushed with anger and he demanded to know where this would end.

McKeever shrugged. There was no good answer to this question. The months had rushed in a tedium of daily wrangles with Mike Taft and in this time he had sent his men out by the score to destroy Tom Canty and to discredit his expected testimony. They were gathering every scrap of information within a radius of two thousand miles, a costly and exasperating task.

"Do you know a certain man?" he asked in his new halting Spanish. "An old one named Sam Trister?"

"Trister?" The *ranchero's* face lighted with a grin. "*Ah, sí! Un loco! Sí*, Sam Trister!" he was pleased to tell. The crazy old desert rat was a known character. With his Navajo woman, he had come along the path four or five years before. No, not more recently. An old man leading a burro. The woman bore a Christian name—Guadalupe. That was all he knew.

"Do you know where he is now?" McKeever persisted in Spanish. "Because we're looking for him. Tell me, for the sake of Don Carlos."

"I do not know," the *ranchero* said with regret.

"Would the Apaches know?" McKeever waved indefinitely to the west. "I have been told he is somewhere out there."

The *ranchero* brought a bowl of thin corn gruel to his mouth and sucked noisily. "The Apache would not tell," he said thoughtfully. "They keep their secrets. I have known them." He held the bowl in two cupped hands and this, for no good reason, struck McKeever as an oddity, as though the cleavage in civilizations cut through to the smallest points of behavior.

"Where could he be hiding?"

"I do not know."

With more of this, McKeever thanked the family and mounted his horse.

"This path, it goes to Polk's Spring?"

The man nodded. "Maybe ten miles, maybe more." No one lived in that direction. The country was a wilderness and the path was kept alive by antelope and wild horses. The Apache country lay too near to tempt settlers into the mountainous regions beyond.

As to whether Douglas Hanna had ever met Carlos de Niza at Polk's Spring before his death, as Sotero Gomez y Gomez had claimed, and whether the two had quarreled, he could not say. "I know nothing," the man shrugged.

135

With a sigh, McKeever gave the child a bag of licorice candies. He left a sack of tobacco for the man and went up the path.

The formations changed as he rode on and with interest his eye caught in the sandstone the faint outlines of a fossil trilobite where tens of millions of years gone by the sea had covered the land.

It was late noon and the heavy overcast had a smell of rain, when finally he heard the splashing which told him that he was at Polk's Spring. He dismounted and walked his horse through a field of brambles. The humming of bees was strong as he glimpsed Florence through the trees. She was singing softly and drying her red tresses beside the pool. His horse whinnied and her head disappeared.

"Who's there?" she called.

When he parted the bushes, she was waiting with a rifle at the ready. "Oh, Link!" she said in a relieved tone. "What are you doing here?" She put down the rifle and inserted a hairpin. "Were you watching me in swimming?"

"I wish I had," he smiled. "No, I came too late for that."

"Why, Link!" She smiled reproachfully. She continued to twine her red braids in a bun. She was wearing a heavy suede skirt, split for riding, and her plaid flannel shirt was still damp. At her feet was a fishing pole cut from a birch sapling. "It's just as well," she added. "I'm not Susanna, by a long shot. The last time I was caught swimming, I was eleven years old."

"What happened?"

She grinned mischievously. "I threw rocks and I spit. Then I came with a stick. He was a pretty sorry boy when I finished with him."

"It must have been worth a beating," he drawled.

"Not when I was eleven," she pointed out.

"True!" he acknowledged. He smiled and looked about. The spring was formed by a vein of water brought by melting snows on the distant higher levels. Here was where it gushed from the rocks to form the headwaters of one of the streams which gave Cuatro Rios its name. The forest with its oak and white birch and towering conifers was almost like New Hampshire. "So this is Polk's Spring," he murmured. In the first blaze of autumn colors it was altogether lovely.

"Is that what brings you here?" she asked.

He answered indirectly. "Do you imagine they could have met here, Carlos and your uncle? How could it happen?"

"Let's not talk about it." Her face darkened. She began to lace her boots with firm tugs of her tanned competent hands. "We'll wind up talking about the case. It's too peaceful for that."

136

"Good enough," he agreed. "H'm! Is that trout?"

She opened a wicker basket. "Five rainbows, the biggest yet. They were just dying of old age. Nobody comes out to catch 'em. They were begging to make someone a meal."

"Well, I'm famished."

The afternoon passed pleasantly. She pan-fried the trout with bacon contributed from his pack. The rainbows, the first he had ever seen, prepared mountain style, were delicious. They hobbled the horses and picked the last sweet blackberries of the season. She showed him a cave with Stone Age paintings. They talked of everything but the subject gnawing at his mind.

"Do you always come out fishing alone like this?" he asked lazily. Above, the overcast was thickening. They were seated on a carpet of pine needles on a slope overlooking the stream. The taste of pine resin was on his tongue. She nodded and smothered a yawn. "I've come here all my life," she murmured.

"Isn't it risky?"

She put a needle in her mouth and chewed. "Nobody comes this way, and if they do, I've got my rifle. We own this land, you know, everything in sight. It's part of the Grant." Her face was tranquil, eyes closed, as though the Grant were no element of the strife they had left at home. "We used to come out here when I was a girl. Pa was a great hunter. He and Uncle Douglas loved this place. I tagged along from the time I could ride a pony. I'll never forget those days. It seemed as though time would never end. I know every trail for miles around. Now Uncle Douglas is dead, and Pa's got this stroke, so I've come alone. This is my first trip since— well, you know." She paused. "I'm sorry I came. It's too disturbing."

They lay on the slope, resting.

"What's your father like?" he asked, taking advantage of the opening. She looked at him queerly. "I don't know, Link," she replied soberly. "I honestly don't. When I was a child, he filled the whole world. He's not a big man, but I thought he was, and his voice was always strong. I remember that and the smell of tobacco. Did you know"—she turned—"that his library's the biggest Spanish collection outside of Mexico City?"

"I've heard of that," he murmured.

"Pa built that library himself. He's read every book, and he never forgets a line. He's done it all without schooling, from the ground up. A man like that has got to influence you. But now—"

"Yes?"

She shrugged. "He's not the same since his stroke. His hand shakes and then he spills ashes and food. Things like that. It's only his eyes that stay the same." She shivered in the late chill breeze. "He seems so small to me these days. He's dependent on me and it makes me feel wretched. I'd rather not talk about it."

"Of course," he agreed. There were other questions, but these he reserved. Was it wise to ride alone? She laughed. Gossip had always trailed her. Local society, especially the old wealthy Spanish families, was stuffy in the extreme. As he had seen at the plaza Saturday nights, young women still strolled with dueñas, fringed shawls trailing, fans fluttering, all that paraphernalia. But she could not be bothered. She was the wilful hoyden, the terrible Hogarth girl, rushing to perdition—a lawyer, twenty-eight, unmarried—and too rich to care. "Does that answer your questions?"

"Only some," he said uncomfortably, and he found his heart beating under her level gaze. Her cheek was as smooth as a pear, faintly fuzzed, her aroma was in his nostrils. She placed her hand on his. She seemed about to say something when a clap of thunder split the skies and a great Douglas fir was riven not fifty yards away. The yellow overcast burst and the rain came down in blinding sheets. There was a rattling of hail. They jumped up.

"Good Lord!" he exclaimed. "Let's get back to the cave!"

She shouted, "There's a cabin ahead! Follow me!"

Somehow, they got the horses, gathered their packs, and made their way through the drenching icy sheets, almost missing the path. There was a shed for the horses, and dry piñon logs had been piled by the Hogarth foresters. Gasping and soaked, they went in, shivering.

"Where's the lamp?" he asked.

She pointed. "Matches on the fireplace! Gosh, this is something!" She shook her wet hair and came up grinning. "Walk into my parlor, Link!"

"You're a wet spider," he said cheerfully. The dash through the rain had excited them. Their eyes met with a smile. "Make the fire," she suggested. "I'll start some coffee."

Later, they sat before the fire, propped against a bench, warmed and luxurious, sipping coffee and talking in low tones as the hail rattled intermittently on the roof. The log cabin was crude but well-chinked and snug. "I love this." She yawned. "Tell me about yourself, Link. You're a strange man."

He found himself talking about his life. It was lonely enough, even before Liz had died. One met thousands of men and women everywhere. He was a celebrated figure. There was excitement and purpose in his work—and yet it had been an empty business devoted to abstractions and fulfilled among strangers.

Florence gazed into the roaring fire. "She must have been lovely, your wife."

"Yes," he said softly, and he realized with surprise that he felt no hurt.

"And now you're back?" she murmured.

He nodded somberly. "It would seem so."

She loosened her hair and let it tumble to her waist. The quickness of the gesture struck him. She looked up. "I'm sorry for you, Link," she said in a low voice. "You take things too hard. You can't win this case. You don't know this country, and you don't understand. This is an old fight between Pa and Carlos. It's got nothing to do with you. Can't you see that?"

"No, I can't," he said angrily.

She sighed and sat back. "I'm sorry you're on the other side. I'd be able to see you more. Link"—she looked up at his face which had gone suddenly grave—"I want to tell you this. I've gone through a bad time of my own. There was a man in England. He was important to me for a time and that was why I stayed there five years. I thought I would marry him." Her eyes were averted, her breath was coming faster, and this, he understood, was something she had been leading to. Her neck was close and the smell of her hair was sweet. She went on. "The trouble was, he couldn't marry me. He was married and there were children. I knew all that but I wouldn't let that stop me. There was a month in Rome. Then other trips. In the end it got too miserable, too involved. Well"— she looked up, eyes brimming—"I came back to take care of Pa. I could never tell this to anyone before. Never had to, till now. I practiced law instead. Is it all right?" she asked urgently.

There was a spell in the cabin as their breaths mingled. The drumming sound on the roof died. He touched her cheek. "Floss," he said gently, "I don't need to know this."

"You should," she said mutely, and her eyes, those of the composed strong-minded woman of affairs, were suddenly pleading and helpless. "Oh Link, darling—" She turned and kissed his hand at her cheek in despair. "Is it all right?"

He had known this was coming, but still, it struck with a shock of surprise. He was astounded and perplexed and almost vexed at his own constraint. Then she raised her mouth and they embraced.

"It's all right," he murmured tenderly. "Floss, dear—"

It was so old, so new, this remembered taste of woman's flesh. Her mouth was hot and searching as he drew her close, crushing her clumsily, breaking her strength, grasping her breasts. She wore no corsets and her waist was supple as she strove with him, clinging,

139

writing, letting the little sounds slip forth. "I love you, Link," she moaned. "Oh now! Now!" Her passion was a surprise. He shook and trembled as he explored her with all his savage hungers. Her hair was like a net about them. Every part of her was his, and it seemed in the end that this in the darkness had always been.

A log crashed in the fireplace. And another. The wood burned to ashes.

They lay finally in the bunk under rough wool blankets, breathing quietly. She threw her head back exhaustedly. "I've wanted you for months," she yawned with content. "Didn't you know?"

He turned his massive head with a faint smile.

"You knew the storm was coming, didn't you?" he murmured lazily.

"M-m, yes," she admitted.

"And you knew where this cabin was?" he accused.

She threw a naked arm across his chest. "That too," she mumbled.

"Well," he drawled, "so did I."

She laughed. "You villain!"

"He who asks equity," he quoted the maxim, "must do equity."

She raised herself on an elbow. "Link, if you were let loose in a harem, I swear you'd be spouting law till the sultan showed, wouldn't you?"

"That's quite likely," he admitted judiciously.

And they lay there, gratified and amazed in the joy of their discovery, talking, joking affectionately, until she slept and the silence on the roof told that the storm had passed.

It was not till morning that she became aware that he was awake.
She murmured, "Link—"

"Yes?"

"Suppose there'd been no storm? Then what?"

"I'd have found a way," he answered. There was something odd in his voice which struck her. She glanced over sharply.

"What's wrong?" she whispered.

He said in despair, "I don't know."

She arose on her elbow. The cabin was cold and dim. In the feeble light, her eyes were encircled and her mouth was bruised. She studied his troubled face.

"You're thinking of the trial!" she said with wonder. "That's been on your mind all this time, hasn't it?"

"I'm afraid so," he sighed. "It's a nightmare."

She thought of this.

"Why is this case so much worse than any other?"

140

He sat up. "I'm afraid of this jury," he said hesitantly. "If I had one witness, it would be different, but I haven't. I've got to depend on destroying Canty. If I could be sure of the jury, I wouldn't care. I know I could do it. But the feeling is too high." He sighed heavily. "I can't forget that it's Carlos de Niza's life. If only—" He broke off. "Do you mind if I smoke, dear?"

"Smoke? No, of course not."

They smiled uncertainly. These were things they had yet to learn about each other. They got up and while he found a broken cigar, she slowly brushed her russet tresses. She thought deeply.

"What's on your mind, Link?" she asked directly. "Did you have a reason to follow me?"

He drew apart and arose.

"Let me build the fire first." He piled the kindling, then the logs, and started the tinder. When his hands were warm, he said, "I want to find a way out for Carlos. I don't want to lose this case."

"I don't understand."

"His wife doesn't want me to go to the jury, that's the thing." She continued to stroke her hair. "How can I help?"

"Well," he said, poking the fire, "the first day I saw María de Niza, she wanted me to see your father. To suggest a compromise. Since then, she's been at me for months on those lines."

"Do you think she's right?"

He shrugged unhappily. "I've got to respect her wishes."

"And you want me to take this up with Pa?" she asked slowly.

"There's no one else I can ask," he said simply. "Bellew volunteered to try on my behalf, as a newspaperman, you know. I had to quash that. Your father would see through that, and we can't show a weak hand. But he might listen to you."

They faced each other a moment.

"I see." She held her hand to her face, drawing the blanket up to cover her breast. "I guess I made a fool of myself," she muttered. "You were thinking of that all the time. While you were making love to me! The case!"

"That's not true," he protested.

"Oh yes!" She laughed without mirth. "You're as transparent as a baby! Dear me, Link, do you think I can't see through a man?" She half smiled at his misery. "Don't make a tragedy of it! I can't help feeling used."

He took her hands.

"You mustn't think that, not for a moment!" he pleaded. "I wanted you for yourself, you must know that. It's just that this other thing never leaves me a moment. The man's life depends on me. His wife

141

and those boys look at me. They're hanging on every move I make, every word. Floss, I don't know which way to turn!" He added in despair, "I should never have had them in the house!"

She said with wonder, "Is it always like this?"

"Not always," he said.

"But usually?"

"Yes—that."

She sighed.

"You're sure you didn't mean to put me in this stupid position, Link? Because I'd feel like an awful fool."

For an answer, he kissed her mouth. Her bruised lips were dry and passive but not wholly untender. Her eyes were partly closed, faintly luminous in the dark. When he was done, she said distantly, "Now hand me my shirt." She dressed quickly and turned, with a thoughtful look. "Talk to Pa for Carlos de Niza? Is that it?"

"Yes."

"Have you thought how I feel?"

He nodded slowly. "I think you've been changing."

She lowered her eyes. "Where's the kettle?" She busied herself at the fire, tossing her hair as the loose strands fell forward. She turned angrily to demand, "Why should I go against Pa? Why shouldn't Carlos hang? Isn't that what the law is for?"

He said somberly, "That's when the law fails."

They faced each other, hostile and cold.

"It wouldn't work," she said finally. "Even if I tried."

"I know that," he agreed.

"And Carlos wouldn't ask it."

"That's true, too."

"Then why?"

He shrugged helplessly. "The law can be made to do horrible things. I don't want you to be part of it. Not you, Floss." He hesitated. "And I've got to know we've done everything possible! I'm sure Carlos is innocent. I'm not sure I can acquit him."

She looked at her hands. "It's a lot to ask," she muttered. "I've never had any doubts before. We're not ready for your kind of thinking out here, not yet."

"Will you try?"

She put aside the coffee things and came to him, holding him at arm's length. The wind was whining at the chimney. "Wasn't there a moment, Link," she pleaded, "one moment when the trial was out of your mind? When you thought only of me?"

"Yes," he said with tender humor, smiling faintly, "there was a moment."

"What will happen to us now?" she whispered.

His face clouded. "I don't know," he said unhappily. "Not till this is over."

She stared at him.

"Your poor wife!" she said slowly. "I feel so sorry for her!" She kissed him and with a sigh buried her head against him. After a time she pushed away with determination. "The trouble is," she decided, "that we're hungry!"

He laughed.

With a brisk air, she filled the cabin with the smells of coffee and sizzling bacon and biscuits. They found themselves lighthearted and ravenous. When finally they turned back to Cuatro Rios, the cold wet trail at dawn seemed filled with beauty. They parted and, as a matter of discretion, took their way home by separate paths.

Months later, on a morning following the bitter news that the Supreme Court at Washington had refused to grant certiorari, thus precluding further appeal from the dismissal of the writ of habeas corpus, McKeever drove out to the old Mission of San Augustine. A young priest showed him to an arbor where a tall man with white hair arose with an expression of pleasure.

"My dear Mr. McKeever," said the archbishop, "this is good of you to join me. Have you had breakfast?" His face was serene and animated by an air of polite solicitude. His shaven features were handsome, although somewhat severe, and from his high narrow forehead, twin tufts of white hair swept back like rays of light. He was dressed informally in a simple black cassock. He turned. "I should like you to meet Father Hawthorne."

An elderly priest, spare and brown, with a humorous face as wrinkled as a berry, arose from the cedar table. "How do you do?" he said in a strong Midwest accent.

McKeever found the breakfast of muscat grapes, cheese and bread and red wine delicious, but not more so than the sweet courtesy with which the two churchmen entertained him. A small bird with a bright yellow throat hopped about for crumbs. There was a sense of serenity as, in a tone of polite banter, they discussed indifferent things, in the realm of current events and of philosophy. They knew his reputation. They were as curious to explore his views as he was theirs. He found in the archbishop a richly furnished mind, quick to seize a point, deep in understanding. The churchman was a practical administrator, a liberal in the French style, a lover of the peoples he served. The priest had a joking style with an earthy practical twist.

143

Finally, the archbishop patted his mouth and came to the purpose. "I do not believe Carlos de Niza can be guilty of a senseless murder," he said firmly. "This crime could serve only the purpose of his enemies. I think that is evident."

"That is the feeling," the priest agreed.

McKeever waited. There was a reason for all this, but what it might be, he could not fathom. "I can't understand all this hate, Your Excellency. Everywhere I turn, I find that feeling. How did it begin? Why does Carlos feel so bitter? He won't discuss these matters. I don't mind saying, his attitude has been a great handicap to me."

"How?" The archbishop twirled a wineglass thoughtfully as his mind searched the past. His memory was like a palimpsest, one screed written over another, but at the bottom lay—what? An original act of violence, bloody reprisal, hatred without end. A treaty of peace violated, promises broken, a desperate struggle for the land. He said, "I have heard a tale that Hogarth came to this land before the conquest as a freebooter, and that he and a group of Texans corrupted the defenses of the Fortress. There was a surrender to the Americans without a shot. You'll find the report in the archives in Washington. It is not generally known, and I'll ask you to keep this information in confidence."

McKeever objected, "That was a long time ago."

The archbishop said seriously, "He came as a guest in the house of Don Francisco de Niza, the father of Don Carlos, who was then a boy. It was an abuse of hospitality. The Spanish feel these things strongly. I may add that Don Francisco was a casualty of that war. When the great *casa* was burned, whatever the cause, his heart failed him." He smiled bleakly. "Does it matter now? Carlos de Niza is a man eaten by a burning sense of injustice. That is the thing. Can you understand?"

"The burning sense of injustice?" McKeever murmured. "Yes, I know what that can do!" It could be a consuming passion, he thought, stronger than love, defiant of the grave, a thing beyond reason. He said somberly, "The land's so big, it seems to swallow my voice. What can a man do when he finds himself talking to the wind?"

The archbishop popped a grape into his mouth. "The problem is not unfamiliar," he said drily. "You have within you a sense of the love of man. When the time comes, this will sustain you." With a twinkle of teasing fun, he added, "I was tempted to say that you have a sense of God, but with your cherished reputation as a skeptic, I will not embarrass you before Father Hawthorne."

McKeever laughed.

The priest smiled and put a question. "Is it essential that you find this man Trister?"

There was a significant pause.

"Yes," the lawyer said slowly, glancing in turn at the serene faces before him. "I'd say vital."

"Can you say why?"

A toad hopped across the gravel path, landed on the lawyer's shoe, and hopped into the shade of the table, its throat bellows working slowly. The lawyer stared at it, unseeing, as he grasped the import of the question. He nodded. "Yes, it's quite obvious. The old man can throw light on the heart of the case. If Carlos de Niza ever met Tom Canty, what actually happened? Trister is the only possible witness to the facts."

"But Trister *might* support the prosecution," the priest pointed out.

"He might."

"Then why do you want him?"

"Because I believe my client is innocent."

"And if not?"

McKeever hesitated. "I will defend him still."

"But it is a risk?"

"Yes."

"I see." The priest looked at his superior, who nodded. "Can you say what Don Carlos has told you of this?" he asked cautiously. "Forgive my question, please."

"Quite all right. The answer is simple. My client has refused to discuss the matter. He simply denies that he is guilty of the murder."

"But what will he say in court?"

"He says that when the time comes, he will know what to say."

"I don't like this," said the archbishop. "Does he consider his wife? Or his sons? Have you pointed that out?"

The lawyer laughed harshly. "I've said everything a man can say! Nothing works!"

"And still you will go ahead?"

"Yes!"

"I think, Father Hawthorne," said the archbishop, turning, "that you should do what you see fit. While I have a certain influence, I cannot interfere in these matters. On the other hand, I do not believe we should refuse to aid Mr. McKeever in his search for justice. I am quite satisfied."

The priest finished his wine. "Mr. McKeever, your trial is pretty well talked about by everybody, you know." His speech was broad Midwestern in marked contrast to his superior's delicate French intonation. His manner was forthright. "I've come down from my mission near Farmington. That's not far from Shiprock. You've heard of Shiprock?"

He was referring to the famous mesa, towering like a battleship over the plains, located west and north of Albuquerque.

McKeever nodded. "Yes, of course."

"My mission is small, but extremely lovely. It was built three hundred years ago. There are twin spires and the old adobe has weathered to a mellow color. I work there among the Navajo. I am devoted to them, and I think they like me."

The archbishop interrupted. "Mr. McKeever is impatient, Father, if you don't mind."

The priest smiled.

"I'm afraid I'm getting garrulous," he apologized. "However! About ten days ago, I was invited to attend a Navajo sing, which is an honor, I assure you. They come from all parts of their land. I wish you would picture that desolation. For miles one may see nothing more than a lonely hogan, a few sheep, a patch of corn, a dry desert of land. Out of this they come, sometimes by the thousands. At the sing, they try to heal the sick, to reject the powers of darkness, to bring forth a sense of harmony and light. It is a part of their life, their tribe, their way of thinking. They are poor, but someday, if you come to my mission, I will show you people who live with an inward grace, who are beautiful to contemplate. I have my difficulties with them, of course, but these are the Navajo!"

"Father Hawthorne!" the archbishop murmured, deprecatingly.

"Yes, yes!" the priest agreed with good humor. "Well, on the fourth day of the sing, I heard something in the large hogan. The name of a woman named Guadalupe."

"Trister's wife? The Navajo woman?"

"Exactly."

McKeever paused.

"Is she with him now?"

"Yes."

"Where are they?"

The priest smiled grimly. He waved a hand toward the west. Out there lay the malpais, the badlands, a tortured hell of frozen lava and drifting gypsum sands where a goat could not live. Unexplored country, trackless and dry, surrounded by Apache lands. Somewhere out there they were wandering, the old man and his Navajo woman.

"How can I get to him?" McKeever asked in a low voice.

The priest shrugged. "It's not possible," he said with regret. "You

146

could look forever. But there is something else. I was told that Trister is afraid to come in for this trial. He feels he might be hung and that's not pleasant. On the other hand, he wants to help Carlos de Niza."

"What can we do?"

"I can send out word," the priest said slowly. "If he will surrender to you, and if you will promise to defend him, there's a chance he may come in. Perhaps not. I understand that the situation is getting desperate."

McKeever drew a breath.

"Well, of course! I'll do everything I can for the old man, you can send him word."

They talked of this until the bell in the *campanario* began to peal. The archbishop paused to listen. "I love the sound," he said softly. "When I came here as a young man, the tower was in ruins, as in so many of the old missions, and it was my first task to restore the bells. Father Hawthorne could tell you some stories. I shall not forget the first Angelus when it was raised. Listen! It is the sweetest sound I know." His eyes lit with pleasure and then he sobered as he placed a hand on McKeever's shoulder. "Now I must say good-by. I shall return to Santa Fe with pleasant thoughts, Mr. McKeever. If you are wondering why I entered this picture, let me tell you that I am extremely fond of Miss Floss. However"—he shrugged—"I could do nothing with her father, but I think this was a good day's work."

"Good-by," said McKeever, reluctant to leave the peaceful arbor. "I can't tell you how grateful I am."

"Stuff!" said Father Hawthorne, smiling.

The archbishop walked him to the gate. "I've been thinking, Mr. McKeever," he said shrewdly, eyes twinkling, "that there's no use getting vexed with my old friend, Carlos de Niza. In essentials, you two are quite alike, you know. And now, go with God!"

As McKeever drove off, he thought with resentment that he did not care for this last remark, not one bit. How could it possibly be true?

Chapter X

A month later, toward midnight in the Calle Alvorado, a wretched alley with a pretentious name, a pianola could be heard plunking away, and otherwise there was silence. On the main street, the saloons were doing a roaring business. The bagnios were running full blast and only Tía María's was closed out of respect to the prisoner in the Fortress of San Felipe. While mounted deputies patrolled the streets in pairs, prudent men and women crouched in bed and allowed the armed Anglos to pass on their way.

Two Anglos passed through the dark street carrying rifles. They were young, no more than boys, and they laughed nervously as they walked about on foot. They were hunting the Spanish. With drunken voices, they hurled taunts into the dark street and then moved on.

It was quiet for a time. There were only the strident crickets to be heard. Three gunshots cracked in the night.

Those who were wise minded their business. But some peered out through their shutters to see a man's body prone in the dust. Squatting nearby was another man who made no attempt to run. In the quick yellow flare of a match, a pistol could be seen in the hand of the man squatting, and then the darkness swallowed up the scene.

There was a silence.

Only half-clad, a girl with braids came running down the dusty street, panting, her face in agony. She paused, twisting her hands. "It is not Luis!" she screamed. "Tell me it is not Luis! *Dios*, tell me!"

The man with the pistol drawled in a slurred voice, "Now, how would I know? Take a look!"

The girl stared, then with relief seemed to reel as she made out the features of the dead man. "It is not Luis!" she cried hoarsely. She saw an older gray-haired man, not the slim boy she loved. "*Gracias a Dios!*" she gasped. Then she ran blindly back into the night. In the adobe houses, the fearful ones considered with their wives. They argued and attempted to return to sleep. They got up and scratched themselves, and finally one bold soul sent for the law. In the meantime, the killer wandered off.

So there it was when the law men gathered. Shots in the night. A man dead. The corpse lay face down in the dust, barefoot, a fat man in a ragged shirt and trousers. The whole matter finally proved to be unimportant. The dead man was a poor railroad section hand, a father with eleven children, a harmless and peaceful man. It was surmised that he had had the poor judgment to discuss the pending trial of Carlos de Niza with the Anglo, but of this no one could be sure. No arrest was made, and none was expected, and Max Kyle scolded the Spanish for provoking such unfortunate incidents. He surveyed the scene and asked some brief questions and raised a meaty paw of authority.

"Now you folks see what happens," he grumbled. "I've been telling you. Don't provoke anybody. Keep off the streets. Leave all your weapons at home. The peaceful Mex don't need a gun or a knife and I don't want to catch anybody carrying one. This man might've been alive if he'd listened to my advice." He waited but the glum circle of dark faces seemed unconvinced and he went on angrily. "I been trying to give you all the protection of my office, but the county gives me so many men and I can't be in every place at the same time. There's a lot of feeling with this trial going on, and it's going to stay that way. You folks refused to cooperate and that's why these unfortunate incidents will happen. This is the third one inside a month. Now get home and get to bed. This is no freak show."

The onlookers were silent. They waited for something to happen but nothing much took place and they dispersed.

On this note the trial began.

In Washington, Amos Tucker waited for the nurse to remove the thermometer and to leave. He propped himself on the pillow and continued to read the letter from Cuatro Rios. . . .

DEAR AMOS:

The town is bursting with workers and witnesses and the curious are swarming like flies. The railroad and stages are running special sections. Extra telegraph lines have been strung down from Santa Fe. The local press has come to recognize the national interest in our little tug of war. This morning Wilby wrote that this case is a test of American justice. I suppose it is, although not in the way he intended.

The weather remains lovely, but the mood is frightening. Each morning we pass through a mob of armed men. They part in silence, close ranks, and the militia take over. As we enter, even counsel are searched for arms. This is an important ceremony. With our frazzled tempers, we guarantee nothing when the fur starts to fly.

A month went in picking the jury, nor am I sure of those we finally got. Our small court is so crowded, we sit in each other's laps. I get some smiles, some glares, but how it is going I cannot say. This is still the frontier, the local code is a real thing. While these men are indifferent to bloodshed, the charge of murder by ambush enrages their sense of fair play. I have hopes only for the sixth juror, a fat little man with blue eyes named Ike Goldman. I keep my eye on him.

The trial has been a horror. Fifty-six witnesses for the Territory and more to come. Sleepless nights and exhausting days and the end seems far off. Taft roars like a Bull of Bashan, quibbles and equivocates, lays it on against me, the Easterner, with a thick trowel. Insults fly like leaves in the autumn wind. We've both got a range of tipsters and hangers-on and hired guards and whisperers. It's become a dirty business, but we've got to fight fire with fire. We tell our people to avoid trouble but of course this is not always possible when passions are running high. My Olympian superiority vanished weeks ago in this bloody shambles.

My one happiness is Jeff whose recovery is now clearly in sight. He spends his days discussing the trial with young Martin, or playing in the garden with De Niza's boys, or stuffing his pet doe with unsuitable foods. I've argued against tortillas as deer food without avail. That it has grown so large is a tribute to something beyond my knowledge.

Miguelito (the older boy) is moody but brilliant, quite a match for Jeff, and violently partisan. They argue incessantly and their more rarefied flights of debate make me feel ignorant indeed. This morning they quarreled quite badly. Miguelito resents Miss Hogarth's visits to Jeff. He feels quite sternly that it is improper for her to visit our house. Ah well, the nuances of Spanish punctilio are outside my grasp, I am afraid. I left the matter to Jeff's good sense.

(He instructs me to thank you for your stamp collection. He has become an avid collector overnight and now your portrait has the place of honor on his wall beside my own.)

Hogarth attends each session, of course. He has remarkable eyes —yellow staring lamps flecked with red. He is shrunken now, a shaggy and untidy old man. He is privileged to smoke, or at least no one dares forbid him, but his hand quakes and he is sprinkled with ashes. His face is dried-up and resolute, pitiless and determined, and as matter-of-fact as you can imagine. I can see now why it was absurd ever to expect a compromise. He told John Macy Bellew— do you follow his accounts of the trial?—that Carlos de Niza is getting nothing more than he would be handing out if their positions were reversed. This may well be true. Hogarth sits at my elbow panting like an old lion and I am conscious of him every moment.

Although this is their first meeting in thirty years, he and De Niza studiously fail to see each other.

The old man takes my attacks on him imperturbably enough. My attempts to prove that the prosecution is a conspiracy directed by him against an innocent man leave him unmoved. Last week I put it so strongly that his daughter was forced to leave the courtroom. As you can imagine, this was a relief, because the scene which followed was quite trying. This judge resents my tactics and shows it. He is honest enough, I believe, but he is a blind and obstinate martinet. We exasperate each other and we clash constantly.

All this is making reversible errors, but I am afraid I no longer wish to depend on appellate courts. I have been too badly shaken by some recent rulings, so farfetched and against the facts as to cause one to wonder. I have my eye now on one thing—the jury's verdict.

So, as expected, it's all boiling down to a single issue. Will the jury believe this monster, Tom Canty, or will they not? It is impossible to say. Five weeks of cross-examination have failed to shake the man. I developed a horrible criminal background, far worse than I had at first believed. Once he admitted that first rape, he freely conceded a whole range of outrages, from the slaughter of cattle to murder. He was well prepared for this by Taft. He claimed that all these crimes were done under De Niza's orders as part of an early campaign of terror to keep out the first Anglos. You can imagine the effect of that Kennedy massacre where a child's hands were cut off before the ranch was burned. I'm afraid that these tactics may have boomeranged. The more monstrous Canty's past, the more inflamed the atmosphere.

But the man must not be underestimated. Our misfortune lies in his complete familiarity with the old affairs of De Niza's pitiful *Partido*. He has an apparent bluff sincerity, and he talks so feelingly of repentance and redemption and a hope for forgiveness, that his fantasies may well be accepted. I believe that he is touched with insanity, and I think this will be the final answer, but will the jury see that too?

I have also been hammering away at the missing Sam Trister. I've challenged Taft each day to produce the man, but of course I've gotten no further than that. He denies custody or control or knowledge of the old man's whereabouts. I've suggested that the governor promise a pardon to induce him to come forth voluntarily. To this there has been silence. Each day this is the message I must bring to Mrs. De Niza. She is quiet and uncomplaining but her agony is the most dreadful burden to carry.

Now tomorrow they will put Mrs. Hanna, the widow, on the stand. They have cunningly kept her for last. Bad as the situation is, I dread this final effect of her blindness on the jury.

And now it is night here in my study, the house is sleeping, and I must beg off. If I take refuge from my burdens in these letters, you must forgive me. It is only because it is sweet to relieve my mind by entrusting part of its agony to one who is wise and understanding. Please get well. Nothing must happen to you. It would not be the same without your voice in the land. . . .

Tucker stared at the letter's end. The signature scrawled off suddenly with a loose flourish which spoke of fatigue. For the moment, the old judge had the smell of the distant courtroom, the press of hostile faces, the vision of McKeever, an angered and weary man, wrestling with an obdurate problem—and then, as his feet felt cold, he put the letter aside and rested on his pillow waiting for sleep to come.

Outside, the snowdrifts were piling high in the streets and this gave him a sense of comfort. It was a feeling unrelated to anything about him, for it went back eighty-five years to his childhood, which now seemed closer to him than it had ever been.

The blind woman sat mute and in darkness with the roaring in her ears. She gripped the witness chair with some sense of comfort for the cool smoothness at her finger tips. A fetid smell was in her nostrils. What could it be? She remembered a mouse which had died in the wall space of her home in Virginia a lifetime ago. She had been a child but she still remembered that smell.

"What happened?" she whispered.

"You fainted," a familiar voice said. "Would you like water, Mrs. Hanna?"

She touched the rough bandages where the sense of pain remained. The two cavities burned with tears which could not shed themselves. She nodded uncertainly. "Yes, Judge Millikan, if you don't mind."

There was a silence and the sound of heavy shoes crossing the court. Someone with a stertorous breath pressed a glass into her hands. "Here you are, ma'am." That would be the rasping slur of the court clerk. With this came a smell of beer and peppermint within the blend of male odors of the crowded chamber. "Thank you, David," she whispered. She sipped slowly while the faintness passed. The darkness was complete.

"Are you ready to go on?" The judge's voice came from her right where the heat of a kerosene lamp touched her cheek. She felt the glass taken from her hand.

"Yes," she whispered, "I'll go on."

Then the harsh voice of the prosecutor came thundering out of the blackness. "Now then, Mrs. Hanna, you were telling us about something your husband said to you before the shotgun went off. Do you recall that?"

"Yes."

"Tell the jury what your husband said."

As expected, the rival voice broke in. "Your Honor, we respectfully object!" The voice was firm but pleasant, a slow nasal drawl fraught with humor. She had gotten to know it well during her afternoon on the witness stand. It was gentle and considerate, laden with kindliness for her plight, but now hoarse and weary. Her husband would have liked that man, she thought.

The judge said crossly, "Mr. McKeever, you will be seated."

"Is my objection noted?"

"The objection is overruled. You will resume your seat."

"May I state the basis of my objection?"

"Beware, sir! There are limits to the Court's patience!"

"With all due respect, this is clearly hearsay."

"And the Court rules otherwise! It comes within the exception."

"I have here a copy of Greenleaf, may it please—"

"It does not please the Court. Keep quiet, will you? That is the trouble. You chatter, chatter all the time."

"I respectfully except."

"Take half a dozen exceptions but please obey the Court and proceed in an orderly way. You are just a lawyer, sir. If you don't like the Court's rulings, take your exception but don't argue. I have been trying to put that into your head for the last three weeks. One exception is as good as fifty."

"May the record show that my demeanor is respectful and that I am resuming my seat."

"Oh, sit down. This grandstand play won't impress this intelligent jury. You cannot make law in this court, and the law you have in mind is simply ridiculous. It is not law at all. The law in this case is what I read to the jury. Anything else?"

"Exception. I will mark this page of Greenleaf, with the Court's permission."

"Suit yourself, sir. But stop delaying the case."

There was a pause while the stenographer marked a page of the text in question. She heard the scratching in the silence, and she groped for the glass of water.

The first voice boomed out of the void, "Now, Mrs. Hanna, what did your husband tell you?"

She felt the trembling within. "Just before the bridge," she said hesitantly, "he told me about Polk's Spring."

"What happened there?"

"He met Mr. De Niza."

"When did this happen?"

"Well, let me see. It must have been after the week of the Feast Day of St. Francis. I'm sure of that because I recall the procession to the Cathedral in Santa Fe."

"That would have been last year, October fourth?"

"Yes, I suppose. My husband came down here for a week's hunting before he went on the circuit."

"And he met Carlos de Niza then at Polk's Spring?"

"So he told me."

"What happened at that meeting?"

The other voice broke in again with weary outrage. "Your Honor, I simply must object!"

"I might have known as much," said the judge. "Can't you let her talk?"

The wrangling resumed, objections were noted, and she was allowed to continue. "My husband told me that he quarreled with Carlos de Niza."

"What about?"

She placed her hand to her temple as the nagging headache overcame her. "The Land Grant Case decisions," she muttered.

"You will have to speak louder."

She waited in the silence. Toward her left, she heard a cough in the jury box. She went on.

"Mr. De Niza resented the decision. Then my husband tried to show him that there was no other decision he could have written. Mr. De Niza did not want to hear this." She was aware of a keener throbbing pain. "He said he was tired of rats in his larder, that he would find a way to get rid of them."

There was an immediate undercurrent of sound. The rear door opened and closed and the clamor of the corridor entered a brief moment.

"Now, Your Honor," the second voice said strongly, "I object to this hearsay testimony on the ground that it is incompetent. Mr. Taft knows that this isn't evidence, and so does the Court."

The judge's voice said, "The Court will reserve decision. Now beware, sir! I'm being patient with you, but you're trying to evade my rulings."

"I respectfully except!"

"Now you obey the instructions of the Court without argument, without comments. Just proceed with your trial in the way the Court

154

directs. If you don't like the Court's rulings, take an exception, but I am going to run this court during this trial."

Mercifully she fainted.

When she resumed the stand, the shuffle of feet subsided. The smell had grown rancid with stale sweat. She placed her hands in her lap to conceal their trembling.

"Your witness," said the prosecutor.

A chair scraped and footsteps approached her. She sensed a quiet and massive personality before her. Her hands twisted and stiffened.

A gentle drawling voice asked, "Do you know who I am, Mrs. Hanna?"

"You're Mr. McKeever," she said in a low voice.

"Did you ever hear of me before this trial?"

"Yes."

"Did your husband ever happen to mention me?"

"I think so. He said you were a good lawyer."

"Thank you. Now, am I right in saying your husband was a fair man?"

"Yes."

"Perhaps stern, but not unjust?"

"I never thought he was stern."

"But in any event, he was an honest and truthful man?"

"Of course."

There was a pause while the footsteps receded, and then the voice came from a greater distance, and she judged that he was standing at the rail near the sixth juror.

"So that your husband would not have approved, either as a judge or as a man, of any attempt to use his death to punish an innocent man to satisfy a political grudge? Is that a fair question?"

"Well—"

As she hesitated, the other voice broke in derisively. "Your Honor, what kind of silly question is that?"

"Oh, let him have his fun," the judge said wearily. "I guess the jury will know what to think of that kind of thing. You may answer, Mrs. Hanna."

She realized that her fingers were aching with the agony of pressure on them.

"That's true," she said quietly.

The voice went on, soothing and pleasant, and she felt the strain ease as it gently established a friendly mood.

"The conversation at Polk's Spring took place, then, at least eight or nine months or even a year *before* your husband's death?"

"It seems so."

"Your husband was alone on a hunting trip?"

"He was supposed to have some friends—"

"But he was alone when he met Carlos de Niza?"

"Yes."

"Yet your husband was not attacked at *that* time, so far as you know?"

"That's true."

"Even though that was as good a chance as any, if Carlos de Niza had any such intention?"

"Yes."

"And the Land Grant Case decision was then fresh in everyone's mind?"

The judge broke in. "Now, all that's just speculation, sir. I don't want to keep warning you."

"I'll withdraw the question," said McKeever. "I'm sure the jury sees the point. Mrs. Hanna, you're familiar with the Land Grant Case decisions, are you not?"

"I just know they went against Mr. De Niza."

"A good deal of land was involved?"

"Everybody knows that. It was the talk of the Territory."

"Including the land on which the Hogarth Ranch now sits?"

The gavel went tapping. "Now, I warn you, sir! Mr. Hogarth is not on trial."

"Isn't he?" McKeever's tone was bland surprise. "Well, then, I'll withdraw the question." There was a trace of drollery and she sensed a chuckle somewhere near the press table. "But wouldn't you say that quite a few families were angry at the decision?"

"I knew they were."

"How was that?" McKeever said quickly.

"We received many letters of protest. My husband paid no attention, of course. He said it was only natural."

"In what way was it natural?"

She paused. She had in mind a picture of her home in Santa Fe before all this had happened. Her husband would be seated at coffee, a fragrant havana making curls of smoke, rustling the morning paper. For all his apparent sternness, his manner was tender and indulgent, and between them lay a score of little jokes. He had teased her that last day for flirting and had gone off humming. If only their children had lived! she thought wistfully.

"No one wants to be driven from the land," she said simply. "My husband understood that. There was just no other decision he could have written, but that did not mean he had no feeling for the old families. That's what he tried to explain to Mr. De Niza."

"Then your husband did not resent the defendant's anger?"

"How could he resent it? He understood the man," she said simply. "He didn't know what was going to happen." Suddenly she bowed her head and wept. "I'm sorry," she gasped finally and blew her nose. "I try not to do this. It's just—" She trailed off.

"One last question. Are you up to it?"

"I'll try," she said faintly.

"As a matter of fact, didn't your husband receive threatening letters even *before* the decision in the Land Grant Case?"

"Why, every judge gets those!" she exclaimed.

"Ah!" McKeever waited before he put the next question. "Did your husband ever get such a letter from this man Tom Canty?"

"I don't know," she said finally. "I just know he got many such letters. I'd like to help, but I simply don't know."

"Then you can't say, one way or the other?"

She nodded mutely.

"May the Court please," McKeever said wearily, anticipating objections, seeing that the point was made, "I have no further questions of the witness."

She sat motionless.

The judge said, "Yes, Mrs. Hanna, what is it?"

She turned timorously. "It's nothing, Your Honor. It's just that this was my husband's court. I'm sure he would not want anything to be done here that wasn't right."

There was a pause.

"I'm sure we all feel that way," the judge remarked. "You may now step down. Miss Hogarth, will you kindly help the witness?"

"Man, was it tough? Say, you got no idea how tough it *was*, mister! Tombstone was nothing! You tell this man, Joe! I'll just finish this good bourbon."

"Well, sir, just like Frank here says, it was tough. It was *real* tough!"

"But tell him *how* tough!"

"Man, there was no limit. Now I owned this here little dry goods store down at Torrence, and by God, I never went to sleep except on top of the overalls. Used to keep my gun in my crotch and come morning, these miners would line up outside. I'd open up, th'ow a gun in the first man's belly, and beller, 'What you want, *mister?*' Even in dry goods, a man just had to git the draw. Never knew what was outside that door. Tough? It sure was!"

"Remember Sheriff Parks? Now *he* was tough."

"No question. Almost had me killed, this old Al Parks. He had these two deputies stole about hundred dollars from my till, and I was stupid enough to swear out a warrant. Well, next morning these same two come for me. Would've killed me except I begged 'em to let me give 'em another two hundred. Tough!"

"It was all that. I remember when old Marshal Bailey's men finally come in. They just stood for nothing. They lined up all the so-called bad men they could lay they hands on, and just marched 'em out in a gang hog-tied in chains by the necks. Only way to handle the situation. Whatever Joe says, you can believe."

"Now you take Jim Handler. In that case, a feller named Miller came into this little bar Jim set up and put a knife in his back, just for nothing. Drunk maybe, or something. Three weeks later poor Jim died and old Judge Dale give Miller five months and a warning. Now I know that for a fact!"

"You can believe that, mister. Course, this Miller paid out a little for that deal, but nobody was excited. Without no family, nobody just plain give a damn, maybe not even Jim his own self. Life weren't worth living then, it was so tough. Many a man expired out of plain desperation. Am I right, Joe?"

"Right!"

"Now Max Kyle was different. Whatever they say, he cleaned up on a lot of them. Folks forget, he got this reputation with the Rangers before he come into the Territory. He lost it with the Williamsons, the way he got them, but that come later."

"I still don't blame him none. With those Williamsons, I would of got 'em any which way—front, back, or sideways."

"With old Ma Williamson looking on?"

"Even so."

"You got a point. Still and all, it was this bragging how he got 'em on the draw after calling 'em out that got everybody sick and tired of old Kyle."

"And don't he know it! Still, this trial ought to make some change. They claim Hogarth guaranteed to set him up for lieutenant governor if it comes out right."

"The word is, the case is a tossup now, but that depends what Carlos has got to say for hisself tomorrow morning."

"So it seems. You got to give McKeever the credit for that. He's a real fighter, not what they told us to expect. Without him, it would've been nothing."

"You got to respect a man like that. He don't take it off nobody. I heard he told off Kyle personally."

"How was that?"

"The way I heard, just this afternoon, Kyle got disgusted hearing himself called a thief and a liar. He caught McKeever at the bridge and told him he'd make an issue did it happen a next time. McKeever just looked at him like a sick dog and said there was nothing personal intended. It was just his feeling Kyle was a wood pussy and his hide ought to be nailed to the barn door."

"Is that a fact?"

"So they say."

"What happened?"

"Kyle let it go at that. In my opinion, he was just talking. He knows this lawyer don't carry a gun. Wouldn't know how to use it if he did."

"You can't tell with Kyle. He's real desperate to win this case. Without that, where is he? He did quite a job lining up all that evidence, and you got to admit, this Canty has been quite a witness. McKeever had him going for weeks, but as far as I can see, he got nothing the man didn't admit, anyways."

"What about all those killings in 'sixty-nine?"

"That was all part of that *quetzal* stuff. He explained all that."

"Even about the Kennedy ranch? You mean to say, Carlos told him to cut off the hands of that baby like he claims?"

"Well, the baby was dead anyways and that was under orders. Would a man make up a thing like that? Anyways, why get so surprised? I saw the same thing back in 'seventy-four when we raided this Apache camp at Salt Springs. They had a white kid they had caught. They was bringing it up for an Apache, the way they do. Well sir, but when this squaw saw us coming, she sliced the kid's belly out. How was that so different from Canty?"

"You got to admit he's a miserable son of a bitch, any which way."

"That, yes!"

"Then how do you figure he got this religious? Is he on the level? It's hard to believe."

"If he ain't, he's the greatest actor alive!"

"Still and all, bringing a man like Carlos into this stuff! Now, you tell me!"

"When you're dealing with a fanatic, it ain't hard to believe. In my experience, the Mex has got a peculiar mentality. He ain't like us. Like Canty testified, once he got the idea that the land belongs to the old dons, anything goes."

"The way I look, it's all up to which way Carlos makes out tomorrow."

"You think he'll take the stand?"

"Hell, yes! He's got to! I don't like Canty, but they never broke him down. Only one man can give the answers, and that's Carlos. Even the Mex know that much."

"Speaking of which, you posted on this talk about a break?"

"Some talk, sure. I hear this Garcia claims he got a hundred men waiting in case it goes against Carlos. But I don't believe they got more than ten."

"Well, we got forty and I got a personal bead on Garcia. Say, mister, what about a side bet on the trial? Oh Juana, what took so long? I'll be right with you. I'm talking business with this gentleman. I'll give even money, and we can let Juana hold the stakes. What do you mean—no pockets? Under the mattress is good enough."

"It's my turn, Joe. One thing about Juana, I admire. She don't ever seem to get tired."

"I was there when they got Billy the Kid, mister. Now let me tell you about that. There was a boy who was plain misunderstood."

"Hey, Juana, that ain't funny!"

Chapter XI

Through the grating the planet shone, white and brilliant in the dark sky, so intense that it cast its separate shadow on the prison floor. Carlos de Niza gazed at it fixedly from his point on the cot. The iron bars were like an astrolabe in which the ascension of the stars could be measured where now the late winter constellations were rising.

Whether he was asleep or not, one could not tell, for although he lay motionless, long ago he had learned to keep a rigidity of limb while his mind went wandering, and this warm nourishing counterfeit of sleep, useful to a wandering man in the saddle, had been cultivated in prison. The iron cot was short and his naked shanks hung out. His feet were cold, but of this he was unaware, for his thoughts were ranging to the point where fate was driving him.

The small lockup was restless. In the other few cells, prisoners were snoring fitfully. One whimpered, and at the sound he turned his head. This was a sixteen-year-old who had been taken, starving, from a freight car by a yard detective and lodged as a vagrant. Earlier in the week, he had been subjected to the ordeal of a kangaroo court, the usual mock trial launched in parody of legal forms by the older prisoners.

Don Carlos stirred with angry recollection. The boy's terror had touched his compassionate heart, and he had volunteered to act as counsel. In the drunken circle, he had arisen, spectacles affixed, clutching his lapels in a mock legal pose. His manner was in perfect mimicry of McKeever, ruffled cowlick, friendly drawl, eyes twinkling. Chuckles passed. The lamps had guttered, the gap-toothed faces had grinned in expectation, as he requested an adjournment.

The judge spat liquidly. "Denied!"

"But we need witnesses," Don Carlos protested.

The judge fell back in amazement. "Witnesses? Next thing, you'll ask for a square deal!" He pointed a wavering finger. "You sound like a troublemaker, mister! How guilty do you plead?"

Suddenly it was not quite amusing. The judge's tone was drunkenly ugly. He wore a tattered wool blanket as a robe, a tin cup filled with a raisin and prune brew served as a gavel. Don Carlos put a reassuring hand on the boy's thin shoulder. He said, "We plead guilty. Now what's the charge?"

The judge squinted. "Prisoner, you're accused of being Paul Wyatt. How do you plead?"

"Guilty with an explanation," Don Carlos announced.

"No explanations! You're charged with being under suspicion!"

"Guilty!"

"You're charged with being handy when we went looking."

"Guilty!"

"You're charged with claiming you're innocent!"

"Guilty!"

"And now," the judge banged the gavel, "is there a good reason not to hand out a stiff sentence?"

All this went on a note of challenge. It was absurd, Don Carlos recalled, but he had found himself shaking. This was meant in sport, a standard prison joke, but it was at the frightened boy's expense and a generous anger was rising. It was suddenly all too real.

"What about a trial?" he had asked sharply.

"A trial? Are you trying to defy this here court, mister?" The judge rose, swaying, and thrust his fist out. "Why, you greaser! Is there any of this that you want?"

In the sudden quiet, the lamps cast enormous shadows on the walls. One of the prisoners complained, "What's this for, Earl? What's the fuss about?"

This was too ridiculous, Don Carlos thought. This was not the courtroom. No issues were at stake. How odd that his heart should be pounding! He turned sardonically. "What can I say? That my client is innocent? That he doesn't want to play the game? That the court has no jurisdiction? That he has had no hand in making the rules?" He threw back his head and laughed harshly. His neck with its naked tendons was suddenly an old man's. "No, this justice is as good as any! We throw ourselves on the court's mercy."

There was an uncertain quiet.

"One dollar," muttered the judge.

"Very fair!" Don Carlos curtly tossed a dollar on the bench. He patted the boy's shoulder and returned to the heap of letters waiting in his cell. He had sat at his bench rigid while his candle guttered and melted, unable to write or think. He could not understand himself. He was a man of mind and discipline, but under the goad, his anger had become a thing with its own will, a force stronger than reason.

He stared at a sonnet of San Juan de la Cruz of the 16th century sent him from Barcelona:

> *¿Qué tengo yo que mi amistad procuras?*
> *¿Qué interés se te sique, Jesús mío,*
> *que a mi puerta, cubierta de rocío,*
> *pasas las noches del invierno oscuras?*

The lines blurred. *Que pasas las noches del invierno oscuras!* He sighed. The dark nights of winter were passing indeed. At his cell door, the boy shivered with doglike devotion. He looked up somberly.

"You must sleep, *hijo mío*," he said softly. "Then they cannot touch you! Eh? Isn't that so? There is nothing one cannot endure, if only sleep comes!"

"Yes, sir," said the boy, sniveling.

The train of thought went on until in the distance a cock crowed, and the white planet disappeared. After a time, a winter sky lighted the cell and it was morning.

"Up, up, up!" came the call. "Everybody up!"

Don Carlos sat up in the cold brisk morning. After his devotions, he bathed carefully and trimmed his beard with care. He did not like his face in the mirror. His nose and cheekbones jutted like red angry things, and his cheeks were sunken. His beard was white. He felt lightheaded as he snipped the hairs of his nostrils with a trembling hand. He dressed in his immaculate best, gulped the cold bitter coffee brought by a trusty to his cell, and was ready for the day.

"That's no way," urged the trusty, an elderly ranch hand convicted of cow theft. "You got to defend yourself in court, Mr. De Niza. If you don't eat, how can you think?"

"Let me be, Frank!" said Don Carlos irritably. How could he explain that he had taken to vomiting his food, that for months he had been living on coffee? He said, "I could not eat." He strode off and knocked. "Ready!"

"Good luck!" a prisoner called.

"Eh?" He looked up, and the circle of faces, ragged and beaten fellows, suddenly stood out clearly as persons. "Why, thank you," he said with surprise. He tousled the boy's head and left.

When finally the gate behind the courthouse swung open, the sheriff was waiting, dressed in dark serge and wearing a black bow tie. Don Carlos measured him and held out his wrists.

"My ornaments," he said with irony.

Kyle tilted back his stetson and scowled. "I swear, Carlos, that ain't funny. Can't you get into your head this is nothing personal?"

"I find it extremely personal!"

"I don't see any call for this resentful attitude. I'm only doing my job. After all"—Kyle puffed his cheeks angrily—"I could let you eat the regular lockup food. I don't have to keep Consuelo cooking for you."

Don Carlos stared with contempt. After inflicting a mortal injury, the fellow was begging somehow for his forgiveness if not, he thought acidly, for approval. Well, it was a thing to expect.

"I could do without this nonsense," he said curtly. "If your wife won't sleep with you, it shows her good sense. Take your troubles to the priest."

Kyle flushed with anger. The strain in his household was not a secret. And his deputies were exchanging covert glances of amusement. Late into the night the fierce quarrels raged, with Consuelo shouting that she could not show her face among her people, for the thing with Don Carlos was a scandal! In the Cimarron country, she screamed, there was a burning resentment and what could she say? For months now, she had slept in a separate room while he smashed the ornaments and in cold fury got drunk and spent the hours at Tía María's, weeping in his beer.

The sheriff thrust his face forward.

"Carlos, I try to be fair, but if you get out of swinging, which you won't," he grated murderously, "I'm making this a personal matter between you and me."

Don Carlos measured him and spat full in the man's face. "*Cabrón!*"

The sheriff stood back and wiped his face and examined the spittle. His great hands opened and closed.

"All right!" he said quietly. "Inside!"

The prisoner was taken through a jammed corridor to the large sparsely furnished office set aside for the defense. A mutter of anger followed him. Outside a light rain had been falling and the stink of wet wool was strong. As the door opened, Doña María turned from the window and they faced each other for the first time in months. Her expression was resentful.

"Carlos," she said in a low voice.

He replied stiffly, "My dear!"

Something had happened to him, she saw. His eyes were touched with pain, they seemed to stare out of burning pools of hate. Her hand went to her heart. "Are you ill, Carlos?"

"Why are you here?" he asked coldly. He nodded formally to his lawyers in the background. McKeever at the window with folded arms. Young Martin at the desk with a book. An unhappy Dominguez was holding a file. He added sharply, "This is no place for you, María, I thought I made it clear!"

She was breathing heavily under strong emotion. "What is this they tell me, Carlos?" she demanded. "How can your lawyers advise you, if you won't help them? Why must you be so impossible?"

He closed his eyes wearily. "I'm in no mood for a scene, María. You're simply making this worse. I want you to go home."

"Home?" She clutched at her hair. "To eat my heart out? Not knowing what you're planning? Not able to help?" She stared at him and burst out, "Oh, no! My feelings mean nothing! Not mine, not the children's! We're less than nothing! What do you expect?"

"You are my wife!" he said quietly. "I expect you to behave!"

She laughed wildly. "Am I your wife? Since when? Do you treat me like a wife? Do you protect me? Or the children? What happens if these men kill you?"

"You will—" he interrupted.

"No, I will not!" she swept on. "These damned ideas of yours! They mean more to you than your family! Am I supposed to thank you? Or feel grateful? They are killing you, these fine notions! Can I sit home while you let this happen?" She pressed her trembling fists to her mouth. "*En Nombre de Dios,* what are you planning to tell the Court?"

Don Carlos closed his eyes. "This is embarrassing, Mr. McKeever. Didn't I make it clear that I don't want my wife here?"

At the window McKeever put aside his cigar. "You've made nothing clear," he said wearily. "Frankly, I asked her to come. We're at the end of the case, and you've put me in a difficult position. Perhaps she can get you to make sense."

Don Carlos turned. "José?"

Dominguez shrugged miserably. "If you won't take legal advice, Carlos, at least listen to María. She has as much a stake in this trial as you. Perhaps more."

Don Carlos clasped his hands behind his back. "Very well! What is the purpose?"

"The purpose?" McKeever rubbed his tired eyes with the hopeless realization that this confrontation had failed. He turned to Martin. "How many witnesses for the Territory, Em?"

The young lawyer opened a buckram ledger. "Eighty-seven," he said with a grim tug at his goatee. "We put in sixty-two."

McKeever resumed his thoughtful smoking. "As many as that?" he murmured. "Good Lord!" Could anyone understand what that meant? Dreary toilsome nights of preparation. Traps and stratagems which so often failed. Lies and moral filth. Things in his own camp he dared not know too closely. Doubts. And all this grinding strife with an unrelenting adversary to be carried with an outward appearance of ease. He looked up with some anger. "All those witnesses, De Niza, and now—you!" He pointed his cigar. "I've got to decide whether to let you take the stand."

"I will give testimony," Don Carlos said harshly. "Those are my instructions."

McKeever studied the long firm ash, wondering wearily how to deal with the impossible fellow. "Regardless of your views, De Niza, I'm not in a position to make a decision. As I told your wife, this case is in balance. It can still go either way. How will you deal with Canty's version of the meeting in the Sierra Blanca last December?"

Don Carlos grimaced sourly. "Canty!"

"I hope you do as well. His testimony was pretty convincing! Right now"—McKeever cocked a brow—"I'm not sure whether you had that meeting or not."

Don Carlos said nothing.

McKeever went on. "If the jury believe Canty's version, they'll convict. If they reject his testimony, they've got to acquit. That's the law."

"Ah, the law!"

"There's no need for irony!" the lawyer said sharply. "That's how the Court will charge. Trouble is, you can never figure what a jury will do. That's true, East or West. Otherwise—" He paused to rub his face stiffly. "Otherwise I'd say we're in fair shape. If the jury don't see that he's a degenerate criminal, we might as well shut up shop." He strode back and forth, slouching, sunk in thought, seeking to pierce the fog of indecision. "He's a lunatic, and in any other case, I'd go to the jury on my summation. But now, I'm simply afraid to take that chance."

There was a silence. In the corridor outside could be heard the tread of heavy men.

"Have you finished?" Don Carlos asked coldly.

"Just about," McKeever said.

"Then may I smoke? María, my dear, you will not mind." He gave a ghastly grin as the sweat burst from his forehead. "My nerves, these days, you know. I've become an addict."

She saw the graven lines deepen, the agonized muscles of his jaw. "I do not mind," she said. "I do not mind anything."

He inclined his head and lit a cigarette with shaking hands. He closed his eyes exhaustedly. "Mr. McKeever, I don't wish to be a difficult client. If I object to having my wife in court, it's for a good

166

reason. I want to spare her this distress, and also myself. It's hard enough as it is." He waited for a throbbing in his head to ease. "I appreciate your efforts, please believe me. Whatever happens, I have no complaints. You've met these problems like a master." He smiled wanly. "You may be an Anglo, but you're a decent enough fellow."

"Thank you," McKeever said drily.

"Well, what do you wish?"

"If you don't take the stand," McKeever put it nicely, "we'll lose the point by default. On the other hand—" He paused.

"Yes?"

"If you don't carry the jury, the whole case can collapse. We've simply got to meet the issue directly. Now"—he thrust out a finger—"what do you intend to say?"

Don Carlos hesitated. From the window came the sound of the mob below, not loud, a mutter of hate.

Doña María put out her hands. "Carlos," she begged, "why are you holding back? Why?"

"Why?" He stared at his ashen wife. "My dear," he said painfully, "is it so hard to understand? These men are talking trifles. Did I meet Canty here or there? How did he get the shotguns? Did we pass a crippled Indian near the spring? Was Sam Trister there? This is all nonsense. If they will believe I could kill the old man, I can't change them. If not, my denials will mean nothing. I am Carlos de Niza. I stand for something!"

"But you must say something!" she cried hoarsely.

"Ah, yes!" He nodded grimly. "I must say something. But all this business of evidence and alibis! It's nonsense and I'm simply not interested! I will take the stand and then they will hear." A red film seemed to glaze his eyes. "They will surely hear, all of them! The truth! The Anglos will hear from me!"

She stood back in horror.

"*Madre!*" she cried. "He is mad!"

"Not mad! Sane! I will know what to say!"

She faced him foursquare, hands on hips. "You fool!" she cried hoarsely. "I'm sick of these gestures. You're not on a platform now, you're in their court, the Anglos. They intend to hang you. Well, let them!" she shouted. "I hope Hogarth has his way! Do you hear, his way! Forget me! Forget the children! But do you know about this man?" She pointed to McKeever. "Do you know what this has cost him? Do you know about the nights he has walked the floor? Do you know about *his* son?"

Don Carlos turned. "Your son? What does she mean?"

McKeever shrugged. "It's nothing."

167

Don Carlos paused with sudden concern, "No, I want to know."

"A little accident last night," McKeever said irritably. "Please don't dramatize it, Mrs. De Niza. It wasn't important."

"Not important?" She laughed harshly. "You're two of a kind!"

She was referring to an event of the night before. They were in the dining room finishing an early supper, smoking and discussing the last phases of the trial. McKeever had been sipping tea, listening to the laughter from the garden. He heard Jeff call, "Here, Niña! Reach for it, girl! Upsy, upsy!"

He took his glass to the window. The others, Martin and Dominguez and the detectives, were reviewing the testimony of a Customs guard at El Paso who remembered the shotguns crossing the border in Trister's pack. It was a pretty sight in the garden. Jeff was standing on a chair teasing the doe with a lump of sugar on a string. Her brown eyes winked moistly as she danced about him, reaching for the morsel. She was now the height of a pony, tame and affectionate and graceful. McKeever was smiling when the thing happened.

For a moment his heart froze. As the doe reared, her sharp hooves hit out like pistons, striking the boy's right side repeatedly. The chair tilted and the boy fell. The doe swallowed the sugar and trotted off, lapping her muzzle. Jeff lay on the grass in pain.

"Oh, God!" McKeever cried. He dropped his glass and rushed out with the others. "Jeff, what is it?"

"Oh!" The boy grimaced. "Nothing, I guess!" he said doubtfully. His hand went to his rib. "I don't s'pose."

"Here, let me see." McKeever opened the shirt. The smooth tanned skin was dotted with small brown moles; the pattern was exactly his own, a series of triangles at the faintly marked nipples. He touched the ribs. There were no contusions but a light swelling was beginning to rise.

"Ow, that hurts!" the boy complained.

"Is it bad?"

"No!" Jeff sweated with pain. "I guess I was surprised, that's all. I shouldn't have stood on the chair."

McKeever looked about, shaken. The others had followed and there was about him a circle of advisers, but no one seemed to know what to do.

As it turned out, it was more frightening than anything else. The pain at first was not too severe, but when, after dark, Dr. Kimball drove up to make an examination, the swelling had turned an angry purple. The doctor grunted and packed his bag.

"Might be a broken rib, might not," he advised. "We'll tape him up and see what happens."

"Is it serious?" McKeever asked worriedly.

"At his age?" The doctor was amused. "No, just painful. It ought to heal in a few weeks. Should teach him not to play with a growing deer. Those sharp hooves are like little axes. Lucky she didn't cut his face. I seem to remember I warned him once."

And that was all. When they put the boy to bed, he complained but he slept soundly and easily and McKeever's agitation subsided. Still, it had been a fright, and he found it hard to work over the thousands of pages of testimony for his expected summation at the end of the case.

Doña María had discovered him toward morning, awake at his desk, haggard and distressed, with the pages swimming before his eyes. The room was chilly and she brought hot chocolate. They sat almost till dawn talking of the accidents of life.

"You are a remarkable man," she said, stirring the bitter unsweetened brew. "I have been watching! I know what I know! *Ya!*"

He raised his brows. "Remarkable?"

"To work as you do!" she pointed out. "This devotion to my husband when your boy is so ill!"

"Jeff will be all right," he answered, rubbing his eyes. "It's you I'm concerned about, Mrs. De Niza! This trial is coming to an end, and I'll be finished with it! But I'm not so sure of you."

Her laugh was melancholy.

"I live for each day as it comes." She stared at her drink. "I cannot think of life without Carlos. Before I was ten, I loved him. When I became a woman, he began to look at me. I knew then I would marry him or none at all. When one has known a man like Carlos, there can be none other. Mr. McKeever," she said in a dry whisper, her eyes shining with tears, "he is a great soul. I am a simple woman, but I have always known his greatness." She placed a fist over her heart. "I have known it here! He has given me unhappiness, but I would change nothing! Yet now—" She paused.

"Yes?" he asked gently.

"I don't know." She made a gesture of despair. "What has it all come to? When he was young, there was an excitement in his work, a hope. There were men around him with ideas. They were writers and talkers. *Dios mío!* How they argued till all hours! Our house was filled with them. Plans! Schemes! I suppose it was always hopeless, but they never thought so." She laughed harshly. "Now where are they all? Pedro Gallegos! Juan de la Torre! Jesús Gomez! Great names once, now all gone. One by one, they died or they fell away.

169

When Carlos had influence, they flocked to him. You should have seen him when his voice meant something! Now he is old and he stands alone. If it weren't for you and Don José and a few others, he would be lost indeed." She looked up. "What will happen?"

"I don't know," he said gently. "As you know, I've never made promises."

"If only it weren't for the children!" she sighed. "*Ay*, prayer does not help." She stared into her cup and her iron-gray braids hung like helpless things. "I shall never forget your kindness to them."

He finished his chocolate. It was in the local taste, but it seemed right. "I've enjoyed them," he smiled bleakly, "and they've been good for Jeff."

"Ah, your boy!" She made a sucking sound of pity. "How cruel we are! I know better than anyone what this has cost you, and even I forget! I too am thinking only of myself, it seems!" She raised her hands. "But if they take my husband, what's the good of it all?"

"The good?" McKeever put aside his cup. "A man is two things, Mrs. De Niza. What he does, and what he is. What's done to him by others, after a certain age, becomes not important. I would think of that." She looked up and saw the compassion in his eyes. She shivered in the chill and nodded. "Yes," she said simply. "I will not forget."

They sat in silence until she returned to her room. He sat alone with his transcripts, drained of all feeling, until he gave up the hopeless work and tried without success to sleep.

McKeever brought his thoughts back to the witness room as Doña María echoed his last words. "It was not important?" she cried. She turned to her husband and told him of the accident. "Carlos, this man feels more for your life than you! In his worst moments, he has never thought of deserting. Do you think of that? Do you consider what you are costing him? No! You are unnatural! I hate you! I hope they do their worst."

He stepped to her. "My dear," he began.

"Don't touch me!" she cried.

"I can't bear that you feel this way," he said helplessly. "I love you, but what can I do?" His hands dropped. "I am what I am."

"Love me?" She turned wildly to the others. "Do you hear? He loves me! Ah, *Madre, Madre!*" She looked about desperately, her face a grimace of laughter. "You—!" She choked and stood wringing her hands. As it had to come, she burst into tears, and deep sobs racked her stout body. She felt her nose and eyes swell with grief as she stood swaying, a middle-aged pallid woman with heavy features, clutching a damp handkerchief. He embraced her and stroked

170

her. "*Querida*," he murmured, and there were other endearments and kissing of her hair until the spasm of grief had flushed itself out.

"Oh, Carlos!" She wiped her eyes and blew her nose. "My love, my husband!"

He raised her head gently. "My dear, you must not worry. I will give a good account of myself, you will see!"

There was an embarrassed moment.

"I told you to expect this," said Dominguez gloomily, his ugly face downcast. "This is Carlos for you!"

The woman turned to the lawyer. "What will you do now?"

McKeever rubbed his face. "I don't know," he said dispiritedly. "There're still some loose ends waiting for us. We'll see." He opened the door and said with haggard humor, "After you, Don Quixote!"

"Quixote?" The prisoner was amused. "Oh, very good!" he laughed. "But after all, why not?" He fluffed his beard with an air of relish. "Don Quixote!"

With a chuckle, he passed shakily through the ugly crowd into the court and another morning of the long trial began.

At this moment, a hundred miles to the south, the cow man turned from the pleasant sizzle of frying bacon to shield his eyes and study the figure in the distance. The morning sun was at his back and the air was clear, but it was too far and too small to make out. It was a black dot against the sloping rusty hills which formed the west wall of the valley.

He poked the skillet and gave this some thought. The cattle about him lowed and bellowed in the grass. A steer lowered its head and pawed the earth; there was a tossing of dust over its flanks and then it trotted off.

He cursed softly, without conviction, and finished a breakfast of bacon and beans and drank his coffee. The fire of cow chips burned low, the acrid smoke drifted into the sky. That black dot now! It had appeared on that distant hill the day before. Human or animal, he thought, it should have moved—but what could it be? Out there occasional antelope or bear wandered; there were wild jack burros and mustangs seeking the grasses at the point where the wilderness of sand and lava beds began, but he did not think it was any of these. The buzzards were still floating high.

Why did it not move? The thing troubled him. He broke camp and mounted his horse and started for the hill at an easy canter. . . .

He found her resting in a patch of yucca. In spring, the rains would bring out the clusters of white blossoms, but now the plants were spiky. She was a Navajo, he decided. What was she doing so

171

far south? She looked up with wary fathomless eyes. He held up his open palm and smiled and dismounted.

"Hello," he said pleasantly. "What's the trouble?"

She lay panting with her back to a boulder. Behind her a path led into a ravine which seemed to pass toward the south. Her flat broad face was seamed with deep lines, wizened, spare; its network of wrinkles told of a lifetime of squinting into the sun. Her long black hair was flat on her coppery forehead. She wore a gingham dress under her blanket. Her only ornament was a necklace of turquoise and silver, the sort sold to *turistas* in the curio shops at Santa Fe.

She stared up at the freckled smiling face. He was to her eyes a simple cow hand, an American wearing a red bandanna and familiar dusty chapparals. Her mouth opened and closed.

"McKeever," she said harshly.

He continued to smile. "Yeah?"

"McKeever."

Her voice was a croak but it was clear enough. He squatted and gently wiped the dried crusts from the corners of her mouth.

"Water?" He smiled. "*Agua?*"

She nodded weakly. Her eyes were on his freckled young face as she let the water overflow and run into her dress. She pointed to her swollen ankle; this and a shrill bray from the ravine told the story. The burro had strayed and her ankle, broken or sprained, had hobbled her. He examined the injury with strong stubby fingers, clucking softly with sympathy. "Oh me, oh my." It was a simple accident but she might have died.

"McKeever, hey?" He smiled. "Well, old lady, I'm a friend of his. What's this about?"

She stared at him. "Friend?" she asked weakly.

He nodded. "You looking for him?"

"Yes."

"You savvy English?"

"Yes." She made a rolling motion with her fingers and pointed to the tag dangling from his shirt pocket.

With his pleasant grin, he formed a cigarette and tapped out the makings. "You want me to take you to him?" he asked. She waited until he had wet the paper. When he had placed the cigarette in her mouth, she smoked a moment and nodded.

"You want to talk to him?" he asked.

"Yes."

"Do you want to tell me about it?"

She smoked hungrily and shook her head. Without doubt, he thought, she had a message. Why else would an old Navajo woman

172

want the eastern lawyer? He had some shrewd idea who she was. His grin widened. *"Cómo se llama?* How are you known?"

She stared at him blankly.

"All right." He knew this stubborn retreat into silence. The Navajo were jolly among themselves; cheerful, hard-working, friendly; they had their jokes, salacious and otherwise, but this imperturbability was the face to show the enemy. He watched a rabbit leap off into the yucca, kicking up puffs of dust. "Take it easy, old lady," he said softly. "I'll take you. Think you can ride?"

She nodded, too exhausted to talk. She sipped at the water bottle while he rounded up the burro. When he returned with the unwilling little beast, she broke out a handful of parched corn which she chewed with a noisy crackling. She continued to rest and when the sun was high, she seemed better.

"Come on, old lady, whatever your name might be," he said. He helped her mount the burro. The beast was small but the Navajo woman was a light burden, all string and bones. She sat sideways on the improvised pack and drew a shawl over her eyes against the sun.

They started down the trail—two dots moving alone in the vast reaches of the valley. Dust and yucca gave way to grasses and then to moist sand as they came to the river. He took the lead, riding easily and singing the mournful songs of the range to pass time, and she followed.

A day passed and then a night.

When finally the path turned and he guided her to the great stone house of the Hogarth Ranch, she realized her mistake, but by then it was too late.

Don Carlos took his seat at the defense table. He locked his fingers behind his neck and stared at the ceiling. The lawyers took their places with practiced ease. Behind the prisoner the bailiffs thrust hands into belts, letting boredom glaze their eyes. At strategic points Kyle's deputies stood about with a display of badges and guns.

The clerk made an impatient gesture. The wall clock showed that they were an hour late. "Are you ready, Mr. McKeever?" he called.

McKeever nodded. "Ready."

The clerk trotted to the rear and opened the door. "All right, gentlemen."

The twelve men filed into place with an easy slouch. Some traces of a smile showed that they had left a moment of laughter behind. They scuffed their chairs, worked tongues over teeth, scratched, stared at the ceiling, and gazed blankly at the cold bright view outside.

173

McKeever studied them somberly. Anglos all, he thought, cattle-men and miners, storekeepers, a blacksmith, the local assayist and one timber cutter. Blue and gray eyes. Eight Protestants, three Catholics, one Jew.

In a way, he blamed himself for the composition of the jury. The venire had originally comprised both Spanish and Anglo names, but mysteriously all the Spanish had appeared delinquent on the collector's roll of taxes for Hogarth County and ineligible for jury duty; and equally so all Anglo taxes had been fully paid. It was a hole he had failed to plug. Ah, well, it was a point for his bill of exceptions. Weak, but still something.

All Anglos? Not quite. Juror Eight was Willie Lopez, a stonecutter, sallow, curly-haired, furtive and a miserable weakling. It was clear why Taft had failed to challenge him. Then Juror Six. Ike Goldman. Dry goods. Snub-nosed, washy blue eyes, pink skin, wispy blond hair. Only his accent told a special story—a man grown since first days as a Galveston peddler from pack on back, selling ribbons and gewgaws in blazing summer and icy winter, to a horse, then a store, until now he sat as a man of substance with a place in the land.

A man named Manuel Garcia made his way through the crowd. His coloring was fair—a clear face with a neat straight nose and white mustaches. He affected the dress of a cattleman, ornate high leather boots, an elegant embroidered shirt, silk scarf and creamy stetson. He took a seat down forward. He folded his arms and idly glanced at a thrush swinging on a twig at the window. McKeever turned away. Officially he had no knowledge of this man's plans.

At the press table, Ida Montgomery gave him a wink of encouragement and he smiled with the gloomy thought that at least in the outside world his stock was high. It was questionable whether this outside support was worth the price of local resentment. John Macy Bellew smoothed his bangs, and his eyes, cool and amused, slid toward the empty seat being held for Florence Hogarth.

McKeever flushed with some sense of wonder at himself. He was a worldly man, an experienced trial lawyer, and here he sat blushing like a schoolboy. It was expected that gossip would swirl and eddy around a protracted trial of high passions. Nothing in that sensitive atmosphere could long remain hidden—nothing at least so strong as the miserable ache for Florence within him. Since the night at Polk's Spring—the thought was a solace!—they had tried in public to remain formal and circumspect, but the world had a way of smelling out these things. Now where was she? he wondered restlessly. This would be her first absence from the trial. He nodded stonily at Bellew and sank into his chair, eyes closed, patting his finger tips gently, excluding everything but the sound of Don Carlos's heavy breathing at his side.

Two loud raps sounded. "All rise!"

Millikan strode in with his usual look of dark displeasure, bunching his robe. He mounted the bench and opened the Bible to his text for the day, which he read silently to himself. His hectoring manner, McKeever noted, had diminished since the day the blind widow had testified. He was less scarlet with passion, more the judge, more respectful to defense counsel. Perhaps the intense efforts of the defense had sobered him, perhaps he was seeking to protect the record. It took a long time, the lawyer thought acidly, to whip some judges into shape, but it could be done.

Millikan busied himself with his minute book—the third since the trial had begun. He studied the proceedings of the prior day, then looked up and pointed his pen. "Will counsel step up to the bench?"

Mike Taft was up first, swaggering his paunch, incredulity in his wrinkled eyes, ready to boom fierce protest. McKeever wearily placed his elbows on the bench. About them clustered the lesser lights, looking as legal as possible. The jury settled down. They had learned to live with boredom. This was the ritual, the daily dance of the lawyers.

The judge said, "I'm now prepared to rule on the admission of the newspaper file, gentlemen. Exhibits numbered 153 to 232, offered by Mr. Taft. *La Luz.* Mr. Wilson"—this was to the stenographer—"will you take this." He turned the pages of the crumbling old newspapers and favored McKeever with a stare.

"Now sir, you've made quite an issue as to the admissibility of these exhibits. You've had a lot to say about the prejudice of this court"—he glanced up with a grim smile—"but I promised a fair trial, and I meant just that. You'll get justice here under the rules." He turned back to the Spanish text. "These editorials begin back in 'sixty-eight. In practically every issue, we get the defendant's views on the operation of our land laws. He takes exception to the legislation of Congress and the actual running of our land offices. Here and here and here"—he fingered the several issues marked by red silk ribbons—"he attacks the Congress itself. I'll skip the next issues. Let's come down to the Land Grant Case decisions we've heard so much about. Now look what he says about Judge Hanna the day the decision was handed down in Santa Fe. Here's a streamer headline." He turned the bound volume about.

La Pena del Talion! Ojo por Ojo y Diente por Diente!

175

McKeever polished his spectacles. *Lex Talionis! Eye for eye and tooth for tooth!* Would it pay to argue that text? In truth the Mosaic rule was one of mercy, not of rigor, one of limitation, not of exaction. It was properly to be read *"Not more than* an eye for an eye." In a harsh primitive society, it forbade more than monetary reparations. It was a shield against extermination and the limitless vengeance of the blood feud—for was not the Lord merciful and gracious? No, he concluded, such discussion here would fall on deaf ears. "I'm familiar enough with the exhibit," he said coldly. "I still press my objection. That last editorial was written two years before this crime. It is simply newspaper comment on a public matter."

Millikan continued to turn the leaves thoughtfully. "I think it's something more! These editorials form an unbroken series of attacks over a period of twenty years. They show a consistent hatred for our whole system of laws, and they end with a direct personal attack on the deceased. They continue down to the murder, and beyond."

McKeever said stolidly, "I don't see why all this should clutter the record. The exhibits speak for themselves. We contend—"

The judge smoothed the corners of his mouth with a hard smile. "We know what you contend. I rule"—he hesitated for a tantalizing moment—"I rule that these exhibits will not be received in evidence."

Mike Taft was taken aback. *"Not* received?"

"You may have an exception, Mr. Taft," the judge said coldly.

The prosecutor clutched at his bony skull which had burst into instant perspiration. "But, Judge! I don't see that, I swear! Here the man calls for revenge. He says the old judge ought to be exterminated like vermin. He even calls him a bastard. If that don't show motive, why, my God! what will?"

The judge said patiently, "The ruling stands."

McKeever cut in. Although the decision was in his favor he disliked the reasoning given. He asked, "May we have the basis of this ruling?"

The judge shoved back his chair on its casters. "There's no actual proof the defendant wrote these editorials. They are excluded as incompetent."

"No actual proof?" Taft protested. "Why, this is a newspaper, Judge! Carlos's name is all over the masthead! Why can't we presume—?"

Millikan said coolly, "We'll presume nothing, Mr. Taft. It's just not competent." He touched his thick brown vandyke with a delicate gesture. "At least, not at this time."

There was a significant pause.

McKeever said cautiously, "Your Honor, I made my objection eight weeks ago on a *number* of grounds. Aside from the question of competency, I urged that anything written twenty years ago is not relevant to a present state of mind. And even the recent issues prove nothing. A man can write an editorial without intending murder."

The judge blew away the brittle yellowing flakes of paper from his desk. "If the Territory can prove that the defendant actually made these writings," he said calmly, "I will allow them in evidence."

Taft suddenly started to chuckle. "Why sure, Judge, that's good enough. I'll take that ruling." With a pleased look, he took his seat.

McKeever returned to his place, shaken with dismay, and sat. Don Carlos asked for an explanation. They put their heads together and spoke in whispers. He said:

"The point is this. Under this ruling, the newspapers are now excluded from evidence. If you take the stand, then Taft can ask you whether you wrote these editorials. If you admit the writings, they'll go into evidence. It's a lot more effective that way from their point of view. The whole thing's a trap."

Evidently this thought had been developed at the prosecution table where a gobble of amusement could be heard.

The defendant followed this reasoning with anger. "I will not deny my own writings! Everyone knows what I stand for! Why else did I publish them, if not to be read?"

"Really, De Niza, I don't know." McKeever rubbed his eyes wearily. "You went the limit there. Some of that fantastic stuff you wrote is unprintable in English. Do you want Taft to rake you over all those old issues? Those files give him a lot of ammunition!"

Don Carlos brushed this aside. "What are you going to do?" he demanded loudly. "I am not afraid of the truth!" His eyes smoldered. "I want to know precisely what to expect! I have changed my mind about nothing!"

"Please, Carlos, the jury is listening," Dominguez begged. "Lower your voice!"

Don Carlos turned his eyes upward with grotesque effect till the whites gleamed. His throat strings were taut. "Be quiet, José! I am talking to the Anglo! I want to know what he plans!" He demanded, "Will you call me to the stand?"

McKeever shook his head with sick anxiety. "I can't take the responsibility," he said desperately. "Not unprepared! Let me ask for a recess—"

"It would change nothing!" Don Carlos retorted.

Dominguez tugged at his sleeve. "Carlos, for God's sake! The whole court is listening. What are you trying to do?"

The judge's voice cut through, "Mr. McKeever, do you have a witness?"

"No—Yes!"

The two voices spoke together. The judge glanced from lawyer to client. "Which is it?"

"Sir Judge, I wish to give testimony!" Don Carlos said strongly.

All at once, everyone seemed to be talking. The defense lawyers were up clustered about the prisoner. The bailiffs went down the aisles motioning spectators to their seats. A man arose from the press table and rushed out.

"The jury will disregard—" Millikan's voice was swallowed by Taft's howl. "It's a grandstand play!" the prosecutor bawled. "They know they're licked! Carlos don't dare take the stand and he knows it!" His goiter went purple with rage.

"Order! Order!"

When calm was restored, the judge turned to the prisoner with an air of curiosity. "You must address the Court through counsel, Mr. Defendant. I have repeatedly admonished you!" He returned to McKeever. "What is this about?"

Don Carlos threw off restraining hands. "I object to this procedure!" he said strongly.

Millikan tapped the gavel. "Be quiet, or I'll have you gagged!" he said angrily. "Your lawyer says one thing. You say another. You can't do both."

Don Carlos pointed a quivering finger. "I have the greatest respect for Mr. McKeever. He's honest and he knows what he is doing. Those are rare qualities in a lawyer—especially in combination." With all his anger, he paused at the flicker of amusement. "But his reasons are not mine!"

"H'm!" Millikan sat tapping his finger tips with perplexity. These outbursts were like dust devils on a hot street—quick stinging whirls of passion arising out of nowhere. Was there some plot of McKeever's in this? Hardly likely. The eastern master had a streak of cunning. He was persistent, indefatigable, ingenious, annoying, fighting for every trifling advantage, but trickery was not his style. The judge said with a reasonable air:

"You can't overrule your counsel, Mr. Defendant. He carries the responsibility here. You'll have to come to some agreement."

"May I answer?" Don Carlos asked ironically.

Millikan nodded wearily, "I suppose I can't stop you. Go ahead!"

"With all respect, unless Mr. McKeever agrees to call me, I shall apply to dismiss him as my lawyer."

"Oh, now!" The judge slipped back his black cuffs impatiently and arose. "You can't do that. You're not qualified. I'd have to appoint other counsel and believe me," he said grimly, "you won't like my choice. You can't do better than Mr. McKeever."

The lawyer folded his arms and bowed with a stony expression. "Praise from Sir Hubert, is praise indeed!"

"Well, well! We've got quite a maverick!" Millikan stood behind his high leather chair, hands resting on its studs. He gnawed his mustache. "Mr. McKeever, what do you say? If you like, I'll let you withdraw. But there won't be mistrial here, if that's what someone is working for."

They formed four points of a quadrangle—the judge gazing across the open Bible; the haggard lawyer; the prisoner trembling with passion; the prosecutor with amused eggshell eyes popping. The others had no wish to speak and McKeever dared not.

The lawyer groaned inwardly at the damage done. How could he risk placing an unprepared witness—even an acute formidable personality like Carlos de Niza—on the stand? What was that experience Carson had had in England recently? Or was it Hall whose client had thrown away his silly life at the Old Bailey? He drew a deep shuddering breath. The court was quiet. In his accustomed seat, Dan Hogarth was watching with fixed attention. Somewhere in the rear Doña María's pallid face was in the clutch of fear.

He sighed.

He could withdraw! It was as though a door to freedom had been opened. Under the circumstances, there could be no criticism.

Why should he not? He could leave this agony and return home to his son. Jeff! A pang gushed through him. No one else, not even Doña María, was aware that the boy had begun again to run a low-grade fever. It had become evident that morning when his rough heavy hand had touched the boy's forehead. It was the expected result of the accident, but possibly—it was the other thing!

And he was tired—tired!

A long interminable moment passed. Don Carlos turned, and the lines of suffering were deeply graven in his face. "I will not reproach you if you go," he said harshly. "This is my decision."

McKeever stared at the floor in the long moment which passed, then turned with somber gravity to the clerk. He said quietly:

"Kindly call the defendant to the stand."

179

Chapter XII

McKeever waited for the silence to deepen as the sound of slow painful steps crossed the well of the court. He adjusted his glasses to study a paper with a thoughtful air. But this was pretense. His eye was cocked to the jury and his mind was racing. The witness was wild, he thought desperately, and anything might be said. It would be necessary to bring him step by step into the heart of his testimony.

The judge leaned over. "Do you need the interpreter, Mr. Defendant?" Since the proceedings were bilingual, José María Alarid, the interpreter, who had been trimming his nails in obscurity behind the jury box, stepped forward. He looked like an elderly bearded schoolteacher with a hunted look.

"Thank you, no!" Don Carlos said harshly. "I prefer to be understood. I will testify in English."

The question had carried a subtle insult; the retort a challenge. The judge sank lower in his deep leather chair. "Swear the witness," he said curtly.

With deep solemnity, the oath was administered by the clerk for the hundred and fiftieth time in the trial. Don Carlos followed the formula with an air of thoughtful concern. "The truth?" he murmured with irony. "The whole truth? Oh, yes, indeed. I think we are entitled to so much."

From the point of vantage, he gazed out at the courtroom. To his right, he had a glimpse of the docket books on the long bench, the pens and inkwells, the carafe of water, the open Bible—

Out there, the faces had changed. In the first days, they had all been Anglos; now the Spanish had taken heart. Some were olive-skinned, dark-eyed; some blond types showed the persistent ancient Visigothic strains of the mother country; others, more coppery, revealed the later infusions. They had separated out: Anglos left, Spanish right—

In the midst of all this, his hand quaking, his privileged cigarillo smoking, the great yellow eyes of Dan Hogarth stared with fixed purpose—

When the clerk's chant had ended, McKeever threw aside all papers and sat back against the rail.

"Mr. De Niza, you are the defendant in this case?"

Don Carlos drew a deep breath. "I am!"

"Where do you live?"

"I am living in the county jail." The witness paused and repeated with deep irony, "The Hogarth County Jail!"

His deep rich voice was trembling almost as though he were nervous. He touched his feathery white beard and then as his hands shook, he placed them between his thighs and cleared his throat. McKeever felt his own heart beat faster with sympathy. He asked:

"And before that?"

"Before this trial, I was detained at the Fortress of San Felipe. It was an illegal place for detention. Part of the time I was in irons."

The judge tapped a pencil. "Do not volunteer information, sir. Just answer questions."

Don Carlos raised his brows. "My answers are my own," he said evenly.

Millikan swiveled to face the far window where the sun was high in the distant valley. "Go ahead!"

McKeever resumed. "Before that, sir, where did you live?"

"Before that?" Don Carlos murmured. "I had a home in the State of Chihuahua in the Republic of Mexico. It was where I moved after my lands were stolen from me."

The pencil tapped. "I must warn you—" the judge began.

The witness said curtly, "My home was last in Chihuahua. That is the answer!"

McKeever raised his hands. "Mr. De Niza, these are just preliminaries. Please bear with me. Did you live there with your wife and children?"

"I did."

"How old are your children?"

"Miguel is fifteen. Juan is nine."

"Is your wife in the courtroom?"

"She is."

The eyes of the jury went to the rear. Doña María was one of the few women in court. She sat with eyes closed. An expression of suffering was in her face. Beside her, with an air of distinction, sat the archbishop of the diocese, his fine eyes liquid and perceptive of the deep currents of feeling at play. McKeever resumed:

"How long have you been married?"

The witness paused. "What have these things to do with this trial?" he asked impatiently. "I am not here to discuss my family affairs, sir."

Mike Taft let a slow grin grow.

McKeever said patiently, "Please answer the question."

"Twenty years," Don Carlos said angrily. "I must say—"

McKeever raised a restraining hand. "Where were you born?"

Don Carlos hesitated. "I was born in Cuatro Rios," he said slowly. "About ten miles away."

"Can that point be seen from this courtroom?"

"It can."

"Is there a landmark now there?"

"Yes. There still stand the ruins of my father's house. The foundations can be traced at the river's bend at the point once called La Puente de las Estrellas. It stands now five hundred yards from the ranchhouse of the Hogarths."

Mike Taft was up bawling objections.

"Overruled," said the judge firmly. "I suppose this will lead to something."

McKeever said in his friendly way, "When was the last time you saw that home?"

"Perhaps thirty or forty years ago," Don Carlos said in a low voice. "I cannot be sure."

"Were you born in that house?"

"I was."

"And your father?"

"My father too."

"And your father's father?"

Don Carlos said grimly, "The house was built in 1743 when the older house burned down. The original hearthstone is still there to be seen. It was placed in 1674 by my remote ancestor, Don Francisco de Niza. That house descended to me upon the death of my father forty-five years ago. I trust that you are now fully informed," he added with asperity. "Let us get on to the matters at hand."

McKeever gazed around.

The spectators now quieted as the witness continued to set forth the origins of the De Niza family. All this went on under his friendly gentle guidance until Don Carlos broke in angrily.

"Are you going to ask about the lands of my family?" he asked in a loud challenge. "Will you develop the circumstances under which they were stolen?"

The judge tapped his pencil twice.

"Not yet!" McKeever held a gush of exasperation in check. "Mr.

De Niza, do you have anything against me personally?" he demanded sharply.

Don Carlos was taken aback by the tone. "Eh? Against you? Oh no!"

"Do you believe I'm acting in your interests?"

"I daresay you're doing your best."

"Are you trying to embarrass me?"

"Certainly not, but—"

"Then permit me to be the lawyer! Suppose you confine yourself to answers. Your chance will come soon enough!"

Mike Taft arose with his broad grin. "Now, Judge, I find this colloquy entertaining but I can't imagine any rule of evidence to cover it. I object to all this stage play. I don't know what they think they're cooking up."

"Denied!" With a puzzled look, Millikan turned to the witness. "Mr. Defendant, I suggest you let Mr. McKeever put the questions."

"Then let's get down to the case!" Don Carlos retorted.

An impossible man! McKeever silently cursed his dogged obstinacy. "Very well!" he said aloud. "I'll let you have your own way, but first let us cover a point. Are you a citizen of the United States?"

Don Carlos drew a deep breath. There was a mutter of surprise. The question was obviously in point and yet it was raised for the first time.

"I acquired that distinction under the Treaty," he said harshly. "In those first years, I believed in the promises made. I thought our lands and titles would be honored. That was before the new land laws were introduced. I was young."

"You never surrendered citizenship?"

"No!"

"Why?"

The witness hesitated. "It was a tactic," he said grimly. "I thought it might help with my work."

"Ah!" McKeever bent over the table, studied his notes, and then looked up over his spectacles. "Now, sir, when, if ever, did you first meet the deceased, Douglas Hanna?"

There was a long pause. This was the first mention of the name of the slain man. Someone in the rear coughed and there was a sound of a door opening and closing.

"Douglas Hanna?" Don Carlos raised a shaking hand to his face. A dim and faded picture seemed to stand vivid in his mind. He looked up darkly. "When they came to take the Land," he cried with a flush of passion. "More than forty years ago! And now, sir, will you permit me—?"

McKeever raised his hand. "Please, Mr. De Niza!" he said strongly. "I will come to all that—"

With a violent gesture, Don Carlos took off his spectacles and smashed them on the rail. The splinters went flying. "No, we will deal with the issues now! You're trying to do too much, sir! You're trying to paint me in false colors. Well, that's ridiculous. These people know Carlos de Niza. I don't intend to hide behind your sentimentalities!"

"I beg you!" McKeever cried in alarm.

"No, sir!" Don Carlos gripped the arms of the chair. "This is almost amusing!" he said angrily. "This jury of Anglos for months has listened to these filthy dogs besmirching me. What am I supposed to answer, hey? That I never knew this miserable Tom Canty? Nonsense! Of course I knew him! In those days, we took any man who could use a gun. He was insane, a liar in his cradle, a mad dog. But he was a Spanish man and he claimed he was with us. That was forty years ago. Am I supposed to pervert the past?"

He shook with the effort. His hoarse strained voice had risen to a shout and he had gone scarlet. Old and forgotten scenes seemed to stand alive before his burning eyes.

"He had a lot to say about the so-called *quetzals!* Why that simple emblem should loom so large, I cannot say. We *quetzals* are a legitimate political party. I founded the organization. I wrote the Sonora Program. The fundamental ideas are mine. Why should I deny that? The restoration of these lands to Spain is the dream of my life. The true Faith is my guide. Do you expect me to spit in my mother's milk? Well, well!" He drew breath with a loud wheeze. "Did Canty join us? Of course he did, just as he stated. It was easy enough. We were being burned and pillaged. We needed every hand. He seemed a likely ruffian and we took him on. I can only plead that he was under strict surveillance until we found him out. I imagine his grudge goes back to a certain day when we stood in judgment on him. If you examine his fat buttocks, you may still see the scars of the lash. Fifty of them! I regret only that we did not carry out sentence of death."

Millikan frowned. "Do you mean to say—?"

"I say nothing!" Don Carlos swept on. "I am talking to my friends in this room and to none else. If you wish that delectable pleasure, you may examine the scars yourself. Should I answer to the Kennedy outrage? There was such an episode! Canty says that he cut off the hands of a dead child under my orders to create a political impression. Should I deny that? And the Wilkinson affair. Am I supposed to answer to this? Did I order him to defile the girl before her father's eyes? If that's what you expect, my dear lawyer, remove the thought from your mind. I have no such intention. I'll say only this. These outrages were against orders. When Abrán Valdez, the son of Onofre Valdez, was castrated, everyone knew the reason."

Don Carlos saw that his finger was bleeding from a glass splinter and the bright arterial blood was falling in drops.

"So much for background. Now as to conspiracy. I concede that the shotguns are mine. I concede that Canty met me in the Sierra Blanca between the Feast Day of Nuestra Señora de Guadalupe and the Posadas. Why not? Out in the hills trails cross. One man meets another. Such things happen. But what was said between us I will not discuss. That man"—he pointed a quivering finger at the sheriff asprawl at the rail—"that man knows what was said. I will throw out a suggestion. That poor devil Sam Trister! Where is he? Why is he hidden? I leave that question for the historians. We will not find out in this court."

"De Niza!" McKeever cried with despair.

The witness glared at a point in space, his breath heaving with passion. "Did I write that Douglas Hanna was fit for death? Indeed, I did. I said it then and I say it now. He was an Anglo among Anglos. He was with them from the beginning, the leader of the soldiers, the friend and brother of Hogarth, the thief of the lands of my family. The one was Faust, the other Mephistopheles. Are we not men, the Spanish? The blood in us runs. See!" He held out a white finger and the bright drops fell. Once and twice and again. He watched the splashes on the oiled flooring and then looked up to McKeever with a hard smile of hate.

There was only the sound of heavy panting. After a moment, the judge picked up his pen and made a brief note. He said quietly, "Please continue, sir."

The lawyer took a step forward and put the next question.

"Mr. De Niza, did you hear the testimony of this man Tom Canty?"

"Eh?" The witness turned a burning eye. "Yes, I heard!"

"Did you in any way conspire with him to murder the deceased, Douglas Hanna?"

"I will not deal with that question," the witness said hoarsely.

"I implore you to answer."

"I decline to do so."

In the rear, a coarse low voice muttered, "Jesus Almighty!"

McKeever stepped forward in the silence. He held up trembling hands. Behind him the asthmatic wheezing of his opponent rose and fell. He said in a strained voice, "I'm sure the Court appreciates your

185

feelings, Mr. De Niza. We understand your resentment, but you must answer to the indictment. I beg you not to be whimsical."

"Ah? I appear whimsical then? Well, well!" With a flourish, almost with enjoyment, the witness lightly brushed his beard. "Why *must* I answer? You have pleaded not guilty on my behalf. Why isn't that enough?"

McKeever stood irresolute. A dull throbbing at his temples felt unendurable. His eye caught the first juror, a strapping blacksmith, staring in bald astonishment. His mind was curiously divided and part of his thoughts were elsewhere. Through the haze, he demanded, "Did you do any of the acts charged in the indictment?"

"The indictment?" The witness continued to stroke his beard. "I do not recognize that piece of paper," he said finally. "Nor do I recognize this court. These proceedings are a parody. What is their moral foundation? Where is their legitimacy? Can law be based on deceptions and broken treaties and theft?" He folded his arms with scorn. "Oh no, my dear lawyer, let the Anglos do what they wish. I admit nothing, I deny nothing. Today I am a victim of force. Tomorrow our time will come. I reject the jurisdiction!"

McKeever cried hoarsely, "Carlos—!"

"Save your breath, my lawyer," the witness said softly. "I am sorry to disappoint you. You have worked hard and faithfully and you deserve a better client. But explain to these dogs? Go into this filth? Nonsense! They would not believe a word I say! There is no truth or honor in them. From the beginning they've had in mind to hang me. Well, I suppose they can. Let the case stand."

In the rear, Doña María covered her face with shaking hands and her lips moved in silent prayer. The hoarse strained voice went on in the silent court.

"It is just as well," Don Carlos said laboriously. "When this farce is over, my death will be a symbol of a truth for the entire world to see. This is our Land. Our Spanish fathers came in the first days. They drenched the soil with their blood. They made it holy with their sacrifices. In God's time, out of the blood of martyrs, the Land will be redeemed. And with it, in the true Faith, will come our redemption. It will surely come."

His voice trembled and then he came back from his vision. "And now a word for my friends," he said softly. "Is this a dream? Perhaps! But there were days when it did not seem so! Not when Maximilian came and the Anglos were warring among themselves and there was a chance! It was not then so absurd as it now seems. Who can know when the chance may come again?"

His trembling voice lowered. "If our sons will it, then it is no

186

dream. But I must tell the truth. I have lived too long. Our sons have dwelt too much among the Anglos. They have lost the Idea with which we started. They have no feeling for these things. The language of their fathers is leaving them. They have left us for the new order of things. The broken treaties, the lying promises, the deceptions mean nothing. Where are our sons?" He closed his eyes and gathered himself. "I am not sorry for myself. It is better to die than to eat this bitterness. As for the Anglos, I have tried to forgive them. I have reminded myself of our Savior's words when He was betrayed. It is no use. I have nothing for them but hate."

Hands on hips, he turned first to the bench, then to the twelve jurors, his beard bristling. He laughed jeeringly and deliberately. "Ha! Ha! Ha!" And again. And again. Each burst was an explosion of hate—more sob than laugh. "Ha! Ha! Ha!"

In the silent court, the archbishop clasped his hands in prayer. The rough spectators stared at the shaking bearded man. Doña María kept her face buried. She had sunk to her knees and her fringed black shawl had fallen from her head. A low moaning sound could be heard.

Dan Hogarth raised his quaking hand in a gesture of respect. Ha! Ha! Ha!

McKeever rubbed his jaw. He dared say nothing. With his trembling hands, ropy with blue veins, and his sunken eyes blinking with rheumy anger, the witness seemed suddenly frail and testy. A clinker fell with a thump in the stove. The lawyer's shoulders bowed. The fool! he thought with numb despair. The obstinate single-minded old fool! He resumed his seat and placed his chin in his cupped hand. In a low voice he said:

"You may examine."

Taft asked with an air of incredulity, "Are you through?"

McKeever shrank down. "Your witness, sir."

"Well, well!" Eyes popping with satisfaction, Taft arose ponderously. He jingled a key ring provocatively, glanced knowingly at the jurors, then advanced toward the witness. With each step his shoes squeaked. He pointed a finger stub. "Now sir!" he boomed. "I'd like a few answers."

The witness turned with hate. "*Sí, Señor Verdugo,*" he grated, "*que quieres?*"

Lawyer and defendant faced each other. *Sir Hangman, what dost thou wish?* The familiarity was an insult. Taft jounced his goiter as his eye caught the pile of newspaper exhibits, the copies of *La Luz* with their poisonous editorials. He hesitated a tantalizing moment, shrugged contemptuously, and sat. Tongue in cheek, he announced to the ceiling, "No questions."

Millikan looked at McKeever. "Sir?"

"The defense rests."

A mutter went about the courtroom.

Taft held a whispered consultation and looked up grinning. "The Territory rests."

In the frozen silence, Millikan glanced at the clock and turned quietly to the jury:

"Gentlemen, I expect that you will receive the case early next week. Until then please be admonished once more. It is your duty not to converse among yourselves on any subject connected with the trial nor to form or express any opinion until the case is finally submitted to you. This Court stands adjourned."

Ha! Ha! Ha!

The echo of the harsh mocking laughter seemed to be ringing as the man was led off. Only then did the court disperse—the Spanish in despair, the Anglos thoughtful. McKeever sat staring at the litter of notes, his hair rumpled. He felt nothing, he told himself, nothing at all. This was the dreary end of the trial—and not the end. Ahead lay the last painful duties: the summation, the making of bricks without straw, the charge, the waiting, the long dreadful slope would lead only to the verdict of the twelve men—

At his side Dominguez spoke. "Coming?"

"In a minute." McKeever looked up drearily. "Look after his wife, Joe. I can't face her."

"I told you what Carlos was like, Link. Don't blame yourself," the old Spanish lawyer said. His ugly face was quivering with the shock of disaster. "You did your best."

McKeever raised his head with a gray smile. "What good was my best?" he said harshly. A knot of newspapermen were clustered at the rail, waiting for comment. The archbishop had a comforting arm around Doña María's shoulder and was leading her out. A bailiff with a pole was closing the windows, where one could see the steel-blue overcast gathering. There was a final subdued hum and murmur. His hands mechanically began the collection of papers. "What will I tell his wife?" he asked. "That I did my best? How will that comfort her?"

Dominguez wiped his watering eyes. "What else can you do but your best, Link? This can happen, you know!"

McKeever gave him a dreadful look. "Joe, he threw the case! I didn't know what to do. He went on and on and *on!*"

The bailiff came over. "We're closing now, Mr. McKeever."

Painfully they gathered their papers. As they emerged, a cold wind was blowing the spare dry snow in windrows and the militia were dispersing stragglers.

Hogarth was waiting on the courthouse steps with a small group of men. "Oh, McKeever!" he called. "Can I have a minute alone?"

The lawyer paused. "I'm not going to try the case on the courthouse steps." This was their first encounter in all these months. "What's on your mind?"

"I only want a minute," Hogarth said. When they were alone on the porch, he held out a gold cigarillo case, with a crooked smile. "Smoke?" He was huddled in a great furlined overcoat, dusted with snow, and his yellow eyes had a curious expression. The stern head came only to the lawyer's shoulders. In those coarse features for the first time McKeever saw something of Florence, a cool detachment, an intellectual awareness—

Hogarth grinned. "You got quite a kick in the belly, McKeever. I could've told you it was coming."

McKeever was still sweating and trembling from his experience and he felt the chill of an icy blast at his back. Stiffly he said:

"I'm in a hurry, sir."

"I just wanted to congratulate you. You put on a good show." Hogarth faced him with his crooked smile which held no irony. His rich voice had a hollow quaver. "Now maybe you see why I said no compromise. Where was the use?"

"Do you still claim De Niza is the killer?" McKeever asked bleakly.

With yellow-stained fingers Hogarth took up a cigarillo. "That ain't the point," he said thoughtfully. "Now it's out of my hands. There's no two ways. He's a man—*muy hombre! Muy valiente!* Whatever happens now, tell him I got it."

"What does that mean?"

Hogarth grunted. "You're a young man, McKeever. You got a lot to learn."

"I don't understand."

"Sure you do! Carlos pulled that stunt purely for my benefit. He waited forty years to spit in my face. He wouldn't give me satisfaction and that's the simple thing of it. Well, you tell him he made his point. You know, I—" He broke off and struck a match and went on in his quaver, "Carlos may not believe this, but I'm willing to help the family. That's what I want to say. I'm sorry for María. Tell him he can write his own ticket."

McKeever said coldly, "He wouldn't let her take a cent."

"I know," Hogarth agreed, "but tell him anyways."

"You can always write a letter," McKeever said abruptly. "Now is there anything else?"

"Guess not." Hogarth continued to smoke, thoughtfully. "This was coming a long time. Carlos had this figured out way back and there was nothing you could do. Now at least there's one thing—it ain't up to me. It's up to twelve men." He paused. "I do believe that's why he's so wild. He's just sore he can't cut his throat on my doorstep!" He looked at his quaking hand with a sad questioning smile. "He's an impossible man, but all the same tell Carlos he made his point."

"I don't think I will," said McKeever curtly.

"All right." The older man stared at his hands, tearing the cigarillo to shreds, thinking. "But I'll tell you something, McKeever, and nobody else knows this, not even Floss. Oh sure, way back before the Mex war, I came here with a load of gold in my belt from Austin. The war was coming, everybody in Texas knew it, and the Mex couldn't win. The only question was, would we take this land with a lot of killing, or could we buy it? Well, I came buying and not a shot was fired. I ain't sorry for that. They knew what I was doing in Washington. But that ain't the thing."

Hogarth paused, thinking back, while the snow settled on his black homburg. "I stayed at the old De Niza *casa* for a spell, and later I tried to swing the old man, but the point is this. It was Christmas and Carlos had a sister back from some convent school in New Orleans. Why, you wouldn't believe how strict they were! Every second thing was a mortal sin, and the girls couldn't even whisper to each other. Well, you can imagine! One thing led to another, and when I lit out, the girl followed me. Died of yellow fever in Galveston. Sixteen years old. Carlos was one year older. Well"—he looked up smiling shakily—"that's the whole matter. A real little beauty full of fire. Just died of the fever. Name was Isabella."

McKeever considered this.

"De Niza never mentioned this," he said finally.

"I know."

"It could have helped him in the court."

"Sure it would."

"Then why is he so secretive? It was a long time ago."

Hogarth smiled bleakly. "I could never convince Carlos," he said slowly. "I could never make him believe I married her before she died. After a time, I stopped trying. How long can you let a man rub your nose in his dirt? I'm sorry because Carlos was a man I liked."

The dry snow flurried across the plaza.

"Why tell me now?" McKeever asked finally. "What's the good?"

The old man shrugged. "I just think somebody ought to know," he said in a low voice. "Someday maybe Floss ought to be told. This is something I could hardly make her see. Right now, we ain't eye to eye. Still"—he tapped a fresh smoke and struck a match—"I don't see what else I could do about all this, I swear I don't! It's sure curious the way things work out. You'll tell Carlos what I said?"

"Would you give back the land?" McKeever asked.

Hogarth looked surprised. "Why no," he said slowly, "I couldn't do a thing like that! Why would I?"

The lawyer measured the remorseless face staring up at him. "Mr. Hogarth, we've got nothing to say. Good-by!"

"All right!" With a curious nod of respect, Hogarth shakily went down to his carriage, a small figure huddled in a great fur coat. He drove off followed by a group of mounted men.

"Now what was that about?" Dominguez asked.

McKeever was suddenly conscious of the chill in his back. He wanted to laugh. It was not something he intended. It came of itself, bubbling from the depths within, arising from the tired reaches of his soul. In the smarting cold wind his eyes grew wet and he wiped his cheeks. He turned to his own group and swore luridly. "Good God, I hate a sentimental villain!" he burst out fervently. "Six months ago this could have made a difference. Joe, what does he want now? A pat on the head? What's he after? I liked him better the other way!"

Dominguez murmured glumly, half to himself: "I don't know, Link. There's something there."

"He's sure bothered," Martin agreed. "I know the old man—he could cut Carlos up for bait. Now why this?"

"Someday I'll understand this place," McKeever muttered. Nothing was simple, nothing clear. Obscure relationships, feuds and hatred, old grudges, a code of violence—

"What about tonight?" Emory Martin broke in. "Do you want to work?"

"Tonight?" With a qualm of anxiety McKeever recalled what was waiting in the sickroom at the house. He hesitated. "I don't think so, Em. Let's meet in the morning."

Martin hefted the bulging brief case. The once-proud black calfskin was now scuffed to shreds in its six months of service. "We can't stop now," he objected stubbornly. "There's too much work."

"What work?" McKeever sighed.

"All right, we had a bad day, but doggone!" Martin said strongly. "You've got your summation!"

McKeever agreed drearily. "Yes, there's the summation."

"You'll think of something, sir," Martin urged. "I know you will."

191

"What would you suggest?" McKeever asked drily.

"I don't know. Something brilliant, sir, unexpected. Let's see if we can figure it out."

"H'm!" McKeever rubbed the bristles of his face. "Something brilliant? Unexpected? I'd like that too. Do you think I'll come up with something?"

Martin said earnestly, "You always do, sir."

"Do I?"

"Well, don't you?"

"*Do* I?" McKeever repeated with tired irony. "No, let's stop pressing for one night, Em. We're running dry. That's no way to get ready for summation."

Martin exclaimed, "You're not laying down—?"

"Emory!" Dominguez said warningly.

McKeever sighed wearily. "No, it's all right, Joe. I understand Em's feelings. He's disappointed and now he wants me to wade in to the finish with a meat ax. Well, it's not done that way."

"What is the way?" Martin demanded.

McKeever rubbed his cold hands. "We're dealing with main ideas at this point, Em," he said patiently. "Maybe De Niza was right in his approach. He's lived a long time in this land and his instincts may be sound."

Martin exclaimed, "Carlos went *loco*. That don't mean we're licked yet!"

"Oh, I'll agree. We're never licked till the verdict is in." McKeever paused as the wind drove the snow in light chill flurries. What could he say to these men? Their childish trust in him was still there. He said, "No, we need a main idea. It can't be too heavy or too light. It needs to weigh like—well, like a sword. It needs the strength and the lightness of steel. Have you that idea, Em? Do you know where to find it?" His voice had a strange quality.

Martin said uncomfortably, "Guess not."

"Well, that's what we need." McKeever started to add something and then his shoulders suddenly bowed. "Tomorrow morning, Joe—Em. Let's meet at eight. I'll think of something. I'm getting back to my son. 'By!" He left them in the shelter of the portico.

Martin stared after him with dismay. "What happened to him?" he cried.

Bellew brought his meerschaum to life with a sucking sound. "You're hitting McKeever's low point now, Em. When he begins a case, all he can see is the grand strategy. If he feels he's right, everything bends his way and he starts at his peak. Then the other side starts slamming away. The facts come in, the unpleasant facts. A brute like Mike Taft doesn't care, because the facts don't count, he just knows he wants to win. But it isn't that simple to McKeever. He sees the two sides of everything. He's a thinking man and he's always looking for the truth. He hesitates in his own mind. He's not sure. But when the time comes, he'll see the thing to do, and he'll do it."

Dominguez stared at the newspaperman with tired wonder. "You think he's worried about that, the truth, an abstraction?"

"I think so," Bellew said.

Dominguez stared off into the swirling snow. "No, it's something else. I wouldn't want to carry his load." He wound his muffler against the wind, and nodded briefly. "Señores, go with God."

The group on the courthouse step dispersed.

McKeever remained sunk in thought and drained of feeling, as his driver, a thin shivering youth wrapped in a serape, drove him home. A knot of hangdogs looked up as he passed them outside the office of the *Herald*. They were neither hostile nor curious. The streets were deserted except for children trying in vain to pack the powdery snow into balls. As he entered the drive, he noticed a familiar ornate buggy with red-spoked wheels. He leaped down and the door opened.

"Hello, Link," Florence said impatiently, "I've been waiting for you." She stood with grave troubled eyes, rubbing her hands against the cold. She had loosened her hair and a scalloped white blouse exposed her throat. He looked at its hollow with gratitude, and somehow he had known it would be like this. "Oh Floss!" He hesitated a moment in surprise and took off his hat. "Did you hear what happened in court?"

"Yes, I heard!"

"He threw the case!" he muttered. "After all that work! Well, he'll deserve what he gets!"

She opened the door wider. "Come into the house."

He looked up at her tone.

"Is it Jeff?" he asked quickly. "Is anything wrong?"

She frowned. "No, not Jeff. It's something else."

He entered and took off his frock coat with some dim unease that the house was empty. He hung up his hat and followed Florence into the living room. There was a forlorn air in the heaps of records and the gaping cabinets, the wall maps and the stacked files, the debris of a battlefield.

"Where is Mrs. De Niza?" he asked.

Florence said, "She's in her room. She's lying down. Now come to

193

the fire, you're shivering." He followed her and took her hands. They were cold and pleasant with the tingle of woman's flesh.

"Where were you?" he demanded hoarsely. "I looked for you in court! What kept you?"

She withdrew. "Please, Link, there's no time. I had a fight with Pa last night and I got here just as soon as I could." She hesitated with some pity for his gray pinched look, then opened the study door. "Come on out, Lupe. It's all right now."

With a look of suspicion, the old Navajo woman limped out, scratching her hands. Her flat Mongoloid face was incredibly wrinkled, the seams crossed her coppery skin in a thousand cracks.

Florence said, "This is Guadalupe Trister."

McKeever stared. "Sam Trister's wife!"

"That's right."

McKeever turned with a dangerous look. "What does it mean? How did she get here just too late? Where's her husband?"

"That's what she came for." Florence explained that she had learned only that morning that her father's men had detained the Navajo woman at the ranch. "I came when I could, Link," she said simply. "They found a message on her for you."

"What was the message?" McKeever demanded. He realized that he was shaking violently.

"The gist was this," said Florence. "Trister wants you to arrange some way for him to testify for Carlos. He's afraid to show up. He wants some guarantee that he'll be safe if he surrenders to you."

"Safe from what?"

"He's afraid he might be killed before he gets to court."

"Oh!" McKeever touched a distracted hand to his face. "For God's sake, what made him wait till now? We closed the case today. I'm not sure the Court will take more testimony!"

She looked at him oddly. "Link, I don't understand this. Don't you want to meet Trister? You built the whole case on that!"

"Not want him?" McKeever's eyes fell on Jeff's baseball mitt in the corner sitting like a mute witness. Not want Trister? It was quite true. This was news he did not want. At least not now, not at this time, not this way.

The Navajo woman clutched her calico dress. "Trister is afraid of sheriff," she said in a heavily accented old voice.

"Kyle?" McKeever exclaimed.

The old woman nodded. "Kyle had Trister in the lockup. One night, he almost killed." She made an expressive gesture. "Trister knows. He tell. He sure you can keep him safe till he get to court. After that!" She shrugged. "He will take chance."

Florence explained, "She means if they try him for murder, he'll want you to defend him."

"What makes him think I will?"

"That was the promise he got through Father Hawthorne," she answered sharply. "Link, I thought you'd be pleased. What's wrong?"

McKeever looked down and saw that he was holding the poker. He strode about the room swinging the iron bar in his great hands like a wand. A gray film was at his eyes. He muttered, "Your father had this news all day? Even back there in the courtroom?"

She nodded soberly. "We had a real set-to, Link, you can imagine."

"He knew you were coming here with this woman?"

"Yes."

"Why did he let her loose?"

She made a face. "Give Pa credit, Link. He wouldn't hold out a witness in this case. It's just that he wants the Territory to get first licks."

He paused. "Do they know where Trister's hiding?"

"I'm afraid so," she said simply. "But it's a question if they can find him. There are no clear trails out there."

McKeever continued to slouch about, rubbing his stiff face, swinging the poker, considering many things. So this had been the thing on Hogarth's mind at the courthouse! He said:

"Are they trying to sidetrack me, is that it?"

"How do you mean?"

"With this news, I'll need an adjournment! Will I get it?"

"Oh, I'm sure!"

"I don't know!"

Florence said firmly, "That's nonsense, Link, and you know it!"

"Yes, I suppose!" he conceded and resumed his pacing, morose and glowering, not seeing the warm decorations. He licked his dry lips and paused.

"How can I leave? How can I go now? Tell me how I can do it!".

"What's holding you?"

"It's Jeff," he said simply. "I can't leave him."

Florence frowned. "But I talked to Dr. Kimball myself, just an hour ago. He told me this fever's just a little pleurisy because of the rib, nothing else. Jeff's gone through that before, hasn't he?"

"It's not just the fever," he muttered.

"Then I don't understand."

"It's hard to explain." McKeever held out his hands, helpless, pleading. "Jeff's so cheerful nobody sees what he goes through, but this morning he was afraid. For a long time, he was convinced he'd

195

never get well. It was only after we got here that he felt he would recover, that he would live. Sometimes at night—"

He paused to swallow. "He's been so well for months that this setback is a shock. He knows it's just a minor thing. But he knows it here, not *here*." McKeever touched his temple and his heart in turn. "He knows what fever means, and he won't distinguish one thing from another. I can't leave until he's well." He stood at the hearth with his face in a torment of indecision. "Oh Lord! Without me he's so afraid! Floss—" he paused, gray-faced, "He's still just a child!"

The Navajo woman fingered a turquoise ornament at her neck. In her wrinkled eyes McKeever saw a quick intelligence he had not at first fathomed. There was faint contempt, as though she had expected nothing else but this, and he could almost see the scene in the desert, the decision by her man to take this risk, the dispute between them—

"I don't know what to say," Florence muttered. "I thought you needed Trister. I thought this would help."

McKeever argued, "I'm not sure it wouldn't be better to let it rest. There's always a risk in every witness. How do I know what the old man will say? This way the burden is on the other side!"

"In that case," Florence said, "you can forget the whole thing."

"Suppose I send Dominguez? Or Martin?"

"No!" said the Navajo woman strongly. "You!"

There was a burst of laughter from the balcony. Miguelito was up there with Juanito. McKeever strode about, swinging the poker. "Does Mrs. De Niza know this news?" he asked in a low voice.

"Not yet, but she will," said Florence and added, "Jeff won't be alone, Link. I'll stay here if you wish."

He stared at her.

"The boy won't like it," he muttered.

She took his hand.

"I'll do whatever you wish," she said gently.

For a long moment there was silence. The Navajo woman's eyes were a fathomless black, liquid and implacable in their pouches. The clattering of pots and a savory smell of cooking came from the kitchen. His shoulders sagged.

"I'll have to tell him," he said in a low voice.

There was further discussion and then he went upstairs. The lamplight in the bedroom was warm and pleasant. The dog raced across the floor, claws clattering. She nestled in the quilting, a weight on the boy's feet, and her bulging eyes were black pearls of sympathy.

The boy felt the bed weight and the acrid tobacco smell. His eyes were hot, too hot, and he lowered the lids as his father explained the decision he had made. He looked up and dreams became thoughts. He turned fretfully on the pillow and winced with pain. "How long would it take, Dad?"

McKeever said, "Three or four days, not more. A week at the outside."

"A whole week!" The boy stared with glassy eyes. "Can't you send somebody else?"

"No, I'm afraid not," McKeever said grimly. "It's something I've got to do myself."

He explained the day's events in the courtroom. Jeff listened attentively with flushed cheeks. "But Dad, you'll win!" he protested. "I know you'll lick 'em."

"Will I?"

How like his mother, McKeever thought, the neat head, the straight nose, the sensitive mouth, the man's face emerging out of the child's—

Jeff waited and it almost seemed that he was asleep. Then he whispered, "Please don't go, Dad."

McKeever swallowed. "You're not afraid, Jeff? It's only the rib. It will heal. It's not the other thing."

The boy shook his head. "No, I'm not afraid—" He trailed off.

"Because it's something I've got to do. If there were another way, I'd send some men. You know that. This Indian woman says Trister wants me, no one else. Otherwise he'll disappear in the malpais. Don't you see?"

Malpais. The mal-y-pie. Land of frozen lava and lunar fantasies. Waterless. Deadly. Cut by a thousand dry canyons. Trackless.

The boy let his head fall on the pillow and weakness began to gather. He stared at the ceiling and the tears rolled down his cheeks into the wet pillow.

"Oh Lord!" McKeever murmured. With a helpless feeling, he took the boy in his arms. He had a sudden longing for his distant New York office, staid and quiet with its black furniture and musty smell of calf bindings, the cheerful young clerks in the library, the letterpress at work, the harbor view from Pine Street, the wind whistling at the casement, and the mewing seagulls—

The portrait of Amos Tucker was on the wall. The fine eyes on him, the soft white beard and fierce mustaches, the affectionate inscription to Jeff—

Lord, he thought, the giants of his life, the landmarks were crashing, the world would not seem the same without that resonant voice, that clear mind—

Aloud he said, "You won't be alone, Jeff. Now I promise you."

197

"Oh sure! I've got Mrs. Blanchard! Some fun!"

McKeever almost smiled. "No, not Mrs. Blanchard, I'll get Miss Hogarth to stay. Now wouldn't that help?"

Jeff turned with a flicker of interest. "Florence?"

"Yes."

"You think she would? Even overnight?"

"She might, if you stop this nonsense!" McKeever rubbed his mouth. Jeff was fourteen. That fuzz meant something. He couldn't be too ill. Well, he thought, he could hardly quarrel with his son's taste.

"I'm sure she will," he said drily. "If you want her."

The boy closed his hot eyes. He felt a forehead kiss and the sound of retreating footsteps, and the room was empty. "Little doggie," he murmured and a wet tongue licked his fingers. His thoughts slid into dreams, and he played an old mental game. He thought of the room—

Each thing in its place. The press book with its trial clippings. College pennants. Indian masks and artifacts, flint arrowheads and war bonnets. Mineral cabinet with its fossils. The stamp collection. The rows of books. Cooper and Scott and Dickens and Darwin and—

Now begin the count! Divide the room into cubic inches of space. How many? Length and width and height. One and two and three. Wall to wall. Floor to ceiling. Three hundred. Eighty-four more. Count lost and try again—

No use.

Try again.

No.

Divide time? Long wide high?

The other game—

Time flies you cannot they pass too quickly. Punctuate and parse! Where the comma? Which the subject object verb gerund? Flies? Thunderstorm and window open and ceiling crawling with black speckles hairy legs compound eyes watching wet soft disease proboscis hide under quilts crying Mummy Mummy all right nothing can happen see the flies gone there there I'm here come bed warm safe nothing outside no end yet soft soap smell wet starch darling darling allright allrightnow—

And when he opened his lids Florence was in the room, abundant in health, filled with vigor, smiling as she sat on the bed and took his hand, and McKeever followed in.

"Gosh, Jeff! This is the woolly West!" she teased. "You can't let a little old busted rib get you down. First thing you know, you'll spoil our good name. Don't you know nobody stays sick out here?"

She had him smiling and sitting up with a bowl of soup and Mrs. Blanchard clucking like a laying hen. He sat there wincing a little, and wiped back his forelock. "Say, Florence, is it true? Did you have a fight about this case with your dad?"

She pushed forward a spoon with a smile. "Sure did, Jeff, but Pa had it coming, and he knows it. He'll get over it. Here, take some more of this good soup."

And so on until he felt more cheerful and willing to release his father for the necessary thing. McKeever sat back while Florence took over with the warmth of her smiling green eyes.

There was a tap.

"We're ready," said Emory Martin. "Packed and saddled."

"I'll be right there." McKeever went to the bed. "Jeff," he said softly. The boy managed a smile. "It's all right, Dad," he answered. "I don't mind now, I really don't." They kissed and McKeever left. Florence followed him into the hall.

"Pa's all right now on this thing," she said seriously. "But I wouldn't answer for the men. Look out for Kyle. And don't worry about a thing here. I'll take charge."

They were alone and her face was close. She seemed expectant. "Floss, I don't want to leave," he muttered. "I don't want to leave at all." She said nothing. He heard the whinnying in the corral. He wanted to touch her hair.

"Look after the boy," he said at last in a low voice.

She kissed his cheek. "Come back soon, Link."

With icy foreboding, he turned and left the house and met his men. When later he passed under the window, there was the sound of laughter, a rich contralto, coming from his son's room above.

Chapter XIII

McKeever had been nodding on the trail and his neck felt the weight of his head. He awoke with a start. In the darkness ahead he made out dim forms swaying in their saddles. Beneath him, the soft sound told him that they were passing through a soil drift deposited by the winds blowing a million years from the west.

Ahead there was the flare of a match. He saw Emory Martin's troubled face, and the darkness closed down. A cold wind was blowing. They plodded up the rise until the sound changed again to steel shoes ringing on lava—

Lava! That light spongy rock which could in a matter of hours tear a man's boots to shreds! The primeval adamantine in which nothing of life could grow!

He was content to let the younger man assume the lead. In Cuatro Rios, Emory Martin had been deferential. Out here he was in his element. He had a fund of knowledge of the land, its geological formations and its living things. It was a scholar's knowledge keenly pursued. They had been crawling—almost forever, it seemed— through endless lunatic formations all of which he described with zest. A score of times the land had heaved to mountain height, only to erode and wash away and sink into ocean abyss. The occasional fossils, the primitive animal remains, the tracks of reptiles, outcroppings of coal, were proof of the eternal cycle which had gone on for five hundred million years.

McKeever tried to listen but it was hard. He sat dejectedly, his chin on chest, swaying in the saddle, letting his thoughts wander. He was pursued by anxiety. This was the third day on the trail and each mile was taking him further from Jeff. His last conversation with the doctor was in his ears. The boy would be in no danger. The fever was low grade, expected, assuredly the bone injury speaking and not the other thing. Yet he had heard the knocking of a giant fist at the door.

With a sigh he looked over his shoulder. The Dipper was tilting low in the sky. It was two hours to midnight, he judged. In the north lay the extinct volcanoes which had mothered these lava wastes. In this wild land, cut and crossed by a thousand arroyos, he felt outside the flow of time. The few living things—the pines, the sprouts of grasses, the starved deer, the lizards were no more than puffs of smoke against the wilderness.

They were following a path of some sort to a rise. Even here men of the Stone Age had gone before them. Boulders had been heaved aside and the flinty rubble had been moved. What had brought primitive man to this desolation? Had there been rain then? Had the climate changed? Or was it something else?

In the darkness a voice said, "Yo!" The small column—they were six men and the Navajo woman—halted. A figure came plodding back and then Martin said wearily, "The old girl's tired, sir. I think we ought to hold up."

"Can't she make it?" McKeever asked.

Martin shook his head. "She's willing enough, but she can't keep going. Besides, we've got two more days, more or less. No sense in pushing too hard."

"Whatever you say, Em," McKeever agreed numbly. "How do we stand now?"

Martin pointed dimly to the south. "Straight ahead, we can cut across the Sands. Going left, we've got more of this damn lava. Between the two there's a pass, she's sure. She'll know better by morning."

"What's the shorter way?"

"Six of one, half a dozen of the other. The Sands are shorter but we can't make time. The lava way is longer but we're better off while we keep this trail."

McKeever rubbed his neck stiffly. "We should rest, I suppose. We'll make better time in the morning, if we do."

Martin called softly, "Bill—Terry." Two of their men joined them. Bill Donovan and Terry Birkett were their best workers, jovial and unassuming Texans sent by their detective agency from Dallas. Although they had worked the West in many capacities—as cow hands, miners, railroad workers—they were strangers to the Territory and they were lost. They received their order impassively.

"Whatever you say," they agreed. "Do we make fire?"

McKeever said, "Let's not take a chance."

For the third time, they made camp. They ate dried meat and chewed on parched corn which crackled in their mouths like gunfire. Water was rationed out and they bedded down on the lava. The Navajo woman ate by herself, wandered off a moment on a call of nature, then curled up apart from the men and drew a blanket over her head.

McKeever rested his head on his saddle and stretched his legs. The moon was rising. Beyond the lava, a gleam of silver showed the drift of the Sands, the gypsum residue of a fossil extinct sea. In the far distance the ridge to which they were headed rose like an endless series of battlements. Martin came over.

"All right, sir?" he asked softly.

McKeever grimaced. "Just saddlesore."

Martin sank wearily beside him and began a pipe. "Well, we're on the right trail, there's not much question in her mind."

"How can she know?" McKeever wondered. "One gulch is worse than the next. By gosh, this is like the desert in the Bible. We could wander for forty years and never be missed."

Martin considered the question precisely. He hesitated. "How can she know the trail? Hard to say how they do it." He continued to smoke thoughtfully, the tobacco hissing in his pipe. "You know, we're just beginning to figure out the Indian. The old-timers here romanticize him, or join him, or kill him. But the fact is—" He broke off.

"Yes?"

He went on hesitantly, "You remember that mesa we passed yesterday? The one like a ferryboat?"

McKeever thought back. "They're all so alike." He recalled the mesa as it had appeared at sunrise, russet and green, moderate in height, covered with sage, not different from a hundred others.

Martin went on. "Long ago, she says, there was a stone marker that made this path. She says that made the path sacred."

McKeever frowned. "I don't recall a stone marker."

"It's not there now."

"Well then?"

"She remembers that marker."

McKeever was interested. "When did it stand? I mean, why was the marker destroyed? Who would want to do that?"

"She's not sure. They tried to hide this path. Maybe a hundred years ago. Maybe a thousand." Martin was half-serious, half-joking.

"That's a long time to remember," McKeever said mildly.

Martin grinned boyishly. He removed his rimless spectacles. They were useless in the darkness but this was his last ritual before turning in. With his studious air, he went on. "Oh, it's all true. When the Navajo says he can remember a thousand years, that's a proven fact, at least the way he means it. He remembers when the timberline was five hundred feet lower down, or where some sacred tree used to stand, or where a settlement got washed away long before Coronado ever saw this land."

"Mighty convenient," McKeever sighed. His own strong memory, he thought, was a mixed blessing. It was a strength that he could recall by volume, page and line any legal text he needed. It was a weakness that he could not forget the things which tormented his soul—

The sudden image of Liz on her deathbed was strong before him— that and the white stricken face of his son that night outside his mother's room—

He shook the pictures from his mind. "Do they ever forget?" he murmured.

Martin said seriously, "In personal things, sure, they're like anyone else. The thing is, the Navajo has a tribal memory too. He's part of his people, and what the tribe knows, he remembers. He's not measuring by himself or today but by the people. That way—what's a thousand years? We're lost because we measure by our one lifetime. That's our scale. We get born, we get old, we die. The Navajo's too poor to own a clock."

McKeever glanced over at the silhouette of the square-faced young giant with respect. Martin was perceptive and thoughtful in a way he had not suspected. "Does the Navajo realize all this?"

Martin grinned. "I'm not sure," he confessed. "This is just theory I've been reading. But if he doesn't, he ought to, because that's the thing of it with him. They say time doesn't mean anything to the Indian. That's not true." He trailed off, sucked his pipe, then said, "The Navajo wants intensity in time. Does that mean anything to you?"

"I'm not sure," McKeever muttered and added, "Why just the Navajo? Or is this true of all the tribes?"

"True enough, I suppose. I just favor the Navajo. He isn't looking to race through time. He wants to absorb its flow, get it to enter him, become part of it. You know the *kiva?*"

McKeever nodded. The *kiva* room was to be seen in the pueblos, an airless pit carved in rock to be entered by its ladder. It was a place of communion—an accumulator box for the forces of the cosmos.

Martin went on, "The Navajo is looking for the deepest feeling he can. That's why they induce visions, starve, eat peyote, wander in the desert."

McKeever asked drily, "Do they eat honey and locusts?"

"What? Oh!" Martin smiled seriously. "The Zuñi will climb down there in the *kiva*," he said. "Just sit and wait and starve himself till he sees his visions. That's the point. He tries to get time to stand still. He tries to absorb it, and get absorbed. He's trying to *feel* in the deepest way he can." He indicated the black soft clouds scudding under the stars. "Our idea is that there's something out there for us to reach. They don't feel that. They don't go to the gods. The gods come to them."

McKeever's pipe was cold. He let it slip from his fingers and waited for Martin to go on. The younger man said softly, "That's why they come to the desert. Out here the visions are strong. It's not an easy thought."

"You can't build too much on their kind of mysticism," McKeever pointed out.

"Why not?"

"We're not primitives," he said drily. "Our intuition is dried up. Our lives are different. We've got reason and common sense. Don't let the obscure become the ineffable."

Martin gave his laugh. "I'm just trying to give you an idea. This is the Navajo's land. He remembers everything about it. Land—gods—people. All one thing." He paused. "You know, when Carlos made that speech in court about the Land, it sounded good. But I'm not so sure. When we're gone—Anglos, Spanish—the Navajo will be here. It starves him and keeps him poor, but it's his land."

McKeever thrust his neck against the hard saddle and looked at the stars. "It's just his luck they haven't found gold yet. It's all true as long as the land isn't worth the taking," he said drily. "Still, it's food for thought, Em."

"Sure is." Martin indicated the old Navajo woman snoring a distance off. "But that's how I know she knows the path." He laughed self-consciously. "Funny how I got to study all this. I used to take the Indians for granted, like anybody else. Just varmints to be wiped out. Then I came across some old decisions of the Court of Claims. Why, do you know," he said with rising excitement, "so many treaties have been busted, there ought to be millions in those claims. Just the Cherokee alone! Let alone Utes and Comanches and Choctaw and Apaches! If a man could specialize, there could be bigger fees than the country's ever seen outside railroad work." At the thought of large remuneration, his honest eyes began to shine with the unbruised exaltation of a young practitioner with all ideals intact. "All we need is some enabling legislation!"

"Ah!" said McKeever wisely. "A small thing!"

"Well, it is exciting," Martin said defensively. "And it does make you think."

McKeever was silent and for a moment Martin thought he was

asleep. He lay considering the matter. Somberly he said, "Em, I'll admit something—"

"Yes."

"I don't want this trip to end, isn't that strange?"

"No, not strange," Martin said.

"While we're on this trip, I feel that everything is standing still. I want it to stay this way. Now why?"

Martin yawned wearily. "I know, I feel the same way."

McKeever said queerly, "When I was a boy I could walk a road and it would never end. I could climb a hill to the sky. When I looked into a pool there was my life. It's like that here."

"It's the desert. Everyone feels it, yet only few talk about it. Don't suppose I would either, except that I just happened to major in English in college. Got me to read some books. Sometimes," Martin said gloomily, "I think that was the worst thing in the world. It's made me a marked man."

"Oh come!"

"Fact! You ought to hear Floss on me. She's convinced I'm a prize poop. Maybe I am."

"I don't think so," McKeever smiled. "Em, when this is finished, if I'm still practicing law look me up. I could give you a good job, that is, if you'd like New York—"

Martin repeated slowly, "*If* you're still practicing—?"

McKeever sighed despondently. "The practice gets harder each year, Em. The way things are turning out—" He broke off and closed his eyes. "I don't want to keep carrying these damn loads!" he burst out.

For a time there was no sound but the wind.

Martin said finally, "You can turn back, you know."

"No, I don't want to do that," McKeever answered.

"But what—" Martin arose on his elbow and in the starlight studied the dim troubled face. "What do you expect we'll get from the old man?"

"It's a good rule not to speculate."

"But you must have a theory!"

"I believe," McKeever hesitated, "I believe that Trister was simply a dupe in all this. Canty probably got him to arrange that meeting in the Sierra Blanca without revealing the purpose. In my opinion—" He broke off.

"Does that mean we concede that meeting?"

"I'm afraid we must," McKeever sighed. "But we can still urge that Canty's offer to murder Douglas Hanna was rejected, and from then on, his malice was directed against Carlos de Niza. That's why the shotguns were stolen and used for the murder. At least," he added, "that's what I hope Trister will tell us."

A horse pawed the lava and whinnied softly in the night.

"Why do you suppose Canty never fled?" asked Martin. "That's the strangest thing in this whole case. Just as though he *wanted* to be caught."

McKeever laughed softly. "Oh Lord, Em, that was his dearest wish! For the first time in his malevolent life, he's got a commanding importance. The world is at his feet. The biggest men fawn on him. Think of it, Em! He strides across the land with giant steps while we scurry like ants before him. His words hold life and death for a man he hates. Not even the gods have greater powers. Caught? That's not the word to use—not in that private universe in which he lives."

Martin pulled his blanket to his chin, shivering. "Why not go back?" he suggested. "We're outnumbered in any case if we hit trouble. Leave me three men. That's as good as four, if it comes down to that."

"No."

"I can handle Trister, now why—"

McKeever said angrily, "We've been over this, Em. I'm sticking. I've come this far, I'll go the rest of the way. I'm sure it's all right back home."

Martin looked at him. "You're not sure at all," he said.

"No, I'm not sure," McKeever admitted miserably.

"Then, for God's sake, why didn't you stay home?"

"I don't know!" McKeever said to himself. "I just had this job to do."

"Well, try not to worry," said Martin after a time. He pulled the blanket over his head and fell asleep. McKeever remained staring at the black sky. Unbidden there came to his mind a text out of his boyhood on which his own father had lingered and meditated. Was it in such a wilderness that the Voice had said—?

> *Take now thy son, thine only son, whom*
> *thou lovest, and get thee unto the land of*
> *Moriah; and offer him there for a burnt offering*
> *upon one of the mountains which I will tell*
> *thee of—*

"Oh my son!" he groaned. "My only son! On what altar are you being offered?"

In the next days the strong wind blew a yellow haze of choking dust. Sunsets were thick as blood and at night the sky could not be

206

seen. McKeever remained sunk in his thoughts. His eyes burned and each muscle was in agony. He blindly let his gray stallion follow the column. Ahead the old woman's form jounced as she searched the trail for markers. They dived through dry gulches and hugged the shoulders of impossible rock-sliding cliffs. The trail rose and fell and skirted stands of ancient forests.

Then when the wind died, they found themselves looking down into a ravine. The woman held up her hand and grunted.

"Huh!"

They gazed in silence at the long narrow valley scoured out of limestone hills by the river. An hour of daylight, perhaps less, remained. The surrounding heights, covered with massive conifers, still gleamed in the brilliant sky. The river bottom in the gathering shadows was lush with thick green grasses, and softer woods, birch and quaking aspen, had sprung up in a wide flat beaver meadow. Lacy cascades of the melting snows filled the ravine with a thunderous murmur.

The woman lifted her chin—it was against her custom to point—and said, "There!"

Directly opposite, a vast ruddy bluff soared from the valley bottom. At its base it wore an apron of rubble, at which a cluster of diminutive figures were gathered. As they watched, there arose a puff of blue smoke and then came the sound of gunfire—the chatter of pistols and the roar of Winchesters. "God damnation!" Martin swore. "That's Kyle!"

McKeever arose in his saddle and shouted down the ravine with fury, "Kyle—Taft! Let up, damn you! You'll kill that man!"

In the clear air the echoes carried his voice and Taft looked up. His frock coat was a distinctive black and his sunburned naked skull was a glowing pink. He waved jovially and shouted something they could not hear.

McKeever said bitterly, "Late!"

His men dismounted. Jim Birkett shielded his eyes dubiously. "Good twenty men down there, Mr. McKeever," he muttered glumly. "I just don't see how we can take on that kind of a party."

"Nor do I!" McKeever said irritably. "I'm not that simple, Jim, and even if I were, I wish you fellows would remember we're not here for a fight."

"Fight might be the thing," Birkett grumbled.

In the distance the law men continued to fire at twin openings of a cave at the head of the talus slope. The woman sat huddled on her mount, a tough bundle of dried sinew and bones. She gazed fixedly ahead and muttered a word in her language. She covered her face reverently and muttered, "*Los Ojos de Dios*"—the Eyes of God.

McKeever saw the scene suddenly in a new aspect. The bluff did indeed resemble a malevolent god mask. The cave—or caves—were divided by a plinth of limestone into staring horrors. A frowning brow of lava made the formation unique. One could understand that here was a place where legend thickened. At his side Martin murmured, "Barlow's Cave."

This then was where Trister had hidden since the murder at Vale's Crossing. A rickety log cabin and a sluice box at the river showed the manner of his living.

The guns continued to fire. In the far distance a thin voice wailed.

"Oh don't! Please don't come near! Oh please—"

The woman turned to McKeever with eyes shining with fear. "Trister! See there!" From the left eye of the stone face a wisp of smoke drifted and seconds later came the crack of a rifle. The men below dropped with ludicrous haste and then Max Kyle arose. His great frame was unmistakable. He cupped his hands and his angry bellow rolled up the slope. "Come on down, Sam! I'm just about losing my patience with this foolery!" He paused. "You hear?"

The thin voice screeched, "Oh Jesus, stay away from me, Sheriff. Please don't kill me! I don't want you to come! I don't! Oh Lord! Oh Lord!" It trailed off in senseless entreaties.

"It sure don't sound human!" Birkett murmured.

Kyle shouted, "I'll give the count of three, Sam! Now that's a fair warning! One! Two!—"

A split second later came the reverberating cough of a rifle. "Damn you!" Kyle shouted with fury. The pitiful begging voice above him wailed thinly.

"Disgraceful!" McKeever exclaimed. "Perfectly shocking!"

Martin kicked a stone aside with anger. "What's the use, sir? Nothing seems to work in our favor. I sure thought we'd get here first!"

"We're not out yet, Em," McKeever said grimly. "At least Trister's alive and that's something we didn't know."

"What do we do now?"

"We'll get down there and talk."

"Oh sure! *Talk!*" Martin said bitterly.

McKeever looked at him oddly. "Why not, Em? Isn't that our stock in trade?" He studied his hollow-eyed men with the thought that they were more ragged than he could have wished. One of the horses had cast a shoe and was limping on a torn hoof. The men were unshaven and exhausted by the lava. He muttered, "Let's get down."

They picked their way among the rubble of flints into the valley.

When finally the immense limestone block loomed above them in the fading light, Mike Taft broke off to meet them. He left the armed men in position and scrambled down the talus slope, his frock coat flopping. He studied the weary party with amusement and boomed, "How was the lava, Link? Thought you'd never make it! I was real concerned about you!" He was in extremely good humor.

"So I see," McKeever said sourly.

Taft wiped his mustaches and wondered whether anyone might not have a good cigar.

"My cigars gave out a long time back, Mike," said McKeever.

Taft grunted philosophically, "Just goes to show this ain't work for an educated man." He followed McKeever's gaze toward the cave where at that moment a lanky bald deputy arose to fire a shot.

"I'm surprised at you, Link, a lawyer of your standing, high-tailing around this way! Why get in a sweat for a thing like this? You ought to've sent some men."

"I see *you* here!"

"That's different. I'm a public official. A lot of dirty work comes my way. Besides—" Taft's gaze turned significantly toward Kyle who remained crouched behind a boulder, gripping his rifle. The sheriff's eyes were dead, immobile, fixed on the cave above, his throat convulsive. The prosecutor wiped his glowing skull. "A watched pot don't boil," he said succinctly.

The lawyers faced each other with professional respect. As a circle of men gathered about them, McKeever made a strong gesture. "Mike, are you trying to kill that harmless old man?"

"Harmless?" Taft boomed with sarcasm just as a screech of rage from above underscored his point. He said affably, "Why no, Link, that wouldn't be the idea at all!" It was quite simple, he grinned. The old man had been going since dawn, crying and singing. He was half-crazed with fear and possibly drunk and no one cared to rush him. The law men were merely drawing fire to exhaust his ammunition.

McKeever stared up the slope at the sheriff, then returned his gaze to the prosecutor. He asked slowly, "Is that the whole story?"

Taft parted his dusty frock coat and thrust his hands into trouser pockets. "What exactly brings you here, Link?" he drawled. "I hope you got no foolish notions."

McKeever shivered in the chill breeze. "I came to take Trister back. I want him as a witness."

"Can't be done!" Taft said decisively.

"Why not?"

"For one thing, you got no standing here at all," Taft said judiciously. "The sheriff's got to take him in. Any move you make would obstruct justice."

"I don't see that at all."

Taft rubbed his nose vigorously. "Kyle's got a warrant for murder," he said softly. "Just as soon as we smoke out the old man, he goes under arrest."

"For murder?" McKeever said skeptically.

Taft nodded solemnly. "I drafted the warrant myself."

McKeever drew a deep breath. "Let me take him back with me, Mike," he said persuasively. "I'm sure it would work out. You could send some of your men along. Make the arrest after we reach home."

"Why not here?"

McKeever gazed up at the sheriff. "I simply want to make sure the old man gets to the court alive. That's why he sent for me. He's scared." He paused. "I don't want to say anything prejudicial at this time."

"Oh?" Taft thought this over, plucking at his lip, studying the matter. "I'd like to," he said finally, "but it's out of the question. I can't let you have him."

"Oh Lord!" McKeever felt overwhelmed by the inferiority of his position. The immensity of the scene oppressed him. Everything was enlarged beyond reason—the forms of animal life, the soaring trees, the convulsions of nature, the passions of men. He had a sudden longing for the wet smell of a New England forest in the rain.

He said in a low desperate voice, "Mike, I want you to let me talk to him. He sent for me and I consider myself his lawyer under the circumstances. Besides, it's in your own interests."

"How's that?" Taft asked skeptically.

McKeever held up a finger. "Listen!" The voice on the heights above burst out hoarsely:

> *"Doo-dooda-day,*
> *Put my money on a bobtail nag*
> *Somebody won on de bay—*
>
> *"Oh, Lordy, Lordy!"*

"You don't know what he'll do," McKeever urged. "He might take his own life. Then what?"

Taft squinted, "What makes you think he would?"

"I know this sort," McKeever said. "If he kills himself, you'll never know the real truth here. If he corroborates Canty, you'll know you tried a clean case. If he doesn't—well, I'll expect you to do the right thing. Let me talk to him first."

210

"You're asking a lot!" Taft said heavily.

McKeever measured him. "You're a lawyer, Mike," he said somberly, "one of the best. If anything goes wrong you'll never forgive yourself."

"You think that would bother me?"

"Yes, I do," McKeever said soberly.

Taft wiped the creases of his pulpy neck thoughtfully. He said irresolutely, "Link, you'll be taking your life in your hands. I can't let you go up there. The old man's crazier'n a coot."

"I'm sure he'll talk to me."

The voice howled:

> *"—other helpers fail,*
> *And comforts flee,*
> *Help of the helpless—"*

Taft shrugged, then bawled to the man on the slope, "Oh, Max Kyle!"

The sheriff turned with a scowl and sat behind a boulder. "I got nothing to say to that twisting McKeever son of a bitch," he called down.

"Come on down!" Taft shouted peremptorily.

The sheriff slid down in a heap of rubble. Despite the cold he wore nothing over his blue wool shirt. Deep circles of sweat were at his armpits. He came stumbling on absurd high heels, panting and wiping his forehead. His eyes seemed rimmed with yellow dust. When Taft had explained the situation, he fished out a sack of tobacco and a cigarette paper. He said:

"After all this work, you mean to say I just sit by?"

"You sit by!" Taft agreed.

Kyle tapped a measure of tobacco into the paper with a trembling hand. "All that sweat goes down the hole?" he asked savagely. "You got any idea what it took to make this case, Mike? Where I had to go? What went into it?"

Taft said calmly, "I ain't interested in that aspect."

"He ain't interested!" Kyle spoke with heavy wonder. He spilled the tobacco and tried again. "That's just fine! This lawyer makes me out the bastard in this case! I'm the one put the word in Tom Canty's mouth! I'm the one framed Carlos!" He shook his head with incredulity. "Now he ain't interested!"

Taft said distinctly, "Shut up, Max!"

"No, I ain't going to shut up!" Kyle licked at the paper with a

211

dry tongue. "It just ain't fair!" he cried resentfully. "I made this case, by God, nobody else! I was there at the beginning. When we didn't have one little lead, I was there! Ask anybody!"

"Max!" Taft said.

"The hardest case of my life!" the sheriff went on, chewing his cheeks vengefully, his eyes blank and staring. "Now everybody grabs the credit, taking advantage, climbing on my back! Where does that leave Max Kyle?"

"Everybody's *always* grabbing the credit!" Taft said wearily. "Forget all that! If you had more'n one idea, you wouldn't worry. Now we got a serious legal situation. This here is no fly-by-night. McKeever's an important lawyer and when he says something, we've got to pay attention. He wants to see his client. Only way to stop that is to go up and make that arrest. You ready to walk up that hill, Max?"

The voice called with despair, "Sheriff? You going to let me be? Oh Lordy! Lordy! What can I do? What's going to happen? How can I help myself?"

Kyle turned with trembling lips. His eyes were awash with rage and self-pity. "I swear it ain't *right*," he choked. His hands opened convulsively and the tobacco spilled at his feet. He glowered at the golden particles. "All right, McKeever, go ahead! I'll be watching! I hope he blows your arse off!"

As he spoke, the swift darkness of night gathered. After a silent moment, McKeever smiled bleakly. "Well, I certainly invited this, didn't I?" he drawled, and then they were at him.

"You're not called to do this," Martin urged. "Let me go up. If anything happens, who'll finish the trial?"

McKeever scratched his chin. "In that case, ask for a mistrial," he joked. "That's one way to win this case."

"Think it over!" Martin urged.

"I'm thinking of a lot of things!" McKeever said heavily. A cook fire had been started and a savory smell was drifting toward them. The darkness was an advantage. He turned to the old woman.

"Lupe," he said quietly.

She came to him. "Huh?"

"Will you come up the hill with me?"

Her wrinkled eyes blinked like a lizard's. "Not safe for you," she croaked. "You listen."

The voice screeched down. "Sheriff, you son of a bitch, keep away from me! You'll never get me!" There was a malicious chuckle and then a singsong chant. "Max Kyle Max Kyle Max Kyle—"

"Damn him!" muttered Kyle convulsively.

212

McKeever studied the slope. At the lower level there was cover—shattered blocks of limestone, some brush and a lonesome tree, all faintly visible. The last fifty yards would be difficult. The unobstructed grade was commanded from the cave. He ran his hand through his hair, surprised that his scalp was wet.

"Let's see what happens," he said. He took her hand and they began the steep climb. She was surprisingly light, no heavier than a child, but there was nothing frail in the clutch of her hand. McKeever found himself panting. He said, "Let's rest a moment."

They crouched behind a boulder. Over the eastern rim of the ravine a cloud drifted aside. The full white moon stared down and the brief hope of darkness was gone.

A stone whizzed past and Trister screeched:

"Go back, Kyle, you hear?"

McKeever looked down. In the cook fires below, he could see the armed men strung out, watchful of his move. A neighing broke from the horses bunched at the river. He turned and called coaxingly:

"Hello, Sam! It's me, McKeever!"

There was a silence.

"I'm coming up," he called. "I'm your friend."

Somewhere a cricket chirred. McKeever paused in perplexity. The Navajo woman was staring at the cave strangely. He said, "Tell him not to be afraid, Lupe. I'm not carrying a gun, tell him that. I only want to talk."

She nodded and arose in the moonlight. She cupped her hands. "Sam!"

There was a pause and then the old man said on a softer note, "That you, Lupe?"

She spoke in her own language—splashy Navajo mixed with occasional Spanish and English words. The exchange went back and forth until she turned to McKeever:

"He think you bring Kyle."

"But that's nonsense!" McKeever said urgently. "Tell him not to be a fool!"

She shook her head. "Kyle shoot at Trister. He ask, how Kyle know this place?"

"Oh?" McKeever rumpled his hair in perplexity. "Tell him I had nothing to do with that. He can't keep this up, tell him that. His only chance is with me."

She paused. "He not believe. He think you bring these men."

"Please try."

"You go back. Trister say he got bullet for self."

"Oh God!" he exclaimed. "He mustn't!"

They faced each other in silence.

In her seamed face he glimpsed a lifetime of lonely wandering in this stark harsh land. How strange, he thought, was the devotion and fear and love he saw for the man of another race. Her eyes were pleading with him. She said, "I am afraid for Trister."

He paused, irresolute. So many things were involved here—a process of events were dependent on the outcome which she could not even imagine. He said somberly, "I'm going up, tell him. If he won't talk with me, I can't help that, but I'm going."

"No," she begged. "He do something to self."

"I'm sorry." McKeever stepped into the moonlight. He said in a low soothing voice, "Sam, I don't want you to be nervous. I'm coming up to talk. I want you to behave—"

There was a silence.

McKeever toiled up the slope. He kept up a coaxing line. "I just want you to sit there, Sam. I've got nothing in my hands. I'm just a lawyer. I'm on your side—"

Crack!

McKeever paused. A bullet smashed the rock at his feet, and ricocheted off. Death had come close and yet he felt only a sense of detachment. There was surprise, then realization. Everything was the same—the silent ravine, the ominous bluff looming above the moonlight, the strident cricket, and yet—

It was like the center of a cyclone, the dead calm eye of the vortex where nothing stirred, nothing spoke, while on the periphery the elements howled—

"Don't be afraid of me, Sam," he said quietly.

This was the first time in his life a thing like this had happened yet it came as no stranger. He had a sense that he was commanded. Clinging to this hillside in the wilderness he was reminded of such moments when in the courtroom a force seemed to speak with his tongue, think with his mind—

He groaned with the knowledge that he would go on. "I'm your friend, Sam. I'm here to help."

Crack!

Trister's white face appeared. They were only yards apart. McKeever could see the whiskered mask of terror and despair.

"Stay away!" the old man cried hoarsely.

McKeever continued to climb. "It's all right. I won't let them hurt you," he said softly.

When he reached the ledge, the cave was empty.

"Sam!" he called.

He was standing, he saw, on the floor of a vast chamber whose gothic vaulting soared out of sight. The embers of a fire were still glowing; its acrid smoke arose in a natural flue. A stack of piñon logs had been piled in the recess.

There was evidence of prehistoric man. A circular rock mescal, cooking pits filled with dust, marked the entrance. A heap of grinding bowls lay shattered beneath crude pictographs. In the dim light he made out a running elk, a vivid painting in black and ochre and red.

"Sam!" he called. "I'm your friend!"

—Friend! Fri-e-e-n-d!

The echoes whispered about him. In the further depths he heard a scuttling noise. An unpleasant smell was in his nostrils. The passage led deeper into the mountain, he saw, but how far?

Fri-e-n-d! Friend—!

There was a bundle of resinous branches. McKeever seized one and set it ablaze. The yellow flame leaped with a dry crackling, warming his cheeks, dazzling his eyes. He held the torch aloft and turned toward the darkness. A cold wind blew in his face.

"Oh!" he cried, startled.

A small black phantom on wings swooped. It fluttered about his head, looping, side-slipping, dancing like a butterfly. He almost dropped his torch. In a moment countless bats were winging in a steady spiral traffic toward the exit behind him. Flock upon flock, in the hundreds of thousands, went darting toward their distant foraging grounds. He now recognized the acrid smell of guano.

He looked down. A ridge of droppings ran down the center of the passageway. To either side the sands were clean. In the soft under-layer he saw the trail of small dragging boots.

The torch was roaring. McKeever saw that it could not last. He took several boughs from the heap and plunged ahead into darkness. In the flaring light, the walls receded and came together and receded again into dimness.

He paused.

A rushing sound came from his right, where one vast ledge of limestone lay piled on another. His eyes made out a shifting motion on the wall. As he brought his torch forward, a tapestry of scorpions dissolved as the scuttling creatures found refuge in paper-thin crevices. "Oh my Lord!" he exclaimed with distaste. Then between two blocks of stone he saw an irregular opening in which the tracks disappeared.

There was no help for it. He thrust the torch ahead and went in, crouching. After fifty yards, the tunnel ended and he paused on a ledge. The torch showed nothing around him but the darkness of

215

space. He waited for his eyes to accept the deeper blackness. He called:

"For heaven's sake, *Sam!*"

Crack!

The flash came from below. McKeever saw Trister in the moment of brilliance—a gnarled ragged old man, pitiful and terrified. The crushing splendor of the limestone fairyland vaulted into reality. It was a cavern of incredible beauty. Frozen rock cascades in white and tan and turquoise blue. Green draperies festooned from the vaulting overhead. A ramp led from his ledge to the floor of the cave.

The darkness swallowed everything. Beyond the range of the torch came Trister's voice.

"Now you're mad at me!" the old man moaned. "I don't want this! Go back!"

"I'm not angry," McKeever called. "Just sit there and wait!"

"No!" Chattering desperately, the old man scuttled off into darkness.

McKeever paused.

This was the bat-cave. Myriads of black shapes clung to the walls about him. The acrid smell was overpowering. His lips felt cracked and his eyes watered with the ammoniac effect. Absolute quiet. Absolute dark. Here no light had penetrated since the world began.

In a shallow Permian sea two hundred million years before, an unending rain of diatomic ooze had laid the limestone formation on the sea bottom. As the aeons passed, the land had risen, the earth's crust buckled, the mountains had sunk, and these limestone ranges had been born. At once the trickling waters had begun their work—dissolving the rock, washing out the carbonate solution, corroding the vast cavern, and then deposition and the slow creation, cycle after cycle.

He looked on this and was oppressed by the weight of time.

He lit a second torch and picked his way down the ramp to the dusty cave bottom. He lowered the torch to study the scuffed trail of boot marks and for the moment the flame seemed to die. Below a certain level the air was dead. A small animal, a dog, would have died in the invisible poison layer. With a shock of fright he recovered the torch and looked around. A sound came from his right.

Trister stumbled further into the wilderness of stone, gasping and weeping. Vast dancing shadows followed. On and on.

"Oh Lordy, Lordy!" he chattered. "Don't let it happen! I don't want this! I'll do—"

He went on crazily, babbling with insensate fear. He turned and raised his rifle—

Crack!

A shower of dust trickled from the ceiling.

"All right, Sam," the voice came. "Nothing to be afraid of. Don't get excited."

"Oh please!" Trister turned, weeping, feeling his way, guided by the light from which he was fleeing.

Through a beautiful little room of spiral cones.

Around a series of domes.

Clusters of needles.

A hall of colors—

"A-a-a-h!" he screeched.

He stumbled and splashed in a sink of icy green water. He stood chattering in whiskered terror on a slimy bottom. He had no idea where the edge might be. He dared not move beyond his depth. He was paralyzed as the flame came closer—

"No!" he cried.

And then, the plough-horse face loomed in the torchlight, sweet and kindly, sorrow in its sunken eyes. "Just give me your hand!" said the deep friendly voice. Babbling and weeping hysterically, Trister fell into McKeever's strong arms and the nightmare came to an end.

"It's all right, old man," McKeever murmured. "You're all right now."

Through an eternity they sought their way back, following the scuffed trail, eyes watering in the bitter gases.

The last torch gave out when they reached the ramp leading to the small tunnel. There was a moment of panic and then, inch by inch, McKeever crawled up the ledge in utter darkness, feeling his way along the wall. He rested frequently, holding the old man's hand firmly. . . .

The party of searchers found them finally in a cul-de-sac, seated in darkness, exhausted and frightened. Martin held the torch aloft. "Well, thank God!" he cried fervently.

McKeever looked up wearily. "Hello, Em," he croaked. "Get us out of this, will you?"

"You'll stick with me?" Trister whispered.

McKeever nodded. "I promised I would."

The small party made their way slowly toward the first light of dawn at the end of the passage. The bats came flocking in their faces, back from their feeding grounds, flopping and darting in an unending stream of traffic.

"Can't make it, mister," the old man said weakly. "My legs give out way back."

McKeever said, "Carry him, will you, Em?"

They strode on, and when they reached the outer cave, Martin put down his burden. Trister shakily stepped onto the ledge, blinking in the fresh morning sun. Below, the law men were about the cook fire, slapping their thighs with laughter. The smell of coffee and bacon was in the air.

McKeever drew a deep breath. A thick dew had settled on the trees. Above the canyon rim, the sky was blue. It was the most beautiful of worlds, he thought, and at this moment Max Kyle stepped from the cave to his left. In a trembling voice, he said:

"Sam Trister!"

As the old man turned, the rifle spoke.

Trister was buried in the valley where he died. A scratched block of lava marked the grave. The parties divided and picked their ways back by separate trails. Max Kyle rode lolling in his saddle, his wrists bound, staring unwinking at the sun.

It was late afternoon at the top of the trail when McKeever turned to look back. In the valley below, the shriveled old woman was squatting at the grave, mourning in Navajo fashion for her husband.

With a sense of foreboding, he turned toward home.

Chapter XIV

Some days later the gray stallion reached for the lathered bit and McKeever let the reins slip away. No, there was no surprise, he thought. Even before Florence had spoken—her face raised in the rain, careless that her hair was wet, her eyes grave—he had known what she would say. In the long hard ride home, the sense of disaster had grown to certainty so that in this first shock, he felt nothing—nothing at all.

His son was dying.

"Oh my dear," said Florence with compassion, "I'm so sorry!"

He held his hand to his face and let his head bow with exhaustion. The rain trickled down his neck. In the warm stables a goat bleated.

He whispered, "How long has he known?"

"Since morning," she said. "We kept it from him, but he's too bright not to know what's happening."

So there it was, he thought, the very end of things. It was the fact.

Or was it? Everything was unreal, the horse beneath him, the neat familiar corral, the circle of faces dark with sympathy, the voices of children, the tamarisk overhead, the cold sweeping rain.

He seemed to be floating in a void. Half of him sought to grasp the fact. Another half sat in judgment, weighing, measuring—

Florence lifted her rain cape higher and peered up. "You'd better hurry, Link," she said, "there's not much time."

"Yes, of course," he said in a small voice.

A man in a bedraggled serape came forward. "*Patrón*, I will look to the horse," he said humbly.

McKeever studied his hands. The palms were covered with black flecks of leather, where days of riding had raised painful blisters. There was a smell of leather and horse's sweat and, in his daze, it occurred to him that he would need to wash. "Come, Link," Florence said. He dismounted and followed her through the unreal garden into the house. In the warm kitchen the steam of a mutton stew was billowing its redolent fragrance. The room was festooned with strings of chile, green and red, and the copper pots were shining. He went on, ashamed that his eyes could still see, his palate still hunger.

He paused at the stairs.

Dr. Kimball came down, heavy-eyed and weary, fumbling at the buckle of his black kit. "Oh hello, McKeever," he muttered despondently. "I'm sorry about this."

"What happened to the boy?" McKeever cried.

The doctor gave a hopeless shrug. "It was just a pleurisy, I thought," he said defiantly. "That's what it looked like. There was no way to tell."

"Wasn't there?" McKeever asked in an odd voice.

"No, certainly not!" The doctor put on his coat brusquely, pursing his lips, frowning with perplexity at this turn of bad luck. It had looked at first like a minor infection, he explained uncomfortably, but now it appeared that the fractured rib had done some damage to the pleural lining. Slowly blood and air had been oozing into the cavity and the right lung was collapsing, thrusting aside the heart and allied organs, crushing the left lung.

"It shouldn't have happened," the doctor repeated defensively. "I'm trying to explain. If I had any idea, I'd have told you, but I didn't. It wouldn't have helped for you to stay, in any case."

McKeever gave him a burning look. "Wouldn't have helped?" he said in a loud voice.

"There was nothing we could do for him!"

McKeever glanced up at the door to the sickroom on the landing. "Oh for God's sake!" he burst out, trembling. "Stop talking! Did you make him comfortable?"

"Of course!" the doctor said stiffly. He picked up his bag, then turned. "I know it's a shock, but I don't think you're being fair. I did my best. I'm sorry you feel this way." Shaking his head and offended, he nodded curtly, and left with the promise to return in a few hours.

McKeever threw aside his wet sheepskin. He walked up the stairs alone and opened the door.

The clock struck two.

Florence shivered and awoke from a cat nap in the living room. The fire had died. The house was cold and silent except for the sound from Doña María's room. She stretched the stiffness from her arms and crossed and tapped lightly on the door.

Doña María was kneeling in prayer on the worn stool and her knees were painful. Her eyes were wet. As she heard the sound, she crossed herself and arose with a final whisper of entreaty to the Virgin and drew her fringed shawl about her shoulder. She looked at her two sons who lay sprawled in bed in tranquil sleep. She went to the door.

"Is there a change?" she whispered.

Florence shook her head. "Not yet."

"*Ay, Madre!*" the older woman murmured dolefully. "If there were something to be done!" She wiped her eyes in a sodden handkerchief. "Would he like chocolate? He must need food, the poor man, he has eaten nothing."

"No, he doesn't want that," Florence sighed. She took the older woman's arm. "Come and sit with me, Doña María. It might help to talk."

They made hot chocolate in the kitchen, a thick bitter brew, and sat drinking beside the warm stove. From the outhouses, a wailing could be heard as the women let their hearts loosen with grief.

The thin minor of a crude ballad could be heard.

> "*Canto del joven*
> *que en esta casa miserable,*
> *Inocente, se muere sin culpa—*"

The chant went on, each line taken by the chorus, thrown back and elaborated, in the mournful strumming of the guitar. The women in the kitchen talked of the dying boy. Florence recalled her first meeting with the McKeevers in Washington and her raillery with Jeff of that distant afternoon. "He had more than a boy's mind," she mused. "He had a man's intelligence. His trouble was, he had feelings which were too large for him to deal with. He was only a boy."

With a start, she realized that she was using the past tense. Doña María caught this. She put aside her cup and the tears suffused her nose and eyes.

"*Ay de mí!*" she wept. "That it should happen to this boy! I feel for him more than my husband. Carlos is old, his life is over, but at least he had chosen his own way. What wrong has this innocent done? Where is the right? And for the father, where is the justice? What does it mean?" She broke off and wiped her eyes. The mournful singing went on:

> "*Vinieron a Cuatro Rios,*
> *El padre y el hijo.*
> *Canto de sus corazones—*"

Florence had no answer for the older woman. The hours passed in the dark night.

The light shallow breathing went on, fluttering the thin nostrils, giving the softest whistling sound. The boy turned in the pillow. He whispered:

"Dad."

McKeever bent over and touched the boy's forehead with his large warm hand. The lips were a distressing blue. He hated the sick smell, hated the cold room, most of all he hated himself—

"Yes, Jeff?" he asked.

The boy's eyes rolled. "What will it be like?"

"Like?" his father murmured, slowly stroking the tangled sick hair. "What do you mean?"

The boy whispered, "Dying—"

With a wrench of anguish he protested, "Now, Jeff."

"Please, Dad!" The whisper could barely be heard. "I want to know."

"Oh?" McKeever shrank back. There was no evading the issue. The boy's mind was still clear, still inquiring.

He said painfully:

"No one knows, Jeff, but it won't be bad. When the time comes, you'll know."

"How can I be sure?"

"Why do you ask?"

"I may fall asleep first."

McKeever patted the boy's hand.

"Well, it's the same thing," he said.

The boy closed his eyes and was silent a moment. A faint smile touched his lips. His father noticed this hopefully and said, "What are you thinking, Jeff?"

"Oh, just that old story about the Tammany judge," the boy murmured. "The one who wanted to mark the actress's leg in evidence. Gee, that was the best!"

"That was a good one!" McKeever agreed. "That judge was so astonished when I joined in the motion! Good Lord, that was a long time ago!"

They smiled at each other.

These stories were a warm thing between them, and McKeever's first manner had been light. He had spent the hours arousing the boy's sense of fun with old anecdotes. He had described his hunt for Sam Trister in the same manner, making it a comical thing, but of course he had not told the truth. So far as Jeff knew, the search had been a success. The old man was alive and prepared to testify in the morning.

But the device was a makeshift. Jeff could not be deceived about himself. The agony was grinding past endurance. He looked up and whispered, "You'll beat 'em tomorrow, won't you, Dad?"

"Oh sure!"

The boy waited. "I'm glad you got here, Dad. I was afraid you might think I was scared."

"No, I didn't think that," his father murmured.

"Because I'm not—"

"You can feel scared if you want to," McKeever said gently. "It's a natural thing."

They were silent a moment.

"I don't mind it," the boy whispered. "I did at first while you were away but not any more."

"I know."

"Maybe I should, but I don't." The boy closed his eyes a moment and resumed, "It's just that I don't know what I'm supposed to think."

McKeever continued to stroke the tangle of sick hair. This was in character, he thought, the boy's fear, not of pain or hurt, but of inadequacy. "It's all right, Jeff," he said softly, reassuringly. "Just remember, this is nothing unusual. It happens to everyone. It's a part of life. There's no particular way you're supposed to feel."

The boy smiled faintly.

McKeever went on. "You wonder about yourself too much, Jeff. About how you'll meet things. You get ashamed of being frightened, but you shouldn't be."

"You'll be here?" Jeff asked. "You won't leave now?"

"I won't leave," his father promised.

There was a whining sound at the door and the boy turned restlessly.

"Can I see my little dog?" he asked weakly.

McKeever said, "Not now." There was a sudden sound and he leaned closer. With alarm he asked:

"What is it, Jeff?"

The boy opened his blue lips, and spoke with surprising strength. "Open the window," he begged. "Please!" His breath came faster.

McKeever looked at the casement. "It's too cold."

"It's stuffy here," the boy gasped fretfully. "I can't breathe."

McKeever made a pretense of compliance. He raised the sash up and down. Outside the night was clear, the rain had passed, the sky was black and moonless. He returned to the bedside. His quiet voice went on, soothing, reassuring, over and over, warm in its deepest timbre. "It's all right, Jeff," he said. "This is nothing unusual. You'll be all right."

The boy's eyes were steady. "Will I?"

223

"Of course."

The shallow breathing went faster and suddenly the boy's voice was strong and clear. "I'm sure of one thing, Dad," he said distinctly.

"Yes, Jeff?" McKeever asked.

He waited but there was no answer. Quietly, in the midst of a loving thought, the boy died.

As the news spread at dawn, men and women began to gather, from the town proper, then from the surrounding farms and ranches. The Spanish were first, especially those who had been close to McKeever in his struggle; but there were also Anglos, sober men and their wives in whom curiosity mingled with compassion. Those who were Catholics crowded the ancient adobe church at early Mass. Those who were not, made directly for the house of death. Gifts of food came in abundance—jellies and smoked hams, fruits and pies and Spanish delicacies.

The older women, Doña María and Mrs. Blanchard, were desolated and Florence stepped in to take charge. She had in fact managed affairs during McKeever's absence and her efficient touch was sorely needed. She hushed the children, kept the kitchen going, seated the visitors and maintained the decorum of the household. Her presence in McKeever's house made her an object of speculation, she was aware, but this was now an accustomed thing.

They filled the house. Heads shook with incredulity, sighs were breathed, the boy's merits, real and imaginary, were elaborately discussed in a pious hush. Mostly they resented the fact that death had come by accident. It seemed grotesque, unfair, more shocking than by the expected means of lingering disease. The consuming of food went on in a busy hum of conversation. Beneath the gravity there were crosscurrents and even low-toned joking.

Florence brought a tray to a group of newspapermen gathered in the study. In low tones they took their coffee and discussed the struggle due to be resumed in the District Court. The killing of the witness, Sam Trister, and the peril hanging over Don Carlos were perplexities. Lon Wilby stirred his cup thoughtfully. He asked:

"How's McKeever taking this, Floss?"

She drew a weary hand across her eyes. "Well enough, I suppose. What can I say, Lon?" She added that McKeever had not yet come down from his son's room although he knew that his associates had gone to inform the Court of the situation.

"What will he do?" Wilby asked.

She sighed, "I don't know, Lon, honestly. Adjourn the case, I suppose. I just haven't asked him."

With a delicate gesture, John Macy Bellew put a raisin in his mouth. "Has he been alone with the boy?"

"Yes," said Florence.

"Strange," Bellew murmured. "I should think he'd want someone with him in the room."

"No, he wouldn't have it," she said dispiritedly. "It's terrible, an awful thing. He's been there all night alone. He just sits there staring. I couldn't get a word from him."

Bellew removed a pit from his tongue. "He'll have to adjourn the case," he decided.

Wilby asked, "Why so?"

"What else can he do?"

The newspaperman had been thinking deeply, scratching his nose, his chubby face concerned. "You can't tell with a man like McKeever. When he first came, I remember we figured he was here for the money—"

"Or the glory!" Florence broke in bitterly.

"Same thing!" Wilby said briefly. "But now I think it's something else, I sure do!" He finished his coffee with some wry recollection of his early adverse editorials on the subject.

Bellew was ironically amused at this change of opinion. He asked drily, "What else could it be? That McKeever means what he says? That he takes things seriously?"

"Maybe," Wilby said and turned to Florence. "What was Trister supposed to know about the case? Have you got any idea?" She gave him a strange look and said, "I don't know, Lon, and that's the truth. He hasn't mentioned a word."

"Sure flummoxes things, don't it?" Wilby drawled shrewdly.

"Excuse me," she said abruptly. McKeever had appeared and had come downstairs. She put the empty cups aside and went through the living room with deep concern. He was standing in the midst of his visitors, smoothing his rumpled gray suit, and his smile was strange. "Thank you," he was saying. "It's quite all right. Everything's fine, I'm sure. It doesn't matter, thank you."

Florence came to his rescue. "Come in here, Link," she said, taking him aside to the small coatroom off the entrance. His manner disturbed her. He said in a tone of wonder, "Why are they here, Floss? Who are they?"

"They're friends," she said softly. "They've come to condole."

"Oh? Is that it?" He scratched his unkempt hair irritably. "Why should they do that now? I'm all right."

"They're your neighbors, Link," she said as though to a child. "They want to help."

225

He shook his head. "They're not here for me, not for Jeff. They're here for themselves." He looked back to the room where smoke was drifting. "Well, I don't need them," he said with rising excitement.

"Don't be unfair," she urged. She closed the door and turned with perplexity. "Link, what's the matter?"

"Matter?" he repeated, subsiding. "Why nothing! I just don't see why they're here!" He fumbled at a bow tie with helpless hands. "Here," she said, "let me." She made the tie quickly and pulled the wings with a firm gesture. "Now sit here where I can see you." Obediently he took the chair and stared up as she combed his hair. He said brightly, "Floss!"

"Yes, dear?"

"At the end it was all right," he said with his smile.

"I'm sure it was," she murmured.

"I was with him and he didn't mind."

His smile lay heavy in her heart. With a gentle hand she stroked aside his rebellious forelock. "Oh Link," she said softly. "Link dearest!"

His lips twitched in his mirthless grimace. "I was joking with him," he whispered, "that was the last thing." He paused and she took his head to her breast and held him close. "I know," she murmured. "I know."

They remained in silence.

There was a tap on the door. Mrs. Blanchard entered holding a soaked handkerchief to her flat humorless face. McKeever looked up with dry eyes.

"Yes?" he asked distantly.

The old woman wiped the tears away. "I prayed the Lord to take me," she said piteously, "if only He would spare Jeffrey."

He arose and the vexation drained away. "I'm sure you did, Rachel," he muttered.

"If he were my own child," she whispered, "I couldn't feel it more." She looked from him to Florence, but as there was no response, she wept and left on painful swollen ankles.

Florence said, "Would you like something to eat, Link? You should, you know. Let me get you coffee."

"I don't want anything. Not now."

"But you must," she protested. "You can't keep this up."

"No!" he said stubbornly. He strode to the door. She followed and asked, "Where are you going?"

"Why, to court," he said with surprise.

"Now? But you can't!"

226

"But I must," he said with perplexity. "Don't you see that?"

"No, I don't. I'm sure no one expects you there."

He said angrily, "I'm going to court!" He stepped into the clear morning air. She followed into the gravel drive. "But why?" she cried. "Emory can handle it. Why must you go?"

"Why?" he asked hoarsely. Curious eyes were on them from the Spanish quarters. Anglos were at the windows. A buggy was coming up the road with a rancher and his wife. "Why?" he repeated, turning, and his smile was a grimace. "Floss, when I left the boy," he said in a shaking voice, "I knew he was going to die."

"Oh no!"

"Oh yes!" he mocked bitterly.

"But you couldn't!" she cried.

"I knew it exactly!"

"Even the doctor had no idea! No one did!"

"I knew it within me!" He smote his heart with a clenched fist. "I knew it *here!*"

"Oh that!" She then looked up suddenly as the deeper significance struck her. "I don't believe it!" she said strongly.

He laughed harshly.

"I denied it to myself! Oh I told myself over and over it wasn't so, but I lied! I knew it as sure as fate!"

She stared at the trembling ashen face.

"Then why did you leave?"

"Why?" He ground his teeth in fury. "Because the case needed me, that's why! No one else could go, no one but me! Link McKeever! I didn't want to go, but I went!" His smile of horror twitched at his mouth.

There was a moment of silence.

"Link," she pleaded, "stay here now."

"No!" he said violently. "There's a case to finish!" He faced the path which led through a cluster of trees to the distant courthouse. He raised his powerful arms, thick as beams, in a blind gesture toward the horizon. "Was it for nothing?" he cried. He stood with the sun in his face, trembling. "Was it useless? Should it go waste? Is that what you're saying?"

After a moment, she bowed her head and stood aside.

He started on foot to the courthouse, a shaggy man with bowed shoulders, grasping his lapels. It was a lovely fresh day. The rains had washed the air and the soil was squashy beneath his tread. The first flowers were splashes of color at the highway, dwarf sunflowers and devil's-paintbrushes.

Humble men swept off sombreros as he passed. A flock of sheep scrambled from his path. He strode along the dusty street and crossed the bridge and his eyes saw nothing.

The military came to attention as he approached the court plaza. He strode up the broad path to the entrance he had last left in swirling snow. All his life as a lawyer he had been punctual and it seemed significant that, as he entered the courthouse, a bell began to toll the hour.

Chapter XV

A black mist swirled as he arose, and then cleared, and he saw the twelve faces in the box sharper than life. Like those in a Flemish painting, they stared at him with cold precise speculation. Over the months, in the small cockpit, a sense of intimacy had sprung up, he had thought, but now he could not be sure. Across the void their alien intelligences were sitting in judgment.

The moment of decision was upon him.

He studied the writing in his hands. In the unseasonable mildness, the heat of the stoves was suffocating. He loosened his collar and turned to the seat of authority.

"May the Court please."

Millikan moved restively, unsmiling. It did *not* please the Court. On the bench the Bible lay open at *Exodus*:

> *Take heed to yourselves, that ye go not up into the mount, or touch the border of it: whosoever toucheth the mount shall be surely put to death.*

The judge thought of himself as a just man, neither hard nor soft, but an impersonal arm of the Law. He was sure that he got no pleasure from these proceedings, that his duties were painful, that the imposition of sentence would grieve him, but the concept that the Law had been handed down at Sinai in fire and smoke, that the mount quaked, that the people were struck with fear, was to his mind right and proper and a source of deep satisfaction.

In all sympathy the Court had suggested an adjournment and this courtesy had been refused. With disquiet, he swiveled and gazed out at the scene of the awakening spring. It was scarcely decent, he felt. The Court was not sure that its dignity was not invaded.

McKeever turned mechanically and bowed. "Mr. Taft."

The prosecutor sat sprawled among his fellows, laundered and barbered and refreshed. The inky locks at his neck gleamed with unguents. For a moment the lawyers' glances met and the distant scene at Barlow's Cave, the death of Trister, the arrest of Kyle, the return from the desert, lay between them. Now why, the prosecutor wondered as he plucked his throat, why had his adversary failed to put these matters in issue? With a friendly blink of encouragement, he parted his frock coat and nodded at the formal salutation.

"Gentlemen of the Jury."

The jurors stirred slightly, embarrassed by the fixed smile, the stricken face. In all these months of proximity, with no barrier but the rail between, this was his first direct address to them since his opening. Until now, all words had filtered through the bench. The burly first juror coughed into his blacksmith's fist.

At the lawyer's side, the defendant sat rigid, clutching his chair, his eyes glinting in a low red light. "*Andale, andale!*" he muttered vengefully. "Get on with it! Finish the business!" He had at first been staggered by the tragic news, but now he was sunk in his own thoughts. His hoarse whisper filled the stagnant air.

McKeever affixed his spectacles and took up a page of notes. He had less room than ever, for an extra row of chairs had been installed within the rail, and he stood amidst the cold-faced men. This was something he disliked, for it spoiled the stage effect. "Would you mind?" he asked wearily. But they remained immovable, and he turned to the jury. His voice was thin and strange in his ears.

"Gentlemen," he said, "I hope you will forgive me if I read a portion of my summation. I don't usually rely on notes. But this trial has been unusually long, and I've been under a strain, and some of my thoughts, I felt, should be prepared. I have here a few words I wrote last week. Forgive me if I turn to them." He adjusted his spectacles and began to read.

"We have now reached the point where it becomes my duty to point out to you the significance of the evidence in this case—one which has no doubt been burdensome to you, extending as it has in all the heat and passions of these many months. It is unfortunate and no one could help it. I will be as brief as I can."

He paused. "It will soon be almost a year since I first arrived in this community to accept the responsibilities of this trial. I have been associated with members of the Territorial bar, my colleagues beside me, whose skill and devotion to their duty have been remarkable. I am proud to have served with them. This Territory is to be congratulated on their selflessness and on their high legal qualities." He gazed at them a moment. A slow flush mounted in Martin's face. Dominguez's eyes were awash, and his ugly face was quivering. McKeever went on. "I should like to mention others who have assisted the defense, some lawyers, some laymen, whose efforts have been outstanding, and whose friendship has been rewarding. But I hope they forgive me if I go to the matter at hand."

He went on in this fashion, laboring through the amenities and introductory matter, lightly touching on themes to come. At the press table, pens went down, writing stopped. Bellew put his head down and noted in a whisper to Wilby the omission of any expressions of gratitude to the bench for the conduct of the trial. It was, for McKeever, a singular departure from graciousness, almost a studied affront. Wilby shrugged. The bench, he admitted, deserved no better.

The lawyer paused to wipe his eyelids of their burden of smarting sweat. Hollow! he thought. His words were formal! The sound seemed swallowed in the suddenly vast spaces of the chamber. He gathered himself and continued to read.

"As you can imagine, this period has been one of remorseless anxiety, not only because a life is at stake, but for an additional reason. As you may know, this man's wife and sons have become members of my household. During this trial, they have lived with me, and a warm affection has grown among us. You have seen Mrs. De Niza in court"—the jurors turned to the rear where she sat, twisting her hands—"and you can easily understand how this feeling has grown up, especially between her sons and my own. Now this, I suppose, has nothing to do with the case. I mention it because it explains the sense with which I must approach the issues. No lawyer is fit to practice law unless he feels personally as though the judgment were against himself. Sometimes we overdo things. Perhaps we talk too much. I don't know. When I say too little, I reproach myself for the things left out. When I say more than I should, I wish I hadn't." He smiled bleakly, an old smile without mirth, in memory of an honored jest. "Well, you must take me as I am, and bear with me."

He could not continue, he thought, for the words were swimming before him. His knees were trembling. The heat of the stoves was oppressive. He stared at the paper, noting the imperfections, the smeared lines of blue ink. He put aside the paper and advanced to the rail. The sixth juror, the blue-eyed man with wispy blond hair, winked rapidly under his gaze.

"Gentlemen," he faltered, "I'm afraid that you've heard somehow what happened this morning in my home. You may wonder that I am here now before you to conclude this trial. Well, I wish it were not so. I wish it were possible to address you strictly on the merits, and without the intrusion of these things. Your task is hard enough. It requires keen judgment, calm deliberation, mature consideration and an impartial decision. I beg that you put the death of my son from your minds." He leaned on the rail and closed his eyes.

The judge stroked his beard. "Mr. McKeever," he said quietly, "this is not proper."

The lawyer turned. "Perhaps not," he admitted, "but it is in everyone's thoughts."

"That is your own doing, sir, not the Court's."

"Yes I know," said McKeever humbly.

"You may still take an adjournment, sir."

There was a pause.

"I am afraid not."

"Well, proceed," said the judge, disturbed, "but do make an effort."

The lawyer removed his glasses and crossed toward the witness chair. "Gentlemen, the Court is right," he said somberly. "I dislike mentioning these private matters, but what am I to do? The Law is not a school for manners. It is a system of justice. It is my profound belief that all things should be considered by the jury. However, I will try to abide by the ruling." He paused, his eyes in dark shadows, thinking of the night's events. He said, "I would gladly have avoided this burden, but in the pursuit of justice, we lawyers cannot always pick and choose our cases. The issues before you are great and solemn. I would feel unworthy of this moment if your verdict were to come, even for acquittal, on any basis other than the strict justice of the case."

He remained wordless, sweating, his eyes vacant with the effort of bringing forth the thoughts he required. At the press tables, the scratching of pens resumed.

"I am sure my client agrees. He too wants no false sympathy. In this period, I have lived with Carlos de Niza. We have met and talked almost daily, from the time he was kidnaped in Mexico till now. I have found in him a rich and varied mind, deeply learned, quite philosophical, and completely without fear. I don't mean that he doesn't love life, because he does. There are few men in whom the joy of living is not more abundant. But he is not afraid to die."

The jurors glanced to his side covertly. The gaunt heavily lined face with its white beard and aquiline features nodded desperately. "*Ah sí! Verdad!* Get on!" If no one else could follow, McKeever thought, at least Don Carlos was in accord. The clock, he noticed, stood at ten.

"Now this man is remarkable," he went on laboriously. "He has a wife who is as dear to him as life. He is widely loved. The arts satisfy him and the whole world is his. But life itself, his wife, and all the world are not prized above some other idea in his mind.

"What kind of man is this?

"What is that idea?

"You must decide those questions. You cannot avoid them. Because the law requires that you decide his guilt for the murder charged in the indictment. His guilt for murder! And that is something you can never, never do unless you know the man. Who is guilty? Who is innocent? No one can say who cannot look into the hearts of men!"

He paused before the fifth juror, a scarlet-faced man of fifty. "Will you tell me, sir, as a former minister, that this is beyond human power? Well, if so, I agree. I am as conscious as you of our human limitations. In all my life, I have never attempted to stand as a judge of men, for that reason. There was a time when I thought otherwise, but now I see how wrong I was." He wiped his eyes with flat palms wearily. "I suppose there are others who are not subject to this frailty. They are content to be the judges. They are gifted with an unshakable certitude of mind. Or so they suppose. I do not object. I am thankful for such men, because we must, I imagine, have judges in this sad unhappy world of ours. But for myself, I can only defend. Because of this I *can* be sure—there is no one who does not need to be defended. No one too undeserving."

The black mist gathered and he waited. "All this is especially important now"—he swallowed, and went on with an effort—"especially because I have not, I am afraid, done the work of the defense too well. It was my duty to find positive evidence in favor of this man. I had hoped to establish some form of alibi. I failed. I had expected to produce a witness to show by direct proof that the Territory's creature, Tom Canty, is a liar as well as a thief and murderer. I failed. At the end of the trial, I must concede that the witness, Sam Trister, cannot be produced, nor is my adversary to blame."

The jurors' puzzled frowns showed that Trister's fate had been kept from them while in the bailiff's custody. They had no idea, he saw, of the old man's death. The judge leaned forward. "Mr. Mc-Keever! I must warn you!"

The lawyer turned. "That will be my only reference to that matter," he said in a low voice. "I relinquish that point."

At the press table, Ida Montgomery cupped her hand and whispered, "John, isn't this a peculiar kind of argument? Is he giving up?"

Bellew removed his pince-nez. "He's only admitting an obvious weakness," he whispered dubiously. "It's really the cleverer way. What else can he do?"

"Well, perhaps." The newspaperwoman returned, unconvinced, to a pencil sketch of the lawyer. It was an idealistic conception of the orator, hand in vest, forefinger upraised, addressing a rapt audience, and wholly unlike the weary laboring man at the rail. She murmured, "I'm not so sure he's clever. Not today, at least."

McKeever was saying, "It was my duty to persuade my client to act as witness in his own behalf. Even here I failed. Good Lord! I could not persuade him to testify, not even to save his life. So that now, bedraggled and worthless as it is, Tom Canty's version of the events in the Sierra Blanca stands without direct contradiction." He looked down, opening and closing his great hands. "Empty! Empty! Well, enough of that," he sighed. "I suppose I can trust Mr. Taft to point out my deficiencies. He'll do a good job, be sure of that."

The prosecutor raised the wrinkled hoods of his eyes inquiringly. He clasped his paunch and settled back, uncertain how to take this tribute. The pens went down. All eyes were on the bowed man striding in the well of the court, twisting his hands as he stumbled for words. The hoarse tortured voice went on, filling the hush of the chamber to every corner.

"I have my excuses. I know"—he made an empty gesture—"I know all the arguments. An innocent man can be helpless against the false accuser. No one can guard against a bolt from the blue sky. No man can arrange his life to provide in advance for witnesses against—what? Against whom? Who can live that way? And a man who wanders alone in the wilderness, who can he bring? There are cases when nothing stands between a man and death except the conscience of twelve men.

"I know all that. But that is not enough.

"And it's not enough to answer that the man may want to throw away his life for his own reasons. This is no excuse. None at all. Not for the Court, nor for the jurors, not for his lawyer. The man did not give himself life. It came to him from elsewhere. It's not his to destroy, or if it is, we cannot admit the fact. It was entrusted to him to use, well or ill, but he cannot embezzle it away.

"And we must not listen to what he wants. We can only do what is right.

"When Carlos de Niza sat in that chair, I expect you heard him with some anger. His words were harsh and cruel, his laughter was bitter and insulting. He refused to explain. He refused to palliate or justify. Why? He was an honest witness, you'll agree. He told you frankly what he thought. He is Spanish. We are Anglo. He is convinced that he cannot get justice in this American court of law. That is his clear belief, plainly stated. Well, you have every reason for resentment.

"But is resentment enough? You must ask yourselves why this man at a time like this should want to antagonize you? Why would he not beg and plead? Why not lick your feet? I think the reason is clear. Carlos de Niza is a man. To this kind of man some things are impossible. I believe you understand that much. Yes"—he peered closely—"I see you do." He stood nodding before them.

"I have been troubled throughout this trial by the outcry that I have come from the East to defend this man's life. I admit that fact. I have come a great distance to assume these burdens. But why should that disturb Mr. Taft? What is sinister about the East? This Territory is occupied by men who have been coming from all parts of the country—East and West and North and South. All accents are heard here. The legal forms reflect the general experience. This is one country. We are bound by the same ties. The destruction of law in any part affects the whole.

"If injustice should flourish here, do you think we are not affected elsewhere?"

The clock struck the half-hour.

McKeever turned to his client and went on. Yes, they, the jurors drawn from the county, had heard Carlos de Niza say that he would be pleased to see the Anglos destroyed to the last man. Did they really believe it was Carlos de Niza talking? Or was it the bitterness of a man in despair? Where was the truth?

He went on in the deepening silence. In the plaza and on the surrounding lawns, the crowd at the open windows was quiet as snatches of his words were relayed back. His voice rose and fell hoarsely, and the morning shadows shortened as the sun rose higher.

Shortly past noon, Florence drove up in her buggy. She paused with surprise at the size of the crowd, and its quiet air of serious attention. She tied her mare to the post and with the help of a deputy sheriff managed to struggle into the courthouse. Breathless and worried, she got up to the second floor and squeezed through. At the door, she touched the elderly bailiff's shoulder.

"S-sh!" He turned and recognized her. "Oh, Miss Floss! 'Fraid there's no room inside," he whispered. "They're jampacked."

"What's the state of the case?"

The bailiff scratched his chin. "Can't say! McKeever's been at it now for hours. He's skinned your Pa alive. I won't even say what he done to Canty. He just showed they want the man in Vancouver."

She shivered with fatigue. "Is he getting across?"

The toothless mouth chewed a liquid cud thoughtfully. "Can't say," he managed, shifting. "That's a tough bunch in there. Can't make out the half of what he's saying. I just know he's got 'em a little sick o' that skunk. You want to sit with your Pa? He's down front."

"No, Fred, but I'd like to slip in back."

He rubbed a stubbled cheek dubiously. "I'll try."

A wave of warm fetid air greeted her as she slid unobtrusively into the rear bench. As though on a signal, the lawyer turned. A pang went through her. His broad face was deathly pale, his hair was tangled. He stood at the rail, leaning heavily, rumpled in his gray suit, speaking earnestly in a quavering hoarse voice of pain. His collar was opened, his neck was exposed. He seemed not to see her. She clasped her hands tightly in her lap and sat back. The smell was offensive.

"Because what"—he asked in his strange voice—"what do all these facts show? Isn't it clear that he wants *not* to be acquitted? Don't you see? He's determined to be hung on the scaffold out there in the prison yard. Why? How can this be? He's not a suicidal fool, not an hysteric looking for martyrdom. No, there's something more. He wants to give his life, not uselessly, not in vainglory, but to prove something. He wants to show that our laws are not instruments of justice, but weapons of force in the hands of men like Hogarth.

"Is he right?

"I'm not concerned with Hogarth as a man. Not at all. It's simply that Hogarth has become more here than one old man whose hold on life is slipping. He stands here as a symbol in my client's mind for a whole order of things. This is what Carlos de Niza hates—the things that symbol represents. Our country and its laws and its institutions.

"Is this so hard to see?

"I can tell you something. I've dealt with symbols all my life. They're part of my profession. I know what they can mean. They are the powerful things of our world. A flag is cloth, a book is paper, a cross is wood. Men in the millions have died for these, and not only men. An idea is—well, who can say? What else is our country but the child of an idea?"

The jurors followed his gaze to the limp flag beside the bench, the Bible before the judge, the crucifix on the breast of Doña María. McKeever let the silence underscore his words.

"He is trying to show the world that force and violence rule not only this case, but all cases of its kind. He rejects our courts and our laws. Through his death he sees a last chance to prove these vindictive ideas. Well, obviously he's got a point. It's not without substance. The prosecution has given the weight to his charge. His laughter was meant to mock this court and the institutions of our life. It was a charge that here, where the man stands before you

236

different in language, and in belief, twelve common men cannot bring in a verdict according to the justice of the case."

He paused, wiping his hands, peering earnestly at the array of stony faces. "Well, in many lands, gentlemen, that's how things are done. But is this such a land? Is there truth to the charge? This embittered man believes there is. He has lost faith in our laws. And this is a pity, a matter of regret, because he is a man worth saving—and he is lost. And if he is right, we are all lost."

He paused again. The going was difficult, and his throat was rasping and cruelly painful. His words seemed not his own. The clock told him he had been talking for hours, an eternity had passed and he had not yet said the multitudinous things swarming in his mind. Was he making an impression? These were waxwork faces—blue-eyed, red-necked, astonished, blinking. Was there thought in them? Emory Martin put a glass of water before him. He shook his head and toiled on.

"Because what," he asked desperately, quavering, "—what does this case turn on? The entire fantasy stands on the word of Tom Canty that my client hired him that day in the Sierra Blanca to commit murder. Unless you believe Canty, you must acquit. I am sure the Court will charge that as the law.

"It won't be easy, God knows! My client gave you a heavy burden when he refused to answer the charge against him. He made this a difficult case. But there is something—something my client said, which you must consider. If Carlos de Niza were an Anglo, you'd fling all this back in Canty's face for what it's worth—filth from the sewers of a degenerate criminal mind.

"Canty!

"This witness for the Territory is a horror. A confessed murderer and a thief, a butcher of children, a rapist, a degenerate. All his life he has lived destructively. He is worthless in all things that make a man. He told you plainly that he knows that he is no good, and that no one likes or respects him. In turn he despises and detests every human being on earth including himself. His only feelings now are hate and fear. Whatever decent instincts he ever had were brutalized and destroyed long ago.

"But now, he claims, he is telling the truth. It is now, under the spiritual guidance of the unfortunate Max Kyle, that he has determined to find a good life.

"Now he seeks redemption, he wants you to believe, through his role in this trial—through the destruction of a man whose superior merits he has envied through a lifetime of monstrous vindictive jealousy.

237

"And he wants you to believe that he committed murder not out of spiteful ambition to take this man's place as the leader of his people—insane as that notion might seem—but to *help* his people.

"To help his people!

"Can you believe that? How would it help his people? How can hatred and murder and burning and reprisals help anyone? Good God! Here are his own words! If you've forgotten, you can consult the record. Here! One thousand pages of testimony and not one word of truth!"

He smote the pile of stenographic transcripts on the table. "No, gentlemen, I won't rehash the evidence again. You know Canty by now, and you see the truth. You have his measure. When you consider what this man was ready to do for money, what can my words add?

"He could kill for money.

"He could commit arson for money.

"He could maim for money.

"He could commit bestialities for no reason at all.

"Then why, when his own neck stands to be broken by the rope, why would not this poor creature lie? Is the swearing away of a man's life so different from these other things? What is truth to this man? Why would he not use perjury to magnify his own personality, and to destroy the man before whom he knows he is nothing but slime?

"This unhappy wretch told you the details of the murder. He went over the night of the ambush. His mind was clear on that. He was not confused. He described the skill with which he aimed the shotguns, those deadly weapons. He recalled the darkness of that night, with all its beauty, the sounds of night birds and the croaking frogs below. The details still were clear, even to the song on the lips of the old woman. And what did that mean to him? Nothing! He had no feeling. Not for himself, nor for what he was doing, nor for the old man and woman. It was nothing. No more, in his own words, than drinking a cup of coffee.

"And so he stood with the rifle in hand, and when the shotguns had done their work badly, he fired his rifle to kill the poor stableboy, Tomás. And then Douglas Hanna. And still he had no feeling. He did all this, he told you, because another man then fifteen hundred miles away had paid him for the job.

"And now they ask you to believe this man.

"Ah yes! He was not altogether bad, he now claims, because he spared Mrs. Hanna from death. He put aside his gun because of

238

sudden pity. Having blinded her, and widowed her, a softer feeling entered his heart. He could not do it.

"I would like to believe in this man's pity. With all my heart I would like to think that a touch of wonder at himself entered his mind. But what is the evidence?

"Where did he turn up next? As fast as his horse could take him, he returned to town. Did he kneel in prayer? Did he consider remorse? It would hardly seem so. There was no time for these things. Within moments, he entered the brothel and what happened next you heard from the mouth of the witness, Juana Malina. I will not go into her reluctant testimony. The pollution of her body is there in the record.

"And now they ask you to hang Carlos de Niza on this man's naked word. Why? If my client were an Anglo, would they have the audacity? In any other case, you wouldn't hang a dog on this testimony—isn't that the phrase?—not if he swore on his mother's grave.

"There is only one issue.

"Against the word of Tom Canty—the personality of Carlos de Niza. Here he sits. Look at him. You know who he is. You know what he stands for. He's not a stranger. He made the issue clear. If you can believe him capable of this murder, why, then convict him, for that's your duty. But if not, then you must acquit.

"If he were an Anglo, one of us, there would be no doubt that he would go free.

"I've examined the records of all your cases in the Territory. Under these circumstances there has never been a conviction before of an Anglo. Will you now give the same kind of justice where the accused is Spanish?

"He thinks not!"

He stood peering at the jurors, fumbling at his mouth.

"Carlos de Niza thinks not!" he cried. "And I must tell you the truth! I no longer know what to expect! Yesterday I would have staked my life on your verdict.

"Today I am not sure.

"All my life has been spent in the courts of our country. I've tried cases and argued appeals in many states and territories. I've won and I've lost, but I never felt that the struggle was not worth the effort. How could I? Can you think of a better or higher calling? I never thought that our laws were perfect. I've seen too many sickening things in our courts for that. Our laws work through men, all sorts of men, sick with hate, spilling with venom, dull in feeling, parts of a machine which grinds us all alike.

239

"And the stupid!

"Against stupidity, the gods themselves battle in vain! How many times are we not tempted to water down our thoughts to the dullness of our courts and juries. Well, I never have. The law is a vast sea of knowledge, but its conceptions are not difficult. There is nothing there beyond the scope of common sense. It deals with human behavior and it represents the accumulated wisdom and experience of our past.

"The knowledge of the law is not beyond you. It needs simply a patient willingness to understand.

"Ah well, I never complained. I always felt at peace in the courtroom. However violent and cruel the world outside, here was sanctuary. Here, I thought, the issues were great and lofty. Here one could serve something greater than oneself. I started with the conviction that the profession of law was the best business which life could afford. To serve justice and to support the principles of this country, to maintain the Constitution against attack, whether from government or from the unbridled mob, to defend the innocent, all this seemed to furnish a goal and purpose worthy of any man. Did this make me happy? I don't know. I can only say it was something I had to do.

"These principles may not always be observed, but they are those of my profession. It is the business of lawyers to compel obedience to their mandate. The law is not a matter of quiddets and tricks but a body of truth as broad as human need, and even beyond. If I had not believed this, I could not have done the work to which I put my mind.

"But now," McKeever went on, looking up with a mixture of cunning and despair, "I must tell you that I am not sure. I felt once that I understood. A man can be poor and sick and take misfortune without complaint. But the sense of injustice is another thing. It can cause a man to give his life"—he turned to stare into the unwavering burning eyes of the prisoner—"his life, and even more. Why? Because justice is the essential thing. It strikes us deepest. The lack of justice can destroy a land more surely than war or pestilence. Ah, yes! We think there's peace in this borderland because a treaty was made forty years ago—but is there? Carlos de Niza does not think so. Peace is not the absence of war. It is the presence of justice.

"Yes," he whispered hoarsely, "I thought I saw all that. But that was yesterday. Now? I considered this during the night, and this morning I do not know."

His massive head and shoulders drooped as he leaned for support on the rail. Florence covered her eyes, his cry of pain was in her heart.

240

The low voice of anguish whispered on.

"You see, I thought no cost was too great—that justice was beyond price. It doesn't come by itself, but it can't be bought. It must be won, but it can't be paid for. So that its value is beyond our thinking. When we stop to measure, we've lost the thing. So I thought.

"But the trouble is, that each trial is a fresh start, and when we walk into court, we begin again each time. And this means something for you, because in our courts, in the criminal law, the verdict must always be given by twelve men. Not scholars, not specialists, not the high-perched few. Plain men from the life around us. If ever the courts get too remote, these men are reminders of their humanity. I wouldn't have it otherwise, but it means that the burden is yours. You cannot look to the judge. Nor to the prosecutor. Nor to me. We can't help you. The verdict is yours!

"So you must think deeply. Will you kill Carlos de Niza? Will you pay him back in kind? Whatever you say now, the hangman will do tomorrow.

"It will be easy enough. The cruel and the thoughtless will congratulate you, and he too"—McKeever turned and pointed—"this man will thank you, because that's what he's invited, and no one will care for his guilt or innocence. You've got evidence enough. You'd be less than human if you were not tempted.

"And why should you not? What difference if the man should die? Why not destroy him? Isn't he the stranger in our midst?"

The thud of his steps was loud as he strode before them, his mouth working fitfully. A touch of spittle was at his lips. He paused before the glowering prisoner.

"Why?" he cried with anguish. "Why must this man's life weigh so heavily on us? Is it so precious? If so, in whose eyes? He doesn't value it himself. He thinks more of his own perverse and obstinate pride of opinion. How much more must we do for this man? Why not satisfy his spite? He doesn't care that"—the snap of his fingers was like a firecracker—"not *that* for his wife or his sons or anyone else. Why not let him have his bitter way? Why not?" His voice arose with an animal hoarseness. "I don't know why not! Not any more! Except that it must not be so! Because, you see"—he turned and held out his shaking hand—"if we take his life, it was all waste. Everything we did. Is that the answer to this man? Is that the truth?" He stood shaking at the rail. "Was that all it meant? Nothing?

"Or have I been talking of abstract things? Are our laws just words?" He paused before the snub-nosed blond juror in the sixth seat. "Abstractions? Why, good God, our laws have terrible powers. They can take this man and put him to the scaffold. They can pull

241

the trap. They can break his neck and forever put out the light of his brilliant flaming mind. Abstractions? Hardly!"

The blue eyes winked slowly like a chameleon's under the outburst of anger. McKeever lowered his voice meaningfully. "Ah, and they have their gentle side. Our laws can take twisted and hunted creatures who come to us from the dark corners of the earth, and when they breathe our free air, their backs go straight, their heads go up, they live like men and lose the cringing look of slaves.

"Oh, our laws are real enough. Those they curse know their weight, and so do those they bless."

The washy blue eyes winked more rapidly.

McKeever stepped back. His head swung back and forth like a pendulum. "But how will you use the laws? I came to tell you the truth. I don't know what to expect from you. Carlos de Niza has invoked the spirit of violence. It would be human to answer on that level. But will you? The case is clear. The issue is justice. You must decide.

"But if you destroy this man, then God have mercy on us all, for then no one can feel safe. If justice cannot be found in this land, where can we seek it? Do you know? Then tell Carlos de Niza. Tell his people. Tell me, for I don't!"

There was a long silence.

He stood breathing noisily. He looked at each juror in turn as though to speak. His dry glassy eyes were urgent.

The clock stood at two.

After a moment, he bowed to the bench and left the silent courtroom. The way parted before him. He passed out unseeing through the throng.

Florence arose and followed.

He strode out and across the plaza and into the dust of the street toward where his son's body lay.

"We will recess for lunch. Mr. Taft," said the judge, "and then you will sum up."

Chapter XVI

The long vigil was unendurable.

The militia were alerted against a possible attemp;t to storm the jail—whether to liberate the prisoner, or to lynch him, the rumor did not say. Flares were set up as night fell, and the nervous commander, Major Prescott, paraded on his spirited mount around the perimeter of force surrounding the courthouse. The shadows of the jurors crossed the blinds of their lighted room.

McKeever sat in solitude. He was motionless in his characteristic pose in the deep chair beside the bed, his arms hanging, forelock ruffled, staring at the faintly smiling face of the boy.

Through the black night a mockingbird sang in the garden.

The guitars were hushed. The defense were heavy-hearted. At their fires, the Spanish recalled the fortunes of the De Niza family in low tones. There were stories of the former splendors of the *casa* at the river's bend, the great *bailes,* the still-remembered wedding of Doña Constancia, the mother of Don Carlos, her dress of white satin with its bodice of costly Chantilly lace, her coronet of pearls, her diamond broach sent from Madrid by the Duke of Alba. Then years later the ornate splendid funeral of Don Francisco. The misfortunes which followed.

Ay, they sighed, where would it end?

"*Santa Madre*," Doña María prayed through the night in the ancient church, "look after the soul of the young one. Protect my husband. Deliver us from evil. . . ."

When the long wax tapers were guttering, some hours before dawn, Florence entered and touched McKeever's hand. He looked up with mute stricken eyes.

"I can't believe that he's dead," he whispered. "Not yet. I feel that he's still alive."

"Yes, dear," she said gently, "but now you've got to come."

Obediently he followed her to the carriage waiting below in the darkness, and they drove off. The courthouse bell was silent. The throng was quietly watchful, their faces dim and curious in the lamps of the park.

The courtroom was chilly when finally Millikan, with a last stroke of his beard, requested that the jurors be brought in. The rear door opened, a streak of light showed, and then the twelve men entered. Impassive. Blank-eyed. Their tread was loud.

The sixth juror glanced at McKeever, then folded his arms and stared at the ceiling, blinking washily.

"Proceed," said Millikan quietly.

The clerk glanced at his docket book where the white page was ready for the decision. He tugged at his cuffs and said in his loud nasal voice:

"Will the jurors please rise."

They obeyed unevenly, clasping and unclasping their hands, gazing enigmatically ahead.

"Who is your foreman?"

The first juror raised a massive hand. "I was elected, Your Honor."

"The defendant will please rise."

There was no response and the command was repeated. Dominguez leaned over and whispered. "Eh? Oh!" the prisoner muttered. With an air of derisive malice, he arose on shaky legs. He leaned one hand on the table for support. His breathing was stertorous. With a gleam of triumph, he faced the twelve men.

The judge turned.

"Mr. Foreman, have you agreed upon a verdict?"

The foreman bobbed a pale face nervously. "We—" His voice broke and he made a second attempt. "We have, sir." He opened his mouth, then thought better, and remained mute.

"Pass up your verdict."

The foreman held up a paper in a shaking hand. "We wrote it out, Judge, like you said."

Millikan read the statement without change of countenance, then looked up. "The clerk will read the verdict."

The clerk peered at the inscription in the dim light, and read in a low voice, "We, the jury, duly empaneled and sworn, find the defendant, Carlos de Niza y Pereira, not guilty. Signed. Jody Mitchell, Foreman of the Jury."

There was a gasp.

Millikan asked harshly, "Mr. Foreman, is this your verdict?"

The foreman nodded, wordless.

The clerk went on in his imperturbable chant, "You say you find the defendant not guilty of the crime whereof he stands indicted, and so say you all?"

"We do," the jurors muttered. "That's right."

Their faces twitched, some looked at the darkling countenance on the bench, others at McKeever, and hesitant smiles began to break.

Still there was silence.

Millikan leaned forward and said in a distinct voice, without feeling, low and peremptory, "The prisoner will be discharged. Mr. McKeever, my congratulations. This court stands adjourned until next Monday." He arose and strode from the bench.

There was then a piercing scream. "He lives!" Doña María shrieked. "He lives! He lives!" She arose and clasped her shaking hands to her mouth. "Carlos lives!"

And then the cheers began.

"*Yahee!*" The shrill cry arose among the Spanish. "*Yahee! Yahee!*" The exultation burst in a great wave of sound. It receded and swelled and burst again. A sombrero went flying. "*Yahee!*" A fat storekeeper, flushed and excited, started to dance with glee, hands clasped at his spine, prancing in the aisle with joy.

"Carlos lives!" the woman cried. "*Gracias a Dios!*"

Among the stupefied Anglos, a grub-faced Guthrie arose. "Wahoo!" he shouted. The joy was contagious, and the rest joined. Sheepishly at first, then with abandon. The jurors, now grinning broadly, pushed through the swaying milling crowd to shake the hands of the defense. Men were climbing over benches and rail. Don Carlos muttered in a daze, "Not this! No! I did not ask this!"

McKeever arose.

Desolation was in his eyes, and the immediate circle were suddenly quiet. He picked out the faces, now flushed and unfamiliar with jubilation. He wondered at himself. In the midst of numbing grief, he felt an unbidden surge of pleasure, a familiar exhausted sense of gratification, a taste of power.

"Carlos," he said in a trembling voice, "you can go."

"No," said the other pitiably.

The lawyer closed his eyes. "Go to your wife!" he cried savagely. "Get out of this place! For God's sake, go!" He gave the man a push and with dry desperate eyes remained behind as Don Carlos went to his wife. He faced her in wordless misery. Laughing and weeping, she embraced him and together they left the courthouse.

As they stepped outside, a great shout went up. "*Yahee!* Wahoo!" The whole world was laughing and cheering. Anglos and Spanish, arms linked, went capering through the streets. There was gunfire and singing and the saloons flung open their doors. Accordions and

245

guitars and pianos started the dancing. Jigs and reels. The music was everywhere.

In the silent courtroom, Florence went forward. Except for the few lawyers and stragglers, the chamber was empty.

"They didn't want his life," McKeever muttered. "Not from the beginning. Not if they were left alone. Why do they always make it so hard?"

"But they did acquit," she said gently. "It's over."

He looked at her with some first sense of release. "I didn't think they'd do it," he said. "I just didn't believe at the end. Why?"

She asked, "Are you ready to leave now, dear?"

He looked at her. "Yes," he said slowly, gazing at the deserted benches, the empty seat of authority, the gaping jury box, a luna moth fluttering at the lamp. "Yes, I think I'd like to go. There's nothing more to do here. Coming, Em? Joe?"

They left and drove off.

"Why hell!" drawled the foreman, Jody Mitchell, "it was all in the cards. I could've told 'em, saved the county all this money, but no! They told us we dassn't talk about the case. Why, thanks, mister! Real cognac? Napoleon? I heard about this."

"Would you say McKeever's summation turned the trick, Mitchell?" Bellew wondered. "No, have another. That's all right. It's on my expense account."

"Don't know if I should. Well, just one more. Then I'm due home." The foreman screwed his eyes in thought. "No, I wouldn't exactly say McKeever, although he made a few points. He was real friendly, and mighty interesting, but too quiet half the times, I'd say. Matter of fact, Mike Taft did a lot better job. Now *there's* a lawyer. Just so happened, McKeever had the right side, otherwise it would've been too bad."

"What made you think so?" Bellew winked at Wilby, who was seated across the table scribbling hasty revisions for his morning editorial. "No, I want you to keep the whole bottle."

"Why, thanks! This is good stuff. Well, it stood to reason. Everybody knows old Carlos. He had every right to feel sore. Those old dons got a raw deal, and naturally they didn't just take it, but only the less intelligent class of Americans would hold that against a man. No, if Carlos had a mind to kill the old judge, he would've took a gun, fixed a time, and banged away. But an ambush? Hell, no!"

Bellew made a note. "But Canty's testimony," he pointed out.

The foreman looked for a place to spit and settled for the floor. "Canty? That's plain ridiculous. Did you notice the way his skull

246

has two bumps alongside the ears? I made a study of that once, and it's my belief that those bumps show a born liar—regardless of race, color or creed. It's a scientific fact. Of course, I'm only speaking for myself."

"Can I quote you?" Bellew asked, smiling.

"Now look, mister," the foreman said uneasily. "I was just one of twelve. It was just our idea to do the right thing. How would we feel in old Carlos's place? We wasn't trying to do anything special."

"Then you don't feel that McKeever had an effect?"

"Well, I wouldn't want to say," the foreman replied, scratching his belly hesitantly. "The truth is, it was hard to follow him. We felt sorry about his kid, but that had nothing to do with the verdict."

"We figured his dying might make a difference."

"Hell, no! We wasn't trying the kid. We was trying the case. Frankly, I don't see what all this excitement is about."

It was a bracing day some weeks later. The sun was clear in the soft blue sky. The flowers at the grave were yellow and wilting but the green sod was taking root with vigor. Florence clasped Mc-Keever's hand.

"You can leave now," she said.

He nodded. "Yes, I feel I can."

The train whistle sounded in the distance. Together they found the carriage at the cemetery gate. Florence drove easily toward the town. Occasionally she glanced at the silent man. His eyes were still strained and painful, he was pale, but now he seemed rested and the hurt was beginning to recede. Something was waiting to be said. When the station was in sight he touched her.

"Floss," he murmured.

"Yes, Link."

"I'm stopping off in Washington."

"Oh?" She waited. "Will you see Tucker?"

"I feel I should. His letter meant a lot. It's not easy for him to write."

"I see." She drove in silence. "Do you still want that appointment?"

He shook his head. "No, I think not. I suppose I can get it if I try hard enough, but I'm not ready to be a judge. Not yet. I just want to keep doing the same thing. The world is full of judges, and there are too few of us."

"I'm sure that's wise," she said soberly as the carriage halted at the station. "Well, here we are."

McKeever took her hand.

"It's too soon for me to talk, Floss," he said in a low voice. "But I've been trying to say this. Will you come to New York?"

She looked into his searching urgent eyes. "When?"

"As soon as you wish."

She smiled. "Of course, my dearest." She put aside the reins and took his face in both hands and kissed him tenderly. "Now don't miss your train. I'll wait here."

His sudden smile came like a burst of light in the lowering gloom. He lifted her hand and kissed it. "I won't change, you know," he warned her. "I'll always be a bad husband."

"Yes, I know."

He got down smiling and crossed the station to the small group waiting to see him off. The engine was building a head of steam.

"Well, good-by," said Mike Taft gruffly, shaking hands with vigor. "You sure reminded me of the old days, Link. It was a good court fight. Not too clean, maybe, but enjoyable."

"I must remember that," said McKeever, still smiling. "I imagine it's a form of tribute."

"Well, it's sincere. And it's not," the prosecutor went on, wiping his throat with a cambric, "not like anything was really lost. This way, we still got Canty to hang with a good conscience, and with poor Max Kyle pleading to manslaughter, that kind of gives this case a happy ending, don't it?"

McKeever considered this nicely. "In a way," he admitted gravely. He turned to the others. "Em, there are some checks in the cabinet, and you'll find the bills initialed. If you run short—"

Martin interrupted. "I'll take care of everything."

"I'm sure." McKeever turned last to Dominguez. They faced each other soberly, thinking of that day in Denver. He said, "Joe, will you tell Carlos not to think too harshly of me?"

The New Mexican lawyer rubbed his eyes with a moist knuckle, but he managed a tremulous smile. "He still feels that you played him a dirty trick, but he's coming around. María sends her best, and so does Carlos, although he don't know it yet."

There seemed nothing more to say.

"I shall miss you all," said McKeever. He waved to Florence and got into the train. She remained watching as it vanished into the east.

248